THE INQUEST

Stephen Dando-Collins

ibooks
new york
www.ibooks.net

DISTRIBUTED BY SIMON & SCHUSTER, INC.

Dan

*For Louise, who has always believed,
and for Richard, who has lit the way.*

An ibooks, inc. Book

All rights reserved, including the right to reproduce this
book or portions thereof in any form whatsoever.
Distributed by Simon & Schuster
1230 Avenue of the Americas, New York, NY 10020

ibooks, inc.
24 West 25th Street
New York, NY 10010

The ibooks World Wide Web address is:
www.ibooks.net

ISBN: 1-4165-0441-9
First ibooks printing February 2005
10 9 8 7 6 5 4 3 2 1

THE INQUEST

In A.D. 71,
Julius Terentius Varro,
a Roman investigating magistrate, or *questor,*
was sent to Judea
to investigate the death of
Jesus of Nazareth
four decades earlier,
with orders to prove that
Jesus did not rise from the dead.

This is the story of that mission.

I

THE DEAD JEW

Antioch, Capital of the Roman Province of Syria. February, A.D. 71

*In the time of our grandfathers, there arose a man of Rome who won the hearts
of his countrymen, a man unlike any who came before him or who came after
him. He was the grandson of Marcus Antonius, yet he was not ambitious. He
was the brother of Claudius, yet he was no fool. He was the father of Caligula,
yet he was not depraved. He was . . .*

A roar from the crowd intruded on Julius Varro's thoughts, dragging
him back from the work of history which for years past he had been aching
to commit to paper. On the sands of the amphitheater of Antioch in front
of him, Jewish prisoners of war had been pitted against each other, with one
prisoner in every pair sent out unarmed. Under the sweltering midday sun,
while many in the 30,000 crowd ate a lunch of juicy Damascus plums and
fresh-baked bread and spicy balls of goats meat provided by the editor of
the games, Jew was expected to butcher Jew, as entertainment for the mob.
To the delight and amusement of the Syrian spectators, some defenseless
victims ran, uselessly, pointlessly from their appointment with death.
There was no escape in the circular stadium. Now, one pair in particular
had drawn the attention and the ire of many in the crowd around Varro.
Spectators gave bellicose voice to their displeasure.

"Run, Jew, run!" came the screeching voice of a woman in an upper
tier.

"Kill him, old man!" called a vicious youth to Varro's right. A thousand
voices raucously concurred.

Beneath a shading purple canopy, thirty-four-year-old Varro, athletic, dark-haired, clean shaven like all Romans of his day, sat in the second row of the amphitheater's official box, the tribunal of the editor of the games. His deep brown eyes were fixed on a scene directly below the box. There stood a tall man, naked but for a thick leather belt. An olive-skinned Jew, broad of shoulder, with the skin hanging from his starved bones, he wore a gladiator's helmet with a metal visor fixed to the front. Peppered with holes for sight and breath, the visor covered the face, rendering the owner anonymous. A tuft of gray beard projected below the visor. At his right side, the Jew held a short sword. He was frozen, with his eyes on a younger, wholly naked man of twenty or so who knelt before him. Here was the cause of the crowd's unease — the young man was begging the other to end his life for him.

Through the baying of the mob, Varro could just hear the young man's plea. He spoke in Aramaic, the language of the region, a language of which Varro had a basic comprehension.

"Kill me, father!" cried the youth. "Kill me now!"

Varro, disinterested in the days' entertainment program until now, could not take his eyes from father and son. He knew the pair would have been numbered among the 97,000 Jewish prisoners taken during the Roman siege of Jerusalem which had all but ended the Jewish Revolt the previous summer. At this public spectacle in Antioch, these were the last of the prisoners to be disposed of. Here, a father had been ordered to kill his own son, and the father could not bring himself to comply.

The hoots and boos of the crowd were increasing to a crescendo. Varro could no longer make out what was being said on the arena sands. By his gesticulations, it was obvious that the boy continued to implore his father to dispatch him. There was no response; the parent remained immobilized. Varro wondered what he would do in the same situation. Varro was childless, not even married. Would his own father have had the bravery and the humanity to swiftly end his son's life in similar circumstances? Varro doubted it. His father had not been a man of courage.

If Varro were the father faced with this dilemma, he now pondered, what then? What if this were his son on bended knees before him, knowing that if Varro did not kill his child someone else very soon would? As Varro watched, the Jewish boy took his fate into his own hands. Coming to his feet, he scrambled the several paces that brought him to his parent's feet, then dropped to his knees directly in front of the older man. Grasping his father's sinewy right arm, the boy brought the sharp tip of the twenty-inch legionary sword to the middle of his chest, above his heart. The youth looked up, and spoke words of parting.

Then, with all his might, the young man pulled his father's arm toward him. The blade pierced the boy's flesh, and slid into his heart. Spectators roared their disapproval. Father and son had deprived them of their sport. As the boy died on his knees in front of him, the father withdrew the sword with an anguished cry, then cast it away. Bloodied, the weapon spun through the air and landed on the sand. Inclining his visored face to the cloudless sky, the old Jew began to scream inaudibly to the heavens.

The standing Jew was quickly surrounded by heavily armed troops. Men of the Antioch City Guard, they came running from the perimeter of the arena. As the soldiers stripped the man of helmet and belt, Varro could see that the elder Jew's face was long, and weathered. The father lowered his head, and locked his tear-filled eyes on the body of his son. Amphitheater slaves in red-striped tunics of white wool appeared around him. The slaves had dashed from a door in the arena wall which opened just long enough to admit them. Some brought buckets of sand, others carried a giant hook of iron. With the expertise of habit, several slaves quickly forced the razor sharp tip of the hook through the body of the youth. It entered at the stomach and exited from the middle of the back. Putting ropes over their shoulders, the slaves dragged the limp corpse from the arena. In their wake, others spread fresh sand over blood soaking the arena floor.

As the soldiers then withdrew, Varro saw that another Jew stood facing the father of the boy. This younger man had been equipped with the father's belt, helmet and sword. Some in the crowd were urging the older man to run, others called for the new executioner to quickly terminate the father for his lack of spirit. The elder man sank to his knees and lowered his head. The second prisoner quickly obliged him. Raising the sword two-handed, he brought it down across the back of the old Jew's neck. To cheers from the tiered seats the gray-bearded head was separated from the older man's shoulders with a single violent slice. With a spray of blood, the head fell to the ground. There it lay, the open eyes still watery with tears.

✠

"Did you see that wretched Jew, depriving the crowd of their entertainment?" said General Gnaeus Collega as he and Varro stepped from the general's litter in the light of spluttering torches held by the general's attendants. Ahead of them, broad steps rose to Collega's Antioch residence on the Augustan Way. Collega, commander of the 4th Scythica Legion and Acting Governor of the province of Syria and its sub province, Judea, was the same age as his deputy Julius Varro. Overweight, short, and losing his hair, Collega looked ten years older. He had been administering the region ever since the governor, Licinius Mucianus, had led an army on Rome eighteen months before to unseat the emperor Vitellius and install the current emperor Vespasian in his place.

"Which wretched Jew was that, my lord?" Varro asked absently. A thousand times over the uneven contests between pairs of Jews had been repeated in the amphitheater through the day's middle hours, with each armed man disarmed to face his own doom as soon as he had terminated his designated victim, until 2,000 Jews had killed one another. In the afternoon, the lunch time diversion of the Jewish extermination had given way to the real entertainment of the day, the professional fighters. None of this interested Varro. He would have much rather been writing his planned history of Germanicus Caesar, Roman hero. Epic poems and turgid histories had been written about Germanicus, but no one had dared to delve into his murder. That, thought Varro, would be a true test of his skills as a writer and an investigator. To solve the mystery, that would be a challenge he would enjoy. There was no challenge, no fascinating intrigue, about the bloodshed of the arena. Its lack of nobility sickened him.

"The fellow who fell on his own sword after separating the old man's head from his shoulders," Collega responded as they went up the stairs. "Most unsporting of him."

Varro nodded in remembrance. "Ah, *that* wretched Jew." Before the soldiers of the Guard could reach him, the decapitator of the father who had grabbed Varro's attention had put the sword to his own throat. Looking up at the crowd, taking in the sight of his tormentors for one last time, he had fallen forward. As the sword's pommel hit the ground the blade punctured the man's throat and rammed on through. The point came out the back of the neck. The Jew had died instantly. The crowd had howled its derision. This, they cried, was the act of a coward; they had been cheated.

Blood and death were like food and drink to most Romans. What made Varro different, he did not know. But, as a questor—a junior magistrate —

and the deputy of the Governor of Syria and Judea, Varro could not afford to show anything other than a hard exterior. So he attended the games, watched the barbarity that passed for entertainment, and put on a Roman face. Especially when he was sharing the official box with the emperor's son; that morning, the gleaming golden chair at the front of the box had been occupied by Titus Vespasianus, thirty-two-year-old general, conqueror of Jerusalem, heir to Caesar Vespasian, and second most powerful man in the world. After viewing the morning session, Titus had departed Antioch, setting out for Alexandria in Egypt where he would take ship for Rome to join his father.

Collega was out of breath by the time he reached the top of the steps. Coming to halt, he put a hand on the middle of his chest. A wince of pain creased his cheek.

"General?" said Varro, halting beside him. "What is it?"

"Indigestion, according to the noble physician Diocles," Collega replied. He had been eating throughout the day as he watched the games; rich delicacies: grilled dormouse dipped in honey, pigeon wings, sweetbreads. "Not that I trust that old drunkard of a Corinthian's diagnoses. He ignores half my ailments and dispenses obscure potions for the remainder, which do me no good whatsoever. Did you see him today, wagering on every contest? And losing. Damned fool!" Collega set off again, walking in through open double doors, ignoring bowing slaves. "Diocles' judgement leaves much to be desired. If I am ever truly ill, he will be last man I consult. He would kill me before my time."

"You know what they say, general: if you want to live a long life, never make your physician your heir."

"Well said, Varro, well said!" Collega cackled. "If the truth be known, Syria is bad for my health. I am more than ready to go home, I can tell you."

Only the previous day Collega had learned from the emperor's son that a new governor of consular rank had been chosen by Caesar to come out to Syria. But, for a variety of reasons, the new man, Petus, would not arrive in Antioch for another fourteen to fifteen months. And, because the new governor would bring out his own staff from Rome, including a questor, Varro would also be going home. Not a month too soon, as far as Varro was concerned. He had already given four years to this post. He could tolerate another year, but no more. With luck, he hoped, now that the calamities and crimes of the Jewish Revolt were in the past, peace and normality would return to the region. He might even find the time to finally expound his theories about the murder of Germanicus, reveal the murderer, and prove himself a writer of note.

Appearing in their path, a short, tubby man with white hair, a closely trimmed white beard and wearing a plain brown tunic which matched his sober bearing, announced, "My lord, you have a visitor."

"I am too weary for visitors, Pythagoras," said Collega, impatiently waving away his chief secretary, a Greek named for the famous philosopher of 600 years before.

"It is Flavius Josephus, my lord," said the secretary gravely.

Collega stopped in mid stride. "Josephus? Here? What does he want?" He glanced at Varro, looking worried. "I thought we had seen the back of Josephus." He grimaced to himself. "Very well, Pythagoras," he sighed, "lead us to him."

Pythagoras conducted the pair to a colonnaded garden courtyard. A slim man stood by a fountain where water spouted from the mouth of a bronze dolphin.

Collega produced a practiced smile as they approached. "My lord Josephus, I had thought you on your way to Rome with Titus Vespasianus."

Thirty-five-year-old Flavius Josephus wore a full beard and a serious expression. Five years before, he had been the Jewish general in command of all partisan forces in Galilee fighting the Roman army. Josephus had changed sides, going over to Vespasian and Titus, advising them on strategies against his former comrades and predicting that both father and son would in their turn rule Rome. His defection had brought him freedom, Roman citizenship, and the ear of the sovereign of the Roman world. "Soon enough, Collega," Josephus said, briefly accepting Collega's right hand. "I will overtake His Excellency's column on the road south. For the moment, there is a matter I would raise with you before I leave this part of the world."

Ignoring Varro, Josephus put an arm around Collega's shoulders and steered the general to a bench at the far end of the garden. Varro could imagine that Collega's skin must be crawling, knowing as he did that Collega despised all Jews. Counting against Josephus too was the invisible brand of traitor against his own people. Titus might trust this Jew, but Collega did not. As Varro watched from a distance, Josephus and Collega sank onto the bench. Now the Jew lay his right arm along the back of the bench, leaned close to Collega, then began to fill his ear with a stream of softly spoken words. After a time, Collega began to reply, in an equally conspiratorial tone.

Curious, Varro edged closer, taking care not to appear to be eavesdropping. He only caught snatches. "Nazarene" was mentioned, and "Jesus of Nazareth," "God of the Jews," "the Messiah," "the Christos."

Then, unexpectedly, Collega looked up and beckoned his questor. "How much of this have you overheard, Varro?" he asked him.

"Er, a little, general," Varro guilty admitted as he came up to the pair.

"You are a smart fellow, Varro," said Collega. "What do you know of this Nazarene? What name did you give him, Josephus?"

"Jesus of Nazareth, his Greek-speaking followers call him," Josephus replied, looking at Varro.

"I have heard of such a man, while in Judea," said Varro. "It is said by some that he worked miracles, my lord, like so many Jewish miracle workers. I believe he was crucified at Jerusalem, during the reign of Tiberius Caesar."

"Miracles?" said Collega caustically, shaking his head. "Pah!"

"Well done, questor," said Josephus approvingly. "This Jesus was indeed crucified during the reign of Tiberius."

Varro felt that Josephus had an intelligent face. Unlike Collega, Varro was not a man of inherited prejudices. He took people as he found them, and on the few occasions that he had met Josephus he had found him a learned if immodest man..

"Crucified? For what crime?" Collega asked.

"The Nazarene was convicted of sedition against Rome," Josephus went on, addressing Collega once more. "His followers insist that he came back to life, two days following his execution, and that is their proof that he was divine, that he was the Messiah, as it is said in my native tongue."

Varro frowned. "Messiah?" he queried. "I'm unfamiliar with that term, my lord."

A smile tickled the corners of Josephus' mouth. His lively eyes sparkled. "The Christos, his Greek followers call him, questor — the 'anointed one.'"

"Anointed for what?" Varro asked.

Before Josephus could reply, Collega interrupted. "This coming back to life nonsense," he said with irritation. "Do these people really believe it, Josephus? We have a few of these Nazarenes here at Antioch. I had classed them with all the other Jews of the city." There were in fact 40,000 Jewish residents in the Antioch population of 250,000. "Do they genuinely believe that he actually rose from the dead?"

Josephus nodded. "They believe that he rose from the dead, that he walked from his tomb at Jerusalem, walked to Galilee, then ascended to Heaven. They say he was a god, Collega. A dangerous claim in these unstable times, you would agree."

"A god?" Collega scoffed. "Did anyone see him, after he supposedly rose from the dead and went strolling around Palestine?"

"It is claimed that a number of his devotees saw him and spoke with him after his execution." Josephus smiled, knowingly. "Obviously, this claim is fraudulent, Collega. Thereby hangs the means of suppression of the Nazarenes."

"You have lost me," said Collega impatiently.

"The beauty of the approach I am about to suggest to you, Collega," Josephus confided, "is that you do not have to execute a single Jew to destroy these people. Here is the crux of the matter..."

So that he missed nothing, Varro took a step closer.

"Prove as baseless the claim that this man rose from the dead," said the Jew. "And you destroy the basic tenet of the Nazarenes' belief. Prove that Jesus of Nazareth was not the Messiah, the redeemer of the Jewish people promised by ancient texts, and publish the evidence the length and breadth of the Empire, and you will make these Nazarenes a laughing stock. The edifice of their belief will come crashing down, and the Nazarenes will have been shown to be mere story-tellers and frauds. Their Messiah will be discredited, and their sect will fade into obscurity."

Collega frowned. "Prove that this Jew did not rise from the dead? You think that would be enough to destroy them?"

Josephus nodded. "Prove the ridiculous claim of the Nazarenes to be the myth it is. Like the myth that Nero Caesar is still alive and living here in the East in disguise."

It was Collega's turn to smile. He was thoughtful for a time, unconsciously tugging the lobe of one ear. Then he turned to Josephus, who had given the general time to consider his words. "What of these claims of miracles that Varro speaks of? Would it not also be necessary to disprove those?"

"Miracles, miracles," Josephus responded with an open-handed shrug and a pout of the lips. "You have been in the East long enough, Collega, to know that this part of the world abounds with miracle workers, all of them nothing more than clever magicians. Even Caesar Vespasianus, when he was at Alexandria last year, performed miracles, right before my very eyes."

Collega looked at him with surprise. "He did? Caesar did that?"

Josephus nodded. "I saw it for myself. He cured a blind beggar, simply by spitting in his eyes. Another, a lame man, he cured by stomping on his foot. Yet, is Caesar making claims of divinity?"

Varro watched as Collega again lapsed into thought. Like the general, Varro was astonished by the revelation about the emperor's miraculous powers. He had met Vespasian when he was a general of consular rank, before he became emperor of Rome. Vespasian had been coarse, as foul-mouthed as a common legionary, and terse; the last person Varro would have credited with heavenly powers. Then again, when he met him, Varro had never imagined that the general would one day be his emperor, either.

"So, you see, Collega," Josephus went on, "this fellow Jesus' miracles are of no consequence when it comes to disproving his divinity. We must concentrate on the unique claim, the obviously ridiculous claim as far as thinking men are concerned, that Jesus rose from the dead. This is the foundation of the Nazarenes' appeal to the feeble-minded. Undermine that, and you will destroy the sect and all that it represents. In doing so, you will be able to guarantee Caesar that you have destroyed a corrupting influence within the Jewish community and brought stability to Syria and Judea, and to the Roman East as a whole." He paused, letting his words sink in.

Collega, obviously uncomfortable with the Jew's proposal, screwed up his face. "What do you have against these Nazarenes, Josephus?"

"The Nazarenes are recruiting followers outside the Jewish faith, making an abomination of Jewish Law," replied the pious Jew. "Worse, for Rome, they are infiltrating the cities and the towns of your domain, Collega."

The general turned, scowling. "Can one dead Jew be so troublesome?" he asked, thinking aloud. "Could right-thinking Romans believe the Nazarene nonsense?"

"Fantastic untruths take root in feeble minds," Josephus declared. "The corrupting doctrines of the Nazarenes cannot be tolerated. Mucianus would approve if you were to act against these people." Ever since he had engineered Vespasian's rise to power, Mucianus, Collega's former chief in Syria, had been the emperor's right hand man. "We both know that Mucianus has no time for philosophers of any kind," Josephus continued. "Most importantly, Collega, Caesar would approve. Eliminate a cause of friction within Jewish communities. Halt the insidious spread of Nazarene influence. Do this, Collega, and you will assure your swift career advancement on your return to Rome."

"Is this Titus' wish?" Collega asked. "The destruction of the Nazarenes?"

From his perspective, Varro could sense the general's indecision.

"These are your provinces, Collega," said Josephus. "What you do in your own provinces is for you to decide. Equally, what you do to advance your own career is for you to decide."

Collega was nodding slowly.

"That career is by no means assured, Collega," Josephus persisted, his voice changing, losing its friendly edge and taking a more distanced tone. Now too he came to his feet.

With sudden concern that the Jew knew something that he did not, the Acting Governor brought his head around to face him. "What do you mean by that?" he demanded.

Josephus shrugged. "There are other men of your rank who served in the Jewish War and won great honors. Certainly, you have performed your duties admirably here in Syria all this time. Your handling of the inquiry into the Fire of Antioch met with Titus' approval." He glanced at Varro as he said this, knowing that the questor had been instrumental in the outcome of that inquiry only weeks before. "Yet, for all that, Collega, there is nothing to match the glory of a military campaign when Caesar comes to decide the new year's appointments. Already, you will be a year or two behind your colleagues by the time you return to Rome." He paused, for effect. "However, if your return were to be preceded by a meritorious achievement, such as the discrediting of the Nazarenes…"

Collega did not reply.

"Your future is in your own hands, Collega," Josephus hissed. "Think on it." With that parting comment, the Jew strode from the garden.

Collega looked up at his deputy, as if seeking guidance. "What do you think of all that, Varro?"

Varro shrugged. "Troubling, my lord."

"Yes, troubling. Is it Titus' wish, the discrediting of the Nazarenes?" Collega pondered. "Or is this all Josephus' idea, and he wants me to think he is doing Titus' bidding?" He tugged his ear lobe. "Troubling indeed."

II

THE ASSIGNMENT

Antioch, Capital of the Roman Province of Syria. February, A.D. 71

As the offensive aroma of a rotting animal lying unseen in floor or ceiling soaks all it reaches, a month after the event the acrid stench of fire still clung to the stones and timbers of the city as Julius Varro was carried in a closed litter through the streets. The Fire of Antioch had razed one fifth of the metropolis, destroying the massive Foursquare Market, its place of origin, gutting the city library and archives, and demolishing all the grand old Seleucid palaces, including the palace used by the Governor of Syria as his official residence. Forced to find a new, temporary residence, General Collega was renting the city home of one of the richest men in Antioch, a merchant and owner of a shipping fleet.

"Make way for the questor!" called Pedius, Varro's gray-haired lictor, his official attendant, who preceded the brawny litter-bearers toting his employer's staff of office. "Make way for the questor!"

As he did every day at dawn, on this morning after the meeting with Flavius Josephus, Julius Varro arrived at the Acting Governor's residence as the sun was rising over Parthia to the east. An ante-room was filled with fifty or sixty of Antioch's leading citizens, all come to pay their respects to the governor, some deep in conversation, others looking detached and preoccupied. Despite the waiting crowd, Pythagoras the secretary ushered Varro directly in to see Collega, in a small reception room overlooking one of the mansion's many gardens. The governor was not alone. As

Collega lounged on one of three couches, munching grapes, a man Varro immediately recognized sat across from him. Curly-headed and swarthy, Antiochus, chief Jewish magistrate of Antioch, was narrow-shouldered and of medium height. A man with a sagging paunch and a double chin, Antiochus had been handsome in his youth. Now, in his middle years, lack of restraint and lack of exercise were changing his physiology with the addition of surplus pounds. His brow glistened, for Antiochus was burdened with a nervous complaint which saw him perspire mildly at any time and profusely when he was anxious. Antiochus smiled weakly at the questor as Varro bade his chief and his guest good morning.

"Varro, my dear fellow," said Collega cheerily, pointing his questor to the third couch, before spitting a pip into a bowl on the table in front of him. "I invited Antiochus here to tell me a little about the Nazarenes."

"The Nazarenes, my lord?" said Varro as he reclined. "For what purpose?"

"As much as I hate to admit it, Flavius Josephus was right," said Collega. "I have therefore decided to proceed with that matter we discussed last evening, Varro. The mission to Judea."

"You have?" Varro was surprised. When he had left the governor the night before he had felt that Collega's reservations had meant he would ignore Josephus' suggestion. "May I inquire why, my lord?"

"Expediency, Varro," said Collega with a wink at his deputy. "Last evening after your departure I discussed the matter with the ever wise Pythagoras. He feels that no harm can be done, while no end of good may come of it. It could make both our careers."

Varro frowned. "*Both* our careers, general?"

"You will conduct the inquiry into the death of the Jewish miracle worker."

"Me, my lord?" Varro protested. He could think of nothing worse than spending months in Judea. For one thing, the rebel Jews down there had yet to be completely subdued; the Roman army were still mopping up resistance. All Varro wanted was to serve out his time in Syria as quickly and as peaceably as possible, then go home.

Collega detected the note of dismay in his questor's voice, and scowled at him. "You are my investigating magistrate. You will lead the investigation, an inquest into the circumstances surrounding the death of the Nazarene."

"But, my lord..."

"Come, come now, Varro." His cheerful demeanor vanishing, Collega sat up straight and looked Varro in the eye "Unlike yourself, I don't have a patron as powerful as Licinius Mucianus. I could order you to go to Judea, and you would go. But, if for no other reason, go willingly to Judea and conduct this inquiry as judiciously as your talents allow, as a favor to me. I will show my gratitude in the future, you can be sure of that."

Under the Roman social system, a man served as the client of an influential patron. Varro's patron was Gnaeus Licinius Mucianus. He had come out to Syria with Mucianus four years before as his questor, but had been left behind to serve Collega when his patron marched on Rome for Vespasian.

"Yes, general," Varro sighed. Silently he cursed his luck.

Collega lazily discarded the remnants of a bunch of grapes; they missed the table and dropped onto the tiled floor. The governor held out his hands. In moments, two servants had materialized. One held a bowl in front of his master. Another poured perfumed water over the general's hands and into the bowl. "*Both* our careers, Varro," the general continued. "A success with this expedition would pave the way for your entry into the Senate on your return. Perhaps the emperor would even appoint you a pretor."

Varro, who had no ambitions to be a pretor, a senior magistrate, did not reply.

Collega washed his fingers then dried them on a cloth provided by the first slave. The task completed, both slaves melted away, the first bending smoothly to collect the refuse from the floor as he went. "Would you not agree?" Collega persisted.

"I imagine so, my lord." Varro's only ambition was to write. But his mother had high hopes for him, with her eyes on the consulship which had eluded his late father.

Collega now lifted a boiled and shelled peahen's egg from a platter in front of him. He studied the egg for a moment, rolling it in his fingers. "A fellow with your abilities and your connections should go far." He swallowed the egg whole.

"Yes, my lord," Varro replied unenthusiastically.

Collega turned to the perspiring Jewish magistrate, who had been a silent witness to the Romans' discourse all this time. "Antiochus, tell him about the Lucius Letter."

"Of course, I have no time for the Nazarenes," Antiochus now gushed, like a torrent unleashed from a great dam. "I would burn them all!"

"The letter, man!" Collega growled.

"Of course, Your Excellency," Antiochus responded. "Forgive me." He turned to address Varro. "As I was telling His Excellency, questor, last year when we rounded up the leaders of the Jewish community in Antioch and fried them at the stadium for complicity with the rebels in Galilee and Judea we caught one or two Nazarenes in the net." He spoke with urgency, making no attempt to hide the pleasure he gained from persecuting fellow Jews. "In the house of a fellow by the name of Theophilus, one of the Nazarene elders, I discovered a letter, written by a Lucius the Physician, a native of Antioch. It gave an account of the life and death of the one they call Jesus of Nazareth."

"An invaluable resource, I would imagine, this letter," said Collega. "You will pass it on to Varro."

"With pleasure my lord," Antiochus hastened to reply. "And, may I be so bold as to volunteer to accompany the questor on his expedition of inquiry, to act as interpreter."

"Interpreter?" Collega pursed his lips.

"I am of course fluent in Aramaic, Hebrew, and Jewish law," the Jew added. "I would have thought that there would be witnesses to question and documents to study."

"Hmm. I will think on it," Collega nodded toward the door. "That will be all for the moment, Antiochus."

The Jewish magistrate leapt to his feet. "Thank you, my lord governor." Bowing from the waist, he withdrew backwards, and left the room.

"Despicable creature!" Collega commented under his breath. He clicked his fingers. "Remove the cushions," he instructed his servants. He pointed to the now empty couch. "The ones where the Jew sat — and dripped. Burn them!"

As the slaves scurried to obey, Collega looked over at Varro. His expression of distaste quickly gave way to a sly smile. "So, it is decided, questor. You will conduct this inquest. And the sooner the better. We both know how much your patron Mucianus detests doctrine of any kind. Stoics and Cynics alike earn Mucianus' ardent displeasure."

Varro nodded. "As I know only too well, my lord. He consistently found new ways to insult the philosophers. He said that they were taking advantage of the name of philosophy to teach doctrines which were inappropriate to our times."

"Can you imagine what he would think of the philosophy of the Nazarene? I do not think we can harbor any doubt that Mucianus would welcome a report which destroys the corrupting influence of the Nazarene doctrine, Varro." Collega now leaned closer and lowered his voice. "Just be sure of this one thing, questor. For it to achieve the goal of the exercise, the report you write must demolish the Nazarene myth. You must come back with proof that this Jesus of Nazareth did not rise from the dead."

✠

Varro's chief assistant, the freedman Callidus, a former slave, was waiting for his master with the litter bearers. "Do we go to Judea, my lord?" asked Callidus, a ruddy-faced Spaniard in his fifties, as Varro came down the steps from the governor's palace wearing an unhappy scowl.

"How could you know about that?" Varro marveled. He had after all only just been given the appointment by the governor.

Callidus grinned. "Freedman's grapevine, my lord." Callidus had served the Varros, father and son, for most of his life, and was efficient in his own crude way, none the least in maintaining low-ranked informants in high places. "May I suggest…?"

"What is it?" Varro asked despondently as he slipped onto the comfortable litter.

"Allow me to round up a few suspected Nazarenes and see what information I can extract from them, about this Jesus fellow." The questor had broad responsibilities, covering tax collection, army recruiting, and criminal investigations in the province, and as the questor's chief assistant Callidus led a team of unarmed freedmen who filled the role of metropolitan police and tax collectors in Antioch, backed by the steel of the City Guard. In this role, Callidus could exercise all his considerable powers of coercion, and his more sadistic urges, to extract information from prisoners.

Varro shrugged. "Yes, yes, question who you will." A thought then occurred to the questor. "But go gentle with them all the same, Callidus."

The freedman frowned at his master. "Gentle, my lord?"

✠

Later that night, back at his quarters, Varro had his secretary, Artimedes, read the Lucius Letter to him. General Collega was right. It proved to be a fascinating document. Not the least because it seemed to indicate that Jesus of Nazareth had gone willingly to his execution, like a lamb to the slaughter. Now, alone in his room and with oil lamps set on the table beside his bed, Varro began to reread the letter for himself. It began:

> *For as much as many have taken in hand to put in writing an ordered declaration of those things which are most surely believed among us, and even though those who originally delivered these things to us were eyewitnesses of the events and ministers of the word, it seemed good to me as well, having had a perfect understanding of all these things from the beginning, to write to you, in order, most excellent Theophilus, that you might have no doubt about these things that you have been taught.*
>
> *There was in the days of Herod, the King of Judea, a certain priest named Zecharias...*

III

THE TRIBUNE AND THE PREFECT

Antioch, Capital of the Roman Province of Syria. March, A.D. 71

With a purple-bordered white cloak flowing behind him like a flag in the wind and the sun glinting on his armor, military tribune Marcus Metellus Martius strode forward. Crossing the elliptical equestrian yard in the gladiatorial barracks complex with long, muscular strides, there was a smile on his face, his hand was outstretched. "So, Julius Varro, you and I are to be companions on an adventure in the south," he said, firmly clasping Varro's right hand. His voice was deep, his delivery measured. Martius was second in command of the 4th Scythica Legion, Collega's legion. The unit was based to the east of Antioch at Zeugma on the Euphrates River, facing the Parthian Empire, Rome's long-term enemy. Collega had assigned the tribune to the Nazarene enterprise, as Varro's deputy and commander of the expedition's military contingent.

For several minutes the questor had been watching Martius exercising on horseback in the small arena, launching javelins from the back of a fast-moving horse with round wooden shields just the breadth of a man's hand for targets. Martius had not missed a single target. Now, as the tribune's groom led away his horse, Varro returned Martius' handshake with enthusiasm. "An adventure in the south?" said Varro. "So it would seem, Marcus. I shall be glad of your strong sword arm."

The broad-shouldered, twenty-nine-year-old tribune was a little taller than Varro, with a strong oval face and thick brown hair. His eyes were a piercing blue. "I'll gladly play Hercules to your Apollo. What will be the chances of a little action, do you think?"

"According to the most recent reports there are still pockets of Jewish resistance in southern Judea. Still, I would have thought you had seen enough action for the time being." Varro and Martius had been friends ever since both served as prefects of auxiliary units on the Rhine almost a decade earlier. Varro knew that Martius had fought alongside Titus in hectic Galilee battles early in Vespasian's offensive to put down the bloody Jewish Revolt, coming out of the campaign with Titus' praise, a Jewish arrowhead embedded in his thigh, and promotion to tribune of the 4th Scythica Legion in Syria.

"There is never enough action for Marcus Martius," the tribune returned with a boyish grin. "Are you going to the baths? I'll walk with you." The pair strolled side by side from the arena and into the labyrinth of buildings which made up the Antioch gladiatorial barracks complex. Callidus, Varro's freedman, fell in behind them. From close by came the sounds of gladiators going through their paces in combat exercises, their trainers bawling insults at them in language salted with curses. "So, Julius," said Martius as they walked, "you make your home in a gladiator's barrack now?"

"Since the fire, the choice of accommodation has been limited."

"Yes, the fire. We heard about it out at Zeugma of course, but seeing the damage for myself when I arrived in the city this morning, it was a shock, seeing the center of Antioch in ruins. You apprehended the culprits, so I hear."

Varro nodded. "A pair of greedy merchants: Priscus and Plancus. Some people were ready to condemn half the Jews of Antioch for the crime, but the evidence led us to the merchants."

"The word is that it was a clever questor, not the evidence, which made the difference," said the tribune with a wink.

Varro shrugged. "I merely asked myself who stood to gain from the fire, and pursued my inquiries accordingly."

Martius was smiling. "A modest questor, too, it would seem. What led you to the merchants?"

"Well, I first became suspicious of Priscus when I learned that he had been celebrating ever since the fire. Here was a merchant who had supposedly lost most of his stock in the blaze, and he was leading a life of revelry. I sent my freedmen around the city asking questions about the high-living merchant, and in time they learned that Priscus and his friend Plancus had removed all their stock from the Foursquare Market and stored it in a warehouse on the river, just days before the fire. Ultimately, their slaves gave them up; they confessed everything."

"What did the merchants hope to gain?"

"It transpired that Priscus and Plancus were hugely in debt. So they conceived a plan between them to rid themselves of their creditors. They had their slaves set the fire in a section of the market which backed onto the city archives, and laid a trail of pitch all the way to the archives itself."

"What was the attraction of the archives?"

"The building contained the records of every debt the merchants owed. Once the fire had swept through the records, Priscus and Plancus were debt free."

"Of course!" Martius threw back his head and laughed heartily.

"Had Priscus not wined and dined his way into my sights," said Varro soberly, "the pair might have evaded suspicion, and retained their heads."

"Not even Mercury will protect a felonious merchant. And now we go to Galilee and Judea to investigate a criminal of a different color. What do we know of this Nazarene? What was he? Nobleman? Slave? Priest? What was his crime?"

"A wandering priest of sorts," said Varro, "leader of an obscure Jewish sect, crucified for sedition. We have a letter written by one of his followers, Lucius, a physician, telling us something of the arrest, trial, and execution of the Nazarene. In addition, my man Callidus has questioned some of the Nazarene's followers here in the city. They are a smug lot, he tells me, and make no attempt to hide their affiliation with the group." He glanced over his shoulder to the freedman walking in his shadow. "Is that not so, Callidus?"

"Yes, my lord," Callidus came back. "Very smug. As if they are in possession of some special secret. They are despised by other Jews, for they introduce non Jews into their ranks. They even claim that one of the Nazarene's followers, a fellow by the name of Cephas, converted a retired Roman centurion into their sect."

"I find that difficult to believe," remarked a skeptical Martius. "A centurion?"

"They said the centurion's name was Cornelius, my lord," said Callidus, "and he had come out of the 1st Legion on the Rhine to live in his retirement at Caesarea. They claim he later went into Asia to try to win more followers for the Nazarene. He went with Paulus of Tarsus, a Jew who first introduced the Nazarenes philosophy to Antioch."

"A Roman centurion would have more sense," Martius gave a dismissive snort.

"Tell the tribune what you learned about the subject of the inquiry from the Nazarene's followers, Callidus," Varro instructed.

"Yes, my lord. This Jesus fellow, whose name in Aramaic was Yehoshua, or Joshua as we would say in Latin, was unmarried, and had four brothers and several sisters. His brother Jacob took on the leadership of the sect at Jerusalem following the Nazarene's execution, but he was stoned to death by the Jewish authorities some time during the procuratorship of Lucceius Albinus…"

Martius was nodding as Callidus droned on, but he was not taking in the details. Varro was the detail man, Martius was a soldier, a career soldier, and all that interested him was soldierly subjects.

"The Nazarene was thirty-five years of age when he was crucified…"

"When was this, Julius?" Martius interrupted the freedman.

"In the latter part of the reign of Tiberius Caesar," Varro answered.

"So, we have to pick up a trail that is perhaps forty years old?" Martius commented, raising his eyebrows.

Varro nodded. "The witnesses to the events in question are probably dead, of old age, or else they perished during the Jewish uprising." He sighed unhappily. "This will not be an easy task, Marcus. The crux of the matter is a claim by the Nazarene's followers that the man rose from the dead two days after his execution, before disappearing. A claim I must disprove to Collega's satisfaction."

"What? Rose from the dead?" Martius roared with laughter. "Not a difficult thing to disprove, I should have thought, Julius, my friend. Since it is physically impossible!"

"Evidence, Marcus," Varro glumly replied. "It will take evidence to destroy the myth that has grown around this man, indisputable evidence."

"So, do the Nazarene's followers claim he still lives? Can we not arrest him and question him? Torture a confession out of him?"

Varro shook his head. "The body disappeared, shortly after the execution. He has never been seen since."

"All very convenient. So, we're looking for grave robbers?"

"I suspect the evidence that General Collega requires is simply no longer there to be found. I didn't ask for this assignment, and now I fear I will fail to come back with the proof that Collega requires. As the Spanish say, sent for wool, I will come back shorn."

Again the tribune laughed heartily. Then he looked at Varro. "You need evidence, you say?" He winked at his friend. "Invent it, Julius. Invent it!"

Now it was Varro's turn to laugh.

"I could have extracted evidence from the Nazarenes I questioned, my lord," Callidus then declared. "Had you permitted me to loosen their tongues my own way."

"A non-productive exercise, as I have told you, Callidus," Varro returned, a little impatient with the freedman's forthrightness. "These people, who told you they never even laid eyes on the Nazarene when he was alive, will send word to their people in the south, warning them that a Roman questor is asking questions about the Nazarene. If you were one of these people and word were to reach you that the questor was applying torture to Nazarenes, would you not go into hiding?"

"Well, yes, I suppose so, my lord," Callidus begrudgingly agreed.

"That is why your master is the questor and you are the freedman, my dim witted fellow," Martius scolded him. "Manumission relieved you of the bonds of slavery, not the bonds of stupidity."

Callidus did not reply. He was not well disposed toward the questor's new deputy.

As the trio reached the entrance to the barracks bathhouse, a tall, gangly officer in a white cloak and wearing a long cavalry sword on his left hip came marching deliberately toward them. As he drew nearer, the officer removed his helmet and slipped it under his left arm, revealing a delicately featured visage and a head of golden curls.

"Here's a new face," said Martius.

"My new cavalry commander, I think," said Varro. "Greetings, friend."

The blond reached out his right hand to Varro, smiling. "Quintus Cornelius Crispus, Prefect of Horse," he cheerily announced.

"Julius Terentius Varro," said the questor, returning the handshake. "Welcome, Crispus. You have brought my cavalry contingent?"

The twenty-five-year-old prefect nodded. "With Decurion Pompieus and thirty troopers of the Vettonian Horse, reporting for duty on the questor's mission to Galilee and Judea, as ordered by General Collega."

"Very good. This is Tribune Marcus Metellus Martius, your immediate superior."

"Tribune." Still smiling, Crispus held out his hand to Martius.

Scowling, Martius briefly took his hand. "You are new to Syria, prefect?"

"I landed at Laodicea from Rome two weeks ago, tribune."

"A green apple," Martius growled malevolently. "Where were you previously, Crispus? With which unit?"

Crispus swallowed hard. "The Second Wing of the Egyptian Horse, in Macedonia, my lord."

"Egyptians! Macedonia? Not exactly a hotbed of action, is it, prefect?"

"Er, no, tribune," Crispus conceded. As the blood drained from his face and the enthusiasm drained from his spirit, and seeing Callidus smirking at him, he turned to the questor for support. "My lord, I, er…"

"We march at dawn the day after tomorrow, Crispus. Have your men ready."

"Yes, my lord. Thank you, my lord. My men are ready now, my lord," he gushed, eager to please the questor.

"The day after tomorrow will suffice," Varro returned.

"Egyptians? Macedonia?" Martius grumbled to himself, beginning to ascend steps to the bathhouse door.

Crispus fell in beside Varro, as the questor also began to climb the steps, and Callidus brought up the rear.

"Would a fellow have much chance of writing a little poetry on this assignment, do you think my lord?" Crispus asked.

"Poetry!" Martius bellowed in front, spinning around to face the others as they came up. "Did you say poetry, prefect?"

"Er, yes, tribune." A fearful Crispus quickly turned to Varro. "I have published an amount of verse, my lord. My friend the noted poet Statius says that my work shows great promise. I had thought, with the Jewish business all but dealt with, there could be a lull or two during this expedition when I might be able to put pen to paper. I had hoped to use the journey out from Rome to advantage, but I am not a good sailor, and composing verse aboard a tossing merchantman is no easy feat."

"I can imagine," Varro responded with an amused smile.

"Poetry!" Martius exclaimed again. "If we do strike trouble in the south, Crispus, you can use that cavalry sword of yours to decapitate a few rebels with poetic flourish! Will that suit you?"

Crispus smiled weakly. "Yes, tribune."

Martius turned and continued in through the bathhouse door. "Poetry!" he spat.

Crispus looked at Varro with a plaintive expression.

"You will find the tribune a harsh critic but a firm friend, Crispus," Varro assured the prefect. "We can count ourselves lucky that he is going with us."

"Yes, my lord," Crispus responded without conviction.

Varro continued on up the steps. He sympathized with the young prefect; they could not all be dashing heroes like Martius, and to his mind Rome needed her writers as much as she needed her fighters. Just the same, knowing that he would have his friend Martius as his strong right hand made him feel a little better about undertaking this difficult mission. Only that morning Collega had informed him that he had accepted the offer made by Antiochus and was assigning the Jewish magistrate to Varro's expedition as his interpreter. Collega was also sending along his secretary Pythagoras, supposedly to help Varro write his report about the death of the Nazarene, even though Varro had a perfectly capable secretary, Artimedes. But Varro knew Pythagoras' brief would be to keep a covert eye on the questor and report back secretly to Collega in Antioch.

IV

AN IMPOSSIBLE MISSION

Antioch, Capital of the Roman Province of Syria. March, A.D. 71

'Come at once,' said the message summoning Varro to the governor's mansion on the eve of the expedition's departure. The questor found his commander playing dice with six freedmen and a youth who looked vaguely familiar to Varro. Collega was never happier than when he was eating or when he was winning at dice.

"Ah, questor," said the smiling Collega, turning on the stool where he sat before the gaming table with the *fritillus,* the dice box, in hand. "Just one more throw," he said, shaking the box. With a jerk of the hand he cast a pair of dice onto the wooden gaming board. All eyes watched the ivory cubes tumble and roll to a standstill. Leaning forward to read each die, Collega roared with delight. "I win!" At the same time, his companions threw up their hands and groaned with despair. "*Par duplex!* Double evens!" Collega gloated. "Pay up, all of you."

As the other players dug into purses, Collega came to his feet. Briefly he winced with pain and put a hand to his lower back. "The old back problem," he said in explanation to Varro. "It is nothing." Then, looping his arm up over the taller Varro's shoulder, he steered him across the room, to stand in an open doorway looking out from a small balcony over a sunken garden decorated with exquisite topiary. Below, water cascaded into a circular pool. The aromas of lush perfumes wafted up from the greenery.

"You depart on the Nazarene mission tomorrow, Varro?" the general asked. It was a rhetorical question; Collega was intimately acquainted with all the details.

"At dawn, my lord," Varro returned.

"Good, good. I have arranged for a physician to join your party. You may need a medical man where you are going."

"Thank you, my lord. That physician would be…?"

"Diocles, the Corinthian. A very experienced and able man."

"Ah, Diocles," Varro responded. Apparently Collega had forgotten that this was the same Diocles he had labeled an incurable drunkard, the same physician whose judgment he had called into question. But Varro could not say as much, could only graciously accept the doctor's appointment even though he suspected the general was only trying to rid himself of Diocles. "Thank you, my lord."

"I also have another military officer for you." Collega beckoned the young man who had been a spectator to the dice game.

The youngster slowly rose up from the gaming table and strolled to join the pair. Wearing an expensive multi-colored tunic, and, on his left hand, the gold ring of a member of the Equestrian Order, he was a handsome boy of eighteen, with rosy cheeks, soft skin, and black hair cut in a severe fringe.

"Questor, this is Gaius Licinius Venerius," the general said in introduction, "the scion of a distinguished family."

"I am the descendant of Licinius Lucullus," the youth pompously announced as he joined the pair.

"Indeed?" said Varro, trying to sound impressed. He knew who the boy's ancestor was; Lucullus had been one of Rome's greatest generals, and one of her most extravagant spenders, in the time of Julius Caesar's youth.

"My father was twice a consul. My uncle is Gaius Licinius Mucianus."

"You are the nephew of my patron?" said Varro with surprise. "It occurred to me that I knew your face, Venerius. I must have seen you with Licinius Mucianus at Rome."

"You are one of my uncle's clients?" Venerius sniffed. "I do not recall having seen you before. My uncle has certainly never mentioned you."

"Quite possibly," Varro returned, determined to remain civil despite having taken an instant dislike to the priggish youth.

"Venerius has been serving out his six-month posting as a tribune of the thin stripe with the 4th Scythica at Zeugma, Varro," Collega advised. "However, Licinius Mucianus has written to say that he wishes his nephew to gain the broadest possible experience while he is in Syria."

"An admirable sentiment, my lord," Varro remarked, dreading what he realized must be coming next.

"It is, is it not," said Collega. "So, I am sending Venerius on your expedition."

Varro gulped. "I see, general." He looked at Venerius, inwardly cursing.

"He should prove useful; you can use another officer," Collega added.

"Yes, thank you, general." Varro tried to give the youngster a diplomatic smile. "It should prove interesting, Venerius. For us all."

"You will find the questor has much to teach you, Venerius," said Collega.

Venerius looked Varro up and down with a contemptuous expression.

"Perhaps you would care to join me for dinner, Venerius," Varro suggested, "at the gladiatorial barracks. All my chief officers and senior freedman are dining with me tonight, as a prelude to our departure tomorrow."

"No, thank you," Venerius snapped back. "I shall be otherwise engaged."

Varro shrugged. "As you prefer." Determined not to say anything he would regret, he turned to Collega. "If that was all, general, with your permission…?"

"Yes, Varro, you must have a great deal to do prior to your departure." Collega walked him toward the door. There was a cylindrical leather document case lying on a table by the entrance, and as they came to it Collega took up the case and handed it to Varro. "Your Authority, questor," he said. "Use it wisely." Then he held out his hand. "I will not be seeing you again before you leave. May the gods go with you." He focused very deliberately on Varro, and lowered his voice. "Be sure to bring back the evidence I seek, Varro. As well you know, much hangs on the success of this mission as far as Rome is concerned." His eyes transmitted the true meaning of his words. Collega was thinking about his career at Rome, first and foremost.

Varro returned the handshake. "Yes, general, for Rome. Thank you. I will do my utmost not to disappoint you."

"Do not forget, I want you back here with your report before the last ship of the sailing season sets out for Italy. I bid you a good night and all success, questor."

"Thank you, general. A good night to you."

As Varro walked from the room with his Authority in hand, he cursed his luck. Collega was not doing anything to contribute to the success of the expedition, saddling him at the last moment with a drunkard and a brat, adding them to Pythagoras the spy and the devious Jew Antiochus. Varro resolved to be on his guard from this moment forward, knowing there would be few in his entourage apart from Martius he could rely on and trust, on what he had become convinced was close to an impossible mission.

V

THE PREFECT'S SHAME

The Road to Beirut, Roman Province of Syria.
March A.D. 71

With characteristic efficiency, Varro had begun as he meant to go on. The questor's column had departed Antioch on time, in the light of a golden dawn. While the main body moved down the military highway at brisk marching pace, the mounted advance guard of ten Vettonian troopers led by their decurion Gaius Pompeius cantered down the road ahead, accompanied by a centurion and several civilians.

Callidus rode with the advance guard, along with another freedman, Paris, the questor's portly cook. The advance guard's task was to clear the road of obstruction and to precede the main column into the place chosen for the next night's camp. There, Callidus would make whatever logistical arrangements were necessary for the expedition as a whole, while Paris the cook acquired food for the questor's personal table.

There was a smile on Callidus' face as he rode. His thoughts were in Antioch, the previous night, in a small attic room in a house on the Street of the Olives, and Priscilla, the love of his life. Priscilla was a slave in the household of Paganus, a freedman originally from Northern Gaul and now a grasping merchant and money-lender. While Callidus had frolicked in plump, playful Priscilla's bed, his master Julius Varro had been below in the bedroom of Octavia, eldest daughter of Paganus. Callidus did not like Octavia. A beauty she might be, but she was arrogant and self-centered. But because she had been the questor's bed partner for a year Callidus was certain his master would take Octavia back to Rome with him when he and Callidus went home, and would keep her there as his mistress even if he married a daughter of the nobility. And if Octavia went to Rome, so too would her favorite body servant Priscilla, and Callidus and Priscilla could be together. It would be a perfect outcome as far as Callidus was concerned.

Callidus smiled too as he remembered the words last evening of Priscilla's mother, the ancient, toothless, sightless Aquila, who shared a tiny upper floor room with her daughter. Paganus had retained the crone because he valued her skills as a seer. The merchant would boast to friends that old Aquila only had to hold of a subject's hands to receive messages containing often astonishingly accurate predictions about their future, and he would charge them for her 'readings.' Last evening, old Aquila had taken Callidus' hands and, wide eyed and perspiring, she had predicted that he would soon go on a journey, and on that journey he would be in danger. The danger would not be from without, she had told him with quaking voice, it would be from within.

Now Callidus laughed out loud as he heard Aquila's words replaying in his mind, so loud that Paris the cook riding beside him looked around with a question on his face. Callidus was as superstitious as the next man, but he had never been convinced of Aquila's so-called talent for divination. For Priscilla's sake he pretended to be awed by the old woman, but her forecasts had never impressed him. And so it was with her latest predictions. Danger, on a journey? He was always going on one journey or another. And in his job when was he not in danger from within? On the strength of that sort of prognostication, Callidus told himself, *he* could go into business telling fortunes.

As Callidus and the advance party rode on ahead, the expedition proper was led by another troop of ten Vettonian cavalrymen, advancing two-by-two at walking pace on neat Spanish ponies. Each man was equipped with a sheathed *spatha,* the long Roman cavalry sword, a round shield, a lance, and a quiver of small throwing spears. Behind the horsemen walked Questor Varro's grim-faced, gray-headed lictor, Lucius Pedius. Wearing a loose white tunic, the former 10th Legion centurion was tanned and fit, with calves like steel and thighs like tree trunks after two decades of military service. A scar down the left side of his neck was a permanent souvenir of that service. The unarmed Pedius bore the questor's full-size *fasces,* a bundle of rods surrounding an ax, all bound with red chord, symbol of a magistrate's ultimate power to punish and to execute. Just two men in all of Syria, Varro and his superior Collega, were endowed with that power. It meant that the *fasces* was a symbol sufficient to send a shiver down the spine of many a traveler standing at the roadside to let the column pass.

Pedius was not a happy man. For four years he had fought in General Vespasian's battles in Galilee, had stormed Jericho, had slogged through the five-month siege of Jerusalem for Titus. Then, the previous December, he had retired at the end of his twenty-year enlistment, glad to leave behind the blood and death of legion life and start a new life with his savings and his retirement bonus. On his discharge he had quickly gone up to Antioch, where, permitted to marry now that he had left the army, he immediately wed Phoebe, a freedwoman and native of the Syrian capital whom he had met and fallen in love with seven years before while serving under General Corbulo. It was then that Questor Varro had offered him a one-year appointment as his lictor.

The offer had been attractive at the time. A good deal of prestige attached to the post of lictor, and it was not overly demanding. Even the annual tax gathering trip around the province was nothing more than a sociable ramble, with the questor and his staff made the guests of the communities they visited. Pedius had not hesitated to accept the appointment. Little had he known at the time that the questor would within three months be setting off on a journey which would take Pedius back into territory that held many unpleasant memories for him. His new bride had not complained. Phoebe had assured Pedius that he would soon be back with her, and had sent him on his way that morning with a loving kiss and a long embrace. He might even be able to do some good on this mission, she had told him. But as far as Pedius was concerned, the sooner this expedition was over and he was back with his new wife, the happier he would be.

Directly behind the lictor marched a bare-headed standard-bearer of the 4th Scythica Legion, proudly holding aloft his *vexillum,* a square cloth banner signifying a legion detachment. On the red cloth was painted the motif 'COHVIII LEGIVSC' denoting an element of the 8th Cohort of the 4th Scythica Legion, together with the symbols of a running boar and a fish. The boar was the legion's emblem, a symbol with great significance to the Celtic ancestors of 4th Legion men, who all originated in the province of Cisalpine Gaul which extended from the Po River in northern Italy to the Alps. The symbol of the fish represented the zodiacal sign of Pisces, considered the legion's birth sign because the unit had been founded in late February.

Three unarmed boy trumpeters of the 4th came immediately behind the standard-bearer, all in a line. Each youth was entwined with a *cornu*, the large G-shaped Roman military trumpet, which was almost as big as its player, and each wore a bearskin cape, with the upper part of the animal's head affixed to their helmet, the front legs crossed over their chest, and the pelt trailing down their back. On the trumpeters' heels came a group of riders. First of all, Questor Varro, wearing a simple tunic and cloak. Then, the tribune Marcus Martius, the prefect Crispus, the junior tribune Venerius, all three in uniform, armor, and helmet. Riding immediately behind the military officers came the secretaries Pythagoras and Artimedes, followed by Diocles the physician, a chubby, pasty-faced man who appeared almost asleep in the saddle, and then Antiochus the Jewish magistrate, wearing a discomforted scowl.

The reason for the Jewish magistrate's discomfort rode directly behind him — a massive, one-armed black Numidian. Columbus was his name, and he was a freedman and former gladiator of the Thracian school who had lost his left arm in the arena. Yet, so powerful was he with just one arm, and so imposing was his almost seven foot frame, that General Collega had employed Columbus as a personal bodyguard. As clear evidence that Collega did not trust Antiochus entirely, Columbus had been sent along with the express task of keeping an eye on the apostate Jew.

Astride mules, a group of freedmen functionaries rode close behind the official party. After them, in marching order, seventy-eight legionaries of the 4th Scythica came swinging down the roadway, their hob-nailed military sandals crunching the stone pavement. Marching six abreast in thirteen ranks, the soldiers wore the blood red tunic and cloak common to all soldiers of Rome's legions. Gleaming segmented metal armor covered their torsos and shoulders, while a red scarf protected each man's neck against the chafing effect of the heavy armor. A sheathed short sword hung on the right hip, a dagger on the left. A curved rectangular wooden shield with a central boss of iron hung on each man's left shoulder. Weather covers of plain leather hid the running boar symbol of the 4th which decorated every shield. Suspended by a neck strap, each man's helmet hung loosely about his neck. Over his right shoulder each legionary carried a long wooden pole. Javelins were strapped to the pole, while from it, behind him, dangled the man's backpack, with bedroll, mess tin, water bucket, entrenching tools, rations, removable horsehair helmet plume, military decorations, and personal items, the lot weighing more than eighty pounds per man.

Immediately in the wake of the last rank marched a single optio, or sergeant major. Quintus Silius was his name. He was identically armed, attired and equipped to the men of the rank and file. Occasionally the duty-bound Silius would bark an order for silence, should a legionary dare to attempt to share a comment or joke with a colleague.

Behind the infantry came the column's baggage train: forty heavily-laden pack mules led by non-combatant freedmen muleteers, then a succession of covered carts, twenty-one in all, carrying heavy equipment and supplies, also in the charge of mule-drivers. Most of the carts carried sacks of grain, full pots of water, jars of olive oil and lamp oil, amphorae of wine, grinding stones, cooking pots, folded tents and lumber for construction. One vehicle was stacked high with wax writing tablets wrapped in damp linen to keep them moist, and virgin scrolls of parchment in protective leather cases — the raw material of the questor's ultimate report. Several carts were devoted to the questor's personal needs, his tent, furniture, armor and clothing, and his silver dining plate.

Between the baggage train and the rearguard of another ten Vettonian cavalrymen walked the thirty male slaves serving the expedition. Some of these men had official duties. One group of three had the sole responsibility of the care and operation of the expedition's water clock by night and sundial by day. Most of the others were the personal slaves of the officers and freedman officials. Varro had instructed his subordinates to keep their staff numbers down, for efficiency's sake, but none had brought less than two slaves. Diolces the physician had brought five, including three medical orderlies. Martius had three: an armor-bearer, a handservant, and a cook. Young Venerius had a similar number. As for Varro himself, apart from Paris his freedman cook, he had brought along just two slaves, Timeus his baker, and Hostilis, a Briton, who, because he was the questor's chief slave, acted as supervisor of the entire slave party.

Before dawn that morning, prior to leaving Antioch, Varro had gone to the city's Temple of Mars. There, the augurs of the temple had performed the *lustratio* ceremony, purifying the 4th Scythica *vexillum* with perfumes and attaching sacred ribbons representing garlands of flowers to bring protection and good fortune to the unit on its mission. Varro had then presided over the obligatory ritual animal sacrifice before he set out on the expedition. The entrails of the sacrificial goat had been found to be clear, and the augurs had pronounced that the omens for the questor's mission were fortuitous. The chief augur had then walked outside with Varro. Pointing to the cloudless early morning sky with its carpet of twinkling stars, the augur had proclaimed that the clear sky also boded well for Varro's endeavor.

Riding the highway now, deep in contemplation of the augur's words, the pragmatic Varro told himself that while the god of war may have been on his side success on this expedition would also depend on the flesh and blood people in his party. He knew from experience that Callidus was utterly dependable, as was Artimedes his faithful Greek secretary. As for Pedius, he had known his lictor for only a matter of months, but he felt sure that the officious former centurion would not let him down.

Pythagoras was pompous, but he excelled as a secretary, and Varro knew he would be loyal to General Collega's purpose in all this. Knowing that Pythagoras would be sending reports back to Collega with Varro's official dispatches, about the expedition and the way that Varro was handling it, Varro would be careful not to allow the secretary entry into his innermost thoughts. As for the military men, Martius would be a solid deputy, and Crispus would do his best to please.

Heading the other side of the ledger was Antiochus. The previous year, to obtain his appointment as magistrate of the Jewish community of Antioch, the man had sworn off Judaism and informed on his father, the incumbent holder of the post of Jewish magistrate, telling General Collega that Antiochus senior and other Jewish elders had been planning to put the capital of Syria to the torch in revenge for Rome's suppression of the Jewish Revolt to the south. Believing the son's accusation, Collega had executed Antiochus' father and other leading Jews of Antioch, incinerating them in the amphitheater. The affair had given Antiochus his position of power, and had given the now deceased merchants Priscus and Plancus their incendiary inspiration for the subsequent Fire of Antioch, which they had hoped would be blamed on the Jews. Varro himself had never run foul of Antiochus, but the man's duplicitous past and the fact that Governor Collega did not trust Antiochus implicitly were reason enough for Varro to handle his dealings with the man with judicious care.

As for the others, the reputation for drunkenness that had preceded Diocles the physician had caused Varro to issue strict instructions that all members of his party were to refrain from excessive drinking during the mission and that Diocles in particular was not to touch a single drop of wine until they had returned to Antioch. Then there was young Venerius, the spoilt, arrogant and lazy thin-stripe tribune. Varro was expecting to have difficulties with him, sooner or later. The other military officers serving under Varro were unknown quantities but came with good reports. Pompeius the cavalry decurion, Crispus's deputy and a man with a fearsome battle scar from right ear to empty eye socket, was an aggressive cavalryman of fifteen years' service. The commander of the 4th Scythica Legion detachment, Centurion Titus Gallo, also appeared to Varro to be a valuable man. The fifty-two-year-old had thirty-two years' legion service to his credit. Right now, the centurion was out ahead of the main column with Decurion Pompeius, Callidus, and the advance guard, setting in train procedures designed to become routine on the march over the coming weeks and months.

✠

Centurion Gallo urged his horse to the gallop. To his rear, the two cavalrymen riding with him, caught by surprise at first, did the same. The stone-paved military road, just fifteen feet across, and built by legion engineers with a slight central camber so that rainwater ran off into culverts at the roadsides, cleaved through the wheat fields to the south of Antioch without deviation. Nobody knows better than an engineer that the most direct route between two points is a straight line.

The wiry, silver-haired Gallo wore the same red uniform and cloak as his legionaries, but his armor and equipment was richly decorated with gold and jet inlay. He also had the additional protection of metal greaves on his shins. His officer's rank was confirmed by the fact that he wore his sword on the left and dagger on the right, the opposite configuration to that of the ordinary enlisted man.

The centurion had parted company with the advance guard near the coast, at a courier station a six-hour march south-west of Antioch, and accompanied by the two cavalrymen he was heading back up the road to rejoin Questor Varro and the main column. Glancing over his shoulder, Gallo grinned to himself as he saw the two troopers struggling to keep up.

Now, with travelers appearing on the road in the distance, the centurion eased back to the trot, allowing the Vettonians to catch him up.

Titus Gallo was a man with a large chip on his brawny shoulder. After joining the 22nd Primigeneia Legion in his native Galatia as a twenty-year-old recruit, he'd risen to centurion of the fourth grade with the 12th Legion, stationed in Syria. A promising career had then met a brick wall under an incompetent general, Cesennius Petus, the same General Petus who was destined to return to the East to take up the governorship of Syria in the coming year. Petus had been recalled to Rome by Nero after his inept performance in Armenia, where he'd as good as surrendered to the Parthians, and many of his centurions had been dishonorably discharged or reduced in rank. Even though Titus Gallo felt that he had served well under a poor commander, he had been demoted four grades by General Corbulo, commander in chief in the East.

Gallo's chance to redeem himself, and his career, had eventually come when the Jewish Revolt blew up. The 12th Legion was included in the task force led south from Antioch by the then Governor of Syria, General Gaius Cestius Gallus, to put down the uprising. But after reaching Jerusalem, General Gallus had led his army on a bloody retreat all the way back to Caesarea, losing six thousand men along the way. Gallus had died shortly after, some said of shame.

Titus Gallo had survived the Jewish campaign, but like many of the officers of the 12th he was blamed for the disaster that had befallen his legion. Transferred out to garrison duty on the Euphrates with the 4th Scythica, he had spent five backwater years cursing General Petus for his cowardice, cursing General Corbulo for unfairly demoting him, cursing General Gallus for his ineptitude, and cursing the Jews for their rebellion. All in all, there were few people Titus Gallo did not blame for his situation, and there was not a Roman officer above the rank of centurion he would put his faith in, or a Jew he would trust. As far as Centurion Gallo was concerned this mission to Judea with Questor Varro had been sent by the gods to make up for past disappointments.

The 4th Scythica had become the butt of jokes among the other legions of the East. 'The Tuskless Boars' and 'the Sleeping Boars' they called Gallo's unit, because the legion had not distinguished itself in combat in living memory. As far as Gallo was concerned there was nothing tuskless or sleepy about the men he led. The legionaries of the 4th Scythica marching into

Galilee and Judea with him were eager for action, conscripts from Cisalpine Gaul enrolled the previous year. Gallo had been drilling them mercilessly ever since in the hope of a call to service against the Jewish rebels. Before long, he hoped, he would put that training to the test.

After Gallo had been riding for a little over an hour, the questor's column came in sight. The centurion and the two troopers soon moved off the road, allowing the leading elements of the column to pass. As the group of officers drew level, the centurion urged his horse forward and eased in beside the questor and made his report on the move.

"There are several old marching camps at the courier station which would be suitable for the night, questor. I have marked out our camp site in one of them. There will be only an hour or two's digging for the men. And your man Callidus said to tell you that the supply situation is adequate."

Varro was hauling supplies with him, but where possible he wanted to live off the land as they journeyed south. He knew from reports from Caesarea, the Judean capital, that food stocks in much of the war-ravaged province had been exhausted, and the time would come when he would have to rely on the supplies he carried with him.

"Very good, centurion," Julius Varro acknowledged.

As Centurion Gallo took up position in the group of riders behind the senior officers, the tribune Martius, riding on Varro's far side, leaned closer to the questor. "You know, Julius, I have been thinking," Martius said. "I read the Lucius letter last night, after we dined."

This surprised Varro. Martius had consumed a large amount of wine at dinner — apparently not enough to dull his brain. "What was your impression of it, Marcus?"

"Informative. You had noted that this Jesus of Nazareth used several different names? What is more, one of his deputies, Simon the Galilean, was also called Petra, or Cephas, as the Greeks say. I ask you, why would you call a man 'rock'?"

"I have no idea," Varro confessed.

"Well, it is apparent to me that these people were engaged in secretive, seditious activities. Why else would they use false names, code names? Answer me that."

"That is one of the many answers we are marching to Galilee and Judea to find, Marcus. It would not be wise to judge too soon. Would you not agree?"

"Perhaps," Martius returned with a shrug. He had already made up his mind that these Nazarenes had been nothing more than covert revolutionaries who had shrouded their activities in a religious veil.

✠

Just before midday they reached a horse-changing station operated by the *Cursus Publicus,* Rome's state courier service. The outpost was on a ridge looking out over the Mediterranean Sea. As Centurion Gallo had advised, there were the remains of several legion marching camps around about the station's stable wings and central accommodation building. This would be the site of the expedition's camp for the night.

A legion on the march built a new fortified camp every night of its journey. These temporary forts were used over and over again by different units traveling the same route at different times. The fort that the one hundred and ten fighting men of the Varro expedition found themselves in on their first day on the road to Beirut was much too large for them to defend in an emergency. So, after a piece of bread and a gulp of water for lunch, the legionaries set to work digging several new earth walls ten feet high and entrenchments ten feet deep to secure a smaller perimeter in one corner of the fort selected by their centurion. At the same time, Prefect Crispus' cavalry troopers fetched water, foraged firewood for cooking fires, and brought in sacks of grain purchased by Callidus from a nearby village.

Once the walls had been completed to Centurion Gallo's satisfaction the toiling legionaries set up the tents of the officers and officials, and then their own tents, following a grid pattern that Gallo had marked out using small purple, red and white flags. Each officer had a tent to himself, while the foot soldiers would sleep eight to a tent, in their squads. Five Vettonian troopers occupied each cavalry tent, with their saddles. Once tents were erected, the troops installed the officers' equipment.

The questor, as expedition commander, had by far the largest tent. This pavilion, the column's *pretorium,* would serve as Varro's private quarters, as the expedition's headquarters, and as the senior officers' mess. Varro's folding metal bed was set up in a corner; enlisted men had no such luxury, sleeping in their bedrolls on the ground. Three dining couches were unloaded from the carts and set up around a low table. A waist-high work table and several stools were set up, and a number of lamps placed on pedestals. Finally, the men reverently set up the questor's portable family shrine, no more than a large box on legs. When the shrine's doors were opened, they revealed three small statuettes of the Lares, the Roman household goddesses, flanking a central statue of Jove. A small wooden box with an amber knob for a handle contained family relics. A pottery incense burner completed the religious equipment.

Freedmen each had a tent to themselves. Non-combatants would sleep in emptied carts, or beneath them. Slaves rigged canvas shelters for themselves between vehicles and set up cooking fires in the open. Hostilis, the questor's handservant, would spend each night in the *pretorium*, sleeping on the ground at the foot of his master's bed.

As the sun was setting, a trumpeter sounded the beginning of the first of the four watches of the night. The sentries chosen by lot by Centurion Gallo and the four cavalrymen of the night patrol who would check that they were not asleep at their posts now hurried to take up their positions. Every three hours, as determined by the water clock set up outside the questor's tent, a new watch would be trumpeted.

At the sounding of 'New Watch,' Centurion Gallo and his *tesserarius,* or orderly sergeant, came to the questor's tent. As they arrived, the trumpeter was departing and four legion sentries had just taken up their posts, two either side of the tent's entrance. Under a small canvas canopy to one side of the entrance two slaves were fussing with the expedition's water clock, setting it so that it would show the start of the twelve hours of the night the moment the sun set out over the Mediterranean. Another slave was lighting a lamp which would illuminate the clock.

Centurion Gallo and the auburn-haired sergeant, whose name was Claudius Rufus, parted the curtains hanging in the *pretorium* entrance and entered the large, square tent. They found Varro sitting at his work table, talking with the tribune Martius and the prefect Crispus. The two soldiers came to attention in front of the questor's table, before Gallo held out a small wax tablet to expedition the commander. "If the questor would be good enough to provide the watchword…?"

To the centurion's surprise, Varro did not accept the tablet. "Where is the officer of the watch?" he asked.

Gallo looked pained. "I, er, I do not know, questor."

"Give Tribune Venerius my compliments," said Marcus Martius beside Varro. "Ask him to report here to the questor." The eyes of the expedition's military commander narrowed a little. "At once!"

"At once, tribune," Gallo repeated. He spun around. Thrusting the wax tablet into Rufus' hands with a scowl, he hurried from the tent.

A few minutes later, the waiting occupants of the *pretorium* heard a raised voice outside before Gaius Venerius, the junior tribune, entered in a rush. He was wearing a casual tunic, and his face was red with rage. Centurion Gallo came close behind.

"This oaf Gallo laid hands on me!" Venerius raged. "I want him charged! I want him punished!" He turned to the centurion. "Buffoon!" he spat.

Gallo did not as much as blink. "Centurion Gallo reporting with the officer of the watch, questor, as ordered," he formally announced.

"I am not the officer of the watch!" Venerius snarled. "Dimwit!"

"Oh, yes you are," said Varro, in a low, controlled voice.

"What?" Venerius' head snapped around.

"As a tribune of the thin stripe, Venerius, you will fulfil the duties of officer of the watch on this expedition, as you would in any legion or legion detachment."

"No, no, no." Venerius looked down at Varro and folded his arms. "As a thin-stripe tribune I am only required to serve for three months during my six-month posting, and I will have you know that I have done my three months. I am excused duties."

"I will have no sightseers on this expedition, Venerius," said Varro, making an effort to keep his anger from rising.

"As a thin-stripe tribune," said Marcus Martius, rising up from his stool and coming threateningly around the table, "you will obey the orders of your superior, or you will face a court martial. Here, in this camp."

Venerius paled. His arms unfolded and dropped to his sides, as if suddenly devoid of their strength. "You, you are joking?" he stammered.

"Am I?" The imposing Martius stood glaring at him. "The court martial of Gaius LICINIUS Venerius for insubordination would be well received back at Rome, would it not, thin-striper? I think not. Now, listen carefully. In a moment, you will run back to your tent, put on your armor, and arm yourself. You will then run back here and report for duty, after which you will pass the watchword to the sentries and report back to the questor when the distribution of the watchword has been acknowledged by all sentry posts." His face was now just inches from that of the young man. "Do you understand, tribune of the thin stripe?"

Venerius' mouth opened, but no sound came out.

"Might I also suggest, questor," Martius went on, straightening and turning to Varro, "that the thin stripe tribune be assigned to the advance guard from tomorrow, to mark out the new camp each day. Centurion Gallo has far more important duties to attend to than camp marking."

"Very well," Varro agreed, trying not to smile. "So be it."

"Might I also take the liberty of suggesting the watchword for the next twenty-four hours, questor?" Martius continued, turning back to Venerius.

"I am always open to suggestions, tribune," Varro replied.

"Perhaps it might be 'Obedience,'" Martius said, raising his eyebrows at Venerius. "Or perhaps 'Humility.' No, no, I think, 'Respect.' What think you, questor?"

"'Respect' it shall be," said Varro. He held out his hand to Rufus. "The *tessera?*"

The soldier handed the wax tablet to the questor. Varro's skinny, bushy-headed servant Hostilis appeared from behind him with a metal stylus. Varro took the writing instrument and quickly wrote 'RESPECT' in the wax. Laying aside the stylus he passed the tablet back to Rufus. Then he looked directly at Venerius. "Respect," he said. He paused, for effect, then added. "You and the tesserarius are dismissed, centurion."

Gallo and Rufus turned and left the tent.

The shocked Venerius stood looking from Varro to Martius and back again.

"Tribune Venerius," Martius now said. "If you have not reported for duty in full uniform and equipment by the time the sun has set, you will be considered in breach of your orders and you will be charged accordingly. Well? What are you waiting for, boy?"

Venerius swallowed hard, then turned and left the tent.

Martius looked at Varro and Crispus the curly-headed cavalry prefect. His severe expression gave way to a grin. "That seemed to do the trick," he said.

"Could you really court martial him, questor?" asked Crispus, in a lowered voice.

"Of course," said Varro. "All that is required is a panel of three officers senior to, or equal to him in rank — you, Martius, and myself."

"I would quite enjoy it," said Martius. Then he frowned. "You don't think I came on a little too strongly, do you, Julius? Any other thin-striper would have felt the back of my hand, but this annoying little monkey is Mucianus' nephew, after all."

"He cannot use his connections to escape his responsibilities," said Varro emphatically. "You were quite right to set the boundaries, Marcus. This is only the first day of the mission; we must start as we mean to go on."

Outside, on their way to the main gate to commence the distribution of the password, Gallo and Rufus were passing along beside the enlisted men's tents, where cooking fires in front of tent doors glowed in the failing light. Every squad cooked its own food, and tonight the men would be eating hot broth and freshly baked bread oozing with a spread of olive oil. As they walked, Gallo and Rufus happened to look back, to see Venerius emerge from the questor's tent then run to his own.

"Little toad!" Gallo growled, halting beside the standard bearer's tent, where lamps radiated light onto the detachment's sacred standard in its portable camp altar. He glowered toward the tent occupied by the thin-stripe tribune. "Accuse me of laying hands on him, would he!" Under Roman military law, this was a capital offense.

"He's a fool, centurion" said Rufus. "You know what the men are calling him? 'Soupy.' Because he's thick and wet." Rufus guffawed.

"He's no fool," said Gallo coldly, "he merely acts foolishly. In his arrogance he doesn't think before he acts. But accusing me of assaulting him was worse than foolish." His face was set in as fierce an expression as Rufus had ever seen on the centurion. "For his trouble," said Gallo, "Venerius has made himself an enemy, for life."

✠

By the afternoon of the third day into the journey, having made better than twenty miles each day, the expedition reached Laodicea on the Mediterranean coast, principal port of the province of Syria. Here, the men of the Varro expedition prepared to spend the night in a regular marching camp outside the city walls, setting up their small camp inside an existing temporary fortress as usual. The legionaries followed camp markers set out by the junior tribune Venerius, who was now riding with the advance guard by day and serving as officer of the watch each night as instructed.

After dinner in the questor's tent, most of the officers and officials returned to their own quarters, but Martius lingered with Varro to discuss the expedition's itinerary. With cups of diluted wine in hand, they each lounged on a separate dining couch. Both agreed that, after visiting Beirut, Sidon and Tyre, they should swing inland, to the city of Caesarea Philippi at the head of the Jordan River. From there, the former King of Chalcis, Herod Agrippa II, controlled a large region with Rome's blessing, from southern Syria down into northern Galilee. General Collega had told Varro to include King Agrippa and his sister and co-ruler Queen Berenice on the expedition's itinerary. Agrippa and Berenice were Jewish, and Agrippa had been Guardian of the Temple at Jerusalem until the Revolt broke out. Both had tried unsuccessfully to prevent the uprising in Judea, with letters, speeches and troops. Agrippa had subsequently led his troops against the rebels, in the Roman armies commanded by Vespasian and Titus, and was considered a valuable and loyal ally of Rome. Agrippa had only been an infant at the time of the death of Jesus of Nazareth, yet it was agreed by Varro and Martius that as an influential Jew he was in an excellent position to shed some light on the Nazarene sect and the death of its founder.

"We will have to dine with Herod Agrippa of course," said Martius. "I hope he doesn't go in for big banquets. I'm not one for meals that last all night. Good wine I can stomach in any quantity." He took a sip from his cup. "But these minor potentates show off with expensive receptions and interminable meals. A man is ill for days after."

"I suppose we should have brought along some musicians or singers, as our contribution to the entertainment on these occasions," Varro mused, "but I really didn't want to weigh down the expedition with supernumeraries. Can any of your men sing or play the flute or lyre, Marcus?"

"I should hope not," returned Martius with a chuckle. "I lead legionaries, Julius, not an orchestra." Then a thought hit him. "You could always prevail on our Prefect of Horse to recite one or two of his poems for the king."

"Now that, Marcus, is an excellent idea."

Martius looked at Varro in mock horror. "I was joking, Julius."

Varro smiled. "I wasn't. We should ask Crispus to favor us with a recitation of some of his work, so we can judge its worth."

"Now?" It was more a suggestion than a question.

Varro shrugged. "Why not?"

Martius grinned. "I shall fetch the poetic prefect." With that, he pulled himself to his feet, set down his cup, then went out into the night.

Outside, it was a pleasantly mild evening. A low hum of conversation lay on the air, rising up from the tents of the camp. Somewhere away to the tribune's right there was a sudden gale of ribald laughter; Martius' men were in good spirits. He walked past his own tent, and that of young Venerius, until he came to the tent of Quintus Crispus. As a tribune of the broad stripe, there was no door that Marcus Martius would hesitate to open, no tent he would not walk into without warning. Parting the entry curtains, he stepped inside Crispus' tent.

In the light of a single lamp, Quintus Crispus stood with tunic pulled up around his chest. Kneeling before him was a young man, naked from head to toe, sucking the prefect's erect penis. The young man saw Martius first. His eyes widened, and he pulled back. "Don't stop!" Crispus wailed. Then he saw the young man's eyes, and turned to follow his terrified gaze. "Martius!" he exclaimed with horror. "I, I can explain."

"With a poem, no doubt, Crispus!" Martius snarled. He strode forward and grabbed hold of the naked young man's right ear with his left hand. "Up, you!" he commanded, dragging him, wincing, to his feet.

"Please, Martius, this is Fulvus, one of my Vettonian troopers," Crispus gushed, pulling his tunic down as he spoke. "He was helping me…"

"So I could see!" Martius sneered, continuing to hold the naked Spaniard's ear, so that he was forced to stand with his head tilted to one side. The black-haired Fulvus was tall, slim, and aged in his twenties. His tawny skin glistened in the lamp light, and Martius guessed that Crispus had rubbed him with oil at the outset of their tryst. Fulvus' jutting penis was slowly lowering, like a flag coming down a flagpole. "Outside!" Martius barked. The tribune dragged the soldier to the door then out into the night.

Crispus hurried to follow. "Please, Martius, don't hurt him!" he wailed. "I beg of you, don't hurt him!"

Outside, Martius hauled the stark naked trooper toward the questor's pavilion.

Crispus hastened in their wake. "Martius! Tribune! Please!" he cried.

"Give me a knife!" Martius yelled with unbridled anger. "A knife, someone!"

"Please, Martius!" Crispus continued to plead.

"There has been a crime committed," Martius called, deliberately elevating his voice so that it would carry. "A crime committed in the camp. Give me a knife!"

As the pair came up, the four legionaries on duty outside Varro's tent looked at the tribune and the naked cavalryman in astonishment. Nearby, the heads of legionaries poked from the doorways of tents, attracted by the shouting. Seeing what was going on, men began to tumble out into the night and run toward the questor's tent.

Martius looked at the nearest sentinel. "Your dagger, soldier," he commanded.

The legionary immediately reached to the sheath belted on his left hip and drew his *pugio,* the standard legion dagger. He held it out to the tribune, vertically, so that the officer could grasp it by the handle. Martius took the weapon from him. "On your knees!" he snarled to Fulvus, using his hold on the young man's ear to force him down. And then Martius waited, for an audience.

Julius Varro now emerged from his tent, with his servant Hostilis just a pace behind. "Marcus, what is going on?" the questor demanded. His eyes flashed from Martius to the naked cavalryman to the distressed Crispus.

"The poet was having his penis sucked by one of his acolytes, questor."

Varro looked at Crispus. "Quintus, you idiot!" he said, more in disappointment than in anger. "Not in my camp."

"Please, please, forgive me, questor, I did not think..." Crispus began. His voice trailed away. He could not defend the indefensible.

Varro looked around them. Scores of off-duty soldiers had quickly formed in a semi circle around the entrance to the questor's tent. "What do you propose to do, Marcus?" Varro asked his deputy.

"These men all know military regulations, questor," Martius returned. "Or they should!" He raised his voice a little more. "In case any of you have forgotten, as this wretch obviously had, I will remind you. It is a capital offense for a Roman soldier to steal in camp. It is a capital offense to give false evidence to a tribune. It is a capital offense to strike an officer. It is a capital offense to be convicted of the same lesser offense three times. And..." he stressed each word that followed. "It is a capital offense, punishable by death, if a Roman soldier, auxiliary or citizen, who, in full manhood, commits a homosexual act!" He looked down at the trooper. "How old are you?"

"I am twenty-eight years of age, tribune," Fulvus replied with a shaking voice, looking up at Martius with pleading eyes. It was the first time he had spoken. He knew his crime would only be exacerbated if he were to speak without permission.

"Then, you are in your full manhood, are you not?"

"Yes, Tribune."

"You are an auxiliary soldier, a non citizen, and you were caught in the act of an homosexual offense in this camp?"

"Yes, Tribune."

"Then, you are condemned by your own words." With that, Martius brought the dagger up, and, without hesitating, pushed it several inches into the left side of Fulvus' throat. Fulvus' eyes bulged with horror. Many of the men watching gasped with surprise.

"No!" Crispus exclaimed.

Martius dragged the blade across the breadth of the Vettonian's throat, left to right, severing his windpipe. He let go of his ear. With blood spurting from the incision, coating his perfect olive skin, and grasping for his throat, Fulvus toppled onto his side. He lay, quivering on the ground, gurgling grotesquely as he drowned in his own blood.

"So die all perverts!" cried a soldier in the forefront of the crowd, looking directly at Prefect Crispus as he spoke. Crispus, unable to watch Fulvus die, looked away.

Martius handed the execution weapon back to its owner. "Clean it thoroughly before you sheath it, soldier," he instructed. Then, seeing Crispus turning away, he strode to him. Grasping a handful of his yellow hair he pulled his head around, to observe the cavalryman's death throes. "This is *your* punishment, Crispus. Watch your lover die!"

Finally, Fulvus stopped moving. A soldier knelt beside the body. "He is dead," he pronounced unemotionally. Legionaries considered auxiliaries lesser beings. An auxiliary executed for a capital crime earned no more respect than a dead animal. "What do you want us to do with the body, Tribune? Throw it out the camp gate?"

"No, string him up on a tree beside the highway in the morning," Martius ordered, "for all the world to see. And put a notice on the corpse: 'DISGRACEFUL FULVUS, VETTONIAN AND PENIS SUCKER.'"

The soldier laughed. "Yes, tribune."

Varro did not say anything. He turned and went back inside his tent. Martius pushed Crispus away with disgust, then followed the questor into his quarters.

"There is only one way for these people to learn what military law and discipline are all about, Julius," he said, as Varro slumped onto a couch. Martius could see that the questor had not enjoyed the summary execution, as much as he might support its legality.

"I know," Varro sighed.

Outside, Crispus backed away from the execution site with the eyes of leering, sneering soldiers following him, then turned and hurried back to his own tent. Once inside, he sank to his knees, and began to shake uncontrollably.

VI

THE QUESTOR'S DREAM

The Road to Beirut, Roman Province of Syria. March, A.D. 71

Two shaggy black goats. Billy Goats. They were old, very old. The little beards jutting from their chins were gray with age. Varro could see the ancient animals standing, looking at him, as if transfixed. From behind him, someone spoke. "Naum," called the voice. "Naum," it repeated, over and over again. Varro spun around to see who had spoken, but no one was there. He turned back to the goats, and watched as a shadowy figure walked up to the animals. The figure drew a sword, a Roman *gladius*, the legionary's short sword, the kind with a pointed tip. And as Varro watched, in horror, the figure used the sword to gouge out the eyes of the two old goats. With that, Varro awoke, sitting up in his bed with a start.

The questor's personal slave Hostilis was almost instantly up from his sleeping place on the floor at the foot of the bed and standing at his master's bedside. The slave held an oil lamp which lit his square face from below and gave him an eerie, black-eyed ghoulish appearance. "You called out, master?" said Hostilis with concern.

"I did?".

"Were you perhaps dreaming, master?"

Now Varro realized that he was bathed in a cold sweat. An image flashed into his mind, of the two blinded billy goats. The recollection caused him to he shiver, briefly, involuntarily. "Yes, yes, I remember now. It was a dream, Hostilis."

Another figure appeared in the doorway behind Hostilis. "Is everything in order, my lord?" It was the voice of Callidus. "I heard you emit a cry of considerable volume while I was taking the night air." Callidus had a problem sleeping; his solution was to walk until he exhausted himself.

"I was dreaming, Callidus," Varro explained. "There is no need for concern. It was nothing but a dream. Go back to bed."

"Ah, a dream," said the freedman, coming to stand beside the questor's bed. Callidus placed great store in dreams, which in his opinion were much more authoritative then fortune tellers. He had once dreamed that he was wearing a crown, and within a week he'd been given his cap of freedom and manumitted by his master. Another time he had dreamed he had to choose between a plump sow and a bowl of fishes, and days later he had for the first time met the ample Priscilla, who had told him he must give up all his other female companions if he wanted to share her bed; which he had. "The dream may have been sent to guide you, my lord," he said, looking down at his superior with a mixture of interest and concern.

"Do you think so?" Varro responded. He had never been one to have dreams, prophetic or otherwise. Not dreams that he remembered, anyway. His mother, on the other hand, frequently experienced them and swore by their predictive powers. She even employed a slave whose sole duty was the interpretation of her nocturnal visions.

"Tell me about your dream, my lord," Callidus urged. "It may be important."

Sitting in his bed, Varro proceeded to describe all he could remember of the dream. He told himself that he did it to humor his freedman, yet the dream had seemed so shockingly real he felt compelled to revisit it, as if to assure himself that is was the product of imagination, not of memory.

"Two goats?" said Callidus pensively once the questor had finished.

"Do you think there is anything in it, Callidus?" said Varro. "I cannot imagine what it could possibly mean. If it means anything at all."

Callidus scratched his head. "Well, of course, goats are sacrificial animals, my lord. It would not surprise me if the gods are telling you that they want you to sacrifice another goat, or perhaps two, to guarantee the success of your mission."

"Perhaps." Varro nodded slowly, unconvinced. The fact that the dream had lodged in his mind as vividly as if it were a living memory continued to trouble him. Swinging his legs over the side of the bed, he placed his feet on the woolen rug covering the floor. "Bring Artimedes," he instructed Hostilis. "He claims some expertise in this area. Perhaps the secretary can shed light on the matter."

When, a few minutes later, a yawning Artimedes was ushered into the questor's room by Hostilis, Varro was standing, dampening his face to refresh himself, using a bowl and pitcher of water which were kept on the side table.

Varro's secretary had been a member of his family's staff for a number of years. Initially, the little Greek had served as under secretary to Varro's mother and been one of her favorites. In the few years before Varro had gone off at eighteen to do his mandatory six months service with the legions as an officer cadet, Artimedes had been the youth's tutor. When Varro's Syrian appointment had been confirmed, his mother had transferred Artimedes to her son to act as his personal secretary. Varro knew that the secretary frequently wrote home to Rome to keep Varro's mother confidentially appraised of her boy's welfare, but he never let on that he was aware of the correspondence. Artimedes, Varro also knew, was a highly superstitious man who shared his mother's passion for horoscopes, omens, and the divination of dreams.

"Artimedes, can you decipher my dream?" Varro asked.

"Tell me about it, my lord," said the secretary, his gravity laced with anticipation.

So, settling on the edge his bed, Varro once again recounted his dream, this time for Artimedes' benefit, with the secretary, Callidus and Hostilis clustered at the bedside bearing studious expressions. "There," he said when he had finished. "What construction do you put on it, Artimedes?"

Even before the questor had reached the end of his telling, the little bald Greek had begun to pace the room with hands clasped behind his back and mind whirring. "To dream of goats wandering in a field," Artimedes now began, "signifies fine weather and an excellent yield of crops. But to see them stationary…"

"As they were," said Callidus. "Were they not, my lord?"

"This denotes," Artimedes went on, ignoring Callidus' interjection, "cautious dealings and a steady increase of wealth."

"Not an unwelcome omen, my lord?" Callidus enthused.

"Yes, but the gouging of the eyes, Artimedes? And the name of Naum?"

Ceasing to pace, the serious secretary glowered at Varro. "All in good time, questor. Have I not taught you the virtue of patience?"

Varro lowered his eyes. His former tutor still had the ability to rebuke him, all these years after the young man had ventured into the world as his own instructor. "Forgive me, Artimedes. Please continue."

Artimedes resumed his pacing. "If a woman dreams of drinking goats milk, she will marry for money, and will not be disappointed," he continued.

Varro made no comment. It was as if Artimedes was working through a catalogue of dreams in his head, discounting each possibility, no matter how remote, before moving on to the next. As Varro had come to learn over the years, this was Artimedes' methodical style; he knew no other way.

"Should a woman dream of riding a billy goat, this denotes that she will shortly be held in disrepute. But, clearly, you are not a woman, my lord. You did not dream of drinking goats milk, nor of riding a billy goat?" When Varro shook his head, the secretary asked, "They were billy goats? Not nanny goats?"

"They were billy goats," the questor confirmed.

"These billy goats did not butt you? To dream that a billy goat butts you signifies that you must prevent your enemies coming into possession of your secrets or plans."

"Ahah!" Callidus exclaimed, as if this was a significant revelation.

"Neither of the two billy goats butted me," Varro said, with rising impatience. "What is the meaning of the gouging out of their eyes, Artimedes? And what is the meaning of the word Naum? Do you know?"

"I, er… I must confess, my lord, that I am at a loss to explain either."

"Ah. Well, at least you are honest, Artimedes, as you always are. Where does that leave me, apart from well married and with fine weather and an abundant crop?"

Artimedes scowled back at his former pupil. "With respect, my lord, if I were you I would treat this dream with the seriousness it deserves. Clearly, we are not sent these messages for nothing. As Cicero wrote, 'If the gods love men, they will certainly reveal their purposes to them in sleep.'"

Varro attempted to look serious. "Yes, of course."

"Might I suggest, my lord, that you consult the Acting Governor's chief secretary? Pythagoras is a far more learned man than myself. I am sure that Pythagoras will be able to reveal the secret of your dream."

Varro knew that an unspoken rivalry had long existed between the two secretaries, and it occurred to him that perhaps Artimedes had made this suggestion in the hope of embarrassing Pythagoras. Alternatively, perhaps Artimedes wanted to be seen to be giving way to his older colleague. Then again, perhaps Artimedes genuinely believed that Pythagoras could unlock the secret of the questor's dream. "Very well." Varro stifled a yawn. "Callidus, bring Pythagoras."

A little later, General Collega's secretary joined the group in the questor's quarters, looking unimpressed at being woken and summoned in the middle of the night. Now, Varro regaled Pythagoras with the details of his dream.

"I see," said Pythagoras once the dream had been revealed. "Obviously, the goats represent the zodiacal sign of Capricorn," he emphatically declared.

"Ah!" cried Artimedes. "Clearly this is the case."

"That does make sense," Varro agreed. "Go on, Pythagoras."

"Two goats, two years," Pythagoras pronounced with certainty. "Your dream, questor, was telling you that you must wait until two years have passed. When the second month of January arrives, something of importance will be revealed to you."

"Yes, that is perfectly plausible, Pythagoras," Varro responded, "but what am I to read into the blinding of the two goats?"

Pythagoras did not reply. This aspect required more thought.

"Might I suggest, my lord," Artimedes then said, "following on from what my learned colleague Pythagoras has said, clearly this means that you will not be able to see what is to be revealed to you until the Capricorn constellation returns a second time."

"Quite so," Pythagoras was quick to agree.

"That would be logical, I suppose," Varro conceded, without complete conviction. "And the name Naum? What am I to take that to mean?"

"Naum may have something to do with the sea," Artimedes conjectured. "Perhaps it relates to the word *naus*." In Latin, *naus* was a nautical term. "Could it be that you will have to cross the sea to learn the answer to your dream?"

"No, I think not," said Pythagoras definitely. "To my mind, now that I think on it, the word Naum has a Hebrew ring to it."

"Hebrew?" said Varro. "Yes, it does, does it not. I had not thought of that. Perhaps I should be talking to Antiochus the Jewish magistrate. Thank you, gentlemen, you have both been most helpful. The dream does seem to make some sort of sense now, thanks to your expert powers of elucidation." Varro was not entirely convinced that the dream's mysteries had indeed been successfully explained, but courtesy and the sensibilities of the two secretaries required that he let them believe they had served him well. Once his staff had left him, he lay back down. He was soon fast asleep.

Next morning when he awoke, the dream was still as fresh in his mind as it had been the night before. So Varro sent Hostilis to fetch Antiochus the Jewish magistrate. In the meantime, Marcus Martius entered the questor's tent and bade him good morning. For Marcus' benefit, Varro again retold his dream, and as he regaled him with the story they were dutifully joined by Artimedes and Callidus.

Martius suggested that the dream had been sponsored by the events of the previous evening. "Crispus and the Vettonian," he said, taking up an apple from the questor's table and munching into it, "acting like a pair of silly goats."

Varro looked questioningly at Artimedes. "Could it be that simple?"

"Anything is possible, my lord," said the Greek. "But I tend to favor the construction put on your dream by my colleague Pythagoras."

The Jewish magistrate then arrived, looking worried as he bustled into the questor's pavilion. "Your man said that you had need of my advice, my lord," he warily began, with his hand at a small leather pouch which Varro noticed the Jew habitually wore on a leather thong around his neck, fondling it nervously, unconsciously..

"Tell me, Antiochus, the word Naum; does it have any significance among the Jewish people?"

Antiochus seemed to squirm inwardly. "With respect, my lord, as you know, I have sworn off Jewish religious practices."

Varro's brow wrinkled in a frown. "Antiochus, am I to take it that in swearing off the religion of the Jews you have emptied your head of Hebrew and Aramaic? That being the case, you will be of absolutely no use to me as an interpreter on this mission, and I will have to send you back to General Collega."

This brought a mirthful snort from Callidus.

"That will not be necessary, my lord," Antiochus smarted. "It is just that the word Naum has a religious significance to some Jews."

Varro nodded. "Please explain."

"As you instruct, my lord." Antiochus' tone made it clear that he was doing this under sufferance. "Naum is said to be the direct descendant of Adam, the first man created by the God of the Hebrews."

"Arrant nonsense!" Martius sneered.

"Yes, tribune, nonsense, as you say," Antiochus hastened to agree. "The beliefs of the Jews are indeed all nonsense. I thank the gods that I was able to see that for myself and repent, before it was too late."

"So, this Naum fellow?" said Varro. "He would not be living? I could not interview him?"

"No, questor," Antiochus replied. "He lived some generations ago."

Artimedes spoke up. "Now that the magistrate mentions it, my lord, I recall some reference to this man Naum in the religious hierarchy listed in the Lucius Letter. May I read from the letter?"

"Please do, Artimedes."

The Lucius Letter was kept in a leather cylinder in the questor's quarters. While everyone waited, Artimedes removed the letter and affixed it to a reading frame. After bringing several lamps close to improve the light for reading, Artimedes scrolled through the letter until he came to a listing of the antecedents of Jesus of Nazareth. "Here it is, my lord, the reference that I spoke of." With an air of gravity, Artimedes proceeded to read the section in question aloud, with his chin jutting, and projecting his voice like a rhetorician declaiming on the rostra in the Forum of Rome. *"And Jesus himself began to be about thirty years of age, being, as was supposed, the son of Josephus, who was the son of Heli, who was the son of Matthat, who was the son of Levi, who was the son of Melchi, who was the son of Janna, who was the son of Josephus, who was the son of Mattathias, who was the son of Amos, who was the son of Naum..."* Artimedes stopped, and looked over to the questor. "Naum, my lord."

Varro nodded. "Yes, there it. So, there was a Naum who was apparently an ancestor of the Nazarene. Food for thought, certainly."

"There can be no doubt now that your dream had a clear and potent meaning, my lord," Artimedes declared.

"A potent meaning, Artimedes?" Varro responded. "That I will accept. However, a clear meaning? No, that I cannot concede. Was the dream intended to warn me, or to guide me? Do I avoid Naum, or do I seek Naum? This is far from clear, good secretary." He became aware of

Antiochus standing there, bearing the pained expression of a man anxious to relieve himself. "Thank you, Antiochus, that will be all."

"Thank you, my lord questor." Antiochus bowed slightly from the waist, then quickly withdrew.

"Perhaps, my lord," said Artimedes as he returned the letter to its protective case, "this was only the first in a series of dreams. Such a circumstance is not unknown. The meaning may become more clear with each passing dream."

"You mean I can expect more such nightmares?" Varro responded with a groan.

"What a lucky fellow," said Martius with a chuckle.

VII

KING AGRIPPA'S THEORY

Caesarea Philippi, Capital of the Tetrarchy of Trachonitis.
March, A.D. 71

The cities of Beirut, Sidon and Tyre all proved unprofitable for Julius Varro. He had held the highest expectations of Beirut, or Colonia Julia Augustus Felix Berytus as it had been entitled on its incorporation as a colony of retired veterans of the 10th Legion eighty-five years before. Varro knew the city from his annual tax collecting visits. And, eighteen months back, he had worked alongside Pythagoras here to organize a conference between his patron Governor Mucianus and Eastern potentates, a conference which prepared the way for the task force which Mucianus had led to Italy against the emperor Vitellius.

Varro had been hoping to find old soldiers of the 12th Legion here. Marcus Martius, a dedicated militarist with a thorough knowledge of the Roman army's units and their stations, had told him that the 12th Legion had been stationed in Judea forty years earlier. As a legion colony, Beirut attracted a number of retired soldiers, and Varro had hoped to find a few old veterans of the 12th living there who had served in Jerusalem at the time of the Nazarene's crucifixion. To his disappointment, despite posting notices throughout Beirut, no 12th Legion veterans had come forward.

As for Sidon and Tyre, the Nazarenes at Antioch had told Callidus that Jesus had visited both, but inquiries there seeking locals with connections with the Nazarene had brought no response. From Tyre, the column had left the coast and marched due east along the main military highway into Trachonitis, a region ruled by King Herod Agrippa II, to his capital,

Caesarea Philippi, near the head of the Jordan River. Here, the questor hoped, his investigation would at last begin to produce results.

Outside Caesarea Philippi the expedition turned north and marched along beside the Banias River beyond the city wall, with Mount Hermon looming in the distance ahead. The column was heading for a camp site identified by junior tribune Venerius and the advance guard. Earlier, the advance guard had delivered the questor's compliments to the king in his capital, and now the main column was overtaken on the road by a mounted military party led by the commander of the king's army, General Philippus.

The general was a long-nosed, sallow-skinned man with his black, shoulder-length hair and beard in ringlets, a style fashionable among many foreigners in the East. Astride a large black horse, General Philippus welcomed Varro on behalf of the king and extended an invitation for the questor and all members of the Equestrian Order in his party to attend a banquet at the king's palace in the city that evening. In doing so, the general reminded the questor that King Agrippa had himself been made a member of the Equestrian Order several decades before by the emperor Claudius. The king's invitation only covered Varro, Martius, Crispus. Varro considered that his two secretaries would have been of more use to him in a meeting with the king than either Crispus or Venerius, but this invitation was more about protocol than pragmatism. Varro graciously accepted the invitation on behalf of his three colleagues and himself.

That night they attended the royal palace, and dined with the king and his senior advisers.

"Do you know, Varro," said Ptolemy, treasurer to the court of King Agrippa, as he wolfed down a roasted dormouse which had been rolled in honey and poppy seed, "my wife almost died at the hands of the rebels." Ptolemy considered himself more than the equal of any Roman questor. "In Galilee, near Taricheae."

"Is that so, Treasurer Ptolemy?" Varro responded, trying to sound genuinely concerned. "How terrible for her, and worrying for you."

In the king's winter palace, situated on a rise overlooking the compact city, a colonnaded banquet hall had been furnished with three curved couches around a circular table. In part of the arc the usual opening for serving and taking away had been allowed. Agrippa himself reclined at one end of the circle, while Varro occupied the other, on the opposite side of the opening. Along with Varro and the king, Martius, Crispus and Venerius reclined around the circle together with Treasurer Ptolemy, General Philippus, Sylla, commander of the king's bodyguard, and the shaven-headed Bostar, a tight-lipped Cyreniacan Jew and eunuch who was chamberlain to the king's sister, Queen Berenice.

In the background a slave orchestra played gentle tunes on lyre, flute and water organ, as swarms of male slaves in expensive purple tunics wafted around the diners. The meal met with Martius' approval, consisting as it did of a conservative seven courses.

Crispus and Venerius were enjoying being treated as men of importance, after coming to the king's palace with dampened spirits for their own differing reasons. The summary execution of Trooper Fulvus had not been mentioned to Crispus by a soul in the Varro camp since that bloody night outside Laodicea, and the prefect had continued to carry out his duties as usual, although he guessed that his men now despised him; not so much for having his penis sucked as being caught in the act and humiliated publicly by Martius. Yet the incident would not be forgotten by Julius Varro or his expeditioners. Likewise, no one mentioned that Venerius had been disciplined on the first night of the expedition and was under threat of court martial if he were to falter in his duties.

To the court of King Agrippa the members of the Varro party presented the façade of a happy family, and all the dinner guests had engaged in small talk as the groaning platters of the first few courses were consumed. At one point, Commander Sylla, a man with massive shoulders and a pockmarked face, had boasted that as a young man at Rome his king had helped Claudius claim the throne left vacant by the assassination of the emperor Gaius, or Caligula as he was more colloquially known, by addressing the Senate and negotiating with the Pretorian Guard and German Guard on Claudius' behalf. Varro had taken this claim with a grain of salt, politely responding that he had not been aware of that fact. Inevitably, the conversation had turned to the Jewish Revolt, which was so fresh in all their minds, and in the course of the discussion Ptolemy had brought up his wife's brush with Jewish partisans.

"In Galilee, you say, my lord?" said Crispus, eyeing off a platter of sow bellies.

"Near Taricheae," the grotesquely fat, wheezing treasurer replied. "She was returning home from Jerusalem. This was just after the Revolt had broken out."

"In that case," said young Venerius, "if it was in Galilee, the men who attacked your wife, Treasurer, must have been under the command of Flavius Josephus." Like many Roman colleagues, the junior tribune had no liking for the former Jewish general who was now the client and trusted adviser of Vespasian and Titus.

"Quite so," Ptolemy agreed. "Had it not been for the fact that my wife is such an expert rider, those people would have cut her throat. As it was, they escaped with her baggage train, which contained her personal fortune! We never did recover it."

"That was unfortunate," said Varro after downing an oyster with the assistance of a small pointed spoon. "Of course, Marcus Martius here fought the rebels at Taricheae."

"Is that so, tribune?" said General Philippus with interest. "You were with Titus at Taricheae? It was my belief that he only employed cavalry in that battle."

"I was Prefect of the Dalmatian Horse at the time," Martius came back, smiling.

"Ah, but of course." The general also smiled, falsely.

"Marcus was severely wounded at Taricheae," said Varro.

"It was nothing," said Martius.

"You still carry a Jewish arrowhead in your hip from that campaign," said Varro.

Martius shrugged. "It does not trouble me. I had all but forgotten it."

"His Majesty was wounded on the right elbow during the siege of Gamala," Philippus remarked competitively. "A rebel slinger's stone."

"In fact, had it not been for His Majesty's army," said the swaggering Sylla, "you Romans would have struggled in Galilee. We played a key part in the campaign."

"It was my understanding," young Venerius countered, "that two thousand of your 'elite' cavalry not only capitulated at Jerusalem, they went over to the rebels! A cowardly betrayal which resulted in the massacre of a cohort of Roman legionaries!"

"Yes, but that was earlier," said Sylla with discomfort.

"Yes, earlier," General Philippus quickly added, "when matters were completely out of hand. Not even His Majesty himself was able to talk the revolutionaries out of the insanity of their uprising."

Venerius let out a disdainful grunt.

"We know that His Majesty and his sister did everything humanly possible to prevent the Revolt," Varro remarked, keen to smooth ruffled feathers. As he spoke, he threw a severe cautionary look in Venerius' direction, causing Venerius to drop his eyes.

"Indeed, indeed," Ptolemy earnestly concurred.

"Everything possible," Philippus echoed.

Varro looked over at the king. Agrippa had hardly spoken during the meal. His mind seemed elsewhere. In fact, from the moment that Varro had greeted the king earlier in the evening, he had felt that Agrippa was a dispirited man. "Rome has always valued your loyalty, Your Majesty," he said directly to the monarch.

"Hmmm? Did you address me?" Agrippa raised his heavy-lidded eyes from the floor, where they had lain for some time. The king, the forty-four-year-old great-grandson of Herod the Great, was a neat, swarthy figure. Raised and educated at Rome, where his best friend had been Britannicus, Claudius's son and Nero's stepbrother, he had adopted Roman ways. Even now he was clean shaven and kept his hair short, unlike his officials.

"I was saying, Your Majesty," said Varro, "that Rome values your loyalty."

"I suppose she does," Agrippa sighed.

"It must have been a great disappointment to you, Your Majesty," said Martius, "for the Jews to ignore you, only to bring about the destruction of Jerusalem."

"Disappointment?" said Agrippa, sounding affronted. "My dear tribune, one can never be merely disappointed by a catastrophe. One is devastated by a catastrophe."

With the king in such a morose mood, Varro decided that he had been making small talk long enough. He had come here to ask questions about the Nazarene, and ask questions he must, before Agrippa lost interest altogether. "Your Majesty, my colleagues and I are bound for Galilee and Judea, to investigate the circumstances surrounding the death of a Jesus of Nazareth, some years ago," he began.

"Oh?" A look came over Agrippa's face which Varro felt suggested either suspicion or intrigue, but he could not tell which. "Why would you do that, questor?"

The question took Varro by surprise. "Well, to, er, set the record straight, Your Majesty. General Collega wishes to have the record set straight."

"Is that so?"

"There is a story we are hearing, promoted by the Nazarene's followers, that he rose from the dead following his crucifixion," Varro explained.

"Yes, I had heard that also," Agrippa said with apparent disinterest.

"Do you believe the story? Is there, to your knowledge, anything to support it?"

"What does it matter what I believe?" Agrippa sighed. He lifted a cup of wine, and took a brief, contemplative sip. "You will find what you will find."

Varro decided to try to approach the subject from another angle. "Your father?" he asked. "Did he have an opinion on the Nazarene?" The king's father had been Herod Agrippa I, briefly King of Judea, until his premature death two decades earlier.

"My father actively suppressed the Nazarene's followers during the three years he ruled Judea. He had one of their leaders executed — Jacob bar Zebedee — and imprisoned another, a Simon Petra."

"Simon Petra?" said Martius, with interest. He knew from the Lucius Letter that Simon Petra had been one of the Nazarene's deputies. "Your father imprisoned him?"

Agrippa nodded. "The prisoner managed to escape. What befell him after that I could not say. I myself have been no friend to the Nazarenes, but I have not gone out of my way to persecute them either. I perceived my role to be that of a guide to the Jewish people, not a tyrant. I tried to advise the people, not impose my will on them." A bitter tone now entered his voice. "But in the end many chose to ignore my advice."

"So, you had little to do with the Nazarenes?" said Varro.

"*Very* little to do with them. I did once interview a Paulus of Tarsus, one of their advocates, ten or twelve years ago."

"Paulus of Tarsus?" said Martius. "Yes, we have heard of him."

"He had Roman citizenship, but also went by the Jewish name of Saul, if I remember. He had been placed in custody at Caesarea by Felix, the procurator, after being charged with blasphemy by the Great Sanhedrin of Jerusalem."

"How did you find him, Your Majesty?" Varro asked.

"I found Paulus earnest and pious. A persuasive sort of fellow, a compelling orator. At one point he almost had me convinced that there was something in what he said." A smile flitted briefly across his lips. "I considered him guilty of no crime. I believe that Felix's successor, Festus, sent him to Rome, to have his appeal heard by Nero Caesar. Yet, when all is said and done, Paulus was no more than a fanatic." His face hardened. "I abhor fanatics of any persuasion, Varro. Fanatics are blind to reality, fanatics are deaf to reason. Fanatics will be the end of Israel."

Seeing the embittered expression which now possessed the king, Varro quickly tried to redirect the conversation to the man who was the focus of his investigation. "You never personally believed that Jesus of Nazareth rose from the dead, Your Majesty?"

Agrippa frowned at him. "Have I not already said as much?"

"May I ask, what do you know of his background, Your Majesty?"

Agrippa shrugged. "One hears many things. As far as I know, his family had connections with the Pharisees, the largest Jewish religious community. The Pharisees believe in life after death, unlike the Sadducees, who dominated the Great Sanhedrin until its destruction. This Jesus of Nazareth was a cousin of Johannes bar Zecharias, who laid claim to being a prophet. Johannes's followers — and I am told that thirty thousand men were at one time his adherents, including his cousin Jesus — they called Johannes 'the Baptist,' because he baptized them in the Jordan River."

"Why would he do that, Your Majesty?" Crispus asked.

"Baptize them? They believed that the act of immersion washed away their sins."

"If only it were that simple," Martius remarked with a snort.

Agrippa cast him a disapproving glance. "The washing away of one's sins in exchange for repentance and a commitment to a righteous life is an ancient rite among the Jewish people, one with a great deal of religious significance attached to it."

"Did Johannes baptize Jesus of Nazareth?" Crispus asked.

"I believe he did, yes."

Martius smirked. "A god admitting to the possession of sins? What is the world coming to?"

"What fate befell Johannes the Baptist, Your Majesty?" Varro inquired.

"Beheaded, by Herod Antipas, my great-uncle, when he was Tetrarch of Galilee."

"For what crime?" Martius asked.

"Johannes voiced opposition to my great-uncle's divorce from the daughter of the King of Nabatea and his subsequent marriage to the widow of Antipas' brother. That was contrary to Jewish Law."

"He was beheaded? Not crucified?" Martius asked with some surprise. "Was the Baptist a Roman citizen?"

"No. The matter was a complicated one. Antipas' bride Herodias asked for the Baptist's head through her daughter Salome, to silence the Baptist and end his criticism of her new marriage. Antipas gave it to her."

"The politics of the sword," said Martius grimly. "We Romans know all about that." Less than three years before, Martius' father, a supporter of the short-lived emperor Otho, had committed suicide following Otho's defeat by Vitellius. Shortly after, Martius' mother and ten-year-old sister, sheltering on the family's estate in Picenum in the east of Italy, had been murdered by marauding supporters of Vitellius.

Varro glanced across the circular table to Martius, and saw a distant, pained look in his eyes. Varro and Martius had spent the evenings of the journey from Antioch talking about themselves and their families. Varro knew how Martius' loved ones had died, and he guessed where his deputy's thoughts now lay. The questor returned his attention to the king. "Your majesty, what, may I ask, became of the Baptist's followers in the wake of his execution?" he asked.

"Some transferred their allegiance to Jesus, I believe. Perhaps one in ten of them. The majority apparently did not believe that the Nazarene had the same powers of prophesy as the Baptist."

"So, Jesus took up the reins of the sect founded by Johannes the Baptist, following the Baptist's death?" Varro established.

The king nodded in reply.

Crispus quickly asked another question. He seemed to have developed a particular interest in the subject of baptism. "Did Jesus also baptize people in the Jordan, Your Majesty?"

"I gather that he left that to his subordinates."

"Your Majesty, what do you know about the circumstances surrounding the arrest and execution of Jesus?" Varro asked.

Agrippa sighed. "I cannot contribute any information in that regard, Varro. I was only three years of age at the time. You must ask people who were there."

"Yes, of course." Varro sounded disappointed.

"I have my own opinion about the execution, of course," Agrippa then volunteered.

Surprised, titillated, Varro leaned forward. "Yes, Your Majesty…?"

"It is obvious to me that Jesus of Nazareth attempted to conform to the prophesies of Moses and the minor prophets," the king solemnly declared.

Varro was mystified. "I am not familiar with this Moyses, Your Majesty. And, the 'minor prophets'...?"

Agrippa smiled to himself. So many Romans considered themselves learned men, but, to his mind, more often than not their learning was confined to their own country, their own customs, their own gods, their own origins. So many insular Roman administrators had come to this part of the world full of Roman notions, only to run head-on into the sensitivities of subjects who saw the world through quite different eyes. "I shall not bore you with a long lecture on Judaism, questor. Suffice it to say, it was written, long, long ago, that a holy man, a descendant of an ancient king of the Israelites, would arise to save the people and become their new king. In Hebrew, the Jewish people call this savior the Messiah, or the 'anointed one' as you would say. In Greek, this translates as the Christos. This Messiah would be divine. To prove his divinity he would be crucified, and would rise again and walk among men two days after his death."

"These prophesies are ancient, you say, Your Majesty?" said Varro.

"Many centuries old," Agrippa replied. "To this day most Jews believe and expect that the Messiah is yet to come, but the followers of the Nazarene believe that Jesus of Nazareth was the Messiah."

"Only a handful of Jews believe that the Nazarene was divine?" Martius asked.

"A small number of Jews, and some Gentiles, or non-Jews, hold that belief, tribune," Agrippa told him. "There are good reasons to be skeptical of the claim that the Nazarene was the Messiah. Very few people, members of his family and some close followers, claimed to have seen Jesus alive following his crucifixion. If you have proven your divinity by rising from the dead, why would you not go far and wide to show the world that you had risen?"

"A good point, sire," said Martius approvingly.

"We have a copy of a letter from one of the Nazarene's followers," said Varro, "in which the author states that the Nazarene *set out* to have himself crucified."

Agrippa responded sagely. "As I have said, it has always been my contention that the Nazarene strove to conform to the old prophesies and so be declared the Messiah. For that reason, he would have willingly delivered himself up to be executed."

"Having attracted only a portion of the Baptist's following," said Martius, thinking aloud, "Jesus felt that if he did not do something dramatic, such as claiming the mantle of this Messiah or Christos, he would always be seen as a mere disciple of the Baptist. As just a soldier, not the general."

"The Jewish people have always been divided by various sects and false prophets," said Agrippa gravely. "It is the nature of their faith that they will be tempted from the true path from time to time, to be tested by Heaven."

"A false prophet?" Varro mused. "Do most Jews see the Nazarene in that way?"

"I imagine that is the case. I cannot speak for all Jews, questor."

Varro shifted his position on the couch, leaning closer to Agrippa. "Your Majesty, in the strictest confidence, I can reveal that my mission is to prove that Jesus of Nazareth did not rise from the dead. Is there anything you could suggest, any line of inquiry I might follow, that would assist me in that quest?"

Agrippa looked at him without replying for a time, pursing his lips, as if deliberating on his reply. "My good friend Flavius Josephus and I have discussed this very matter at some length," he then said. "If I were you, questor, I would ask myself two questions. Firstly, can I find witnesses who would testify that those who claimed to have met and spoken with Jesus following his execution lied? In other words, prove that the Nazarene prearranged for friends to fabricate this story following his death to comply with the prophesies and confirm the myth of his divinity."

Varro nodded. "I must admit," he said thoughtfully, "I have wondered how the Nazarene's followers could accept this story of the resurrection with so little evidence to support it. Nazarenes in Antioch seem to believe in it implicitly, yet they could not tell us why. A thinking man must conclude that it would take either great faith or great gullibility to believe that a man could rise from the dead, without substantial proof. The balance of probabilities would seem to point toward this story being a concerted fabrication. So, yes, that is a line of inquiry I must pursue — prove that the witnesses lied. The other question, Your Majesty?"

"The other question you might ask yourself, questor, is this. Did Jesus somehow fabricate his death, so that he was in fact not dead when he was taken down from his cross? This, of course, would have enabled him to appear to followers several days after the execution, and so confirm the prophesies."

All four Romans looked at him with surprise bordering on astonishment. None had even considered this possibility.

"How might that have been achieved?" a disconcerted Varro asked.

"You are saying that the execution was a sham?" said Marcus with disbelief.

Agrippa shrugged. "I merely suggest that the question might be asked, tribune."

"How could the Nazarene's execution have been a sham?" Martius queried, making no attempt to hide rising anger. "Surely, that would have required the complicity of the *Roman* authorities at Jerusalem? That is a strong charge."

"I could not say how it might have been done," Agrippa coolly replied. "I merely point it out as a possibility to be explored. You might ask, where did the Nazarene go following his so-called resurrection? If he did rise, why did he so abruptly terminate his teachings? In my experience, fanatics cannot help themselves, they require an audience. They will loudly proclaim their doctrine, ignoring the likely consequences. As I said previously, fanatics are blind to reality and deaf to reason."

"If he did not die on a cross, however that might have been achieved," Varro said, speculating aloud, "he would have had to go into hiding or leave the province. If he were found alive, he would have been rearrested and executed all over again."

"Ah, but if he were a god, as his followers claim," said Martius, with a smile which broadened into a grin, "the Nazarene could not be killed. We could have put him on a dozen crosses, and he would have risen time and time again. Surely?"

Venerius, who had held his tongue ever since receiving the withering glance from Varro earlier, let out a cackle of laughter. Then, seeing no one else laugh, he quickly and self consciously wiped the smile from his face, and lowered his eyes once more.

There was now a poignant silence. All the diners had stopped eating. Varro realized that none of the king's retainers had entered into the debate about the Nazarene. Was it through deference to Agrippa, he wondered, or was it because they preferred not to enter into speculation about the death of Jesus, for one reason or another?

Agrippa now lay aside his napkin and pulled himself to his feet. Having had enough of the meal and the conversation, he was departing. His eight guests all respectfully came to their feet.

"To my mind," said the king, "Jesus of Nazareth was a learned, pious and well-meaning teacher, a man with a prophetic gift, and a talent for deception. Nothing more." He cast a cursory glance around the circle of men. "I wish you well on your quest, my lords." Agrippa paused to allow servants to help him into slippers, then walked across the tiled floor and out the door. With his departure, Varro and Martius looked at each other, sharing the same thought: Was it possible, as Agrippa had suggested, that Jesus of Nazareth had fabricated his own death?

VIII

QUEEN BERENICE'S BARGAIN

Caesarea Philippi, Capital of the Tetrarchy of Trachonitis. March, A.D. 71

The two Romans lay naked but for a coat of thick gray mud. After working up a sweat tossing around a medicine ball, Varro and Martius had progressed through the Caesarea Philippi bathhouse's three baths, ice cold, tepid, and steaming hot, then stretched out on tables, side by side, face down, while slaves fastidiously coated them with mud before dragging it off again with scrapers of sharp-edged animal bone.

"Where is Crispus?" Varro asked as they lay there undergoing the uncomfortable treatment. "I expected to see him here at the baths. He mustn't be allowed to hide away."

"I had him escort your man Callidus," Martius replied. Varro had that morning instructed Callidus to post notices throughout the city asking anyone with knowledge of the circumstances surrounding the death of Jesus of Nazareth at Jerusalem during the reign of Tiberius Caesar to come forward. According to the Lucius Letter, the Nazarene and his chief followers had come to Caesarea Philippi and other towns of the area in search of converts, so there was a chance that someone here might have useful information. "Besides, Crispus has no need of the bathhouse." There was amusement in Martius' voice. "He informs me he took a dip in the Jordan River this morning."

"In the Jordan River?" said Varro, surprised. "Can he swim?"

Martius shrugged. "He probably neither knows his letters nor how to swim, as the saying goes."

"But, why take a dip in the river?"

"The Jews seem to think the waters of the Jordan have certain powers." Martius smirked. "I asked lover boy if he thought his dip might wash away his sins."

Varro frowned. "Crispus' misjudgment on the road here is in the past, Marcus," he said disapprovingly. "Let him be."

"As you wish," the tribune responded, smiling still.

Varro now became aware of his chief slave standing near. "What is it, Hostilis?"

"Master, Bostar, Chamberlain to Her Majesty Queen Berenice seeks a word," the slave advised. Roman bathhouses were common places for business and social meetings.

"Very well, send him to me," Varro responded, and Hostilis withdrew.

"Can *you* swim, Julius?" said Martius as the slaves continued the mud treatment.

"A little. My nurse felt I should. And you?"

Martius shook his head. "Like most Romans, I can only tolerate water in the bathhouse. As for sea voyages, they leave me cold." He was thoughtful for a moment. "Did you know that Gaius Julius Caesar saved himself during a battle against the Alexandrians by swimming to safety, after his own men capsized his boat?"

Varro nodded. "I have read his *Commentaries.*" Varro was not as avid a student of military history as the tribune, but, like his colleague, he had been schooled on the campaigns of Julius Caesar. "Not that I necessarily believe it. He must have been in full armor at the time; he would surely have sunk like a stone."

Martius laughed. "Shameless, outspoken, and questioning. I do believe you have the makings of a first class Cynic, my friend."

Shortly after, the tall, bony eunuch Bostar approached, clad in a saffron-colored robe and adorned with a necklace of gold. His shaven head glistened with perspiration.

"Greetings, Bostar," said Varro from the scraper's table.

Bostar bowed. "I bring greetings from Her Majesty Queen Berenice," he said formally, in Greek, as he straightened, without looking at the nude questor. His voice was nasally, almost comic. "Her Majesty bids you dine with her tonight at her palace."

The questor glanced at Martius. "Just myself?" he asked, with a hint of concern in his voice. Varro knew that the queen was reputedly a fabulous beauty and temptress, that she had been married three times, and that she had been the mistress of Titus, the emperor's son, for the past four years.

"Yourself, Tribune Martius, and Prefect Crispus, my lord," Bostar replied.

"Ah." Varro was relieved. The idea of a lone tryst with the queen had been a worrying one. For one thing he did not consider himself in Titus' league. "Not to Tribune Venerius?" he asked. "He too is a Roman knight, Bostar."

"No, my lord, the invitation is extended to you three alone. It does not include Gaius Licinius Venerius."

Varro could not imagine why Venerius was excluded, not that it mattered. "Of course, my colleagues and I shall be pleased to accept Her Majesty's kind invitation."

"I shall inform Her Majesty." Now Bostar dropped his eyes, and his formality. "If I may say, questor, Her Majesty has been very low since my lord Titus departed. It will be a tonic for her to have Roman officers to dine." He looked Martius' way. "Especially officers who fought alongside Titus Vespasianus." His narrow eyes flashed back to Varro. "Might it be possible for your lordship to provide some form of entertainment at the banquet? Her Majesty needs cheering."

"Entertainment? What manner of entertainment, Bostar?"

"Her Majesty has cultivated tastes."

"I see…" Varro had an idea. "Yes, of course. Prefect Crispus is an accomplished poet, and has published extensively. He shall recite for the queen."

The eunuch's stone features gave way to a wide smile. "That would be most acceptable, my lord. Most acceptable indeed. We must make every effort to help Her Majesty take her mind off her troubles."

✠

Queen Berenice's palace was adjacent to that of her brother Agrippa. It was a deferential distance down the slope, but just as elegant, just as Roman. Like Agrippa, Berenice had Jewish roots and Roman tastes. Like Agrippa too, she had been an astute political player, often interceding with the Roman procurators in Judea on behalf of the province's Jews in the frequent disputes which arose between Jewish and gentile residents and between the Jews and the Roman authorities, yet always remaining faithful to Rome. Both Agrippa and she had kept a palace at Jerusalem, and had frequently gone there. Now, like Jerusalem as a whole, the royal couple's Jerusalem palaces had gone to dust.

On their arrival at the queen's winter residence, Varro and his three companions were ushered into a dining hall which had as its centerpiece a pool spread with yellow pond lilies. The vast room's walls were decorated with murals depicting rural and agricultural scenes. Three dining couches of solid gold were arranged in the traditional 'U' around a low square table. A female chorus, anonymous behind stage masks, occupied a balcony overlooking the hall, delivering austere Greek songs without accompaniment, their voices echoing around the tall walls and marble columns. At the door the Roman officers were met by a flock of servants, all female, and all modestly attired. As was the custom in homes rich and poor throughout the Roman world, the women removed the men's footwear, then washed their feet and provided slippers.

Varro deliberately ignored the servants as they performed the chore — it was considered equally embarrassing to both slave and visitor for one to look the other in the eye. For his dignity and the servants' comfort the questor chatted with his companions as if the slaves did not exist.

Once one slave girl had completed this task, another, more senior female slave came to the questor and took his hand, to lead him to his place at the banquet table. For a moment, as he placed his hand in hers, the eyes of Roman knight and slave met, and Varro was hit by the striking beauty of the girl. It was more than the fact that he had not seen a woman without a veil for weeks, not since he had last visited Octavia at her father's Antioch house. This slave girl was seriously arresting. Her smooth olive skin seemed to glow. Her jet black hair, plaited and wound around the top of the head in the style of a Roman matron, shone with vitality. She had the perfectly proportioned face of a goddess, and capacious eyes which dragged Varro in like the net of a fisherman. And then she smiled. The affect left him almost breathless. It was the strangest feeling, unlike anything he had ever before experienced.

Never having been able to determine a woman's age with any accuracy, he could not be sure whether she was a teenager or in her twenties. Bedazzled, he allowed himself to be led by her to one of the dining couches, to the honored position on the left, beside the low fulcrum. There, she let go of his hand. In that parting of the hands it was if sparks flew. She then handed him a napkin, which he accepted dazedly. Lying down beside the head of the couch and resting his left elbow on a cushion, he watched her move away, his head turning to follow her as she glided past the ornamental pool to the end of the hall.

"One must give all credit to the queen," said Martius as he reclined beside Varro, having been led to his place by another exotic Eastern beauty, "her taste in maidservants cannot be faulted. These women are a feast for the eyes. Would you not say so, Julius?"

"You said something?" said Varro, reluctantly looking around to Martius.

"Comely beauties, Julius," Martius said with a wink. "Berenice surrounds herself with comely beauties."

"Yes." Varro nodded. "Beauties."

"I wonder if the queen herself is as beautiful as they say," said Crispus in a half whisper as he took his place beside Martius. He also secretly wondered whether the queen would like his poetry. He had chosen what he considered to be his eight best shorter works to recite tonight as the Romans' contribution to the evening's entertainment, pieces he knew by heart. All on the theme of love.

"I hear she is in her forties," said Martius. "Past her best, one would expect."

As he spoke, curtains at the far end of the room parted, and a slim, elegant woman swept into the hall, a shimmering gown of golden thread trailing behind her. Maidservants trotted in her wake, concerned with the train of the dress, and Bostar the chamberlain followed close behind. The three Romans quickly came to their feet.

"Good evening, my lords," said Queen Berenice as she reached the central couch. "I cannot tell you how happy I am that you were able to dine with me. We see so few Roman knights." With the maidservants fussing over the spread of her dress, she reclined on the central couch.

Berenice was forty-three years of age. She had two sons in their twenties, fathered by her second husband, the late King Herod of Chalcis in Greece. Yet, she looked barely out of her twenties herself, with soft, pampered skin, and not a wrinkle or imperfection to be seen. The secret of her faultless complexion was rumored to be Canopus ointment, from a town in Egypt famous over centuries for producing an oil for embalming and preserving the dead. Her eyes were the queen's crowning glory. They were huge, like dishes, and dominated her face, drawing the viewer's attention away from the fact that her nose was a little over long in comparison to the rest of her face. And when she smiled, as she did now, so beguilingly, it was as if the entire room lit up. In those first few moments, as they soaked in Queen Berenice's radiance, Varro and his companions knew why Titus had fallen for a woman thirteen years his senior.

"It gives my colleagues and myself great pleasure to be able to take advantage of your invitation, Your Majesty," said Varro.

"Then, we should all have a jolly time, questor," said Berenice breezily as she made herself comfortable and the maidservants retired. She waved for her guests to resume their places, and as they returned to the prone position Bostar reclined alone on the third couch.

Food and wine was now delivered to the table in relays of slaves from the palace kitchens, and the three slaves who had escorted the Romans from the door on their arrival reappeared, each to become a personal servant to the man she had placed, to attend to his every need throughout the meal. So it was that the beauty who had led Varro to his place, the girl with the magnetic eyes, became his silent accomplice for the evening. Varro could not take his eyes from her as she now brought a plate of purple damask plums and held the fruit in front of him.

"I believe, Marcus Metellus Martius, that you were with Titus Vespasianus when he fought the rebels at Taricheae," said the queen as she nibbled a date.

"Yes, Your Majesty," Martius returned, taking a plum. "I served him during the battles for both Taricheae and Tiberias."

"Were you with him when he suffered his wound?"

"Yes, Your Majesty. I was standing close by; no more than the distance between Chamberlain Bostar and myself now."

"It was a stone, I believe. He would not tell me anything of it. I only know that it left his arm a little weakened."

"Yes, Your Majesty, it was a stone, launched from a rebel catapult on the city walls. A missile about the size of your hand." He glanced at her hands, and, noting that they were dainty, added, "Or more the size of mine." He held up his right hand in a fist. "It hit him here…" Now he touched the biceps of his left arm. "On the unprotected arm. The blow was enough to knock him from his feet. We all ran to him, but he quickly picked himself up again, sending away the physicians and telling us all to pay attention to ourselves. Not a word of complaint did we hear from him, then, or later."

"He is not one to complain," Berenice said, her voice full of affection and pride.

"Your Majesty must be missing my lord Titus," said Martius, "now that he is returning to Rome."

Varro jabbed his companion in the ribs. It was obvious that Berenice was pining for her lover, but it was insensitive to remind the queen of the fact that Titus was on the way back to Rome, leaving her behind here in the East.

"My lord Titus' presence brightened all our days," Bostar interjected diplomatically.

"Yes, brightened all our days," the queen echoed sadly.

"We enjoyed dining with your brother, King Herod Agrippa, last evening, Your Majesty," said Varro, quickly trying to change the subject, and trying to maintain his focus on the conversation and ignore the beautiful girl who hovered so close to him at times that he could almost drink the rich perfume which wafted from her skin.

"I understand that you asked my brother about Jesus of Nazareth, questor," said the queen.

"Indeed I did, Your Majesty. Acting Governor Collega has commissioned me to undertake an investigation into the circumstances surrounding the death of the Nazarene."

"So I understand." Her eyes flashed momentarily to Bostar, betraying the fact that her chamberlain was the source of information about the Romans and their quest.

Varro made a mental note: this chamberlain must wield more than elementary influence with the queen. It never paid to underestimate a servant or their covert power, he reminded himself, no matter how servile or unobtrusive they may be. "I was hoping to find a resident of your fair city who might have been in Jerusalem at the time," he said.

"Four decades ago?" she commented with a flicker of a frown. "It would seem much too long ago for witnesses to have survived, questor. Has anyone come forward?"

"Not as yet, Your Majesty. But it is early days yet."

"I wish you well on your mission, questor, but I very much doubt that you will learn anything of value on this journey of yours. You are bound for Jerusalem?"

He nodded, holding out his cup for the beauty to pour wine and water in equal measure. "In time, Your Majesty."

"There is nothing there, questor," said Berenice, sounding just a little scornful. "Not any longer. The city has gone. The Temple has gone. The people are dead, or in chains, or fled."

"I can only seek the truth, wherever it lies, Your Majesty."

"The truth?" She raised her eyebrows. "Whose truth do we believe, questor? You must believe what you choose to believe, and must do what your conscience dictates." She took a sip of wine. "I believe that your patron is Gnaeus Licinius Mucianus."

"Yes, Your Majesty. I came out to Syria as questor to Licinius Mucianus."

"You will be returning to Rome soon?"

"In the new year."

"On the arrival of Cesennius Petus?"

He nodded. "Yes, Your Majesty." She was remarkably well informed. It occurred to him that perhaps she was in regular communication with Titus, that Titus was keeping her appraised of the decisions and appointments made by his father and himself.

"That will be in the spring or summer?" she asked.

"Most probably the summer, Your Majesty."

"Petus is bringing the 6th Gallica Legion back to its station in Syria, is he not?"

"Yes, Your Majesty. The 6th is not expected to be ready to commence its march to the East before next spring."

"After which you sail for Rome? You will be glad to be going home, questor."

In front of them, bowls of fruit were being replaced by platters of fresh water fish from lakes to the south.

"Yes, Your Majesty," Varro agreed. "It has been a long and eventful posting."

"You have family back at Rome? Responsibilities? Family clients?"

"As you say, I will resume my late father's responsibilities to family clients."

"You will be in a far better position to assist those clients now. Before, you were a mere Roman knight with an ex consul for a patron. Now, Marcus Terentius Varro, you are the client of Caesar's most trusted, most powerful deputy."

"Yes, Your Majesty, indeed."

"You must enjoy an excellent relationship with your patron."

"An excellent relationship, yes. Some find Licinius Mucianus a difficult man…"

"I can testify to that," she said, washing her hands.

"Ah. Personally, I have always had the most cordial relations with him."

"That is because you are a man, Varro, and young, and presentable."

Varro had heard rumors that Mucianus disliked women, and that Mucianus' sexual inclinations were toward men and boys, but he had never seen any evidence of that for himself in all the years he had known his patron. He had even heard it said that Mucianus and Titus were supposed to have had sexual relations, but he had never believed it, and he doubted that Berenice would either. "I can only speak as I find, Your Majesty, and I have found Licinius Mucianus a most generous and agreeable patron."

"I am glad of it." She began to eat a delicate slice of Coracin fish with her fingers. "Questor, I am contemplating going to Rome, to join my lord Titus," she announced.

So, he thought, the queen was either pining for Titus so much that she planned to follow him to Rome like a discarded pet, or she had prearranged with the emperor's son to make the journey and reunite with him at the capital. One way or another, it was an interesting proposition. Under Roman law, Berenice, a foreigner, could never marry a Roman. Titus could never make her his wife. At best, Berenice could only be his mistress; unless Titus chose to ignore Roman law. This had all the connotations of the disastrous liaison between Egyptian queen Cleopatra and her Roman lover Marcus Antonius. Varro realized he must step very carefully with Berenice, must watch what he said and what he did not say. Diplomacy of the highest order was called for here. "You would be made most welcome at Rome, I am sure, Your Majesty," he said, "as your royal dignity demands."

"One would expect so," she said. "Do you all think that I should follow my lord Titus to Rome, my lords?"

The question took her guests by surprise. The three of them looked at her, uncertain as to how they should answer. It occurred to Varro that perhaps Berenice had not discussed the matter with Titus after all.

"Tribune Martius?" the queen persisted. "Do you think that it would be wise of me to follow Titus to Rome? How would the Roman people view me, if I were to do so?"

"Well, I, er.. that is, Your Majesty…," Martius floundered, looking to Varro.

Berenice turned to Martius' neighbor. "Prefect Crispus? What is your opinion? Would the Senate resent my presence, do you think, if I were to take up residence at Rome…?" Again her eyes flashed to Bostar; this time, they conveyed a look of censure. "As some are telling me," she added, for Bostar's benefit.

Crispus paled. "Actually, Your Majesty, as a mere prefect, I could not venture an opinion on the attitude of the conscript fathers of the Roman Senate," he responded.

Impatient with the lack of response, the queen returned her attention to Varro. "Questor, should I go to Rome? I was thinking that perhaps I might take a ship to Italy in the summer. That way, there would be a seemly gap between my lord Titus' arrival and my own. Should I sail to Brindusium, or land at Micenum and then continue from there to Rome? Or should I go all the way to Ostia, and then take a barge up the Tiber, as many noble Romans do? Then again, I could perhaps take a house at Brindusium and send a message to my love that I had arrived, and await his call to Rome." She leaned toward him, an expectant look in her eyes. "What do you think, questor?"

Varro hesitated. He told himself that if the emperor's son had not arranged for Berenice to follow him, he must have his reasons. A major personal embarrassment for Titus and an equally major diplomatic incident for Rome must be avoided. It now occurred to the questor how to respond. "Your Majesty, I think that Caesar would welcome a visit to Rome by you and your brother the king, at a suitable time."

"My brother the king? Ah, but of course." Obviously, she had been thinking of making the voyage alone. The inclusion of Agrippa would be tiresome for her, but, seen as an official royal visit by king and queen, it would be less likely to upset the establishment at Rome. Such an official visit would also require an invitation to be first issued by the Palatium, a time-consuming process. "Yes, of course," she said again, absently now. Her disappointment was obvious. "At a suitable time, as you say."

"As to the exact timing of such an enterprise, I could not really advise you," Varro added. "Not being at Rome, not knowing the circumstance there…" His voice trailed off. What else could he tell her? He held out his hands for washing.

Berenice bestirred herself, as if invigorated by a new thought. "Questor, you are absolutely right." She nodded vigorously. "Yes, it would be too soon this year. Next year perhaps, when Caesar and Titus have come to grips with Rome and all the problems that beset her at present. You have a wise head on young shoulders. No wonder Licinius Mucianus and Gnaeus Collega have placed such trust in you."

Varro smiled, a little embarrassed. "Thank you, Your Majesty." His eyes went to the beautiful servant as she poured water over his outstretched fingers with one hand and held a bowl beneath them with the other. He wanted to touch her, almost to convince himself that she was real; but he dare not.

"The question is," Berenice pondered, "how would one know when it was precisely the right time to go to Rome?" She looked over at Varro for further guidance, then followed his eyes to the servant in front of him. The queen smiled to herself. "Her name is Miriam," she said.

Varro's eyes left the servant, and went to the queen. "Your Majesty?"

"The slave. Her name is Miriam. A beauty, is she not?"

"Well, yes, Your Majesty," Varro replied with embarrassment. "I hadn't really…"

"She is yours."

Varro blinked. "Er, I beg your Majesty's pardon?"

"The slave is a gift, from me, to you. In thanks for your kind advice here tonight.'

Varro's eyes flashed to the slave. Obviously disconcerted, Miriam would not look him in the eye. He returned his attention to the queen. "Your Majesty is very generous, but, I have no need of a female attendant. All in my party are male."

"I will not take no for an answer, questor." With that, the queen beckoned Miriam. The slave hurried to the queen, and knelt so that Berenice could whisper something in her ear. As she listened, the slave nodded impassively.

Beside Varro, Martius leant close. "Accept the queen's gift, Julius," he urged in a whisper. "It's the diplomatic thing to do."

"It would be awkward, taking a female slave with us," Varro whispered in return.

"Be gracious, my friend, take the beauty. You can do what you like with her once we leave here: sell her, bed her, or drown her. Or…" He winked. "Give her to one of your friends."

"So, questor, Miriam shall be delivered to your camp tomorrow," said the queen, as the slave, blank faced, straightened and resumed her duties. Berenice looked over to her chamberlain. "Arrange it, Bostar," she instructed.

"As Your Majesty commands," the chamberlain formally replied.

"Your Majesty is most generous," said Varro, conceding to the queen's wishes with a resigned sigh.

"Now, questor, there is a favor that you can render me in return," said Berenice.

Varro was suddenly consumed with dread. What could she possibly want him to do now that he was in her debt? "Your Majesty?" he responded with trepidation.

"It is clear to me that I need someone to be my eyes and ears at Rome, Varro. Someone with impeccable connections, someone who can send me messages alerting me to the appropriate time to apply to Caesar, or to set off for Rome, advising me when the atmosphere at Rome was right for either or both. I could not think of anyone better placed than a client of Licinius Mucianus. I want you to be my eyes and ears, Julius Varro."

"Ah." He felt like an animal caught in a trap.

"Neither Licinius Mucianus nor anyone close to him can know of our arrangement. It will be our little secret." Berenice cast a cautionary eye to Martius and Crispus, to emphasize the need for confidentiality. "No one at Rome can know. No one!"

Now Varro realized that this arrangement had been in the back of the queen's mind all along. That was why she had excluded Venerius from the banquet; as nephew to Mucianus, he could not be permitted to know that Varro had been commissioned to be the queen's spy in Caesar's court, a spy whose role was to report on, among other things, Mucianus' thoughts and actions. Whether Berenice had planned to entice him with the gift of one of her female slaves was debatable. Varro suspected that perhaps his own straying eyes had betrayed him and the perceptive queen had quickly seen an opportunity.

"Say 'yes,'" Martius hissed to Varro from behind his hand.

"Your Majesty…" Varro began, sounding conflicted.

"I know that my lord Titus will be eternally grateful to you once he and I have been reunited," said Berenice, eyeing him with a gaze which had become intense.

It was now apparent to Varro that she had set her mind. He felt a jab in the ribs from Martius beside him, as his colleague reinforced his belief that Varro should agree to whatever the queen wanted. Varro reluctantly decided to accede to her request. The mention of Titus had been the final straw. If Titus and Berenice did reunite, sooner or later, Varro reasoned, then it might not go well for his family if a refusal to help the queen burdened his record. "Your Majesty, it will be my honor to do whatever I can for you...." He said it without enthusiasm, but he said it none the less, and meant it.

The queen beamed. "Thank you, Varro. Thank you. You will not find me ungrateful." She turned to her chamberlain. "Do you hear what the questor said, Bostar?"

Bostar nodded gravely. "Your Majesty should be very pleased," he said.

With that the queen was ready to depart. Beckoning her maidservants, she said to her guests, "Please, my lords, enjoy the remainder of the banquet. I am tired, and will retire for the night." When she came to her feet, the men did swiftly the same.

"I bid you all a restful night." She smiled Varro's way. "I look forward to receiving illuminating correspondence from you at Rome in due course, questor."

And then, having achieved her objective for the evening, the queen departed.

✠

A trio of litters provided by the queen waited in a courtyard. Pedius the lictor and freedmen in the employ of the three Roman knights including Varro's man Callidus quickly came to their feet as their masters descended toward them. Across the courtyard, a troop of dismounted cavalrymen of Crispus' Vettonian command huddled in the gloom.

As Crispus ordered the troopers to mount up, Martius took Varro aside.

"For a moment there, Julius, I thought you would not agree to be her agent."

"What choice did I have, Marcus?" Varro sighed unhappily.

"Just the same, I did briefly have a vision in my mind's eye of an ax hovering above my neck. If the queen does resume her place in Titus' bed, my friend, she will wield immense power beyond the bedroom, including the power to have our heads. If you had not agreed, you would have marked us all for destruction."

The three of them climbed into the litters. The cavalry troop went ahead at the walk, while, with torch bearers lighting the way and with Pedius preceding them, the litters passed through the little city to its northwestern gate, then out into the countryside and along the road a short distance to the camp of the Varro expedition. As they went, the thoughts of the three Romans were very different.

Martius was thinking about the slave girl Miriam who was soon to become the questor's property. In his estimation she truly was a head-turning beauty. Martius envied his superior; he would gladly have accepted a gift of one of the queen's beauties.

Crispus lapsed into despondency on the brief journey. The queen had left the banquet before he could recite a single poem. What an opportunity lost! To have recited before the famous Queen Berenice. After she had left them, Crispus had suggested to Varro that he might voice some of his works anyway, for their entertainment, but Martius had quickly spoken against the idea, and Crispus' verse had never reached his lips. Stomping into his tent on the return to camp, Crispus ordered his servants to stand in front of him. He then proceeded to recite all the poems with which he had intended to regale Queen Berenice that night. He concluded the eighth poem two hours later.

Varro returned to camp thinking neither of poetry nor of the bewitching beauty who had been gifted to him. His mind was troubled by his undertaking to the queen. It was dangerous to be a spy at the best of times, but to be a spy in matters of the heart, involving the emperor's son and heir, this was doubly dangerous.

IX

THE ROAD TO NAZARETH

Northern Galilee, Tetrarchy of Trachonitis.
April, A.D. 71

The rhythmic tramp of marching feet on the flagstones attracted giggling children to the roadside to watch the Roman column pass. The expedition was leaving Caesarea Philippi. No one at Agrippa's capital had come forward in response to Varro's request for information, and both Agrippa and Berenice had politely declined invitations to dine with the questor at his camp. After several fruitless days, Varro had decided to move on.

The party had been joined by Miriam, slave from the court of Queen Berenice. She had been delivered by Bostar the day following the dinner at Berenice's palace. The young woman wore a shrouding headscarf and veil, but all the same Varro found her presence unsettling, for himself and for his men. He had put Callidus in charge of her, and arranged a tent all her own. On the march, he decreed, she would ride a spare pack mule. Then on a Saturday, several days after Miriam arrived in camp, Callidus had come to say that she was refusing to leave her tent. It was the Sabbath, she said, the day of rest. Miriam was a Jew. In the light of this, Varro had decided to make Antiochus responsible for her; as a former Jew, he should know what customs she would need to observe.

Predictably, Antiochus had objected. More than merely protesting that he was no nursemaid, he had said that he had abolished the day of rest for all Jews in Antioch and saw no reason why this slave should be treated any differently. Varro thought otherwise. He knew that Titus had even permitted the Jewish residents of cities he was besieging in Galilee to observe the Sabbath, ceasing operations on Saturdays to accommodate them. It had not altered events; Titus had inevitably triumphed. Equally, Varro saw nothing threatening or offensive in piety, and told Antiochus that Miriam could honor her Sabbath day as she saw fit. Antiochus had wanted to argue, claiming the girl would require special lamps and food prepared in a certain way. But Varro waved away the objections and told Antiochus to do what he could to accommodate the girl, warning him that he would be held personally responsible for Miriam's welfare.

Now, with the column well into its second hour on the road west and commencing to cross a bridge over the swift-flowing Jordan River, the girl was some distance behind the questor, covered from head to foot and riding at the rear of the freedmen on a mule led by a muleteer. From this point on, Varro vowed to himself, he would not think about Miriam until this mission was at an end. A sudden commotion behind Varro drew him from his thoughts and caused him to turn in the saddle, to see that Diocles the physician had tumbled from his horse. Suspicious of the cause, and preferring not to halt the column, Varro called to Martius. "Look to the physician, tribune," and kept riding.

Martius turned back, and as Diocles' five attendants came running from the rear the tribune dismounted and strode to the doctor, who lay on his face at the roadside near the river. Pushing back the slaves as they panted onto the scene, Martius knelt beside Diocles. "Drunk!" the tribune spat with disgust when he rolled the fat physician onto his back and found him mumbling incoherently, his breath reeking of wine.

Martius stood, looked at the river beside him, then called for Optio Silius and four men. As Silius and a quartet of legionaries came at the jog, men of the passing cavalcade looked down at the supine doctor with a mixture of curiosity, amusement, and disgust.

"Into the river with him!" Martius ordered when the soldiers arrived, pointing to a pond-like eddy beside the bank formed around the bridge's piles by silt carried down from Mount Hermon by the fast-moving waters.

The four legionaries lay aside their equipment, took an arm or a leg of the mumbling physician, and then threw Diocles into the Jordan River. He hit the water of the eddy horizontally, making a thunderous splash, then submerged. For a moment, it appeared that he would not resurface. Then his head appeared. Gasping for breath, floundering in panic, he spluttered frantically in Greek, "I drown! I drown!"

Martius motioned to the soldiers, who slipped down the bank and went in after the physician. The eddy waters where he was struggling turned out to be no more than knee deep. Dragged to the riverside, Diocles lay on dry ground like a beached whale. Shaking his head, Martius stood on the bank glaring down at the sodden doctor. "You will not drink on this expedition, physician!" he called with tempered fury. "That was the questor's directive, Diocles, and you will obey it. If I again find that you have flouted that order, I shall personally tie a thong around your penis and pull it tight. That will stop you drinking; you will never pass water again!"

Laughter erupted from the soldiers standing around Diocles. As for the doctor himself, his dunking had sobered him somewhat, and his eyes now widened in terror at the tribune's threat. Diocles groaned, knowing that Marcus Martius was not one to make idle threats; the doctor had seen the body of Fulvus the Vettonian cavalryman.

Martius had not finished. He glared at the physician's anxious servants. "As for you useless nitwits, I should be drowning the lot of you. Be aware; if I find that your master has touched another drop of wine, you fellows will have to become accustomed to passing water *without* a penis." To emphasize his point, he patted his sheathed sword.

The servants shrunk back from him with horror-stuck looks on their faces.

"You have been warned!" Martius added, before swinging on his heel and striding back to his horse. As Martius was gathering the reins of his mount, Prefect Crispus came riding back to check on the doctor's condition.

"What is Diocles' condition, tribune?" Crispus inquired with concern.

"Wet," Martius returned, motioning for one of the nearby soldiers to give him a boost up into his saddle. "Perhaps the Jordan will wash away his bad habits," he said with a scowl in Crispus' direction once he was up. Looking down at Diocles, now being helped up the bank, he called, "Optio, put the physician back in his saddle. We have dallied long enough."

"If he cannot stay on his horse, tribune?" Optio Silius asked. "What then?"

"Tie him to the saddle if you must!"

Eight miles due west along the Tyre road from Caesarea Philippi the column came to an intersection with the main north-south highway. North, the road led to Sidon and the coast. To the south lay Galilee. The column turned south. Ten miles on, the expedition camped beside the road for the night.

Next day, the expedition passed along the lush upper Jordan River valley and entered northern Galilee, part of Agrippa's realm. The countryside here was among the most fertile that Varro had ever come across. Stretching away either side of the river were trees of a variety the likes of which he had never before seen in the one place. Date palm plantations competed for space with walnut groves, while fig tree orchards stretched to the slopes of the Galilean Hills where olive trees and grape vines flourished.

Like most members of Roman nobility, Varro had received a solid education in agricultural matters. He was expected to oversee the family's estates, one at Capua in Campania, south of Rome, where he had been born, and several others near Forum Julii in southeastern Gaul. Part of his correspondence while stationed in Syria had been with his distant estate managers, covering everything from plantings and harvests to farm buildings and runaway slaves. How he wished he had an estate here in the Jordan basin. Varro turned to Pythagoras and Artimedes, who were riding not far behind him. "I would not have thought that palms and walnuts could grow in the same place," he remarked. "Surely, one requires hot air, the other cold?"

"The goddess Ceres has blessed this land," Pythagoras commented sagely.

"A farmer I met in Caesarea Philippi, my lord," Artimedes remarked, "told me that the fig trees and vines of this area produce fruit for fully ten months of the year. The Hebrew people certainly chose a bountiful place for themselves."

The column reached the town of Capernaum, on the northern shore of a body of fresh water in the shape of an inverted pear called Lake Tiberias by Romans and known as the Lake of Gennesaret to the Jewish people who had inhabited the region for centuries. More generally it was called the Sea of Galilee. Capernaum had been a major regional center when Herod Antipas was Tetrarch of Galilee, the base of a fishing fleet and a port for trading craft which plied between the towns fringing the lake, and the site of a customs station. It had also been the home of a squadron of light, fast warships, vessels with a single bank of oars and the task of combating lake pirates. Wherever there is commerce there are thieves, and just as the roads of Galilee had frequently been ravaged by bandits its lakes had attracted brigands in small boats who had plagued trading vessels. In earlier times too, Capernaum had been home to a force from King Agrippa's army and to small detachments of Roman troops, mostly cavalry, under a centurion who had charge of the entire district.

The Revolt had changed Capernaum. Because it had remained loyal to Agrippa and to Rome it had not suffered material damage in the fighting, unlike some towns and cities of the region which had gone over to the rebels and subsequently been besieged, overrun, looted and sometimes burned. Still, many of the Jews of the town had fled to the partisans or away from the Romans during the first year of the Revolt, and few had survived to return. Now, Capernaum was occupied by a mixture of Jew and non-Jew, some, refugees from the carnage in other places, others, opportunists who had come in search of a better living. There was a stone fortress in the town which Varro found occupied by a detachment of auxiliary cavalry of the Nervian Horse from Belgian Gaul and a cohort of Agrippa's archers. The Nervian unit's prefect was away at Caesarea.

The questor gave instructions for his column to pitch a camp outside the town, and once quarters had been prepared Varro called his chief subordinates together and reviewed their one precious piece of written evidence, the Lucius Letter. The document mentioned Capernaum several times, telling how the Nazarene had used it as a base of operations over several years and had recruited a number of his followers here, among them his deputy, Simon Petra. The obvious first task, said Varro, was to locate sites which could be connected with the Nazarene.

That task was made easier when, next day, the commander of the archer cohort stationed here told Varro that the town records had survived the Revolt, hidden in a vault by one of Agrippa's officers. The records were located, and Pythagoras and Artimedes set to work studying them. Within hours the documents yielded results. From poll tax records it was possible to identify a large house near the lakefront which had been the home of a Simon bar Jonas, who, during the reign of Tiberius Caesar, had lived here with his brother Andreius, their mother, Simon's wife and children, and Simon's mother-in-law. Matched with the Lucius Letter, this information pointed to Simon Petra. The letter indicated that Jesus had stayed at this house whenever he was in Capernaum, so, on Varro's orders Centurion Gallo and several squads of his men temporarily ejected the current occupants, who were unrelated to the Bar Jonas family, and then searched the house, looking for anything which might prove useful. Nothing of interest was turned up.

On the second morning in Capernaum, Varro went walking in the town's streets, accompanied by just Callidus and the lictor Pedius, to post notices seeking information and to obtain a feel for the place. Apart from Pedius' wooden staff, they went unarmed. To begin with, Varro deliberately sought out the town's Jewish synagogue, where, said the Lucius Letter, Jesus had taught his doctrine.

Here, in the silent, empty, colonnaded building, Varro lingered. For the first time, now that he was treading the same stones that the Nazarene had trod, he tried to imagine the man who was at the center of his quest. A man of a similar age to Varro himself. Pythagoras had assured the questor with authority that this man would have assumed the appearance of a Greek philosopher, allowing his beard to grow long, going barefoot, and wearing a coarse cloak of goatskin or the like. From the pages of the Lucius Letter a picture emerged of a seemingly gentle man, a man without malice, yet this was at odds with the fact that the Nazarene had been executed for sedition, for bearing arms against Rome. Was the Lucius Letter a fabrication, Varro wondered? Just how reliable was the letter's information, which Varro was using as the basis of his inquiry? Time would tell.

As the questor and his companions moved on, they came to a tavern plying its trade. It was a typical pavement wine shop, open to the street with shutters thrown open. A stone bench separated customer from server. Stools of stone lined the pavement. A side door led to back rooms where more private pursuits could be followed. There were pots for hot food set into the bench top, with round wooden lids. At the back of the room there was a line of long, narrow wine amphorae in cradles, which could be tilted for pouring. Several listless slaves waited to fill drinker's cups. There was not a customer in sight, and two sprightly old men with white hair behind the counter, apparently the tavern's owners, beckoned the trio of passers-by.

"Come, gentle lords, and try our best wine," said one.

"A special price for distinguished visitors," said the other, having noted Pedius' staff of office and an Equestrian's gold ring on Varro's left hand.

Varro led Pedius and Callidus to the counter. Declining wine, he had Callidus give the tavern keepers a coin and asked for walnuts and figs. They soon had a bowl of freshly cracked nuts and another of figs in front of him.

"Your accents are not local," said Varro as he motioned to his colleagues to sample the nuts and figs. "From where do you hail?"

"We are Roman veterans, Your Lordship," said one of the pair proudly. "We are both retired centurions of the 3rd Gallica."

"The 3rd Gallica?" said Pedius, impressed, crunching a nut. "A renowned legion."

"None moreso," said one of the tavern keepers proudly.

"You are a living testament to the legion life," Varro said. "You both look exceedingly healthy."

"How old would Your Lordship say we were?" said one with a wink to the other.

"Oh…" Varro looked them up and down. "I would estimate that you have passed… sixty-five years, perhaps."

Both of the old men beamed.

"Eighty-four, this very year, the pair of us," one of them announced.

"No!" Pedius exclaimed. "Truly?"

"I would hardly credit it," said Varro with genuine surprise.

"I must confess, I would have lost a considerable amount wagering on it," said Callidus, with a fig in his mouth. "Considerable."

"It is true," one of the pair said earnestly. "As Your Lordship says, we can thank the legion life for our longevity. All that marching was not wasted on us."

"How long have you been in business here, old soldiers?" Varro asked.

"Since Nero was a boy, Your Lordship," said one octogenarian. "Ever since we retired from the Gallica. We went to friends at Ptolemais when the rebels started their uprising at Jerusalem, and have not long since returned."

"Why in the name of Jove we bothered to return is beyond me," said the other. "Business is not what it used to be. The town is a shadow of what it once was, and as for the troopers we now have stationed here, those buffoons of Belgae are of no value to tavern keepers whatsoever. They are an insult to Bacchus!"

"They don't drink!" said the other with disgust. "Imagine a Gaul or a German who doesn't swill wine? They give the armies of Rome a bad name. You would have thought, with soldiers stationed in the town, we would be run off our feet. But, not so."

"Why do they abstain?" Callidus asked.

"It is their custom," said one of the pair, shaking his head. "Can you believe it? The Nervians say that wine makes men weak. Weak? Molly-coddles, the lot of them!"

"We hear," said the second tavern keeper, lowering his voice to a conspiratorial level and leaning closer to the three men on the other side of the counter, "that a new colony of legion veterans is to be established in a pass in the hills of Samaria. Flavia Neopolis, they say it will be called. Do your lordships know if this is true?"

"I could not say," Varro responded. "I have no knowledge of it, but that is not to say that it is not true. New colonies are the exclusive prerogative of Caesar."

"If it were true, we were thinking of packing up and trying our luck there. Legion veterans know how to drink!"

"But we are no longer youngsters," said the other, who was obviously not as enamoured with the idea. "The thought of moving our old bones to a new location is not an appealing one. It might be the death of us."

"Abstentious Belgian troopers will be the death of us!" the other countered, bringing a chuckle from Callidus.

Varro now instructed Callidus to produce several more coins.

The eyes of the pair lit up. "Will it be wine after all, Your Lordship?" said one.

"No," Varro replied. "I will have information."

"What manner of information?" said one old man warily.

"There was a centurion stationed in this town during the latter years of the reign of Tiberius Caesar," Varro said, recounting a story he had read in the Lucius Letter and watching the faces of the pair for their reaction. "This centurion was on good terms with the local Jewish community, and even endowed their synagogue. On one occasion, he sent to a Jewish priest, a man called Jesus of Nazareth, and asked him to cure a servant who was unwell. Do you know anything of the centurion, and that event?"

Both men were blank faced. "That was well before our time here, Your Lordship," said one cautiously, with his eyes on the money which Callidus had placed temptingly on the counter in front of him.

"You have not heard of the event, of a miraculous cure for the centurion's servant by Jesus, or Joshua, of Nazareth?" Varro persisted.

"We have heard of Joshua of Nazareth," said the other, "or Jesus as the Greeks call him. A miracle worker, some say, a bandit according to others. Galilee always had more than its fair share of Jewish bandits. Like a plague of locusts, they were."

"There was a bandit leader by the name of Jesus in these parts just before the Revolt," the first man remarked. "Jesus bar Shaphat. I think he was captured by Caesar Vespasianus at Tiberias."

"We have heard of the centurion Your Lordship refers to," said the other, with his eyes on the money. "As far as we know, he died here, many years ago."

"You cannot confirm that Jesus of Nazareth cured this centurion's servant?"

"We would like to, Your Lordship," the less greedy of the two replied. "We would very much like to be able to help you. But, we cannot lie to a Roman knight."

Varro nodded. Despite their lack of useful information, he pushed the money across the counter to them anyway.

The greedier tavern keeper quickly scooped up the money and slipped it into the leather purse hanging at his waist. "Your Lordship is a generous man. Would you care to visit us again this evening? We might be able to provide a little excitement for you in the back room, if you fancy your chances with the dice."

Varro looked at him with surprise. "You can see that my man is carrying a lictor's staff?" he said, pointing to Pedius' *bacillum*. "I am a Roman magistrate."

The old man grinned stupidly. "Yes, but even magistrates need to relax."

Varro burst out laughing. The irony of it amused him. He was the Questor of Syria, responsible for policing all illegal gambling in his provinces, and here was this man risking a fine of four times the value of the stake money found on the gambling table by inviting him to play dice in the tavern's back room. "I will pretend I did not hear your invitation," he said. "Just don't let me catch you hosting a gambling session. In return for my temporary deafness, you can render me a service. Give them a notice, Callidus."

Varro's freedman produced a piece of vellum from the cloth bag slung over his shoulder and handed it to the tavern keepers. The two of them read the notice, penned by Artimedes, which contained the by now usual call for anyone with information about the circumstances surrounding the death of Jesus of Nazareth at Jerusalem to come forward.

"What does His Lordship wish us to do?" said one old man uncertainly.

"Post it, man!" Varro returned. "Nail it up here, beside your counter." He patted a wooden post. "Display the notice where your customers can see it."

"Oh, yes, we can do that," said the tavern keeper. "Rely on us, Your Lordship."

"Give us some more," said his partner. "We'll post them all around here."

✠

Within a few days the expedition packed up and moved on. As was becoming the norm, no information had been offered to the questor. Varro could not be sure whether it was because nobody existed who could provide the sort of information he was looking for or because informants were too afraid to come forward.

The column passed ten miles along the western shore of the Sea of Galilee to Tiberias, a city at the bottom of a bare hill at the lakeside. Tiberias too was in Agrippa's realm. Four years before, because its rebel defenders had capitulated to General Vespasian, Tiberias had been spared from looting and destruction, although because of its narrow gate the Roman general had knocked down the southern wall to provide better access for his troops. Here King Agrippa had recently built a wide new southern gate.

Varro camped in the remains of one of Vespasian's fortified positions south of Tiberias, between that city and Taricheae, scene of bitter fighting during the revolt. Conveniently, there was a hot spring here at the fortress site, with a bathhouse recently restored by Agrippa. The questor had the usual notices posted in both Tiberias and Taricheae, and at Callidus' suggestion also paid a market crier to go through each city calling out the same message as that contained in the notices. Despite these initiatives, the days passed without any informants presenting themselves to Agrippa's city governors in either Tiberias or Taricheae.

"The fighting around here was the most bloody I can remember," said Martius, after he and Varro had gone into Taricheae with an escort of infantry and cavalry led by Centurion Gallo. They stood on a sandy beach below the city wall, beside the lake, looking across the water to the rocky Golan Heights looming over the eastern shore.

"It was here that you were wounded?" said Varro.

Martius nodded. "I felt nothing at the time, just broke off the arrow and continued on." He pointed in the direction of the hill behind the town. "We had two thousand archers of our own up there, raining arrows down on the city walls. And there we were—Titus, General Trajanus of the 10th, a few of his centurions, *me*, and four hundred cavalry. We were supposed to be waiting for Titus' father to join us with the main force, but Titus said, 'What are we waiting for?' He had been hit by a stone from the wall, and the injury had made him angry. So, with just four hundred men, we went over the wall." There was no emotion in Martius' voice. He retold the story like an historian, in an impartial monotone, keeping to the facts. "The odds were something like twenty to one against us, but we fought our way through the city, driving most of the defenders down here to the water. The rebels escaped out onto the lake in boats and on rafts."

"They escaped completely?" Varro asked.

"No, they stayed out on the lake, waiting to see what we would do next, waiting for an opportunity to return and make a counter attack. Next day, Titus' father sent us some light warships. So, the four hundred of us went on board and off we went, after the partisans on the lake. It was a battle unlike any you can imagine: in the boats, on the rafts, in the water. We fought like madmen. We slaughtered thousands of them out there. Some fled back to shore, so we gave chase and caught them here on the beach. Not one survived. They stood on the heaps of their dead to fight us, and not one survived. When we counted the bodies, it was something like seven thousand of them we had killed, in the city, on the lake, and here on the beach."

Varro nodded slowly. He said nothing, just looked at the sand, and imagined it stained red with rebel blood.

"We left them where they died," Martius went on. "On the shore, and floating like lilies out on the lake. It was the height of summer. The corpses soon bloated, and then over the next few days they quickly putrefied. The stink hung over the place for weeks."

Varro turned and walked back toward the city's water gate, and Martius followed a few paces behind. Standing a little way up the beach, with the end of his staff resting on the sand, was Lucius Pedius the lictor, and as Varro came up to him he had a strange, faraway look in his eyes.

"Is anything amiss, Pedius?" Varro asked, stopping in front of his lictor.

Pedius blinked, and then he looked at the questor. "No, my lord," he assured Varro. "Nothing amiss. Just reflecting."

"Well then, lead on."

"Yes, my lord. Forgive me, my lord." Pedius led the way up into the city.

✠

Pedius was cursing the boy, and the boy kept swinging a sword at him. He may have been nine or ten years of age. His face was baby pink. He had gone overboard from one of the Jewish rafts, and among all the men thrashing in the bloodied water he somehow managed to both stay afloat and swing the short sword in Pedius' face.

"Throw away your sword!" Pedius was yelling as he leaned over the low side of the war galley toward him. "Throw away your sword and I will save you, boy!" As he spoke, he lay aside his shield, freeing his left hand.

The boy reached up with his left hand and grabbed hold of the side of the boat.

"Now throw away the sword!" Pedius called.

But the Jewish boy only made another swipe at the centurion of the 10th Legion. Pedius reeled back, feeling a stinging sensation at the left side of his neck. Dropping his eyes, his could see his own red blood flowing. "You little swine!" His anger boiled. He swung his sword down over the boy's left wrist. With a crunching of bone, the razor-sharp blade cleaved off the youth's hand, the hand holding the side of the vessel.

Soundlessly the boy slid from view.

Pedius looked over the side. The child was floundering. The sword had disappeared from his remaining hand. "Now, give me your good hand, you little fool!"

The boy ignored him, grasping hold of the boat's side with his right hand.

Pedius reached over to grasp the boy's forearm and pull him inboard, to safety. "Better to live with only one hand than not to live at all, boy," he called.

The youngster looked up at Pedius with eyes filled with hate, and spat in his face.

Again Pedius reeled back, as if the boy's spittle was poisonous. Again, anger welled. "You spit in my face, when I'm trying to save your worthless hide!" Again the centurion brought down his sword, on the boy's right wrist.

The severed right hand fell into the boat, and the boy disappeared from sight. Looking over the side, Pedius saw the top of the child's head. The handless boy was trying desperately to stay afloat. To Pedius, life without hands was no life at all. Reaching over the side, he put his left hand squarely on top of the bobbing head, pushed the boy under, and held him down. For a time he felt the boy struggle. Then, he ceased to resist.

Gasping for breath, bathed in cold sweat, Pedius sat up: in his bed. For a moment, he had no idea where he was. Then it came to him. He was in his Varro expedition tent, camped between Tiberias and Taricheae, and he had just experienced the same nightmare that had haunted him for four years since that summer's day when he had fought alongside Trajanus his general, and Titus, and Martius, out there on the lake, killing the defenders of Taricheae. During his twenty years in the Roman army, Lucius Pedius had killed many men, and the occasional woman and child. None of those children had come close to killing him. None had even tried to do battle with combat-hardened legionaries. Lucius Pedius never had cause to regret a single act while under arms for Rome, never had a sleepless night, until the death of the defiant Jewish child of Taricheae.

The lictor pulled himself from his bed, and called for his servant, Austinus.

"Water," Pedius croaked when the man, a slender Ethiopian, appeared in front of him. "Water, and a change of tunic."

✠

At last, a stroke of luck. Just as Varro was planning to resume his march and move on to Nazareth, birthplace of Jesus, a resident of Tiberias came forward offering information. The city governor sent him to Varro's camp escorted by a squadron of Agrippa's cavalry. The informant was an elderly man, a gnarled Galilean Jew who went by the name of Laban bar Nahor. Bald, bent, and crippled, he walked with the aid of a myrtle stick. When he stood in front of Varro in the questor's tent he swayed uneasily on his feet. Varro had Hostilis provide him with a stool.

"Your Excellency," said the old man once he was seated, locking bony fingers over the top of his stick, "I do not know if what I have to tell will be of interest. I cannot personally testify to anything about the death of Jesus of Nazareth. I did not know him." He cast his eyes around the other Romans in the tent, Martius, Crispus, Pythagoras, Artimedes, Callidus, and Pedius, as if to gauge their reaction to his words. "Yet, I am familiar with one who did know him, and who could tell you of his death, for he was there, at the execution. He once told me so."

Varro nodded. "His name?"

"His name is Boethus bar Joazar, Excellency, and he was at one time a neighbor of mine. Boethus came from Capernaum after the Revolt began. He resided in Tiberias until recent times, when he traveled to Caesarea. He has a daughter living at Caesarea."

"What connection did this Boethus bar Joazar have with Jesus of Nazareth?" Varro asked, glancing to Pythagoras on his right to satisfy himself that the secretary had noted down the details. As if reading his mind, Pythagoras, working with stylus and wax tablet, nodded confirmation that he had the man's name.

"Boethus told me that he had been a follower of a Johannes, who was called the Baptist. When the Baptist was imprisoned at Cypros and then Macherus by Antipas, Boethus took messages back and forth between the Baptist and Jesus of Nazareth, who was a cousin of the Baptist. After the death of the Baptist, Jesus continued his work, and my neighbor Boethus became a follower of his doctrine."

"He was present at the Nazarene's execution?" Varro asked.

"That is what he told me, Excellency."

"Did he also claim to have seen the Nazarene alive following his execution?"

Old Laban smiled. "No, Excellency."

Martius asked a question. "Are you a follower of the Nazarene, old man?"

Laban continued to smile. "Do I look like a Nazarene, my lord?"

"What does a Nazarene look like?" Martius countered.

"Not like this shriveled old prune of a Jew," Laban returned with a weary smile.

"What did Boethus tell you about the execution?" Varro asked.

"Only that he had been a young man at the time, and that he had watched the Nazarene die on the cross. He saw him taken down, and taken away to be interred."

"Jesus was dead?" Varro asked.

Laban pulled a face. "Why would he be taken down if he were not, Excellency?"

"Boethus did not say anything to indicate he thought the Nazarene still lived?"

"Boethus told me that he believed that the Nazarene rose from the dead two days after his death on a cross."

"So, he believed that Jesus was the Jews' so-called Messiah?"

"I understand that Boethus thought so. We agreed to differ in that regard."

When Varro paused to reflect on what Laban had told them, Martius asked another question. "What reward do you seek, old man, for your information?"

"I seek no reward, my lord."

"You wish to cause trouble for this Boethus, is that it?" the tribune suggested.

"No, my lord. I assure you…"

"What then? You came here with a reward in mind. Admit it! Speak up now!"

Tears began to form in the old man's eyes. "I have a son, and a grandson. They went to Jerusalem five years ago for the Passover, and they never returned." He turned to Varro. "Your Excellency, if there is anything you can do… If they still live, perhaps your Excellency can help them. I know that you are a good man. If you could send them home to me, Excellency, this is all I ask. Their names are Baruch and Tobias. My son Baruch, and Tobias, the son of Baruch. I beg you to save them."

Varro looked into the old man's swollen eyes and sighed. "You know that a great many people died in the siege of Jerusalem, or were made prisoners? It is very likely that your son and your grandson are no longer alive, or have been sent into slavery."

Laban attempted a brave smile. "I know, Excellency. Yet, I am a foolish old man, and even at my age I can still believe in the power of prayer."

"Very well. We have the names of your son and grandson. If they live, and if it is in my power to do so, they will be sent home to you."

The old man closed his eyes, so the Romans would not see him cry.

"This Nazarene, Boethus bar Joazar," said Varro. "You say he is in Caesarea?"

Without opening his eyes, the old man nodded slowly.

X

THE NAZARETH INFORMANTS

Territory of Southern Galilee, Roman Province of Judea. April, A.D. 71

On the route south through the dry hills, just below the junction with the road to Ptolemais and the Mediterranean, lay the village of Nazareth. Before the Varro column reached the place, the disfigured decurion Pompeius rode back from the advance guard.

"The people in the village are preparing to flee, questor," he reported. "They must know that you are coming. Do you want my men to round them up?"

"Yes, bring them to the center of the village. But take care not to harm anyone."

The cavalryman urged his horse forward, and went galloping off to rejoin his waiting troop. The hillside village, with many of its houses in ruins, was deserted when the column reached it a little later. Soon, villagers began to make a reluctant return, some leading mules laden with their belongings, others burdened with all they could carry on their backs, all herded along like sheep by Pompeius' troopers. Little more than thirty in number, the elderly and women with children, they were brought to the middle of the village, where Varro, his officers, freedmen and advisers waited on horseback. The other elements of the column had halted south of Nazareth.

Varro called Antiochus forward, instructing him to address the villagers in Aramaic, with a request for relatives of Yehoshua bar Josephus, also known as Joshua bar Davidus and Jesus of Nazareth, and for people with

information regarding the death of Jesus forty years before. None of the
clearly terrified villagers moved a muscle after Antiochus' call, so Varro
asked for any followers of the Nazarene to identify themselves. Again there
was no response. With increasing frustration, Varro asked for anyone who
knew anything at all about Jesus, adding that they would be well rewarded.
Again, Antiochus translated the questor's request to the villagers.

After a pause, a long-faced man in his sixties stepped forward, dragging
his unwilling wife with him. He wore a simple tunic, she a long gown belted
at the waist, and, like all the women, a modest head covering. Nervous, but
in good Latin, the man identified himself as Malachi, and his wife as Doris.
Then he said, "If we were to show Your Lordship the house where Jesus was
raised, my wife and I would be rewarded?"

"Indeed," the delighted Varro quickly agreed. Progress at last.

"We would not be punished?" The man's eyes flashed around the
Romans.

Varro shook his head. "You have my word that neither you nor anyone
else in the village will be harmed in any way. Lead on. Show me the
house."

The couple conducted the Roman officers to a tumbled-down house
not far from the center of town. "The house of Josephus bar Heli, father of
the one you call Jesus," said Malachi. "While the boy was growing up here
we knew him as Yehoshua."

"This is the house of Jesus' family?" said Varro with interest, dis-mounting
to take a closer look at what had once been a substantial residence on two
floors. He beckoned Pedius, indicating that the lictor should precede him
on the inspection.

"Yes, this is it, the palace of the Messiah," said Malachi mockingly, his
confidence growing.

Pedius had handed the *fasces* to his servant Austinus for safe keeping,
and now equipped with his staff of office he went ahead, pushing aside the
remains of a front door, allowing the questor to enter a long rectangular
courtyard, desolate and overgrown.

"Where is the family now?" Varro called.

While his wife waited outside, Malachi ventured after the questor and
his lictor. "They all left Nazareth when I was a young man," the Jew said
as he followed Varro into the courtyard. "The father died when Yehoshua
was in his twenties. The mother Miriam, the sons, the daughters, they all

left after Yehoshua was executed. It was quite a scandal at the time. Their neighbors would not talk to them. Everyone was afraid they would bring the authorities down on us all. After all, the man had been convicted of sedition."

Varro and Pedius had walked to the far end of the courtyard. "The family left no relative here at Nazareth?" the questor asked, as his eyes traversed the time-weathered stone walls and invasive creeping vines.

"Not one. The family was not from here originally. They did not mix well. They were a very devout family, and people here thought they had airs about themselves. Miriam was related by marriage to Zecharias, a Pharisee and one of the senior priests at Jerusalem. Zecharias was numbered among the councilors of the Great Sanhedrin, and while he lived was a man of standing and influence."

Using his staff, Pedius pushed aside fallen roof timbers in a doorway so that his chief could take a look inside the shell of the house. The flat roof and upper floor had caved in some years before. Roof tiles had been pilfered; only rotting timbers remained.

"Tell me about the brothers and sisters." Varro stepped into the gloomy interior. In his head he imagined the chattering voices, the bickering, the laughter, of a family of nine or ten filling these rooms. Crumbling wood crunched beneath his careless tread.

"Five boys in all," said Malachi, following on Varro's heel. "Apart from Yehoshua, there was, let me see, as you would call them — Jacob, Joses, Simon, and Judas. As for the girls, I cannot recall their names. We saw little of them; Jewish girls do not leave the house. All the boys except Yehoshua helped their father with his carpentry business. Josephus went around the Jewish cities and towns, working on building projects, producing items of furniture; but he stayed clear of the unclean Greek cities."

"Jesus, or Yehoshua, or Joshua, did he work as a carpenter?"

"No, he was encouraged from an early age to follow the religious life. Miriam's cousin Elizabeth used her influence with her husband Zecharias to ensure the boy received the best instruction regarding Jewish Law. Yehoshua left Nazareth before he reached his twenties. I heard that he and his cousin Johannes studied with the Essenes in the wilderness. This cousin was the Johannes they call the Baptist. The Baptist remained with the Essenes until just two or three years before his death, but Yehoshua went to study with the Pharisees and the Sadducees, as a devout Jew should, but then joined Johannes when he began to preach his particular doctrine throughout the Jordan valley."

"Did Jesus frequently return here, to the village?"

"Very rarely. I remember the last occasion well, only a year or two before his death. He was known to have been studying the Law, so, on the Sabbath day, he was invited to read from the holy books at our synagogue. I was there. What a disaster it was!" Malachi threw his hands in the air. "Yehoshua so upset the people of the village by what he said… You would not believe how angry the villagers were."

"What did he say that upset the people?"

"Oh, all manner of sacrilegious things. How he had been chosen by the Almighty to lead the people; things of that nature. He was thrown out of Nazareth, and told never to come back. And in no uncertain terms, I can tell you. Good riddance, I said."

"Where did the family go after they left Nazareth?"

"The mother had relatives at Jerusalem and also at Bethany, the father at Bethlehem, so we assumed they went to one or other of those places. We later heard that several of the boys were living at Jerusalem. Jacob, the second eldest, had also been given religious training, and he took charge of the sect that Yehoshua had inherited from the Baptist, the sect they now call the Nazarenes. Jacob was later stoned to death. I have not heard what happened to the other brothers, but I think they must all be dead by now."

Varro stooped and took up the weathered remains of a simple wooden stool. All three legs had been broken off. Perhaps Josephus had made it, and perhaps his eldest son had sat on it. Perhaps not. "I have seen enough," he said, discarding the piece of wood. Passing through the courtyard he walked back out into the street, where his officers waited. Hostilis boosted him back up into the saddle and handed him his reins.

Malachi and his wife came to the questor's horse, looking up at him. "Was the information of value, my lord?" Malachi asked plaintively. "A reward was mentioned."

"Your information was scant," the questor replied. "Next to worthless."

Malachi and his wife looked at each other.

"If you want more, I can give you more," Malachi's gray-faced wife Doris then announced, becoming vocal for the first time. "His followers say that Yehoshua was such a wonderful man, and a descendant of King

David," she said, in a venomous voice, "but they fail to tell you whose seed he really came from."

"Tell me, then," Varro urged.

"How much is it worth?" She stood with her hands on her ample hips.

He thought for a moment. "A gold piece."

"Two!"

Varro shrugged. "Very well, if the information is good, two gold pieces."

Doris rubbed her hands together. "You have a bargain, Your Honor. The true story is this: Miriam was betrothed to Josephus when she fell pregnant. Yes, and a great scandal it was. Her cousin Elizabeth was then six months into her own term with her son Johannes, the one who would become the Baptist. Now, instead of putting Miriam away as an adulteress, as he could have, and should have, old Josephus, Miriam's betrothed, he goes ahead and marries her anyway. Silly fool!" Her face became decorated with a wicked smile. "Now comes the best part, Your Honor. The rumor at the time was that Miriam had been deflowered by a Roman soldier by the name of Panthera, the centurion in charge of this area. He lived at Capernaum, I think."

"No, wife, the centurion was from Sepphoris," her husband contradicted her. "In those times, Galilee was ruled from Sepphoris."

Doris turned to her husband with a scowl. "No, I think it was Capernaum," she persisted. "Not that it matters." She looked up to Varro again. "What is important is that if the rumor is true, my lord, then Yehoshua bar Josephus, or Jesus of Nazareth if you prefer, was the bastard son of a Roman centurion!" She roared with laughter. "The Nazarenes' holy Messiah was half Roman!"

Behind him, Varro also heard young Venerius burst into laughter. Whether the junior tribune was sharing the woman's derision of the Nazarene or his mirth was directed at Doris, the questor neither knew nor cared. Varro frowned down at the woman. "What proof do you have of this?"

Doris' laughter subsided. "As I said, it was a rumor. A widespread rumor, just the same, Your Honor. It was on everyone's lips."

Varro shook his head. "For factual information I pay two gold pieces. For gossip… Pay them what they are worth, Callidus. Martius, order the column forward."

Varro rode on. Callidus reached into his purse, pulled out a single gold coin, and tossed it at the feet of Malachi and Doris. As the couple dropped to their knees and scrabbled competitively for the coin, the freedman urged his horse forward.

The questor halted his steed at the top of the street, and there he waited for the column to roll past, on the move again and bound for the coast. Before long the body of the expedition swung into and through the village. Looking back down the dusty thoroughfare toward the house of the family of Jesus, he saw Miriam the slave girl behind the freedmen, riding on her mule. Her eyes were fixed on the house where the Nazarene had been raised, where the townspeople clustered still. When her mule drew level with Varro he spurred his horse into motion, and moved in beside her on his taller steed.

"What was your interest in the house of Jesus of Nazareth?" he asked.

Her head tilted up to him. She studied him for a moment from behind her veil, then said, "Was that the house of the Nazarene? He was, by all accounts, a good man."

"Do you believe that Jesus rose from the dead and was a god, Miriam?"

"I believe that the Almighty is all-powerful," she said with certainty and conviction. "A Roman like you, with all your gods, you could not possibly understand."

He laughed. She was spirited and courageous as well as beautiful, he told himself, and his special treatment of her was allowing a defiant streak to emerge. Miriam could not know that when first she had joined his party Varro had thought of sending her up to Antioch, to join the servants in the household of Paganus the merchant, but Martius had talked him out of it; if Queen Berenice were to find out that Varro had given the girl away, the questor's deputy had cautioned, she might be offended. Varro said no more to the girl. He urged his horse to the trot and quickly moved up to the head of the column.

Without a backward glance, Varro left the village of Nazareth behind. Yet, as the expedition made its way through the hills, Varro lapsed into deep thought, inspired by his brief exchange with Miriam. He considered himself a devout man, and certainly no less devout than the Jews. He observed all the feast days of the gods, he performed all the required sacrifices, he honored his mother, he revered the memory of his ancestors.

Every morning, whether at home or traveling, he paid obeisance at his family shrine. The concept of a man becoming a god was not alien to Varro, or to other Romans. Julius Caesar and many of the emperors of Rome who came after the dictator had been deified after their deaths. They had their own temples, their own priesthoods, their own sacred days and festivals. Not that Varro was convinced that any of them truly were gods. As for this Nazarene, he was no Julius Caesar, he was no Roman emperor, and no Roman emperor had come back from the dead. An unconscious smile appeared on the questor's lips. That would truly be an event to convince him that a mere mortal had godly powers, if a Caesar were to rise from the dead.

The expedition camped in the ruins of the town of Gaba on the road to Caesarea. Once his officers and freedmen had departed his tent after dinner, Varro decided he would take in the night air. Summoning Pedius for company, he wrapped himself in a cloak against the unseasonable chill then wandered the camp streets, lingering in the shadows to listen to conversations around the men's campfires, hearing opinions about chariot racing and gladiators and the likelihood that this mission they were on was a wild goose chase.

Varro and Pedius moved on. As they approached the parked baggage train, behind the horse corral, they heard a woman's voice, raised, and tinged with alarm. There was only one woman in the Varro camp. Varro and his lictor quickened their step. Hurrying around carts and wagons, they came on the tent of Miriam. The girl stood outside it, a bronze water bucket in one hand. She was using the other hand to fend off three unarmed legionaries, mere youths the lot of them, and all of them laughing and jesting.

"What's going on here?" Varro demanded.

The three soldiers spun around, with fear suddenly painted on their faces.

"We were only having a little bit of fun," said one of the men. "That was all."

"You will address the questor with due deference, soldier!" Pedius snapped.

"Sorry… my lord questor," said the man, hanging his head. "We meant no harm."

"It was high spirits, nothing more," Miriam spoke up in the soldiers' defense.

"I did not chose to bring a female on this expedition," said Varro. "But proper decorum will be observed by you men at all times." He thought he could see the girl's eyes smiling at him through her veil, as if she found his effort to protect her amusing.

"I am perfectly capable of looking after myself, questor," she declared. "Do I have your permission to retire?"

"Yes," he answered, smarting at her lack of gratitude. "Go."

She turned and slipped into her tent.

"What do you want to do with these malingerers, my lord?" Pedius asked, wagging his staff at the trio of worried legionaries.

Varro briefly studied the young soldiers. "Send them on their way," he sighed.

"As you please. Consider yourselves lucky, you lot," Pedius cautioned the legionaries with the gravity and authority of a former centurion. "Step out of line again, my lads, and, I guarantee, you will feel Centurion Gallo's vine stick across your backs." He raised his staff. Shaking it in their faces, he growled, "To your tents with you! Smartly now!"

The three young men gratefully hurried off at a fast walk.

Pedius turned at Varro, shaking his head. "The young colts deserved a beating."

"They committed no crime," Varro irritably returned, his thoughts still on the young woman. "Come." He strode off toward his quarters, leaving Pedius to follow.

As Varro reached the edge of the collection of carts, a figure stepped out into the light of a lantern hanging on a post. It was Marcus Martius. "The charms of the Jewish girl are difficult to ignore, are they not, Julius?" said the tribune.

"My interest is merely that of a concerned master, Marcus," Varro returned.

Martius grinned. "Ah, then you would not mind if *I* were to bed the girl?"

"I think we should all be keeping our minds above our waists," Varro bristled, resuming his progress. "Let us all leave the girl be. Come, Pedius."

Pedius gave the tribune a censorious glance as he passed and hurried to catch up with the questor.

"Not even a lictor can protect a man against himself, Pedius," Martius called after him. With a chuckle, he cast a glance toward the girl's tent, then turned, and ambled off.

XI

THE HOUSE OF THE EVANGELIST

Caesarea, Capital of the Roman Province of Judea. April, A.D. 71

Strong, but warm, the wind blew in from the west. Bracing against the gusts and feeling the spray of the Mediterranean on his face, Julius Varro walked the broad white stone breakwater as the sea pounded against the massive manmade barrier with an angry roar.

On this sandy stretch of Mediterranean coast, where no safe haven had previously existed between Tyre in Syria and Ascalon in Idumea, Herod the Great had built a port to serve the inland city of Sebaste. Until then, there had merely been a lookout tower here, built long ago by the Phoenicians. With the help of Roman military engineers, Herod had created a city for the shore and a shipping basin for the depths. It had taken ten years and a massive feat of engineering to realize Herod's designs, using glistening white Palestinian stone. At twenty fathoms, a curved sea wall two hundred feet across had been arrayed, using huge stones fifty feet long. A second, inner breakwater was more for the defense against man than nature, containing a crenellated wall and towers which could be manned by troops. Within the circular enclosure of sheltered water created by outer and inner walls two docks had been built, one for Herod's battle fleet and visiting Roman warships, the other for cargo vessels. An arcade lining the quay which encircled the docks provided homes for seamen. Above the arcade a variety of official buildings rose. The most impressive, a white temple dedicated to Caesar and to Rome, could be seen for miles out to sea and was used as a beacon by seafarers. The opening in the breakwater, facing the gentle north wind, was flanked by a huge turret and giant stones.

Through this opening a long slim Roman naval trireme now slid, its three banks of oars manned by paid freedmen. The warship's mainsail and bow sail were furled. The weather out on the Mediterranean was looking threatening, and the craft was heading for the safety of the harbor. As it passed, with its perfectly synchronized oars slowly rising and dipping to the lazy beat of an unseen timekeeper, marines, sailors and officers on the warship's upper deck gazed with idle curiosity across at the party on the breakwater.

From the massive barrier of stone Varro and his companions looked back over all the vessels crowding the harbor, warships, and roundships, as Romans called the tubby merchantmen. Beyond the teeming quay, where goods of every kind were manhandled by hundreds of laborers, the city of Caesarea loomed. A massive white fortress hung over the port. The headquarters of the Roman administration, it housed the palace of the procurator and several other palaces besides, as well as administrative offices, Herod's Judgment Hall, a prison, the city's library and archives, massive underground storage vaults, and quarters large enough for an army of thousands.

Before the Jewish Revolt, the province's resident legion had kept five of its ten cohorts at this fortress. Today, with the resident legion based up at Jerusalem, there was a hodgepodge of different units of varying quality stationed here, mostly auxiliary light infantry and cavalry ranging from barefoot slingers from Spain's Baleric Isles to Numidian troopers who had learned to ride without either saddle or bridle. The standards of the units of the procurator's garrison stood displayed on a rampart of the highest tower of the citadel. There was room enough in the fortress for official Roman visitors and their entourage, and the members of the Varro expedition found themselves with regular quarters beneath a solid roof for the first time in weeks.

Varro had been to Caesarea before, always on official business. He admired the city's neat layout and its purpose-built public works. Fountains flowed throughout the city, fed by an aqueduct twenty miles long running from Mount Carmel in the north. To the south stood the city's amphitheater, capable of seating twenty thousand, and, close by, a chariot-racing hippodrome with a similar capacity. A graceful drama theater for five thousand, in the same shimmering white stone as the other buildings of Caesarea, had been built into the sea cliffs, with the seats tiered up the slope overlooking a stage almost at beach level. It was the most picturesque theater that Varro had seen anywhere.

"It would have been here at Caesarea that Herod Agrippa's father executed the Nazarene's brother Jacob, my lord," bald little Artimedes the secretary said, standing close to Varro's shoulder on the breakwater and raising his voice to be heard above the pounding waves. "It was also here, not long after, that Herod Agrippa's father was himself struck down. His heart failed him, while he was at the amphitheater. They say he lingered for five days before he died."

Varro nodded. His thoughts were in the fortress. The Procurator of Judea, Publius Terentius Rufus, had not met him when he arrived in the city, and Varro had gone on his sightseeing tour with just his own senior men and without an escort provided by the procurator. Not that the questor had been entirely ignored; Rufus had sent Varro a formal invitation to bring his officers and freedmen to a welcoming banquet at his palace that evening. Varro thought that it should prove to be an interesting occasion, for the Procurator of Judea was the questor's cousin.

✠

Three sets of tables awaited the dinner guests. Varro's party numbered thirteen. Not only had the questor brought his senior officers and freedmen, he had also included Centurion Gallo and Decurion Pompeius. For his part, Procurator Rufus had summoned all the prefects of the military units stationed at the capital and his most senior freedmen. It meant that all twenty-seven places at the dining couches were occupied. Before long the banquet developed into a noisy, boisterous affair.

Varro reclined beside his host, in the honored left-hand position on the central couch of the central table. At twenty-nine, Rufus was five years Varro's junior. In rank too he was subordinate to Varro. Until recently he had been the military tribune and second in command of the 15th Apollinaris Legion, having served with the unit through the last two years of the Jewish Revolt. With his family's inherited auburn hair, a narrow face, a small mouth, and intense, suspicious eyes, Rufus was short and slight.

Rufus' father Gaius was the younger brother of Varro's late father. Since childhood, Rufus had been jealous of his cousin. Rufus' father had never advanced past the rank of Roman knight. That Gaius Terentius Rufus had not entered the Senate of his own volition and instead had gone to live the life of a farmer on his estate at Nola, had not altered his ambitious son's envy of the success of the Varro family. The pair had not seen each other in five years, yet Rufus could only remark on meeting Varro in the dining hall, "You have lost weight, cousin. It does not suit you." From the moment the banquet began, Rufus had addressed himself to the other members of the questor's party, Martius in particular, speaking loudly and imbibing to excess, ignoring his guest of honor.

"Titus told me to level Jerusalem after he left, so, I leveled Jerusalem!" Rufus declared midway through the meal. " 'Leave nothing standing,' said he, so, I left nothing standing. Now the Jews are calling me Turnus." He snorted in his wine. "Turnus! You know why of course, my good lords? They name me Turnus after the king of the Rutilians!" To the surprise of all around him, the procurator then suddenly came to his feet and jumped up onto his dining table, kicking plates and bowls aside so that they crashed onto the tiled floor and contents spilled and splashed onto servants and guests. With a slopping wine cup in his hand, Rufus began to recite from the Aeneid, a century-old work by Vergilius familiar to every Roman schoolboy.

> " 'Cries for fire, and grasps, himself on flame,
> A blazing pine torch. Then to work they fall,
> Spurred on by Turnus' presence, the whole troop
> Arm them with murky brands, the hearths are stripped,
> The reeking torch sends up a pitchy glare,
> And Vulcan wafts the sooty lees to heaven.' "

All heads in the room had turned to watch, all ears to listen. Now, as Rufus took a bow, members of his audience clapped politely. Young Venerius made himself conspicuous by applauding enthusiastically. With his recitation at an end, the procurator fell back onto his place on the couch, spilling wine over a slave, without apology.

As the night progressed, Rufus continued to drink heavily, and a little later he made another outburst. "Not content with humbling me with non citizens for soldiers," he ranted to no one in particular, yet still drawing the attention of everyone at his table, "now, the Palatium informs me, Caesar is sending Liberius Maximus out to replace me. A damned freedman, I will have you know! There is precedent, they say: other freedmen have administered Judea in the past. Precedent be damned! At any other time, in any other place, I would have been more than insulted, but, my lords, let me tell you, there is no one more glad to be free of this damned place and these damned people than Publius Terentius Rufus! Or, should I say, Publius Terentius Rufus *Turnus!*"

Eventually, Rufus' chief freedmen came to him and urged their chief to retire for the night, and after initial argument he gave in to persistent whispers and agreed to leave.

"I am reminded by my people that I have a busy day ahead tomorrow," he slurred to the guests at his table. "So I bid you all a tolerable night, my good and gracious lords." His freedmen helped him up, then supported him when he stood on wavering legs. Around the room, the other diners respectfully came to their feet. Now Rufus squinted at Varro through bleary eyes. "I regret, questor, that the business of government will prevent me from devoting time to you while you are in Caesarea. Can I safely assume that before you take any action in my province you will have the courtesy to consult me?"

"Rest assured, procurator," Varro replied, "you will be consulted as and where appropriate. I will of course require full access to the city archives for my secretaries."

"Yes, yes, yes," Rufus responded with a dismissive wave of the hand.

"And a local guide, an officer with an intimate knowledge of the province."

"An officer? A guide?" Rufus looked mystified, until his chief freedman whispered in his ear. "Ah, yes, a good suggestion, my good man," he acknowledged. "Publius Alienus shall be your guide, cousin." He told his servants to have the officer brought to him, then began to make his staggering way toward the door.

A tall, well-built man in his thirties was summoned from the third dining couch, and as the other diners resumed their places and their reveries he hurried to join the procurator at the door. Rufus put an arm around the man's shoulders, looking up at him like a child to an adult. "You will serve the questor, as a guide, while he is in Judea, Decurion," Rufus instructed, finding difficulty manipulating his tongue.

"Very good, my lord," Alienus acknowledged.

"Yes, but…" Rufus lowered his voice and waved a solitary finger in the air, "you see, I do not know the true purpose of the questor's visit here, good Alienus. Whatever he may say, I suspect that my cousin has come to secretly investigate my service in the province, now that I am recalled to Rome, to find fault in my administration." Rufus glanced back toward the questor. "Varro never did like me," he sneered. He pulled the big man closer, so that his mouth touched his ear. "Listen well now, loyal Alienus. Consider yourself of *duplicarius* status; your pay is doubled, from this day forward."

"Thank you, procurator, most generous of you."

"Generous, yes, but in return I expect to you to be my agent in Varro's camp, decurion. As soon as you learn what he is looking for, or that he has found something which might, shall we say, incriminate me, you must alert me, so that I may take the necessary action in my own defense."

Alienus nodded. "Very good, my lord. You may rely on me."

✠

Next day, Varro and his inner circle met in Herod's Judgment Hall to plan their next course of action. Pythagoras and Artimedes would sift through the city archives in search of pertinent documents. Callidus would distribute the usual notices throughout the city. Martius would ignore Procurator Rufus and his subordinates and have Centurion Gallo and his men scour the city for several key figures. Top of his list were the Nazarene Boethus bar Joazar, the man mentioned by old Laban in Tiberias, and the daughter Boethus supposedly had living here in Caesarea. Another figure of interest was Philippus the Evangelist, a Nazarene Callidus had heard about during his interrogations at Antioch. With their tasks assigned, each man hurried to ensure speedy accomplishment.

In the afternoon, Centurion Gallo reported back to Martius to say that many Jews living in Caesarea had apparently gone into hiding; news of the questor's approach had been enough to raise fear and dread. And no one would admit to even knowing either Boethus, his daughter, or the Evangelist. A little time later, the optio Quintus Silius brought in an elderly couple who had admitted to being Nazarenes. The couple was taken before Varro in Herod's Judgement Hall. Identifying themselves as Enoch and Haggith, they told the questor that they had been converted to the

Nazarene faith by Simon Petra, and that they had known Cornelius, a Roman centurion originally from Sebaste who had retired from the 1ˢᵗ Legion and settled at Caesarea. Enoch said he had heard that the centurion had died in Asia.

"What became of Simon Petra?" Varro asked, his voice echoing around the vast, colonnaded hall.

"I believe that he was executed at Rome, my lord," the flush-faced Enoch said, "together with Paulus, toward the end of the reign of Nero Caesar."

"Did you ever meet Jesus of Nazareth?"

A sad smile came over Enoch's face. "No, my lord. More is the pity."

"Do you believe that Jesus of Nazareth rose from the dead?"

"Oh, yes, my lord."

His wife spoke up excitedly. "Oh, yes indeed, Your Lordship."

"Do you know anyone who saw him after he supposedly rose from the dead?"

"Simon did, my lord," Enoch replied. "He was one of the first to see our Lord after the resurrection."

"Simon Petra told you that?"

"He himself did, my lord."

"Did he say that Jesus displayed any physical signs that he had been crucified?"

"He said that he saw wounds on His hands and feet, where our Lord had been nailed to the cross."

"Nailed? Not tied?"

"Yes, nailed, my lord."

"Do you know a man by the name of Boethus bar Joazar?"

Enoch looked mystified. "No, my lord, I do not know such a man."

The questor went on to ask whether the couple was acquainted with Philippus the Evangelist. Clearly suspicious of Varro's motives, they said they did not know the man. To reassure the couple, Varro stressed that his inquiries had nothing to do with the Jewish Revolt; he was only interested in learning more about Jesus of Nazareth.

Varro's questioning was now interrupted. Pythagoras came hurrying in holding aloft a parchment scroll. "*Eureka!* I have found it, questor!" Pythagoras victoriously declared. "I have found the warrant, for the execution of Jesus of Nazareth." He hurried across the hall to a table where he could unravel the document, and Varro joined him. "The archival records have been meticulously kept, all the way back to the founding of the province in the reign of Augustus Caesar," Pythagoras explained. "All I had to do was go to the criminal records section for the years during the last half of Tiberius' reign in which the execution was most likely to have taken place. A few diligent hours looking for the execution of one particular resident of Nazareth, and here we are!"

Varro and his colleagues crowded around the table as Pythagoras fixed the document in question in a reading frame.

"When is it dated?" Varro asked.

"The day and month correspond with the beginning of the Jewish Festival of Unleavened Bread, or the Passover as it is also called. As for the year, it was…" Pythagoras read aloud, "in the reign of 'Tiberius Julius Caesar Augustus, in the consulship of Aelius Sejanus and Cassius Longinus.' That places the execution forty-one years ago. Now, see here…" He pointed to the name of the convicted man, "'Joshua bar Josephus, native of Jerusalem.' This is our man, questor."

They read the details, which stated that Joshua bar Josephus had been condemned to death by crucifixion for sedition, in that he had borne arms against Rome. The warrant had been authorized by Gaius Pontius Pilatus, Prefect of Judea. A note, in a hand other than that which had written the warrant as a whole, certified that the execution had been carried out and that the body of the prisoner had been handed over to his family for burial. That note was certified, 'Longinus, Centurion.'

"There is more, questor," said Pythagoras. "There are also warrants in the archives for the execution of three other Jews from Galilee that same day, similarly for bearing arms against Rome. Also, dated that same day again, a pardon, for one of these other three, a Joshua bar Abbas. All under the seal of Prefect Pilatus."

Varro was thrilled. "Well done, Pythagoras. Find me more written evidence of this quality. At last, we are making progress."

As Pythagoras hastened back to the archives to rejoin Artimedes in the search for further relevant documents, a messenger arrived from Centurion Gallo. It transpired that late in the day, information from a slave had led Gallo and a party of his legionaries to a large residence in a block of houses and tenement buildings in the Jewish quarter of the city. This, according to the informant, was the house of Philippus the Evangelist. Gallo sent word to the questor that the door was barred, and that no one inside the house would respond to his calls to open up. Varro and his colleagues hurried from the fortress to the Jewish quarter, bringing the remainder of Gallo's soldiers and Crispus' cavalry.

"I sealed off front and rear of the house with the men I had," the centurion reported as his superior arrived, "but occupants may have escaped across the rooftops."

Most of these homes stood empty, after a number of Jewish residents had either gone to Jerusalem for the last fatal Passover Festival or joined the partisans in the uprising, and the buildings showed signs of a lack of attention over the past five years, with dusty walls, flaking paint and encroaching weeds. But the house identified as belonging to Philippus the Evangelist seemed to have been tended with care.

Varro sent Gallo's men against the barred front doors with a timber battering ram ten feet long brought from the fortress. After the ram shattered the wooden doors, soldiers poured in through the opening with swords drawn. The two-story house was searched from top to bottom, but not a single occupant was found. Yet, in master's quarters and servants quarters alike the furniture was in place, and food, clothing and personal possessions had been left as if the residents had only stepped out briefly, and hurriedly. To question everyone passing in and out of Caesarea for news of Philippus, Varro now sent some of his troops to join the guards at the city's gates. Leaving Gallo and some of his men searching the dwelling thoroughly for evidence, Varro returned to the white fortress. Several hours later, with darkness descending on the city, the questor was preparing for dinner when a message arrived from Gallo: he had found a horde of documents in the Evangelist's house. Varro and his colleagues hurriedly rejoined him.

In a small undecorated room at the back of the house the centurion had noticed a loose stone in a door lintel. Removing it, he had discovered a hollow space, and in the space he located a long, thin leather bag filled with documents. When the questor and his party returned, they found that Gallo had brought in most of the lamps in the house to light the room and had laid the newfound documents on a high, narrow table. The questor instructed his senior secretary to inspect the find.

"Copies of letters, some written in Greek, some in Hebrew," Pythagoras pronounced after an initial perusal.

Varro summoned Antiochus, and, while he read the Hebrew letters, Pythagoras concentrated on those in Greek. The room was too small to comfortably accommodate more than a few people at a time, so Varro had it cleared of all personnel other than Pythagoras and Antiochus. He himself took a seat on a wooden bench outside the door, and waited for the analysis. As the questor sat there, gazing absently into the room, his mind wandered, to the first time he had laid eyes on Miriam, at Queen Berenice's palace. All of a sudden, something curious caught Varro's eye and brought his mind back to the here and now. Some of the oil lamps in the little room stood on the reading table, some on wall ledges, some on the floor. Several lamps on the tiles at the back of the room fluttered occasionally, doing a wavering dance that bent their orange flame and sent a slender tail of black smoke snaking toward the ceiling, before resuming their normal upright glow. Yet, the flames of the other lamps hardly deviated from the vertical.

A man with an eye for detail, the questor rose and took one lamp from a ledge and placed it in the open doorway, then resumed his seat. The lamp in the doorway did not flutter, suggesting that no significant draught was entering the room via the door. Varro sent for Martius, and when the tribune joined him he pointed out the phenomenon of the fluttering lamps. "What do you think? Varro asked his deputy. "Is it my imagination?"

"I think that something is definitely not as it should be," Martius concluded.

So, Varro instructed Pythagoras and Antiochus to step out of the room, and told Centurion Gall to investigate the cause of the fluttering lamps while Varro and Martius stood in the doorway and watched him at work. Behind them crowded soldiers and other members of the questor's entourage, craning their necks for a view of proceedings. Gallo, on his hands and bare knees and with his head touching the marble-tiled floor, peered at the bottom of the wall at the back of the room. Feeling a draught hitting his eyes, he ran a finger along the base of the wall, between wall and floor. At one point, the tip of his finger slipped into a narrow crevice. "There is a narrow gap here, my lord," he called. "A gap the width of a small doorway." Then he stood, and ran his hand over the stuccoed wall, which was painted a flat, bland green. Putting his nose to the wall, he sniffed it. "The paint is fresh, my lord, and so too, I would wager, is the stucco beneath it. This section of the wall has recently been rendered and painted." He rapped the wall. "Hollow," he proclaimed. "There is a cavity behind this wall, questor."

"Bring down the wall, centurion," Varro instructed.

Soon, Gallo and alternating teams of bare-headed legionaries were attacking the wall with entrenching tools and iron bars. The men, and the room, were soon covered with dust. The lime, gypsum and fine sand of the stucco coated their hair, penetrated their eyes, and forced them to regularly spit to keep lips and mouths lubricated. But before long a rectangular block of stone tumbled out of the wall. Calling a halt to demolition work, Gallo instructed one of his men to take a look in through the gap. Nervously, the young soldier, on one knee and with a lamp in hand, pushed his head and the lamp in through the cavity in the wall. Perspiration stood out on the legionary's brow at the vulnerability of his position, and his muscles tensed as he prepared to recoil in an instant if some weapon or missile were to come his way.

"A man!" the soldier suddenly cried. "There are steps, centurion, and at the bottom, I see a man. No, two! Perhaps more." He quickly withdrew back into the room.

"Are they armed?" Gallo queried.

"Not that I could see."

Gallo had his men resume work on the wall. Before long, a gap large enough for a man to pass through was created. In the light of lamps held at the opening, it could be seen that on the far side, at the bottom of a set of narrow stone steps, three pale and frightened men, apparently servants, cringed around an elderly figure with a white beard. The aromas of foul air, urine and feces escaped from this uninviting hole in the ground. It was if Gallo's men had tapped into the city's sewer.

As Varro came to the opening, his men stood aside. "Are you Philippus, the one they call the Evangelist?" he called down.

"I am he," came the weary reply from the bearded man. "I am Philippus. I will come out, but please, I beg of you, do not punish my servants. They share my house but not any guilt which you may attach to me for hiding from you."

"I guarantee that none of you will be harmed in any way. I merely seek information. You have the word of Julius Terentius Varro."

The old man struggled up the steps, followed by his servants. The centurion helped him into the room.

"Bring a bench for Philippus," Varro commanded, and soldiers carried in the bench which he himself had used.

"Thank you," said the old man as he gratefully sagged onto the seat, ashen-faced and exhausted. His servants emerged from the hole and knelt on the floor around him, looking up at him with a mixture of reverence and concern.

"How long have you been in there?" Varro asked, standing looking down at Philippus as his colleagues crowded the doorway behind to watch and listen.

"Several days," Philippus replied.

"You had yourself sealed in there?" said Varro in a reproving tone.

"It is an old passageway," Philippus revealed, "built during the time of Herod. It emerges beyond my neighbor's house, and a little fresh air enters from outside; enough for survival. I was trying to protect my people. I do not fear for my own life. I have four daughters, and all have the gift of prophesy. Each and every one predicted the destruction of Jerusalem, but none foresee my death for many a year yet. One of my daughters lives at the city of Tralles, in the province of Asia. Do you know it?"

"I know of it."

"My daughter at Tralles has predicted that I will die in her arms, so perhaps I will go to Tralles one day." He smiled, as if sharing a joke. "One day, but not yet a while."

"That being the case," said Martius, lounging in the doorway at the forefront of the onlookers, "it would pay you never to go to Tralles."

"I am told that you knew Jesus of Nazareth," Varro resumed.

Philippus' smile lingered. "I knew Him. I know Him still."

"He is still alive?" said Varro with surprise.

"He lives in me, and in many like me."

Varro frowned. "Is he dead, or is he not?"

"He no longer walks this earth, if that is what you mean."

"How was it that you came to know him?"

"I was one of His seventy original disciples."

Varro felt a thrill of elation. He was drawing closer to his quarry. "You are one of his followers still?"

"I remain His humble servant."

"Did you witness his execution?"

"I was here, at Caesarea, at the time of the crucifixion. I regret to say that an illness prevented me from going up to Jerusalem for the Passover that year."

"You believe that he was the Messiah, that he rose from the dead?"

Philippus smiled again. "Whether I believed it or not, it would still be true."

"You were intimately acquainted with him during his lifetime?"

"During the last years of His time here with us, yes."

Varro was thoughtful for a moment. "You will be tired, and hungry," he then said.

"That is true," Philippus replied. "But that is a small trial, in a life full of trials."

"You will go now to the fortress. Not as a prisoner, but as my guest. You will eat, and sleep. Tomorrow, refreshed, you will testify to all you know about the Nazarene."

"What of my people?" Philippus asked, casting a hand around his disheveled servants. "I care nothing for myself, but they are innocents."

"Answer me truthfully tomorrow, and they shall go free."

Philippus looked at Varro a moment. "You appear an honest man. If I know that you are bound by your pledge of honor, then I shall testify willingly, and truthfully."

"You have it. In front of these witnesses, you have my word that your servants shall go free if you testify truthfully."

"Be certain of this one thing," Philippus added. "I will answer with an open heart, but I will incriminate no man."

"I seek the truth, Philippus. Nothing more, nothing less. Until the morrow, then."

Leaving the room, Varro called Centurion Gallo and instructed him to take the Evangelist to the fortress where he was to clean him up, feed him, and to allow him to obtain a restful night's sleep in preparation for further questioning next day. "Bring Philippus before me in the Judgment Hall tomorrow morning at the third hour," Varro ordered. "Keep his slaves apart from him, and chain him to one of your men at all times. There must be no opportunity for him to abscond or to harm himself. And, you may release Enoch and his wife. Let it be known that no harm comes to my informants."

Gallo hurried to obey.

Martius had been listening to all this, and now, with an unhappy look on his face, he watched the Evangelist and his servants being placed in manacles and led from the house. Unable to hold his tongue any longer, he confronted Varro and voiced a nagging concern. "I think that you are being too lenient with these Nazarenes, Julius," he said, within earshot of several of their companions.

Varro scowled. "Oh? How so?"

"If it were me, I would be torturing information out of these people!"

"I will have more success by winning their trust."

Martius shook his head. "They will never trust us, so long as we rule here. And we will never trust them!"

"Keep your thoughts to yourself, tribune," Varro coolly returned, pushing by him.

Martius, smarting at the questor's rebuke, watched him go.

Antiochus now appeared at Varro's shoulder, walking beside him. "The tribune is right," he growled. "These people have no rights. You must put Philippus and the other Nazarenes to the torture and force all they know from them."

Varro stopped in his tracks and swung on the Jewish magistrate. "Mind your business, Antiochus!" he snapped. "My methods of investigation are not yours!"

Antiochus' eyes flared. "You are in sympathy with the Nazarenes! I suspected it all along. I will write to General Collega and denounce you as a Nazarene sympathizer. I will tell him that you are prejudicing his mission. Do you hear me, Julius Varro?"

The questor now displayed uncharacteristic anger. "You will confine yourself to reading the Hebrew documents found in this house! You will then report to me in the Judgment Hall tomorrow at the commencement of the second hour with a full analysis of their contents. If that analysis is not to my liking, I will send you back to General Collega with the report that you did not satisfactorily perform the duties of translator, the duties which Collega sent you on this expedition to fulfil. Do *you* hear *me*, Antiochus?"

A sudden look of fear washed over Antiochus' face. Instinctively, his right hand went to the leather pouch hanging at his throat.

The questor was storming away. "Pedius, where in the name of the gods is my conveyance?" he called with obvious aggravation.

✠

Martius stood, observing his seated armor bearer Placidus sharpening the tribune's sword on a whet stone. It had been a long time since Martius had drawn his sword in anger. Daily, he used it in exercises with Placidus, having trained the slave to be proficient with sword and shield. As he watched the man work, Martius sensed that someone stood in the doorway. He looked up, to see Artimedes the secretary.

"I hope Your Lordship will excuse my intrusion?" said the little Greek.

After the events of the latter part of the day, with his brief but unpleasant confrontation with Julius Varro, the tribune was not in a congenial mood. "What do you want, secretary?" He returned his attention to the sharpening of the twin-bladed sword.

"The tribune will be aware that I have been in the service of the questor's family for many years," Artimedes began, entering the room. "Before I was employed as Julius Varro's secretary I was under secretary to his mother, Julia, and when he was a youth I fulfilled the duties of his tutor. An able and willing student he made, too."

"What of it?"

"In knowing of my lengthy connection to the questor's family, you will appreciate that my thoughts very naturally flow in the direction of his welfare. In fact, I will confide to you that I regularly write to his mother at Rome and Capua to reassure her as to the state of her son's health and appraising her of his achievements in his post here. The questor is unaware of this, so I would appreciate that knowledge remaining *sub rosa*."

"Come to the point, secretary," Martius impatiently returned. "In all my days I have never known a long-winded dissembler to compare with you."

Artimedes seemed unaffected by the insult. "In being aware that my loyalties lie very firmly with the questor, Your Lordship must not misconstrue what I am about to say, for clearly it is as much in your interests as it is in my lord Varro's interests...."

"In the name of Jove, spit it out!" Martius exploded. "What have you to say?"

"Tribune, you should not have disputed with the questor today, in front of others who are subordinate to the questor and to yourself. This was clearly an error of judgment, if I may say."

Martius' eyes narrowed. "Is that so?"

"You demean my lord Varro's authority by public acts of dissension.

The questor values your opinion, but when it is expressed in private, not in public."

"Have you finished your lecture, tutor?" Martius snarled.

"We have many days and weeks ahead of us still on this expedition, and the questor must be able to depend on your discretion as much as on your loyalty. Meditate on that." With that, the little Greek turned on his heel, and was gone.

"Thank you for nothing, secretary," Martius angrily called after him. "When I need your advice, I will ask for it!"

"Meditate on it, tribune," came Artimedes' voice, echoing down the stone-walled corridor. "Believe me, you are as wise as you are earnest, Marcus Martius."

✠

Out to the west, where the Mediterranean met the horizon, an electrical storm was silently invading the night with flashes of light which illuminated the clouds with sudden and brief intensity. Watching the display, Varro stood alone on a terrace of one of the white Herodian palaces which he was using as his quarters in Caesarea. Less than half a mile away, below, and to his right, beyond the port, the city's theater was packed with an audience from Caesarea and the surrounding district. A troupe of Greek actors all the way from Epirus had come to the city as a part of a tour of the Eastern provinces. Many among the packed audience sitting on cushions on the tiers of stone ranging down to the beach had lost interest in the tragedy being acted out on stage and had lifted their eyes from the stage and out across the sea to the drama of the lightning show. Varro could hear 'Ooo's' and 'Aaah's' of wonder and delight rising up from their entranced ranks.

The questor had dined alone, quite deliberately. He was not happy with himself for losing his temper in front of his subordinates earlier in the evening. He could excuse Antiochus for his ignorance and Martius for his unbridled enthusiasm, but as expedition leader he had aimed to stay above the pettiness and pointlessness of argument. Suddenly, he was a aware that he was not alone on the terrace. Turning, he saw a figure slowly walking toward him from the door which led to the palace apartments.

"Do you mind if I join you, Julius?" It was Marcus Martius.

"If you wish," Varro replied, without enthusiasm. He leaned on the terrace's balustrade and looked out to sea, turning his back on the tribune.

Martius came and leaned on the balustrade beside him. "Do you think the gods are angry?" he asked, watching the flashing show of light on the horizon.

Varro shrugged. "Perhaps Jove is putting on a performance to show off his power to the theatrical producers of Caesarea," he suggested.

Martius nodded. For a time they watched the lightning together without speaking, before Martius said, "You knew the fate of the general Strabo, father of Pompeius the Great, a native of Picenum like myself? He was struck down and killed stone dead by lightning on the Campus Martius, when Pompeius was still only a young man."

Varro nodded absently. "So I remember reading."

"Strabo must have offended the gods very severely, you would have thought," Martius remarked, "to deserve an end like that."

"Perhaps the famously arrogant General Strabo felt certain that he would not be struck down by lightning," Varro countered, "and in his arrogance tempted the Fates by going about a military camp outside Rome in full armor during a thunder storm."

"Perhaps so, perhaps so," Martius chuckled. Again he lapsed into silence for a time, watching the lightning and listening to the reaction of the distant theater crowd. "I wanted to apologize to you, Julius," he began anew. "It was wrong of me to disagree with you there at the Evangelist's house, in front of others."

"It was indeed," Varro agreed, without looking at him. "Express your views to me privately by all means, Marcus, but do not demean my authority in public."

"It won't happen again, you have my pledge. I do not make the same error twice."

"I am glad to hear it."

"You know that I am in earnest?"

Varro turned, smiling. "I know of no one more earnest."

Now Martius also broke into a smile. "My earnestness usually serves me well, but it will have to be bridled, I think, if I am to achieve my ambitions and emulate Rome's most famous generals."

"You will make Rome proud one day. In the meantime, Marcus, I need all your support on this mission. There are some in our party whose only interests are their own."

"I know who they are. You do not have to name them."

"So, you and I must work together. You cannot publicly question my judgment."

"You will never have cause to doubt my loyalty or support."

"Thank you, my friend." Varro patted the tribune on the shoulder. "We will not speak of this again, Marcus. Tomorrow, we start afresh."

"Agreed. And I do believe our luck has turned, Julius. First Pythagoras unearths the documents in the archives, and then we dig old Philippus from his burrow. I will be interested to hear what the Evangelist has to say tomorrow."

Varro nodded thoughtfully. "You and I both, my friend."

XII

THE TESTIMONY OF PHILIPPUS

Caesarea, Capital of the Roman Province of Judea. April, A.D. 71

Two large wooden tables stood below the judgment platform. At one table, the knights' table, sat Martius, Crispus and Venerius. Four officials sat at the other. Firstly, with stylus poised, Pythagoras, wax tablets set up and ready in a writing frame in front of him. Beside him, Artimedes, acting as custodian of numerous documents piled in front of him, and then, Callidus. Antiochus, smarting at being put with the freedmen, sat at the end. Between the two tables, directly below the judgment bench, stood Pedius, with the end of his lictor's staff of office resting on the marble floor. Questor Varro took his place on Herod the Great's judgment seat, and his servant Hostilis seated himself on the floor behind. It gave Varro a modest thrill to occupy the seat first used by the famous king of the Jews and great friend to Marcus Antonius, Julius Caesar, and Caesar Augustus, a man, who, Varro had been told on a previous visit to Judea, was acquainted with power from an early age; Herod's father Antipater had made the boy governor of Galilee at the tender age of fifteen. From the judgment seat, the questor could look down on his subordinates at the tables below, and on the witness bench facing him.

At the outset Varro noted with satisfaction that Crispus had also brought along a writing tablet. It appeared that his Prefect of Horse would make notes of his own during the witness' testimony, but as the questioning progressed Varro would note that Crispus' writing did not keep pace with the questions and answers. Then Crispus would not write for some time and seemingly gaze off into oblivion, before again writing with sudden energy. Or, he would erase entire lines with the blunt end of his stylus. It eventually dawned on the questor that Crispus was writing poetry. Varro would forgive him. As long as Varro himself remained focused on his task, he told himself, and while Pythagoras made his meticulous notes, that would be all that mattered.

Once Varro had taken his seat at the second hour, Pythagoras and Antiochus reported their findings concerning the documents discovered in the house of Philippus. There were three key sources to the letters, they said. One was Philippus himself; most of the letters in both Hebrew and Greek had been addressed by him to followers of the Nazarene in Judea and surrounding areas. All related to religious instruction and did not contain any new information of value to the questor's investigation. Two other letters, copied identically several times in both Greek and Hebrew, had originated with different authors, with each being similar in many respects to the Lucius Letter, giving accounts of the life of Jesus of Nazareth. These two anonymous letters also contained material which was additional to that found in the Lucius Letter, while some of the content also conflicted with Lucius Letter material; in the most obvious discrepancy, one showed Jesus' grandfather as a Jacob rather than a Heli. In some aspects too, these documents conflicted with each other. Varro had the two testaments put to one side for further study.

At the third hour, Philippus was brought in by Centurion Gallo. The Evangelist looked less haggard than he had the previous evening. He wore a new tunic, there was color in his cheeks and life in his eyes. He was guided to the witness bench, then, once the manacles on his wrists had been knocked off, Gallo and his men withdrew.

"Good morning to you, Philippus," said Varro, smiling down from the judge's platform. "You slept well, I trust?"

"I bid you a good morning, my lord. I spent a restful night, thank you." Philippus cast his gaze around the vast, near empty chamber. "Do you know, the last time that I was in this place, it was thirteen years ago."

"Under what circumstances?" Varro asked.

"I stood in a crowd at the back of the hall and listened while Procurator Florus and King Agrippa questioned one of my brothers in Christos, Paulus, in response to charges laid by the Great Sanhedrin of Jerusalem."

"Paulus of Tarsus?" Varro queried, recognizing the name of a leading Nazarene.

"The same, my lord. Florus and Agrippa both found that Paulus had committed no crime. You see, there can be no crime in speaking the truth."

"I could not agree more. Are you are ready to speak the truth in answer to my questions here today?"

"That I am, my lord."

"Very well. I will begin by asking you about documents found at your house."

Before Varro could become specific, Philippus volunteered a description of the documents in question. They were, he said, for the most part copies of letters written by him, or which were written on his behalf, to members of his Nazarene 'flock.' Varro had the two letters apparently not written by Philippus shown to him. Philippus partly unraveled both and studied them briefly, then told the questor that the oldest of the two epistles had been written by Marcus, a scribe at Jerusalem, at the outbreak of the Revolt, in the months prior to the coming of Cestius Gallus and his Roman army.

When Varro asked who this Marcus was, Philippus answered, "One of the seventy original disciples of our Lord, as I was. We of the seventy were a council of elders." He went on to say that Marcus had noted down the parables and lessons that Jesus imparted to the people, so that they might be copied and distributed. These parables and lessons were indeed distributed and declaimed by the disciples for a number of years, but, with the outbreak of the Revolt, Marcus felt sure that a prophesy by Jesus that the Temple would be destroyed must soon be fulfilled, as indeed it was. Marcus had decided to remain at Jerusalem come what may, but he felt that someone should record the story of Jesus' life, suffering, death, before all who had been witnesses to these things perished. "This epistle is that testament of Marcus. It came into my possession five years ago."

"Is Marcus still alive?"

"I expect that he perished at Jerusalem, like so many others."

"Who authored the second letter?"

"This was written by Matthias, one of our Lord's twelve apostles."

"Explain the purpose of these apostles," said Varro.

"Our Lord chose twelve from among us to be His chief messengers to the people, and sent them far and wide. We call these twelve, and others that followed, Message-Bearers, or, in Greek, *apostolos*. Matthias was one such apostle. He felt that as one of the chosen twelve he would have a broader perspective than Marcus, so he wrote his own account of the life, suffering, death, and resurrection of our Lord, soon after that of Marcus. To the best of my knowledge, Matthias is also now deceased. I made no distinction between the two testaments; I have distributed copies of both to our brethren."

Varro then asked if Philippus was familiar with a Nazarene by the name of Lucius, a physician. Philippus said he knew Lucius, but his tone did not contain the warmth that was apparent when he had spoken of Marcus and Matthias. Lucius was a native of Antioch, he said, a friend, secretary and co-worker to Paulus of Tarsus. In years past, Lucius several times stayed in Philippus' house at Caesarea, with Paulus, and alone. Philippus said he had never seen a copy of the Lucius Letter; he was unaware that Lucius had even written his own account of the life and death of Jesus.

"Where would Lucius be now?"

"I had heard that, after Paulus' death at Rome, Lucius went to Greece, but more than that I could not tell you."

Varro moved on from the documents, and learned from Philippus that as a young man had been attracted to the teachings of Johannes the Baptist, and had then followed his successor, Jesus. He had seen and heard Jesus preach many times, he said. "I have seen Him perform wondrous miracles, including the raising from the dead of Jesus' relative Eleazar of Bethany."

Young Venerius the junior tribune let out a ridiculing snort. "Miracle cures are easy enough to fabricate," he remarked. "If one pays enough."

Varro deliberately and loudly cleared his throat, as a way of cautioning Venerius against making any adverse comment which might stem the flow of information from the witness. "Proceed, if you please, Philippus," he urged.

"I have broken bread with Him, I have spoken with Him on many occasions." But, in answer to Varro's specific question on the subject, he did not claim to have seen Jesus following his execution, but said he knew of others who had, although he declined to name them. He said these people were all now deceased or in far away lands, spread throughout the provinces of Rome, and in Parthia.

"Conveniently," Venerius muttered.

"I would not be surprised if I am among the last of the original seventy," Philippus remarked.

Antiochus looked up to Varro. "May I ask a question of the witness, questor? On the subject of this council of seventy Nazarene elders?"

Varro nodded. "Very well."

Using an attacking tone, Antiochus hurled his question at Philippus like a spear. "Why did the Nazarene choose to surround himself with a council of seventy, and, from these, select a group of twelve innermost associates?" Before the Evangelist could reply, Antiochus went on. "Was the latter to represent the twelve original tribes of Israel? Were there seventy of you, and the Nazarene besides, because there were seventy priests and a high priest on the Great Sanhedrin of Jerusalem? Was this intended to be the Nazarene's alternative Great Sanhedrin when he overthrew the Jewish authorities in the revolution against Rome that he was plotting? Further, if the Nazarene's intent had been to gain control of the Temple, as seems clear to me, how can you excuse the fact that your sect has since his death encouraged Jews to eat with the uncircumcised and introduced non-Jews into its ranks without requiring them to conform fully to Jewish Law?"

Philippus sighed, and looked up at Varro, as if seeking relief from the barrage.

"You may answer," the questor told him.

"Very well. Our Lord rarely revealed why He did anything. It was written that the Messiah must do certain things, and this is what He did. I have always believed that everything our Lord did was governed by divine will, and I have never questioned anything He said or did. As for the gentile members of our congregations, our Lord told us to take His message to all peoples in all lands, and this is what we have done."

Antiochus had not finished. "I have heard it said that at one time, in answer to a question from a Pharisee, the Nazarene held up a Roman coin and asked his audience whose head was on the coin, and the people said that it was Caesar's head. The Nazarene then said that the people should pay their taxes to Caesar but should give the God of the Jews their undivided loyalty. Have you heard this story?'

"I have heard something like it, yes."

"Did you witness this event?"

"No, I did not."

"Do you believe that this genuinely took place?"

"I have no reason to disbelieve it."

"How could it have taken place? Look at this." Antiochus held up a silver coin. "In my hand I hold a sesterce piece, of the kind that circulated at Jerusalem prior to the Revolt, acquired by me here in the markets of

Caesarea. It bears no graven image, no portrait of Caesar. All Roman coins circulating in Judea were similarly devoid of images, as Rome generously strove to appease the ungrateful Jews of the province and mollify their stupid dread of graven images. How could the Nazarene have held up a coin bearing the image of Caesar, when no such coin existed in Judea?" A smug smile had come over Antiochus' face. "Is this story of the coin not a fabrication, like the other stories surrounding this man, including the story of his rising from the dead?"

Philippus seemed mildly amused. "The prohibition of coinage bearing the image of Caesar in Judea was introduced by Rome during the reign of Claudius Caesar," he answered. "Our Lord lived during the reigns of Caesar Augustus and Tiberius Caesar, when coins bearing images of the Caesars freely circulated."

Antiochus flushed red in the face, and said no more. He did not have sufficient knowledge about the coinage of Judea during the reigns of Augustus and Tiberius to contest the Evangelist's assertion. The Evangelist had lived in Judea at the time, and Antiochus had not.

"We shall move on," said the questor. "Philippus, from whom did you first learn that Jesus had apparently risen from the dead?"

Philippus answered that he had heard of the resurrection from Simon called Petra, from his fellow disciple Cleophas, and from others who had seen Jesus alive following his execution. He claimed that eleven of the twelve apostles and several of the other disciples later saw and touched Jesus, and they had all been convinced, he said, that Jesus was flesh and blood, not merely a vision or a ghost. When asked if he had expected Jesus to rise from the dead, he replied that he had not been aware of Jesus' intention to submit to crucifixion so he had not expected either his death or his resurrection. Yet, he had believed Jesus to be the promised Messiah. "It would not have taken His resurrection for me to have believed it. From the scriptures, from his miracles, and knowing Him as I did, I knew that He had been sent by Heaven to be our savior."

"You believed him to be a descendant of King Davidus of the Jews," said the questor, "through the line of his father Josephus?"

"Through the line of His earthly father, yes."

Varro's eyes narrowed. "His *earthly* father?"

"He had a Heavenly Father, and an earthly father. He was the Son of God."

Varro paused. So much of the theology of the Nazarenes begged exploration, clarification, and perhaps even demolition, but that was not his mission. He quickly determined to maintain his focus on Jesus' execution, but in doing so he had to firmly establish the motives for the man's claimed return to life following that execution. "Jesus told you and the other disciples that he had been sent to be the next king of the Jews?"

"We knew it as a universal truth."

Varro leaned forward, and elevated his voice a little. "How did you *know* it? You did not all dream it? Someone must have told you as much."

"I first heard it from Andreius, the brother of Simon called Petra, and Philippus, who were apostles of Johannes the Baptist. The Baptist recognized Him as the Messiah."

"Andreius and Philippus told you that Jesus was to be your king, and that the Baptist confirmed this? Yet, no king can be crowned without the consent of Rome? How, apart from consent, or revolt, could any man be crowned king of the Jews of Judea?"

"No earthly power could make or unmake His kingship. Heaven crowned Him."

"I see. We have heard that Jesus willingly submitted to crucifixion, to prove that he was this predicted king. How could he rule the Jews if he were dead, crucified?"

"He is not dead, and He does rule, from Heaven."

Varro could see another diversion into theology looming, and determined to stay on his temporal course. "You say you were called to Jerusalem after the crucifixion. When was that, and why was that?"

Philippus said that Jesus stayed among the people for forty days, and then, after He had ascended into Heaven, the apostles Simon called Petra and Johannes bar Zebedee became the leaders of the seventy. They enlarged the body of disciples, the council of elders, to one hundred and twenty, from a following which numbered some five thousand. They selected the disciples Josephus bar Sabas, a Temple priest, and Matthias of Galilee, as men who had accompanied Jesus since his baptism by Johannes, and as men who had seen Him after the resurrection. These two drew lots to see who would replace Judas the betraying apostle as one of the twelve, and Matthias was chosen in this manner. The apostles made decrees that were committed to writing, concerning the dissemination of Jesus' teachings and the observance of Jewish Law. Philippus said that it came to pass that some among the faithful complained that they were being daily neglected by the apostles, so the apostles called all the disciples together and appointed seven deacons, to serve at table, to aid the widows, to act as shepherds to the flock and to minister to the faithful while the apostles devoted themselves to spreading the message, and Philippus had been appointed one of those deacons.

He had remained at Jerusalem, until Stephanus, a fellow deacon, was arrested by the Great Sanhedrin, convicted of blasphemy, and stoned to death. With much persecution of the Nazarene's followers by the Sanhedrin, the disciples had scattered throughout Judea and Samaria. Philippus had come into Samaria, where, among the many he baptized in the name of Jesus was a magician called Simon. He returned to Jerusalem for a time, and baptized the chamberlain of Queen Candace of Ethiopia, then continued his mission in the south, from Azotus. Simon Petra and Johannes bar Zebedee had then directed him to return to Caesarea, where he had remained ever since.

Martius now spoke up. "Permission to question the witness, questor?"

Varro granted his deputy permission, and Martius came to his feet. As he posed his questions, he prowled back and forth in front of the tables like a caged lion, sometimes looking at the witness, sometimes addressing his questions to the rafters.

"Philippus, do you believe that Jesus was a god?" the tribune began.

"He was and is the Son of God."

"You people believe in just a single god? A commendably economical concept. Answer me this: if your man Jesus was the son of your God, as Apollo is the sun of Jove, then as Apollo is both a god and the son of a god, so then Jesus is a god and the son of a god, and you have two gods, not one." He smirked. "Am I not correct?"

"No," said Philippus calmly. "The Son and the Father are one."

Martius screwed up his face. "How can that be? That is a nonsense, old man!"

"It is the truth. The two are indivisible. There is but one God."

"Arrant nonsense!" Martius countered with rising frustration. "Two gods in one? To any educated, thinking man, such a concept makes no sense at all. I am my father's son, old man, but I am not my father." He glared at the Nazarene with arms folded.

Varro now intervened. "If we were to enter into a debate about differing philosophies, I fear that we would make no headway at all. I have yet to find two philosophers who can agree on little more than what day it is, and even then they will find a reason for dispute. We should concentrate on the central matter, and confine our questions to the circumstances surrounding the death of the Nazarene."

Martius let out a long, exasperated hiss of air between his teeth. "Very well, questor," he then said. "May I continue to address questions to the witness?"

"If the questions are relevant."

Martius turned his now cold gaze on Philippus. "If your man Jesus was a god, or half of a god, or part of a god, how is it that he allowed himself to be executed by mere mortals? Why not just fly away, or strike down those who would harm him?"

"He was a man of peace, so He would never strike anyone down. Secondly, it was written, long ago, that the Messiah would be crucified, and would then rise on the third day. So the ancient prophets had decreed, and so it had to be."

"Let me be absolutely clear about this. Jesus wanted to conform to these prophesies, to be able to claim to be this Messiah of yours? Is that correct?"

"By conforming to the prophesies, He proved that He was the Messiah, yes."

"Now, according to the Lucius Letter," Martius continued, "the Nazarene was charged with blasphemy by the Jewish authorities. However, the Prefect of Judea, Pilatus, found him guilty of a crime under prevailing Roman law, that of sedition, because he was found in possession of weapons when arrested by the Jewish authorities. Do you deny that your man of peace was armed when arrested? This is and was a clear and blatant breach of Roman law in any part of the Empire, as you well know, and a capital offense."

"Two swords were recovered when our Lord was taken into custody by the Temple Guard, that is true," Philippus replied, unruffled.

Martius swung on the Evangelist, glaring at him. "So, your man Jesus was no more than an armed insurrectionist! This 'priest' was a bandit and a rebel, just like the two other men we know to have been executed alongside him."

"No, for the prophesies to be met, it was necessary to be convicted of bearing arms, not of blasphemy, to ensure execution by crucifixion, not by stoning."

"This sounds to me like a very ungodly way of manipulating events." Martius resumed his pacing. "Surely, if you are a god, you can will things to occur?"

"His God-given powers would come later, after He had risen. This was His trial."

"Surely, he must have used divine powers to perform the so-called miracles?"

"Those were the only divine powers granted to Him, and to His apostles."

Martius raised his eyebrows. "His apostles had divine powers as well? Soon you will be telling me that you too are a god, Philippus!"

Philippus smiled. "Heaven has indeed seen fit to empower me to perform powerful works of healing in His name."

Martius shook his head. "I refuse to be drawn into your world of sham and magic, old man. Jesus had divine power to perform miracles, yet had no power to save himself?"

"That is how our Father in Heaven ordained it should be."

Martius chuckled. "You give Heaven as your answer for everything that is inexplicable, old man. You are a true philosopher."

Philippus shrugged. "This is the truth as I know it."

"Your version of the truth is suitable only for the theater!"

"Tribune," Varro interceded, "the arrest, the trial and the execution should be the focus of our questioning, I think. Let us not stray too far from the path."

"Agreed, questor," Martius responded with a sigh. "Old man, help me clarify one thing if you will. Jesus and several of his apostles took two swords with them on the night he was arrested, to ensure that he was convicted of carrying weapons. Is that what you are saying? Did the apostles know that Jesus had deliberately set out to be arrested?"

"He had reminded them of the prophesies. Some of the apostles, such as Simon called Petra, definitely knew what was planned, prior to the event; he told me so later."

"And the betrayal was also planned?" Martius continued. "According to the Lucius Letter, one of the apostles, a fellow named Judas, betrayed Jesus to the Jewish authorities, *with the Nazarene's full prior knowledge.* Jesus took himself to a suitably remote spot, in possession of weapons, and accompanied by only a few close associates, and waited to be arrested. The arrest took place outside the city, at night, when he was not surrounded by the usual mob of followers who could have put up resistance. Would you not agree that Jesus seems to have carefully planned his own arrest?"

"I would agree that our Lord made his arrest possible, and was expecting it to take place. I do not agree that he prearranged the arrest with Judas. Judas betrayed Him."

"What became of Judas?" Varro asked from the bench.

"As far as I know, my lord, he took his own life shortly after his act of betrayal. I have been told that, overcome with remorse, Judas returned his betrayer's wages to the priests of the Sanhedrin, and they used the money to buy a potter's field outside the city, as a place for the graves of strangers. Some say Judas died in that field, others that he hanged himself from a tree. I cannot testify to his fate. He was never heard of again."

"What do you believe happened to him?" Varro asked.

"I only know that he was not heard of again, and that is nothing I regret. Only the Lord God knows the truth. He is all-knowing."

"Oh?" Martius raised his eyebrows. "Is he indeed? Did your all-knowing man of peace know that one of his associates would strike and wound a member of the arresting party by cutting off his ear? According to the Lucius Letter, one of those with Jesus used his sword against a servant of the Jewish High Priest in that manner. Do you dispute it?"

"This is true. It was Simon called Petra who wounded Malchus the servant of the High Priest with the sword, but our Lord healed the man's wound on the spot."

"A miracle, was it? The man's ear grew back? Or Jesus picked it up and magically affixed it to the side of his head once more? Why did this 'miracle' fail to convince the other members of the arresting party that Jesus was indeed a miracle worker and a god? Surely, in that event, they would have recognized him as the Messiah and set him free? Either that, or they would have run as fast as their legs could carry them in fear for their lives from this man of superhuman powers!"

"Perhaps the others did not see the wound heal. It was dark. Perhaps our Lord did not want them to see it. It was his objective to be arrested, if you remember."

"Very well. Explain to me why Simon Petra was not also arrested for bearing arms and for striking the High Priest's man with a sword."

"He escaped. Simon later confided to me that he had intended to also be arrested and share our Lord's fate on a cross, but that his courage had failed him at the last moment and he had run away."

"Very noble of him," Venerius sneered.

"Did Simon Petra also expect to rise from the dead?" Martius asked.

Bearing a faint but perceptible expression of ridicule, Philippus slowly shook his head. "I would not have thought so, tribune."

"Yet Simon Petra was prepared to die on a cross, even though he knew his leader was planning to somehow come back from the dead? A useless gesture, would you not say?" When the Evangelist did not reply, Martius went on. "When Jesus alone was arrested, he was found to be in possession of arms. Despite this, the Jewish authorities seemingly hid the breach of Roman law and charged him with blaspheming against Jewish Law. Is that the case?"

"The Sadducees were determined to stone him to death, as a demonstration of their authority to all the Jewish people," said Philippus. "You must understand, our Lord had to be very careful not to blaspheme while being questioned by the priests, so that he would be convicted under Roman law and sentenced to crucifixion, to meet the prophesies. Despite this, the Sanhedrin produced false witnesses who testified that He had blasphemed, and on that basis the Sanhedrin convicted Him and sentenced him to death by stoning. To his credit, Prefect Pilatus recognized the worthlessness of the false witnesses, and dismissed the Sanhedrin's charges and invalidated their sentence. The evidence on the charge of bearing arms could not be disputed, and our Lord quite deliberately offered no defense, leaving Pilatus no choice but to convict Him."

"Your man Jesus wanted the Roman death sentence, and so duped our Prefect into giving it to him; is that what you are saying?" said Martius.

Philippus replied with an open-handed gesture.

Martius nodded in the direction of Pythagoras and Artimedes. "I understand from our secretaries that according to the official records of the province Pontius Pilatus served as Prefect of Judea for ten years, and that he would have been in the fifth year of his posting in Judea at the time of the trial of your man Jesus. So, Philippus, for Tiberius Caesar to have retained Pilatus so long in his post would suggest that the prefect was neither inept nor stupid. Yet, you say he allowed himself to be manipulated."

"I have heard it said that Tiberius Caesar left all his appointees in their posts for many more years than had his father Augustus before him, but

I would not suggest that the prefect was either inept or stupid. I have in fact heard it said that Pontius Pilatus later became a follower of our Lord, at Rome."

"What!" Martius exclaimed. "Now you truly test my credulity and my patience, old man. Do you have proof of such an outrageous claim?"

"Can you disprove it? As for Longinus, the centurion who had charge of our Lord's execution, it has been said that he recognized our Lord's divinity and deserted his post not long after the execution."

"Oh, this is too much!" Martius cried, his eyes flaring. "The Roman procurator who condemned him and the Roman centurion who executed him both becoming his followers? Is there nothing you people will not invent to suit your ends?"

"There is more," said Philippus calmly. "Longinus was arrested by his own troops after his desertion, and was executed claiming our Lord as his savior."

"I have had enough!" Martius exclaimed. He turned to Varro. "Questor, I shall not waste my time any further with this duplicitous old man." Martius sat back down. Refusing to even look at the Evangelist, he averted his eyes and folded his arms.

"Thank you, tribune," said Varro. Bearing a grave expression, he addressed the witness. "Philippus, I came here seeking evidence that Jesus of Nazareth rose from the dead. To date I have seen nothing or heard nothing that would confirm that he did indeed rise. Is there any undeniable proof that you can offer to that effect?"

"I know it to be true, in my heart. If you could see into my heart, my lord questor, you would have your undeniable proof."

"We should take the old scoundrel up on his invitation," Martius muttered to Venerius at his table. "Have Diocles the physician open him up with a knife, and then we shall take a look at his heart."

Venerius let out one of his high-pitched cackles.

✠

The questioning of Philippus continued throughout the day, with the questor crossing and re-crossing the ground already covered, looking for anything that may have been missed, until, in the eleventh hour, with the sun dipping low in the western sky and with nothing new having emerged, he called a halt to proceedings.

"Philippus, you have answered all questions put to you since the third hour this morning," he said. "In return for your cooperation, I shall instruct Centurion Gallo to release your servants, as I promised I would."

"Thank you, my lord Varro," Philippus acknowledged, his faced drained white by the day's mental gymnastics.

"Yet," Varro went on, "so many questions remain unasked, so many answers remain to be found. I may have further need of your truthfulness, Evangelist. For the time being then, I will ask you to remain as my guest. You will not be mistreated, and you will be permitted unrestricted access to visitors. That is all for the moment." The questor rose up, departed his chair, and strode from the chamber, with Hostilis close behind.

Before long, Martius and Venerius came to the questor in his quarters, each with differing purposes. Venerius sought the expedition's watchword for the next twenty-four hours. Varro gave him a quotation taken from the poet Vergilius — 'The age of godhead hale and green' — then sent the junior tribune on his way.

Martius lingered behind. "May I speak, Julius?" he said, as the questor sprawled wearily on a divan.

"Proceed, my friend," Varro replied, accepting a cup of water from Hostilis.

"That old scoundrel Philippus has been playing us like a flute. He knows much more than he has let on."

"Possibly so."

"Put him to the torture, Julius. Drag the truth out of him."

Varro looked at his deputy for a moment, then said, "Let me ask you something, Marcus. Is Philippus to your mind a clever man?"

"Very clever."

"Is he determined?"

"Very determined."

"Is he passionate about what he believes in?"

"Frighteningly so. Though, how any man could believe such babble..."

"Have you ever seen a clever, determined, passionate man tortured? I have. A man like that will willingly die with his secrets rather than reveal them to a torturer. Such a man actually seem to gain a perverse pleasure from denying his tormentor the one thing he seeks. It is their last victory."

"Then, where does that leave us?"

"We are left with Philippus in our custody. He appears to believe that the Nazarene rose from the dead, but his belief is based on hearsay. Philippus may yet prove a key to unlocking the truth, but what we need is a witness who was actually involved in the execution of the Nazarene, or in any plot relating to it."

"If not through the cunning Evangelist, how do we find such a person?"

Varro smiled. "We must keep asking questions, my friend. Questions always father answers. We keep asking questions until we find the answers we seek."

XIII

THE SECRET REPORTS

Caesarea, Capital of the Roman Province of Judea.
April, A.D. 71

In the white palace overlooking the sea, Varro's seven chief subordinates gathered at his quarters. Sitting on divans forming a square in the spacious sea-view room, they had come for the reading of important new documents. Pythagoras and Artimedes had made a fresh discovery in the city archives, a horde of secret reports addressed to Prefect of Judea Pontius Pilatus. Neatly written in Latin, they provided information about Johannes the Baptist and Jesus of Nazareth and their leading followers, and warned the prefect that these people posed a threat to the peace and stability of the province. Many of the reports had been sent to Pilatus by Ananus ben Seth, one-time High Priest of the Temple of Jerusalem and head of the Great Sanhedrin. Others had originated with Josephus Caiaphas, son-in-law of and successor to Ananus as High Priest, and the man who had held the supreme post at the time of the arrest, trial and execution of Jesus of Nazareth.

Pythagoras pointed out to the questor that Ananus was apparently a very influential figure at the time. According to the records, even after Ananus had stepped down as High Priest not only did his son-in-law subsequently fill the post of High Priest, but four of Ananus' own sons had also been High Priest at various times, making it likely that Ananus ruled the Sanhedrin from behind the scenes for a number of years. Among these secret reports the secretaries found a letter from Ananus to Pontius Pilatus congratulating the prefect on consigning Jesus of Nazareth to his death. In this letter, Ananus had assured Pilatus that even though Jesus had been brought by the Captain of the Temple Guard to Ananus' house for questioning following his arrest, Ananus had not been aware that the Nazarene had been arrested in possession of weapons, and that was why he had sent Jesus on to High Priest Caiaphas to be tried for blasphemy. Had he been aware at that time that Jesus had been bearing arms, Ananus wrote, he would have had no hesitation in sending him directly to the prefect to be tried under Roman law.

There were so many of these secret reports that Pythagoras and Artimedes had spent days sorting them into rough chronological order and then sifting the occasional reliable piece of intelligence from a sea of hysterical priestly accusation and defamation. As a result, the secretaries were able to present the questor with some gems of information. Among the most important of the documents was a report from Ananus which gave a motive for Jesus of Nazareth's 'rebellious activities' and another from the same source which listed Jesus' 'chief accomplices.'

Describing the Nazarene as a man who had undergone considerable religious instruction, the first of these two reports said that Jesus was bitter because he had been denied entry into the Jewish priesthood. Ananus wrote that, unlike his distant cousin Johannes the Baptist, who was the son of Zecharias, a priest of the order of Abijah, Jesus was not a direct descendant of Aaron, brother of Moses and founder of the Jewish priesthood. Under Jewish Law, only Aaron's descendants — Levites, they were called — could become priests. Ananus told Pilatus that Jesus had decided to overthrow the Great Sanhedrin and proclaim that any Jew could become a priest, and then appoint himself High Priest, although Ananus provided no proof of this assertion.

According to the former High priest, after taking over the remnants of the Baptist's band, Jesus had found his support with the people waning because he lacked Johannes' priestly credentials. At the height of Johannes' popularity, said Ananus, the Baptist had attracted a following of thirty thousand men, but of these only some three thousand had attached themselves to his cousin Jesus. As a consequence, Ananus warned the Roman prefect, Jesus was likely to commit a desperate act in order to assert his claim to the leadership of the Jewish people. The most likely time for that act, Ananus wrote, would be during the Passover Festival at Jerusalem, when the city was crowded with pilgrims, a number of them potential recruits for the Nazarene.

Ananus wrote that the Nazarene was known to use secret sympathizers to pass messages and to make preparations in advance of his visits to various towns and villages. Among those preparations, said Ananus, was the recruitment and payment of people including Jesus' own relatives to pretend to be afflicted with various illnesses which he would then proceed to 'miraculously' cure. Jesus was known by a number of different names said Ananus. Apart from his Aramaic birth name, that of Yehoshua, or Joshua in Latin, he was known as both Joshua bar Josephus, or Joshua the son of Joseph, and Joshua bar Davidus, Joshua the son of David. The latter designation was designed to imply that he was descended from David, ancient and revered king of the Israelites.

Pythagoras next read aloud the list of the Nazarene's twelve chief associates provided by Ananus to Pilatus. "'The Nazarene has an inner circle of three. The first of these is Simon bar Jonas, also known as Simon of Galilee, also known as Simon Petra, also known as Petra, also known, to Greek speakers, as Cephas. Simon is a native of Capernaum, where he and his younger brother, also one of the Nazarene's followers, are involved in their father Jonas' fishing partnership. Simon is married, with young children, and his family has large houses at both Capernaum and Jerusalem which the Nazarene regularly uses. The other two members of the inner circle are the brothers Jacob bar Zebedee and Johannes bar Zeberdee. They are also known as 'Sons of Thunder.'"

"Sons of thunder?" Martius interrupted. "All these alternative names, questor! As you would expect of revolutionaries. They probably also wrote their messages in cipher." He looked over at Pythagoras. "You would know all about ciphers, secretary."

"Indeed, tribune," Pythagoras replied without inflection. He was in fact expert at using transposition codes of the kind first employed by Julius Caesar one hundred and thirty years before, where one letter of the alphabet was substituted for another. He was using just such a code in the written dispatches he was sending back to General Collega.

"Continue reading the list, Pythagoras," Varro instructed.

Pythagoras resumed. "The brothers are also fishermen of Capernaum, and are involved in their father Zebedee's fishing partnership with Simon's family. Both have apparently been the close friends of Simon and his brother Andreius for some years. Johannes and Andreius are former close associates of Johannes called the Baptist, the relative of Jesus, and it is believed that it is this connection which brought Johannes bar Zebedee into Jesus' trust.'"

Martius interjected again. "This information implies detailed knowledge from someone close to the Nazarene. The High Priest had an informant in the fellow's ranks."

"Obviously, it was Judas the betrayer," said Antiochus.

"Quite possibly," Varro conceded. "Yet, despite the fact that Philippus the Evangelist brands Judas a betrayer, and despite the Lucius Letter's endorsement of the same sentiment…"

"As do the Marcus and Matthias documents, my lord," said Artimedes.

"Yes," Varro acknowledged. "Still, I have my doubts about Judas' real role in this affair. The testament of Matthias states that Judas was paid thirty pieces of silver to betray the Nazarene. That is barely two days' wages for a common laborer."

"The thirty pieces of silver is an amount mentioned in one of the ancient Jewish prophesies, questor," said Antiochus. "That of the prophet Jeremiah. In the context of the Matthias document, I think that thirty pieces of silver is a symbolic amount, inserted by Matthias to imply that the predictions regarding the Messiah were fulfilled."

"You are saying that in reality Judas was paid more?" Varro asked.

"There can be no doubt that Matthias lied, questor," Antiochus replied. "Of the three authors, Matthias was demonstrably the most prone to invention and exaggeration throughout his text. He wrote that all the bodies in the tombs outside Jerusalem rose up and invaded Jerusalem following the Nazarene's death. This ridiculous nonsense was his way of making his testament superior to that of Marcus."

"If not thirty pieces of silver?" Varro prompted. "How much was Judas paid?"

"Both Philippus and the testament of Matthias make mention of a potters field being purchased with the money, my lord," said Antiochus. "If that were true, the actual amount had to be considerably more than thirty pieces of silver."

"Here I have to agree with the Jew," said Martius, begrudgingly.

"As do I, my lord," said Callidus, a man who knew the value of a sestertius. "No potter sells his field so cheaply."

"Certainly not a Hebrew potter," added Venerius with a guffaw.

"Irrespective of the amount received by Judas from the priests," said Varro, "everything points to Jesus having prearranged his arrest with Judas.

It is clear from the Lucius Letter that when Jesus sent Judas to 'do what he had to do' they were still dining at a house in Jerusalem; possibly Simon Petra's house. Jesus must have told Judas that following the meal he would go to the grove on the Mount of Olives outside the city. How else could Judas have known where to lead the Temple Guard to make the arrest? Was Judas in league with Jesus, and hoodwinked Ananus and Caiaphas by pretending to betray his leader?"

"According to the letter and the two other testaments, questor," said Pythagoras, "none of the apostles knew of the existence of any such arrangement between Jesus and Judas. It had to be a secret shared only by the two of them."

"That being the case," said Martius, "to ensure that the priests never realized they had been tricked into arresting Jesus, Judas had to keep up the pretense, long after the execution. Permanently, in fact. If the collusion had become known, doubts would have been cast on the whole process. Not an easy thing to do, maintaining the pretense when both sides consider you a traitor. A man's life would be a misery. Such an act of self-sacrifice would have required a good deal of courage."

"Or stupidity," said Callidus.

"Or loyalty," said Crispus, chiming in for the first time.

"Had I been this Judas," said Venerius, "I would have run away and become an outlaw. I would have joined a rebel band in the desert."

"Provided they would have had you," Martius commented dryly.

"Philippus, in his testimony," said Pythagoras, "suggested that Judas died shortly after the crucifixion, and by his own hand."

"Perhaps that was a story," Crispus suggested, "circulated to protect Judas and allow him to start a new life in some far distant place."

Varro smiled to himself; at least Crispus had taken in some of this business, despite his predilection for poetic diversions. "Perhaps so," he mused.

"A story circulated by whom?" Martius asked. "If eleven of the apostles were not a party to the deception, as it appears, surely not a story circulated by them?"

"Someone outside the apostles, then?" said Crispus, thinking aloud.

"Who?" said Martius. "One of the seventy disciples?"

"The priests?" Varro postulated. "As part of the arrangement with Judas? To protect him and allow him to start life afresh somewhere."

"The priests?" Martius mused. "I suppose it is possible."

They all looked at each other, mystified.

"It is worth thinking on," said Varro. "Continue reading the list of accomplices."

Pythagoras began again. "'The Galileans Philippus of Bethsaida…'"

"Not our Philippus the Evangelist," Martius reminded the others.

"'…and his friend Andreius bar Jonas, brother of Simon Petra, both former deputies of Johannes the Baptist. Nathaniel bar Tolmai, also known as Nathaniel of Cana, a native of Cana in Galilee. Thomas, also called Didymus, who has a twin brother whom is also a follower. Levi bar Alpheus, also known as Matthias, for many years a customs duty collector in the service of Herod Antipas, Tetrarch of Galilee, based at Capernaum until he left his post to join the Nazarene's band. Jacob bar Alpheus, the brother of Levi cum Matthias. Thaddeus bar Jacob, also known as Jude, also known as Lebbeus, son of the preceding and believed to be a former member of the *sicarii*, the Daggermen revolutionary band also called the Zealots. Simon of Cana, also called Simon the Zealot, Simon the Sicarius, and Simon Sicarius, also a suspected former member of the Daggermen. The treasurer of the group is Judas bar Simon, son of the preceding, also called Judas Sicarius…' Here we have the betrayer '…believed to have at one time been a member of the Daggermen, and, like his father, also from Cana in Galilee.'"

"Do you know, three things stand out from that list," said Martius.

"They all seem to have come from Galilee," said Venerius.

"Yes, that is one thing," Martius acknowledged. "More importantly, the band includes several former members of the Daggermen, sworn enemies of Rome, and several former followers of Johannes the Baptist. Could it be that the Baptist was in league with the Daggermen? Could it be that under the guise of spiritualism he was secretly spying for the Daggermen and raising recruits for a revolt against Rome?"

"The Nazarene merely took up the revolutionary activities where the Baptist left off?" Crispus added.

"Possibly so," said Varro, sounding unconvinced.

"There is more here relating to the apostles, questor," said Pythagoras. "From a secret report by the High Priest Josephus Caiaphas." He turned to another document on his table and read aloud. "'Under the Nazarene's leadership these men all follow the beliefs of the Pharisees, that division of religious philosophy which believes in a strict observance of Jewish law but which also concedes in favor of resurrection. The Nazarene has been known to commune with and to eat with leading Pharisees in the past, but of late he has fallen out with many of these men on matters of religious philosophy and more particularly in relation to observance of the Law. As an example of the irreligious nature of these people, unlike the Pharisees, the Nazarene and his followers fail to observe all the fasts required by the Law.'" Pythagoras looked up from the document. "The Letter and the testaments all indicate that the Pharisees, or some of them at least, became bitterly opposed to the Nazarene," he summarized.

Varro nodded. "The Pharisees believed in resurrection," he reflected, "yet in the end they fell out with the Nazarene. I wonder why? Surely not merely because the Nazarene's followers did not always observe the required fasts?"

"What I find interesting," Martius remarked, "is that all the men listed by the High Priest, apart from Judas, are said to have seen the Nazarene after he supposedly rose from the dead. Now, it is easy to believe they might have lied and were a part of a plot to make it appear that Jesus had risen, to fulfil the prophesies. Yet, many of these apostles seem to have been ignorant of the original design, the arrest and execution, which was also intended to fulfil the prophesies. Why would they be a party to the final deception but not the first? The implication is that Jesus kept his closest associates in the dark about certain aspects of his plans, and they were only brought into the plot after his execution."

"Speculation, Marcus, speculation," Varro mused, coming to his feet. "What I seek is cold, hard fact." He looked across at Pythagoras and Artimedes. "These documents are helpful, to a point. Find me more facts, learned secretaries. More facts."

✠

A day later, Artimedes made several more useful discoveries in the archives. He had moved to the military section, where there was a record of every single Roman military unit to have been stationed in the province of Judea since its inception seventy-five years before. The records attested to the fact that the most senior of six centurions stationed at Jerusalem at the time of the execution of Jesus of Nazareth was a Centurion Julius Longinus, commander of the 2nd Cohort of the 12th Legion, which provided the garrison unit at Jerusalem. Varro and his military companions knew that a legion's first three cohorts were its most senior. The 1st Cohort always remained with the legion commander, and in Judea that officer had been stationed at Caesarea, the provincial capital. In recognition of the importance of the Jerusalem posting, the 2nd Cohort was garrisoned at Jerusalem, quartered in the Antonia Fortress, adjacent to the Temple. As Artimedes pointed out to Varro, the Antonia had a number of roles, serving as Roman *pretorium,* citadel, courthouse and prison in Jerusalem. The Jewish authorities had their own separate court and prison within the Temple complex.

From the records, Artimedes was able to establish that the 12th Legion had undergone a blanket discharge and reenlistment three years prior to the Nazarene's death. This meant that the four hundred and eighty men of the 2nd Cohort had spent twenty years as conscript soldiers and at the time of the execution of Jesus of Nazareth they were three years into a second, voluntary enlistment of twenty years with the 12th Legion.

Martius was to remark that if these men were anything like the men of other senior cohorts in other legions they would have been tough and arrogant soldiers, men who looked down on the inexperienced conscripts of the junior cohorts. When they themselves had been junior cohorts, they would have been based at some or all of the five other fortresses used by the resident legion in Judea. Martius quickly calculated that in the year in question the rank and file members of the 12th Legion cohort stationed at Jerusalem, the men who had physically carried out the execution of Jesus of Nazareth, had been in the vicinity of forty-three years of age.

✠

"You realize of course, Julius," said Martius as Varro and he discussed this new evidence on a walk on the terrace after dinner, "the men of the 2nd Cohort of the 12th who were present at the Nazarene's execution would have retired more than twenty years ago."

"If they were still alive, they would be aged in their eighties today."

"Most of them would have retired throughout Greater Syria, or even gone home to Cisalpine Gaul. It could take years to track down any survivors, and even then there is no guarantee they will be in any state to remember a solitary thing about those days. My maternal grandfather was as lucid as a pumpkin by the time *he* reached his eighties."

"Years I do not have, my friend," Varro sighed. "Time is not our ally. As you know, Collega has ordered me to be back at Antioch with my report by the autumn. Yet, without the evidence of eye-witnesses, there is little to report."

"Look at it another way," Martius suggested. "While there may be little evidence to support the contention that our man did not die on a cross, there is precious little to prove that he did. To my mind there is a good case to be put that somehow the Nazarene pulled the wool over peoples' eyes. For one thing, the business involving Judas is most suspicious. As you suggested, Judas and Jesus seem to have had a secret understanding."

"Facts, Marcus," Varro responded with exasperation. "I must write of facts, not of suspicions. It is an unavoidable fact that the centurion in charge of the execution certified in writing that the crucifixion of Jesus of Nazareth did take place. That would seem compelling to most people, without any firm evidence to the contrary."

"A pity we could not manage to stumble on Centurion Longinus himself. Then you would have some answers."

"Longinus is dead, apparently executed. Remember?"

Martius jovially poked his colleague in the ribs. "Unless we can resurrect him." He chuckled to himself. "Mind you, Julius, we do only have the word of that crafty old dissembler Philippus that Longinus was executed."

"I may be able to contribute to that debate, my lords," came the voice of Artimedes as he approached along the terrace. In one hand he held a lamp, in the other a document. "I have been burning the late night oil at the archives, looking for any reference to Centurion Longinus."

"Well, there's a choice coincidence," said Martius.

"I was particularly interested to locate any record of the death of the centurion." Artimedes held up the document in his hand. "And here it is, my lords! Dated in the same year as the execution of Jesus of Nazareth."

"No!" Varro exclaimed, half way between surprise and delight.

Varro and Martius now each took an end of the small document and unraveled it under the light of the secretary's lamp.

"This is the warrant for Julius Longinus' decapitation," Artimedes informed them. "Issued under Pilatus' seal, and carried out in the late autumn of the same year that Jesus of Nazareth was executed."

"For what crime?" Martius asked.

"Desertion." Artimedes pointed to the relevant line in the text.

Martius scratched his head. "Centurions do occasionally desert the army, I admit, but very rarely in time of peace, as it was then in Judea. What would make a senior man turn his back on his legion like that? He was well paid, he had seniority and was close to promotion to the 1st grade. He may well have ended up chief centurion of his legion, an enormous prize for an enlisted man. It is not as if he would not have known that he and his head would part company if he were arrested for deserting."

"Philippus did say that Longinus joined the Nazarenes," said Varro. "Would that have been motive enough for deserting?"

Martius looked pained, as if in receipt of a personal insult. "I find that hard to believe, Julius, I really do. A hardened soldier, succumbing to the Nazarene nonsense?."

"Certainly, my lords," said Artimedes, "nothing in this document confirms the assertion made by Philippus that the centurion died a follower of the Nazarene."

"It does however confirm Philippus' testimony about the time and nature of Longinus' death," said Varro. "We have yet to make a liar of Philippus."

"On factual grounds, at least," Martius was quick to add.

Varro nodded. "It is a pity that Philippus was not in Jerusalem at the time of Jesus' execution. As I have been saying all along, what this investigation desperately needs is an eyewitness. That must be our unrelenting goal. An eyewitness."

XIV

THE GETHSEMANE WITNESS

Caesarea, Capital of the Roman Province of Judea, April, A.D. 71

Unlike Rome, or Antioch, there were no daylight traffic restrictions in the Judean capital, so that wheeled vehicles serving the port passed to and fro incessantly while riders and pedestrians jostled for room to move around them. Mounted and on foot, people had poured in from as far away as Sebaste before the public holiday next day on April 21 closed down commerce and the courts in the city. The holiday numbered among the one hundred and sixty holy days on the Roman calendar when no business could be conducted. It would bring a double observation, the Parilia, feast day of the god and goddess Pales, protectors of flocks and herds, and the celebration of the anniversary of the foundation of Rome by Romulus eight hundred and twenty-four years before.

As Marcus Martius pushed through the throng, few people realized that he was a Roman officer. He went bare-headed and wore a simple cloak over his tunic. The cloak served to disguise his rank and to conceal the sword belt slung over his shoulder. He was accompanied by just a single man, Publius Alienus, the cavalry officer loaned to Questor Varro by Procurator Rufus to be his guide in Judea. A swarthy, well built Egyptian of twenty-eight, Alienus was the eldest son of a wealthy Alexandrian family whose Roman ancestor had served with Pompeius the Great. Alienus, who carried a cloth bag shouldered beneath his cloak, led Martius through the thronging streets. Their mission was to visit every tavern in Caesarea. As soon as the owner of the first rowdy drinking house discovered Martius' identity, he offered the two officers free wine.

"Why?" Alienus returned with surprise.

"In honor of the Pales, and Romulus," said the tavern-keeper with a wink, "and any other god or notable person you care to name. You are Roman officers, after all — *senior* Roman officers — and we have to look after our brave soldiers."

As Varro had required, Martius had been limiting his wine consumption on the march. But this, he decided, was different. "We cannot be accused of being irreligious, my dear Alienus," he said with a wink. "Accept the landlord's generous offer."

So Alienus handed the tavern keeper a notice to post offering a reward for information about the death of Jesus of Nazareth, and the landlord handed the two officers diluted cups of his best mulled wine. The offer of free wine was repeated at every tavern they frequented, and never declined. Martius found Alienus an excellent drinking companion, swapping jokes and matching him round for round. By the time they had visited thirteen taverns, Martius and Alienus had become increasingly merry. And as they moved on from one establishment to the next, singing bawdy legion songs in two-part harmony, they attracted a growing crowd of dirty-faced children and assorted beggars who limped and crawled in their wake. As the pair tunefully came away from the latest drinking house, they were confronted by a beggar in his forties, a grubby, skinny individual with a forked tree branch for a crutch and dragging his left leg.

"Spare a coin for a hapless cripple, my good and generous lords," the beggar wailed in a pitiful tone, as he stood in Martius' way.

"You are lame, good fellow?" said Martius, a little unsteady on his feet as he looked the beggar up and down.

"If only it were not so, my lord. I have a wife and eight children to support, and it is not an easy thing for a man with a handicap such as mine."

"Eight children?" Martius returned. "You have been a busy fellow." He put his arm around the decurion's shoulders. "Did you hear what Caesar Vespasianus did while he was in Alexandria last year, Alienus, my friend?"

"I heard that Caesar did many things in my home town last year, tribune," the decurion replied. "To what thing in particular do you refer?"

"There was one sublime and superlative act which stands out from all the rest. Allow me to demonstrate." Martius focused his attention on the left leg of the bemused beggar. "Your left limb is lame, I take it? The leg, and the foot, quite useless are they?"

"Perfectly useless, my lord," the mendicant answered with a sigh. "Dead as a piece of wood, leg and foot, ever since I was run down by a builder's cart."

"Ah, well then, let me see what I can do to help you." With that, Martius raised his military sandal, then stomped on the beggar's left foot with all his might.

The man howled with pain, grabbed at his left foot, and went hopping away, accompanied by the uproarious laughter of all the children gathered around.

"Did you see that, Alienus? I have cured the beggar!" Martius declared with glee. "He feels pain in the dead foot! It is a miracle!"

The limping beggar paused, wincing, at the street corner. "A curse on the pair of you!" he called back to Martius and Alienus. "May you suffer a cruel and painful death!"

"On your way, imposter," Martius growled, pulling back his cloak to reveal the sword on his hip. "Or it will be you who suffers a cruel and painful death."

The beggar quickly turned and disappeared.

As Martius and the decurion went to move on they were surrounded by the children, who all now clamored for money. One enchanting child of no more than nine or ten, with short, rough-shorn black hair and large, round, green eyes took Martius' hand.

"My grandfather, Ishmael, has things to tell you about the Nazarene, master," said the child, looking up into his eyes.

Martius looked down in surprise. "The Nazarene?"

"Grandfather says that you must come alone."

Alienus' suspicions were quickly aroused. "Come where?"

"I will take you there," said the child to Martius, "but you must come alone."

"Be careful, my lord," Alienus cautioned.

"All is well, decurion," said Martius. "I'm not afraid of children, or of grandfathers." He leaned closer to Alienus, and spoke softly, so that the child could not overhear. "Follow at a distance, Alienus. Hold back, unless I call on you."

Then, still holding the child by the hand, Martius allowed himself to be led off down the street. Alienus gave them a brief start, then, with his hand on his sheathed sword, he followed the pair at a distance as instructed, ready to melt into the scenery if the child should look back. As he went, the light-headedness that had accompanied the decurion from the tavern vanished, lifted like a morning fog melted by the new day's sun. The child, walking with small, rapid steps and the occasional backward glance, led the tribune from street to cobbled street, then down a narrow back alley toward the city amphitheater. Alienus became increasingly worried. With the beggar's fatalistic prediction ringing in his ears, and fearing repercussions if he were to permit anything to happen to a tribune, he decided he did not dare hold back any longer. Quickening his pace, he began to overtake the pair.

"Tribune, I think that it may be a trap," he called.

The child stopped.

Martius turned around. "Alienus, I told you to hold back," he said unhappily.

"There is danger here, my lord." As he spoke, Alienus cast a wary gaze around them. "This is the worst part of the town. Cutthroats lurk at every turn."

"Grandfather Ishmael will speak to you, and you alone, master," said the child.

Martius looked down at the small face, and saw only innocence. "Go back to the white fortress, Alienus," Martius instructed. "I will return later."

"My lord, I cannot desert you here," Alienus protested.

"Go!" Martius growled. "I order you. Do it now!"

Alienus unhappily obeyed. He turned several times to look back as he retraced his steps down the alley. Each time, he saw that the tribune and the child had remained stock still and were watching his retreat. Then the decurion slipped from view.

Again the child set off with the tribune in tow. Martius found himself led to the arcades beneath the northern side of the amphitheater. In all Roman cities, amphitheater and hippodrome arcades like these attracted the dregs of society, the homeless and the lawless. To pimps and prostitutes, male and female, higgling hucksters and sleazy shell-game artists, street acrobats and clowns and their pickpocket accomplices, these dark, dank, rat-infested arcades were both home and place of business. The holidays were their best days, when festival games were celebrated in the arena, bringing customers and victims flocking here in their thousands looking for sordid pleasures and cheap thrills.

Under the shade of the arcades, the child led Martius to a small, bald, much wrinkled figure with an untidy beard and jaundiced skin, who sat on the stone pavement floor with his back to the wall. Around him lay refuse and human waste. The eyes of the elderly man flickered open. There was a hollow, deathly look behind them.

"He is here, grandfather," said the child, kneeling at his feet.

"You are Ishmael?" Martius inquired, looking down at the ancient.

The old man looked up at him with a searching gaze. "You are the tribune?" His voice was weak and wavering.

After a precautionary look around him, and satisfied that there was no imminent threat, Martius said, "I am he. How did you know to send the child for me?"

"It had been said within my hearing that a tribune of Rome was this morning going around the taverns, seeking information about the Nazarene."

"You have information for me?"

"There are things I can tell you, but whether this is what you seek, I cannot know. I will try to help you as best I can, but I will only tell *you,* and I will only tell you here. If I were to go to the citadel, word would soon spread. The cutthroats here would only think that I had gone to inform on them, and my life would not be worth a muleteer's curse."

"Why would you want to help me?"

"Look at me, Roman," old Ishmael replied. "I try to survive here among the whores and the hawkers, the performers and the parasites. It is quiet here now, because the worst of them have gone to the hippodrome. Tomorrow is race day. Rufus will celebrate the Parilia, and my neighbors will have much custom tonight and tomorrow. Two days' hence, the corrupt and the corrupters will return. I ask you, is this any place to raise a granddaughter?" He cast one hand around his squalid surroundings.

"Granddaughter?" said Martius with surprise, looking at the infant. "I took the child to be a boy."

"This is Gemara, daughter of my son Jonathan," said Ishmael, reaching out and taking hold of the green-eyed child's small hand, "who took his family to Jerusalem for the Passover five years ago, leaving his little one in my care until his return. No longer do I have my son or any living relative apart from this sweet child. They have all been taken from me. I am old, I am frail. If by speaking what little I know of events that interest you, I may be able to prevail upon the tribune's generosity..." His voice faded away.

Martius doubted that much would come out of this, but he was here now. "Very well, tell me what you know, and I will see whether it is of interest to me."

Ishmael let out a deep sigh, and then began. "In the time when Pilatus was Prefect of Judea, I was a servant of Josephus Caiaphas, High Priest of Jerusalem."

Martius was interested. Very interested. Keeping one eye on the neighborhood, he eased down onto a knee beside the soft-voiced geriatric. "Go on."

"Came a night, the night before the Passover, when the Captain of the Temple Guard was sent by Caiaphas to arrest a man who had been preaching blasphemy in the Temple, a man who had disrupted the business of the merchants who sold the sacrificial birds and animals to the pilgrims. That man was Jesus of Nazareth. Caiaphas sent his scribe Malchus with the captain and his officers and the soldiers of the Guard. Malchus was my cousin; I assisted him in his duties. I too was in the party which went to the Mount of Olives to make the arrest."

"You were sent there with your cousin?"

Ishmael shook his head. "It was my choice to go. I admit, I was curious. I had heard about this man, the Nazarene. On the one hand I had heard that he had performed miracles, on the other, I had heard the High Priest and others among the priests say that he was nothing more than a clever magician and a deceiver. I suppose I had hopes of seeing him perform some miraculous act to escape his arrest. Either that, or I was ready to laugh when I saw him struggling to be free, unmasked and powerless."

Martius was wishing that Pythagoras or Artimedes were here, taking notes. His head had cleared, but he worried that his wine consumption might affect his power of recollection once he left the informant. For a moment he thought about dragging the old man to the fortress to testify in front of the questor, but old Ishmael looked as if he might die at any moment, so Martius decided to extract all he could from him now while he had the opportunity. "What happened on the Mount of Olives that night?" he asked.

"There were a great many of us. The captain and his officers were armed with swords, as Roman law allowed, and the men of the Guard carried their staves. We were led to a place on the mountain by an informant, a Galilean."

"A Galilean by what name?"

"Judas. His name was Judas. It was told to me by one of the soldiers that this Judas was secretly in the employ of Ananus, father-in-law of High Priest Caiaphas, but I had never seen this man before."

"Judas led you all to the Mount of Olives?"

Ishmael nodded. "In those times there were olive presses on the mountain, here and there among the groves. In the early hours of the morning — it would have been some two hours before dawn — we went quietly out of the city. We crossed the holy brook of the Kidron in the darkness, and climbed up into the olive groves directly overlooking the Temple Mount, to a clearing where one of those presses was located."

"Judas knew exactly where to take you?"

"So it seemed. He led us to this place, called in my native tongue *got shemanin* — place of the olive press. The Greek-speakers render this as Gethsemane. The Nazarene was there, as the informant Judas had led us to believe. He seemed to be expecting us."

"Was the Nazarene alone?"

"There were three others with him that I could see. Two were older and wore beards, like teachers of the Law, but the other was quite young and clean shaven."

"Did you recognize the Nazarene, or any of those with him?"

"None was familiar to me. It was a dark night, but we carried a number of torches and lanterns between us. I myself carried one of the lanterns. So it was that I was able to see them all quite clearly. One of these three was a large man with bushy eyebrows and a fierce countenance whom I later came to know was called Simon Petra."

"Did the Nazarene identify himself?"

"No. As had been prearranged with the Captain of the Guard, Judas went forward and identified the Nazarene by kissing him on the cheek. He then departed."

"Did the Nazarene resist arrest?"

"He did not resist. In fact, he offered to go peacefully, even putting his arms out for the shackles that the men of the Guard had brought with them. He told the soldiers to put up their staves and told the officers to return their swords to their sheathes. I was disappointed at the time; no miracles were performed, and neither was he made to look a fool. But the one called Simon Petra, he put up a fight. He pulled back his cloak, and drew a short sword, and one of the other two did the same. The captain warned the two of them to give up their arms, but Simon Petra raised his sword and brought it down on the person nearest to him. That person was my cousin Malchus, who was not armed. Malchus went to dodge the blow, moving to his left…" The old man reenacted the moment, leaning to the left as if he were Malchus. "But he was not nimble enough to avoid the blade. It came down here…" He touched his right temple. "It took off his right ear, as neat as you like. I am certain that Simon Petra meant to kill him, and would have succeeded had Malchus not moved as quickly as he did. Poor Malchus looked down and saw his ear lying on the ground, and let out a terrible wail, then collapsed."

"Did the Nazarene attempt to help your cousin with his wound?"

"How could he? The manacles had already been fixed around his wrists."

"So, there was no miraculous cure for your cousin Malchus?"

"Would that it had been so. Poor Malchus was deformed for the rest of his days."

"Is he still alive, your cousin?"

Ishmael sighed. "Malchus was taken by a fit some years ago."

"What took place after your cousin was struck?"

"The Nazarene told his people to lay aside their weapons. Simon Petra threw down his bloodied sword and ran off. The other man also dropped his sword, and all three of the Nazarene's accomplices fled into the trees. The soldiers of the Guard gave chase. There were people running everywhere in the night, with much shouting and confusion. They caught up with the youngest one, but somehow in the tussle he slipped out of his robe and got away — perfectly naked, some of the soldiers told me later. I felt for him, because it was a cold night."

"Then what took place?"

"The Nazarene was taken in chains back into the city, to the house of Ananus."

"You also went to the house of Ananus?"

"We all did. Someone told me to take up Malchus' ear from the ground, but I could not bring myself to do it. Someone else took it up. They said they would give it to a physician, to sew back on. A physician did later try just that, but the flesh of the ear was dead and they took it off again. The soldiers also took up the two discarded swords."

"What took place at the house of Ananus?"

"The Nazarene was taken before Ananus, and Eleazar, and Jonathan, and Theophilus, and Matthias, the sons of Ananus, all Sadducees and councilors of the Great Sanhedrin like their father. There were also other members of the Sanhedrin present, including some Pharisees. They had all been waiting for the Nazarene to be brought in, and they quizzed the Nazarene about his activities, before taking him to Caiaphas."

"They had been expecting his arrest?"

"So it seemed to me."

"Were you a witness to his questioning?"

Ishmael shook his head. "While the priests conducted the questioning I went down to the kitchens in the basement, where there was a warm fire. There I waited with the soldiers and others for the outcome of affairs above our heads. It was by that time into the twelfth hour and coming on toward dawn. While I was warming myself, one of Caiaphas' maidservants who was known to me came to me and said, 'Look there, that man is a Galilean and I am certain that I have seen him with the Nazarene before today.' She pointed him out to me in the crowd, and I recognized the man as Simon Petra."

"Did you speak to this man?"

"Plucking up my courage, I went over to him and said, 'Were you not with the Nazarene in the olive grove tonight, and did you not strike my cousin Malchus?'"

"What did he say to that?"

"He denied it. Vehemently."

"Did you believe his denial?"

Ishmael shook his head. "Yet, what proof of my accusation could I offer? There was also the fact that he was a large and powerful man; much larger and more powerful than I. He was without doubt a Galilean; his country bumpkin's accent betrayed him. Later I thought to find one of the others in the arresting party, someone who had also seen him near the olive press. I went upstairs and told one of the officers of the Temple Guard. By that time it was too late. The officer and I went back down to the kitchens, some little time after sunrise. The trumpets of the Temple Guard — the 'cockerels,' we called them — had only a little while before sounded the hour and the end of the last watch from a Temple tower, and this was echoed by a Roman trumpeter at the Antonia. The man I had recognized as Simon Petra was nowhere to be seen. The officer thought that I must have imagined seeing the Galilean, but as I have told people since I have no doubt to this day that I did see Simon Petra there, and so did the maidservant."

"What do you think Simon Petra was doing there?"

"At the time, I thought he must have been planning to break his master free."

"This Simon Petra was to claim to have seen the Nazarene alive after his execution. Old man, tell me truly, do you think that the Nazarene was the Jews' Messiah, and rose from the dead?"

Amused, Ishmael smiled gently. "Tribune, I am still waiting for the Messiah."

Thoughtful, Martius came to his feet, comparing the old man's information with the other evidence the investigation had produced to date. That evidence seemed to corroborate all that Ishmael had told him. Even the reference to Simon Petra following the Nazarene to the house of the former high priest rang true with information contained in the Lucius Letter and the Marcus and Matthias documents. He looked back down to Ishmael, and asked, "What more can you tell me, about the death of the Nazarene, or events that followed his death?"

"There is little to tell. Caiaphas officiated at the Nazarene's crucifixion, and I accompanied him. He and I saw the Nazarene put up, but Caiaphas did not remain after that. He did not wait for the Nazarene's death. A crucified man does not die quickly, as you surely would be aware. Caiaphas and I went back to the High Priest's house."

"Did you hear anything to suggest that Jesus of Nazareth did not die on a cross?"

"He died up there true enough. It was what happened to the body that concerned Caiaphas most. He and Pilatus had agreed that all the prisoners would be dispatched and brought down before the Sabbath. I should tell you that Caiaphas did not hear until some time later that the legs of the Nazarene were not broken to hasten his death, as was the case with the other condemned men that day. That annoyed Caiaphas, but did not concern him as much as the body snatching. You see, it was Caiaphas' fear that the Nazarene's followers would steal the body and say that he had risen from the dead, to further the claim that he was the Messiah, the anointed successor of King David."

"As proved to be the case," Martius remarked. "Why did Caiaphas fail to take steps to prevent the body being stolen?"

"Steps *were* taken. Caiaphas went to Pilatus and asked for troops from the Roman garrison to guard the tomb, but Pilatus told him that the Temple had its own soldiers of the watch, in copious number, and that he should use those. That is what he did."

"Guards were posted at the tomb? Yet still the body disappeared?"

"It later eventuated that these men of the Temple Guard were bribed to leave their posts, and it was then that the body was removed. They later claimed they had fallen asleep, but the truth was different."

"Bribed by whom? Removed by whom?"

"By the Nazarene's followers. The Temple soldiers involved were all dismissed, but the damage had been done..." Ishmael's voice trailed off. "That is all I know, tribune," he said weakly. "Please go now, before you attract unwelcome attention to me."

Martius reached to the purse on his belt, loosened the leather tie, and inverted the purse over his cupped hand. Silver and gold coins tumbled into his palm. He knelt again briefly, pressing the coins into the old man's hand. "Take care of your granddaughter, old man," he said, before standing and walking quickly away. As he went, he looked back, to see that the old man had lain his head against the wall and closed his eyes. The child was watching Martius go. Her face was impassive, but her emerald eyes shone into his heart.

As soon as he returned to the fortress, Martius sought out the questor and imparted all that he had learned from Ishmael. Varro felt that despite the old man's concern about his own security the value of his information made it necessary to question the former servant of the High Priest with secretaries present. Centurion Gallo was ordered to take forty men to locate and bring in Ishmael.

Leaving shields and javelins behind, the legionaries hurried through the city at the jog. Once he reached the amphitheater, Gallo went looking for an old man and a green-eyed girl meeting the description provided by Tribune Martius. Despite an extensive search, they found no sign of either. Ishmael and his granddaughter had vanished.

✠

Varro was dining with his officers and freedmen that night, discussing the testimony of Ishmael, when a soldier of the watch came with a message for Martius. A child had come to the fortress gate begging to see the tribune; a green-eyed girl. Martius immediately sought Varro's leave to depart the table and hurried down to the fortress' decuman gate. Little Gemara sat on the stone pavement just inside the closed gates. When she saw him striding toward her, the child quickly came to her feet. In the lamp light, Martius could see that her cheeks were stained by tears.

"Master," she said. "It's grandfather. Please help me."

Summoning Centurion Gallo and several squads of his men, Martius went with the child as she trotted through the city streets. She led them not toward the amphitheater, but down to the docks. At the quayside, Gemara pointed to the arcades where seamen lived. "Over there," she said. "Men were hurting grandfather."

Martius and his legionaries fanned out along the stone dock, turning out sailors and laborers lying beneath the arcades as they sought the child's grandfather. It was apparent to Martius that for safety's sake the old man had changed his abode, fearful that he had been seen talking with the tribune. The troops searched the arcades several times, but not a sign of Ishmael did they find.

Then, from the dockside, there arose an urgent shout. "Tribune, over here!"

Martius and his men hurried to the edge of the pier and followed a soldier's pointing finger. A figure could just be seen floating in the water between two docked merchantmen. Face down, and unmoving, it was the figure of a small, bald man. One of the few soldiers in the group who could swim volunteered to go into the water, and after stripping off his equipment the naked legionary eased down into the water then swam out to the figure. "Dead!" he called, stating the obvious, once he reached it. Grasping the corpse's tunic, he towed it to the dockside. Willing hands reached down and dragged the body up onto the dock; others hauled the dripping soldier from the water.

As the body was laid on the stones in front of him, Martius recognized the face as Ishmael's. There was a savage wound from one side of the old man's neck to the other. Martius turned to see Gemara standing, white faced, looking at her grandfather's corpse from the arcades. "Take her back to the fortress," he ordered Optio Silius.

Centurion Gallo searched the body. "Not as much as a single *ass*, Tribune," he reported when he had finished. "You say he had money on him this afternoon?"

"Too much money," Martius sighed. "It cost the old man his life."

✠

"You want to keep the child?" said Varro with astonishment, after Martius had returned to the dining chamber and brought him the news of the death of their best witness, and then informed him of his desire to retain little Gemara with the expedition. "You are not an uncharitable man, Marcus, but even so you surprise me."

"Put it down to guilt," said the tribune. "I made an orphan of the child."

"Not you — the cutthroats of Caesarea. What are we going to do with a child in our midst? Does she not have family we can pass her onto? A child is best with her kinfolk, Marcus, you must agree."

"The old man was her last living relative," Martius advised with a helpless shrug.

Varro peered at him, as if trying to discern a motive that had yet to emerge. "Are you sure that is all there is to it?"

"Let the girl travel with the slave Miriam," Martius suggested. "They will be company for each other. Both are Jewish, after all. We already have one female encumbrance, so another is not going to make so much difference."

Varro smiled to himself. "That would give you an excuse to visit Miriam," he said, "to look into the child's welfare. I know that Miriam has caught your eye, my friend." An astute person would have picked up a hint of jealousy in the questor's voice.

"No more than you, Julius." Martius was sounding exasperated. "Look, you force me to admit it — the girl reminds me of my little sister. No man showed Domitilla any compassion; the swine slit her throat. It is the least I can do to help the girl. There, you have it. Does that satisfy you, questor?"

Varro suddenly felt foolish. "I'm sorry, Marcus. It was insensitive of me. Very well, I may possibly live to regret this, but, yes, she can join the party. As you say, she can travel with the slave Miriam." Summoning Callidus,

Varro gave the freedman instructions to make the necessary arrangements. But instead of hurrying off to carry out his instructions Callidus lingered in the doorway, as if wanting to say something.

Varro saw his freedman's expression. "What troubles you, Callidus?"

"Troubles me, my lord?" Callidus responded. "Well, to be truthful, something that troubles me considerably. You may have had much too much on your plate to have noticed it for yourself, but while we have been in Caesarea, Gaius Venerius and Antiochus have been spending a considerable amount of time in each other's company. I worry that they may involve themselves in some sort of mischief together."

"Is that so?" By his tone, the questor did not seem overly bothered.

"They do make the most surprising bedfellows, my lord — a Jew who has sworn off his faith, and a young knight who has not hidden his dislike for the Jews."

"Dung will always attract insects," Martius remarked.

"Quite so, my lord, but…"

"I cannot see Venerius becoming too intimate with Antiochus," said Varro. "The boy dislikes anyone he does not consider his equal. Fear not, faithful Callidus, once we are on the march again, the thin-striper will be far too occupied to cause trouble."

"I hope you are right, my lord. I raise this concern because, before we left Antioch, I had occasion to consult a seer of considerable perspicacity. She warned that there would be danger on this enterprise. Danger from within."

"We always knew this expedition would have its dangers, Callidus," Varro responded with an impatient scowl. He knew Callidus as a meddler by nature. "Thank you for your concern. Now, the arrangements concerning the child, if you please."

Callidus fought down a sudden wave of resentment at having his concern dismissed so lightly. "Very good, my lord," he sourly returned, before hurrying away.

✠

Procurator Rufus strode into the room followed by an entourage of freedmen assistants. He had sent word that he wished a meeting with Varro as a matter of urgency. "Cousin, we have not seen enough of each other since your arrival in Caesarea," he declared with the most convivial air.

"We both have much to occupy us, Rufus," Varro replied. "As you can see."

Varro reclined on a divan, Pythagoras sat at a table writing, with Artimedes at his elbow, while Martius was pacing back and forth, in mid flow as he dictated all he could remember of his exchange with Ishmael in the arcade beneath the city amphitheater.

"I was wondering, cousin," Rufus began again, "when did you have a mind to be moving on from Caesarea? You must have much to do, many places to visit outside the capital. If it were me, I would not waste any time before I went up to Jerusalem."

"There is nothing there, Rufus," said Marcus Martius. "The place is leveled."

"As well I know," said the procurator with his 'Turnus' smile. "However, General Bassus is at Jerusalem, with three thousand Jewish prisoners. There may be some among the prisoners who could provide the questor with information." From Decurion Alienus, Rufus had learned that the questor was asking questions about the death of a Jew at Jerusalem four decades earlier. "What you would not know, is that Bassus is planning to soon leave Jerusalem and take the 10th Legion campaigning against the last rebel strongholds in the south, and I gather he will be taking the prisoners with him to maintain his lines of supply. I would not tarry before I went up there, Varro. You will miss him."

"Thank you for your advice, Rufus," Varro returned.

"Pleased to be of help, cousin. Any time." Wearing a wicked smile, the diminutive procurator strutted from the room; his silent retinue trotted along behind.

"The little worm wants you out of his hair, Julius," said Martius.

"I know. Yet, if what he says about Bassus is true, we should not waste any more time here. Once the festival is out of the way tomorrow we shall move on to Jerusalem."

✠

In the dead of night the questor sat up in his bed, in a cold sweat. "Not again," he groaned to himself. Hostilis had heard his master cry out in his sleep, and appeared in the doorway with a lamp. After satisfying himself that the questor was safe and well, he took it on himself to summon Callidus and Artimedes.

"Another dream, questor?" said Artimedes when he and Callidus arrived. "I did say there may be a series of them. Clearly, you are being given messages by greater powers than ourselves. Shall I send for Pythagoras to assist in the divination?"

"No, that will not be necessary," Varro responded with a yawn.

This pleased Artimedes. "Then, perhaps you would be good enough to relate the details to myself," he said, assuming the air of an authority.

"Oh, very well," Varro wearily agreed. He had too much respect for his former tutor — and even a little residual childhood fear of him — to refuse.

As the two freedmen stood at his bedside, Varro sat and described as much of this latest dream as he could recall. It had not been a complicated dream. He had seen a finely decorated chariot, drawn by high spirited horses, and driven by a figure in black. Then, watching the chariot, he had seen a group of anonymous people, all clad in black as if they were mourners at a funeral.

"That was all the dream contained?" Artimedes then said, sounding disappointed.

"The decorated chariot could mean that you can one day look forward to celebrating a Triumph, my lord," the always literal Callidus suggested.

"There were only two horses, Callidus," Varro replied. "Not four. It was not a triumphal *quadriga*."

"What number of mourners, my lord?" Artimedes asked.

"Four, I think. Perhaps five. Four or five. They were very indistinct."

"Hmmm." Artimedes began pacing the room with his hands clasped behind his back. "I cannot discern a clear connection with your earlier dream. We must treat this as a separate case, I think. Now, to dream of falling from a chariot, or to see others falling from a chariot, this denotes a displacement from a position of authority."

"No one fell from the chariot," Varro assured him.

"Were you the driver of the chariot? Or were you a passenger in the chariot?"

"Neither."

"A pity. This foretells favorable opportunities, if used to the good. The mourners, then. To dream of going in mourning clothes to a funeral denotes the loss of a husband or wife. Clearly, as you are not married, that does not apply. To witness a funeral denotes an unhappy marriage or sickly offspring. Again, that is not applicable. To dream of a funeral of a stranger, this warns of unexpected woes."

"I cannot be sure that it was a funeral, Artimedes," the questor sighed.

"The horses, then. The horses offer some promise. Many, many things can be divined concerning horses in dreams. Horses seen drawing a conveyance generally denote wealth, although with some encumbrance. What color were the horses? This is important, questor. Were they black, or gray, or white, or spotted, or dappled…"

"I cannot remember, Artimedes," said Varro, his patience running thin. "I honestly do not think the color of the horses is significant. Perhaps I merely dreamed of a chariot because of the chariot races tomorrow, and perhaps the spectators were dressed in black because… Oh, I don't know! Let us pass it off for now. Go back to your beds."

"Chariot races, mourners," mused Artimedes. "Perhaps death awaits you at the hippodrome tomorrow, my lord." The questor was duty bound to attend the festival races.

Varro looked up at him, in two minds. One half told him to dismiss his dream as nothing more than a fantasy. The other half told him to take heed of the dream, to treat it as a genuine premonition, as he knew his mother would.

"You will remember what happened to Gaius Julius Caesar after he ignored the warnings of a seer, questor," Artimedes pressed. "It would be advisable to stay some distance from the hippodrome tomorrow."

Varro looked to Artimedes, in two minds.

"Aristotle once said that we cannot credit what sometimes can be divined from our dreams, questor," the secretary said. "There was no man more learned than he."

"Very well, very well," the questor exclaimed, throwing his hands in the air. "I shall not go to the hippodrome tomorrow. There, does that satisfy you?"

"What will you tell the procurator, my lord?" Callidus asked.

"Tell him… Tell him…" Varro swung his feet from the bed. "Tell him that the questor's column marches tomorrow. He recommended that I make haste to find Bassus and his prisoners, and so that is what I shall do."

"Tomorrow, my lord?" Callidus looked and sounded appalled. "The provision situation! With the holiday, it will take time to secure supplies, considerable time…"

"Then begin your preparations now," Varro instructed, coming to his feet. "Alert the officers. Work through the night. I want to be marching out of this city by no later than the beginning of the fourth hour tomorrow."

Callidus looked bemused. "How many days' rations, my lord?"

"Enough rations for fourteen days. And Philippus the Evangelist is to travel with us; he is too valuable a source of information about the Nazarene's activities to let slip from our grasp just yet. Philippus may yet solve a mystery or two for me." He looked at Callidus, scowling. "Well, what are you waiting for, man? We march for Jerusalem!"

XV

THE BROKEN ROAD

Roman Province of Judea. April, A.D. 71

According to his guide, Decurion Alienus, the questor would make far better time if, rather than take the inland route, he followed the coastal road down the Maritime Plain beside the Mediterranean to the town of Joppa, and then swung inland ten miles to Lydda. At Lydda, another road winding east up into the Judean Hills would lead the questor to Jerusalem. Originally a Jewish town, Lydda had been burned to the ground by General Gallus during the first year of the Jewish Revolt. Since then, it had been partly rebuilt by non Jewish settlers.

At Lydda, the column met a squadron of Thracian Horse cavalry coming down from Jerusalem, escorting dispatches from General Bassus bound for Rome. The squadron was led by Decurion Alaus Scevola, a big-nosed Gaul. Joining the questor at his Lydda camp for dinner, Scevola informed Varro that Bassus was departing Jerusalem for southern Judea just as he and his troopers were setting off on their journey. When Varro asked whether Bassus had taken all his Jewish prisoners with him, Scevola said he had; the general was planning to put the prisoners to work hauling his water. There was very little fresh water up there in the hills, said the decurion. South of Jerusalem in particular, the province was as dry as dust. Scevola urged Varro to take along plenty of water for his expedition, and to gather firewood for his cooking fires before he climbed up into the desolate hills. Much of the south was a wasteland, he said, but even around Jerusalem there was not a tree for miles, for Titus had cut down every single tree the previous year to use as firewood and building material during the siege. Jerusalem itself was an inhospitable place, said Scevola with distaste, and he was glad to be leaving it behind. The very ground there, he said, smelled of death.

Scevola and his troopers passed on, but not before the decurion told the questor about an old Jewish rabbi living at Jamnia, twenty miles down the coast. The Jew had been permitted by Titus to leave Jerusalem during the siege and travel to Jamnia with a handful of religious students. According to an amused Scevola, to escape the clutches of the Jewish partisans holding Jerusalem, who would not let non combatants leave the city, the rabbi had arranged to be carried out in a coffin, as if to his funeral, with his students as pall bearers, and then gave himself up to Titus. Titus had subsequently permitted the rabbi to set up a Jewish academy of religious instruction at Jamnia.

It occurred to Varro that the rabbi may have been at Jerusalem in his youth, during the last days of the Nazarene, and this warranted an interview. At dawn, he sent Crispus and his entire cavalry contingent down the highway to Jamnia, to bring the rabbi back for questioning at Lydda. While he waited for Crispus to return, Varro had his men multiply the expedition's water supplies and cut and load firewood. Riding hard, Crispus should have achieved the round trip to Jamnia and back that same day, but it was not until the early hours of the following morning that horsemen dismounted at the camp's *pretorian* gate then helped an elderly man down from a spare horse. Varro was awoken by Centurion Gallo with the news that Crispus was back.

Crispus reported that he had brought an old Jew who identified himself as Johannon ben Zakkai, a 'teacher of the Law.' The rabbi, Crispus informed his leader, had refused to leave Jamnia at first, and Crispus had spent several fruitless hours trying to talk the Jew into coming with him. It had taken his one-eyed decurion Pompeius to lose patience with his prefect's civil approach and threaten to crucify one of Johannon's students before the rabbi had agreed to budge. Varro told Crispus to bring the Jew to him.

A fragile-looking man, tall but very thin, bald with a gray beard, was ushered into the *pretorium*. Varro estimated that the man was perhaps in his seventies. Sitting on a couch, the yawning questor offered the Jew a stool, but a severe-faced Johannon shook his head, choosing to remain standing. "Were you present at Jerusalem some years ago when a man known as Jesus of Nazareth was crucified?" Varro then began.

"I am a teacher of the Law," Johannon testily replied. "As approved by General Titus Vespasianus, I study my peoples' Law and I instruct my students in the Law, at a house of learning at Jamnia, the *Beth Hamidrash*. This is all that interests me."

"Yes, but were you present in Jerusalem forty-one years ago? That is not a difficult question to answer, Johannon."

"It is not of interest to me."

"It *is* of interest to *me*," Varro came back, tired and irritated. He pulled himself to his feet, and began to walk around the rabbi. "Prior to the Revolt, had you always lived at Jerusalem? It is a simple enough question. Yes, or no?"

"Yes."

"Good. We are making progress, teacher. Have you heard of a Jewish teacher by the name of Jesus, or Yehoshua, a native of Nazareth in Galilee? Yes, or no?"

When the man again replied in the affirmative, Varro asked if he had been present in Jerusalem when the Nazarene was crucified?

"Many trouble-makers were crucified, in those times and later. I could not tell you where I was when any of them were executed. This Nazarene was a trouble-maker. I am not interested in trouble-makers."

"You are aware that his followers claim he was your Messiah?"

"He was not the Messiah," Johannon answered definitely.

"How do you view the followers of this Nazarene, teacher?"

"They are not of the true faith. They do not observe the Law."

Despite further questioning, this was as much as Varro could extract from the rabbi. Johannon dismissed the Nazarene and his followers as irrelevant, and had no information to offer. That was that. After an unproductive hour, Varro gave orders for the Jew to be taken back to his academy, his students, and his Law.

Crispus and his troopers set off to return Johannon to Jamnia. Varro was impatient to overtake General Bassus and considered commencing the march up into the Judean Hills before his cavalry rejoined him, but, counseled by Martius to be cautious, he thought better of the idea. Scevola had warned that isolated partisan bands may still be in the hills. With mounted troops his most effective weapon against Jewish fire and fly tactics, Varro realized that going up into the high country without his Vettonians was like crossing the sea in a boat without a sail. He paused at Lydda another day.

✠

The column crawled along the snaking, inclining road with grunts of exertion from the men on foot and the animated cries of muleteers driving their beasts of burden. Now that they had left the lushness of the plain behind, it was as if they had entered another barren world. The sun reflected harshly from white Judean rock, forcing the men to keep their eyes lowered. Clouds of choking yellow-white dust thrown up by the column filled the air and coated men, animals, carts and equipment. The troops pulled their red neck-scarves up over their mouths, wiped the grit from their eyes, and toiled on.

Varro had hoped to camp this next night at the hill town of Emmaus, a seemingly easy march of twelve to thirteen miles from Lydda, but it had been well into the morning before the column had struck camp at Lydda. Now, the weariness of the cavalry's mounts and the general slowness of the climb into the hill country made Varro's goal seem even less achievable. When the sun was almost directly overhead Varro submitted to the inevitability of not reaching the town that day and sent a message up to the advance guard ordering Venerius to mark out a site at the roadside for that night's camp. As the messenger galloped away, the questor eased his horse to the side of the road, to watch the column struggle by and satisfy himself that men, animals and vehicles were in good order. The mounted members of his entourage followed suit. The infantry slogged past, their equipment swinging and clattering on the poles over their shoulders. The men were perspiring profusely, their rolling sweat cutting little rivers through the pancake of dust on their faces. But their step did not falter; their iron legs drove them on.

The baggage train came abreast of the questor. First the strings of mules passed him, then the carts rolled by, one at a time. The very last cart was open. The front was filled with upright sacks of grain. In the back sat Philippus the Evangelist. There was a manacle on his left wrist, and a chain ran from this to a rail on the side of the cart. Dust-covered and downcast, Philippus did not look at the questor or his party as his conveyance trundled past.

Varro waited until the exhausted troopers of the rearguard were almost on him then urged his horse forward. In single file, the questor and the riders with him slipped along beside the column, heading back to their usual position in the order of march. Varro swiveled in his saddle as he rode, to look back down the column. At that moment, Antiochus, next to last in the line of riders but for Columbus, was passing the rearmost cart of the baggage train. Unaware that the questor was watching him, Antiochus leaned over and spat on the head of Philippus as he passed. Without a word, the Evangelist wiped the spittle away with one hand. Antiochus looked up. Seeing Varro's critical gaze locked on him, he quickly dropped his own eyes to his horse. Unhappily shaking his head to himself, the questor returned his attention to the road ahead.

✠

Titus Gallo's eyes suddenly opened. Something had woken him as he lay in his bedroll. It was as black as pitch inside his tent; the night was without a moon. Gallo collected his thoughts. He was in the Varro camp on the road from Lydda, and he had been dreaming. His dream was still painfully fresh in his mind. He had been fighting the Jews again, on this same road, five years before. General Cestius Gallus had led his army back down the road, retreating from Jerusalem toward the coast. There was a village called Beth-horon, not far from Emmaus, and Gallo and his 12th Legion comrades had fought their way to it. The Jews had attacked them at the front and rear of their long straggling column of twenty-seven thousand men, and all along the flanks. The partisans had focused on the 12th's 1st Cohort, going after the legion's sacred golden eagle standard, eventually wresting it from its dying standard-bearer. The legion's shame at that loss still wounded Gallo. He had been farther along the column in the 8th Cohort, but he had seen the eagle go, had seen legion commander and hundreds of 1st Cohort men fall.

The partisans had surrounded the Roman force at Beth-horon. That night General Gallus had called for four hundred volunteers to fight a rearguard action. Gallo had immediately stepped forward, but Gallus' junior tribunes held the centurion's military record, and they pointed out that Gallo had been demoted after Petus' disastrous capitulation at Rhandeia in Armenia years before. The general had sent Gallo back to his tent. To the centurion, this lasting shame, of being overlooked, had been like a wound to the heart. It had not mattered to Centurion Gallo that the four hundred volunteers chosen by the general never survived. Those men bravely sacrificed their lives giving the rest of General Gallus' army enough time to escape to Lydda. Gallo would have gladly died to win the glory of such a sacrifice, to have put the shine back on his tarnished reputation.

Lying in his bed now, Gallo was revisited by the humiliation of Beth-horon. For years he had suppressed the memories. Now, just miles from the scene of his shaming, it was all he could do to prevent himself from screaming with rage. Gallo made a pact with himself as he lay there in the dark. Never again would he allow a commander to humiliate him the way that General Petus had at Rhandeia, the way General Gallus had at Beth-horon. He did not care who his commander was. If Questor Varro were to put him in a position where humiliation threatened, Gallo would not stand for it. He would allow no one to put him through that again. Every man has his limit. Gallo had reached his.

As he lay there now, the ground beneath the centurion began to move. It was a sideways movement, as if some prankster was beneath his bed. Again the earth moved, more violently this time. In the corner, Gallo's upright shield fell to the tent floor with a woody bang. From outside the tent, there came the sound of yelling voices.

"Earthquake!" someone bawled in terror as they ran past the centurion's tent.

Gallo threw back his blanket and jumped to his feet. Parting the tent flap, he stepped outside. In the light of lamps in the streets he could see that the camp was in uproar. In Gallo's experience there was no man braver that a Roman legionary, and none more superstitious. The legionary feared little that roamed the surface of the earth, but powers above and below it were a different matter. Again the ground moved beneath Gallo's feet. From the corral came the neighing of frightened horses. Then, from somewhere behind the centurion, came the sound of something crashing to earth; one of the temporary wooden guard towers at the camp's *pretorian* gate had come down.

A young legionary without a stitch of clothes on and wide-eyed with terror ran past the centurion. Gallo grabbed him by the hair and pulled him to a halt. "Where in the name of Hades do you think you are going, soldier, naked as the day you were born?"

"Earthquake, centurion!" the man bellowed. "Earthquake!"

"It will pass. Go back to your tent. Put on your tunic and your equipment. Then report with your squad to the tribunal. Now, soldier!"

The youth was suddenly more afraid of the officer than he was of anything else. Besides, the earth had ceased to move. "Yes, centurion." He ran off.

Gallo strode toward the questor's *pretorium,* close by. In front of the tribunes' tents there was a dais formed from sections of turf laid one on top of the other. This was the camp tribunal, the focus of morning parade. Gallo hoped that his men had enough presence of mind to remember their training, that in an emergency they should assemble in front of the tribunal. When he arrived at the earthen platform, he found Tribune Martius there ahead of him.

"Soldiers! There is no need to panic!" Martius calmly called. "This was merely an earth tremor. Fall in by squad. Soldiers, listen to me. Fall in!"

Men were milling in front of him, most in just their tunics, all highly agitated.

"The gods of the underworld are not happy with us!" one man called.

"Pluto is punishing us!" cried another.

"Why would Pluto be punishing you, soldier?" Martius responded.

"For going to Jerusalem, tribune," came the reply.

"We are being warned not to go to Jerusalem," said another.

"The place is stained with the blood of Roman soldiers," someone else called.

"Might not the gods simply be reminding us of their power?" said Martius.

"How so, tribune?" a soldier came back.

"Think about it. It was not so long ago that the Jews celebrated their Passover Festival at Jerusalem at this time of year, flocking to their Temple from around the world to pay homage to their lone god. Yet now, there is no Temple. Why? Because the soldiers of Rome razed it to the ground."

"He's right," came a rank and file voice. "The legions destroyed Jerusalem."

"Where do they celebrate their Passover now?" said another, with mirth in his voice, catching the sudden change of mood.

"In Hades!" someone said, bringing a chorus of laughter.

"The gods are not warning us away from Jerusalem, tribune?" called a doubter.

"The gods were only reminding you that the soldiers of Rome have destroyed the heathen Temple and changed the lives of the Jews forever," Martius responded. "Believe me, you men can march into Jerusalem without fear, and proud to be legionaries of Rome, the finest soldiers that the world has ever seen! You are the rulers of the world!"

This brought a boisterous, resounding cheer from the soldiers.

"You heard the tribune," said Gallo, now striding into their midst. "Fall in!"

Without further comment the men began to file into their infantry squads and cavalry troops and form up in neat formation, as others hurried from throughout the camp to do the same. While Martius had been marshalling the men, Varro had emerged from his tent, and as his staff joined him he had listened with an approving smile to the way the tribune had handled the situation. Now Martius saw him, and yielded the tribunal.

As Varro went to step up, Callidus slid in beside him. "Could it be that it was Pluto you saw in your dream, my lord?" he asked. "In his chariot. To my mind there is a considerable possibility that you were being forewarned of tonight's events."

"Possibly so, Callidus," Varro replied. In reality, the figure in his dream looked nothing like the image of Pluto with which all Romans were familiar, and the horses drawing the chariot in the dream had not been winged like Pluto's steeds. Varro had by this time come to the conclusion that his dreams had a life of their own and did not warrant either explanation or divination. He climbed up onto the tribunal. "By the end of this watch I want full and accurate reports concerning the injuries and damage caused by the earth tremors," he announced to the assembled troops. "Now that we are all awake, we shall remain on our feet and make all necessary repairs. I want to be able to march at dawn. If there is another tremor in the meantime, I expect you all to act like the soldiers you are. Centurion Gallo, you may dismiss the men."

✠

Varro stood looking at the crevice which cut across the road at an angle. To continue east, to reach Jerusalem, the column had to cross this divide.

With daylight, the column had begun to move again, none the worse for wear after the earth tremors. Two men had been injured when the guard tower came down. Until they recovered, they would ride in a cart. All other personnel were fit and well, including Miriam and Gemara — as Varro had been quick to ascertain during the night.

Now, just ten minutes march from the camp site, the column was stationary, as Varro and his officers and officials studied the gap which the tremors had opened up in their path, at a point where the road had been carved from the side of a slope, with an almost sheer drop, a hundred feet or more, to the valley below. Small crevices had also opened in the roadway, but the largest posed the problem. The fissure was five feet wide at its narrowest, ten at its broadest. A man and a galloping horse might hurdle the gap, but pack animals and baggage carts were a different matter.

"Bridge the gap," Varro ordered.

Timber carried on the carts for temporary camp gates and towers was quickly recycled, and within an hour a narrow bridge spanned the gap in the road. The infantry crossed with ease. Some pack mules were nervous, and they unsettled their companions, so the mules were left to last, to be taken across singly. The carts were dragged over the bridge, unhitched from their mules and manhandled by teams of legionaries while Varro and his mounted companions watched from the western side of the gap.

As the first of the mules were being led across, blindfolded, there was a sudden cry of alarm from behind the questor. Varro turned, to see muleteers and slaves rushing to the edge of the road and looking over the precipice, down into the ravine below.

"The slave girl, and the child," someone called. "They have gone over the side!"

With pounding heart, Varro rapidly dismounted and pushed through the throng at the edge of the road.

"I am leading up their mule, my lord," a white-faced Syrian mule driver hurried to explain. "Before I can stop it, the stupid animal goes and put its foot in one of the holes in the road. It topples over. I hear its leg crack. It goes over the side, and it takes the two females with it. Just like that! There was nothing I could do to prevent it, my lord! It was not my fault. I swear to Baal…!"

Dreading what he would discover, Varro looked over the side of the precipice. Then he saw Miriam and Gemara. They had landed on a ledge some fifteen feet down the slope. The mule they had been sharing had not been so lucky. It had bounced from the ledge and fallen all the way to the bottom of the hundred foot drop. Its shattered body lay on the rocks below.

"Are you hurt?" Varro called down to the pair on the ledge. As he spoke, Martius appeared beside him.

Miriam had picked herself up and dusted down her simple white belted gown. Her headpiece and veil had gone the way of the mule. Her silky black hair cascading over her shoulders swayed as she shook her head in answer. Again Varro was taken by her beauty. Pulling Gemara to her, she looked dazedly up at the faces peering over the edge of the roadway at the pair.

"Any bones broken?" Martius called, echoing Varro's concern.

Again Miriam shook her head.

"Neither of them appear to be injured," said Varro, "just shaken."

"Leave them there," came a voice from behind Varro.

The questor recognized the voice, and swung to see Antiochus sitting on his horse among a group of riders behind the anxious crowd. "What did you say?" Varro called.

"Tell them to ask their God to save them," said Antiochus.

This brought a cackle of laughter from Venerius, mounted close by.

"Get down!" Gallo ordered, striving to rein in his anger. "You too, Venerius! Get down, the pair of you. You can help retrieve the females."

Venerius' smile disappeared, and he quickly dismounted, but Antiochus did not move, just remained in his saddle, glaring at Varro. The questor glared back.

"I would not put *my* life in the hands of either Antiochus or Venerius," Martius growled. "I will go down after the females."

"Very well," Varro conceded.

The tribune called for Centurion Gallo and gave orders for a length of strong rope to be brought from the baggage train. When the rope arrived, Martius tied it around the two front horns of the saddle on Gallo's horse. He tied the other end around his waist. With Gallo in charge of the horse, the tribune went over the side of the precipice. As the centurion carefully eased the horse back a step at a time, reassuring it with pats and a soft voice, Martius was lowered to the ledge. There, he removed the rope from his waist and tied it around Gemara. Then, with Varro telling Gallo when to start easing his horse forward and when to stop, the child was hauled back up the road.

A cheer rose up from the soldiers and civilians lining the edge of the road. Varro realized that all other work had ceased while everyone watched the rescue operation, and he now ordered Crispus to supervise the resumption of movement across the bridge. Then he sent the rope back down to the ledge, where Martius and Miriam stood side by side. Miriam was brought up next, and finally Martius was hauled up. Varro then called on Diocles to examine the females for injuries. The doctor dismounted and briefly examined Miriam and Gemara, pronouncing them uninjured but for grazes and bruises, for which his assistants ran to fetch ointments on the questor's instructions.

After ordering the non-combatants to take their turns crossing the bridge, Varro looked to the waiting horsemen. "I told you before, Antiochus," he called. "Get down!"

Antiochus did not reply. He folded his arms. Tired of taking orders from Julius Varro, and having worked to establish cordial relations with the junior tribune Venerius, nephew of the all powerful Mucianus, as Callidus had warned his master, Antiochus had been preparing for this confrontation.

"Get down now!" Varro ordered. "Give up your horse to the women."

"Have you taken leave of your senses?" Antiochus retorted. "Put them on another mule, or a spare cavalry horse. General Collega and Licinius Mucianus…"

"Neither General Collega nor Licinius Mucianus commands here," Varro resolutely came back. "I do! Give up your horse, Antiochus."

"You are talking about a slave. Have you forgotten that I am a magistrate?"

"Get down, *magistrate,* and give up your animal."

Antiochus continued to ignore his order.

"I will not tell you again!" Varro barked.

"I will write in the most censorious terms to General Collega, to Licinius…"

"Get down!" boomed a deep, dark voice, the voice of Columbus, Antiochus' massive Numidian guardian. His role had been to be unobtrusive but alert, and now, sitting on a large horse behind the Jewish magistrate, he edged closer. "You heard the questor. Get down now, or I will knock you down!"

Antiochus looked at the former gladiator, and realized that he meant every word. Fuming, the Jew slowly swung one leg over the horn of his saddle, then slipped to the ground. Columbus also dismounted, and took the reins of Antiochus' steed.

Varro turned to Miriam. "The horse is yours," he said.

"I don't want his horse," she replied.

Varro did not care what she wanted. "Columbus, put her up, and the child."

Columbus wrapped one gigantic arm around the girl. As he lifted her off her feet, Pedius the lictor, who had been caring for Gemara since her rescue, stepped up and helped the Numidian place Miriam in the saddle. Between them, the pair then lifted up little Gemara and set her on the back of the horse behind Miriam.

"Now what am I supposed to ride?" Antiochus whined.

"For your insubordination, you should walk."

"Walk! Me?"

"Callidus, bring a mule for the Jewish magistrate." The questor strode to his horse, and the waiting Hostilis boosted him up into the saddle. "Now, all of you," Varro called, "attend to the business at hand. Too much time has already been wasted."

XVI

THE TESTIMONY OF THE SCRIBE OF EMMAUS

Emmaus, Roman Province of Judea. April, A.D. 71

The flaccid Greek, an apprehensive, balding man, entered the tent and stood at the open end of the table in front of the questor and three of his officers. Aged in his sixties, he was pudgy and pale. There was a prominent and disfiguring brown mole the size of a sesterce coin on his right cheek. The Varro expedition had camped an Emmaus, which Titus had established as a colony for soldiers of the 15th Apollinaris Legion, veterans of the Jewish Revolt who had gone into retirement following the siege of Jerusalem.

"You are not a former soldier," Varro said, looking the man up and down. The questor had stood before an assembly of 15th Legion veterans that morning and called on any man who had information about the death of Jesus of Nazareth forty-one years before to seek him out. This pasty-faced specimen did not have the look of a former legionary.

"No, my lord," said the man apologetically. "My name is Aristarchus. I am a freedman. By profession, a scribe." The Greek spoke rapidly, in short, nervous bursts. As he did, his eyes roved over the lounging officers, and then moved to the two secretaries waiting at a table with moist wax and glittering stylus at the ready.

"You are a resident of Emmaus, Aristarchus?" Varro asked.

"I am, my lord, having only recently settled here. I serve the veterans. I write their wills and their letters, and certify their bills of sale. Previously, I was at Caesarea."

"You have information for me?"

"I do, my lord. I heard that you sought information. In relation to a Jew. A Jesus of Nazareth. About his execution, during the tenure of Pontius Pilatus."

"You are looking for a reward, fellow?" Marcus Martius asked suspiciously.

Aristarchus shrugged. "A hardworking tradesman would never say no to a little coin in hand, my lord. However, if the questor were to make it known, among the veterans of the 15th, that Aristarchus the scribe had been of service to him... The questor's endorsement would be of inestimable value."

"You shall have your endorsement, and cash in hand besides, if your information proves of value," Varro assured him. He sounded impatient; the questor could not imagine what information a Greek scribe might have that would be helpful to his investigation. "What is your connection with Jesus of Nazareth, if any?"

"Forty-one years ago, I was a slave. In the service of Pontius Pilatus when he was Prefect of Judea." The questor and his associates were suddenly all ears. "At the time of the execution of this Jesus of Nazareth, I was with Prefect Pilatus at Jerusalem."

Martius looked at Varro, smiling. "We have to be lucky occasionally, do we not?"

Varro immediately recognized the man's potential value. "In what capacity were you with Pilatus at Jerusalem at that time?" he asked.

"As an under secretary, my lord. Pilatus brought me out from Rome with him. Diamedes was his chief secretary. However, at the time that Pilatus went up to Jerusalem for the Passover Festival during which this Jesus fellow was executed, Diamedes was ill at Caesarea. I served as the prefect's secretary during that particular visit to Jerusalem."

"The secretary Diamedes was ill?" Varro mused. He remembered that Philippus had claimed to have also been prevented by illness from going up to Jerusalem for the Passover in question. "Was there much sickness in Caesarea at that time?"

"Quite a wave of sickness, my lord. People died. Such an epidemic in the low-lying areas is not uncommon following the winter. It was much healthier in the hills."

"Tell me about that visit to Jerusalem at the time of the Passover Festival."

Aristarchus said that he had gone to Jerusalem that year in a party which comprised the prefect, his wife, his household, and several cohorts of the 12th Legion. Pilatus always took reinforcements up to Jerusalem for the Passover. Many Jewish pilgrims went to the city for the festival each year, as many as a million in some years, he estimated. Some, he said, came from as far away as Parthia.

"What do you know of the circumstances surrounding the execution of Jesus of Nazareth?" Varro asked, as he noted the two secretaries dutifully recording proceedings.

"I was present, in the Judgment Hall at Jerusalem, my lord, when Pilatus heard charges against four Jews accused of sedition, in the days leading up to the Passover Festival." Without prompting, Aristarchus then explained that the Roman Judgment Hall at Jerusalem was at that time located in the Antonia Fortress, beside the Jewish Temple. This hall was called 'the Pavement' by the Jews. They had their own Judgment Hall within the Temple complex itself, where they judged matters relating to religious law.

"You said that four rebels were brought before Pilatus?"

"I did, my lord." The scribe testified that all four had been charged with sedition. All were Jews from Galilee. Roman cavalry had captured them under arms in Galilee, and they were brought to Jerusalem for trial before the Roman prefect. On the Thursday, they were found guilty and condemned to be executed next day.

"What of the fourth prisoner?"

Early on the Friday morning, Aristarchus explained, the fourth man had been brought before Pilatus. He was a Jew like the others, but he was no ordinary outlaw. He had been charged by the High Priest with blasphemy. This prisoner was said to be a holy man from Nazareth, the man known subsequently as Jesus of Nazareth. "He was charged under the name of Joshua bar Josephus," he said, looking over at Pythagoras. "Joshua bar Josephus," he repeated for the secretary's benefit.

"Joshua bar Josephus," Pythagoras repeated. "I have it."

Aristarchus continued. Shortly after sunrise, he said, during the first hour, the priests of the Great Sanhedrin had demanded an immediate hearing before the prefect. This was because their holy day would begin at sunset. The chief priests wanted to execute the prisoner at once. They had already found him guilty of transgressing Jewish Law by making blasphemous statements. Aristarchus later heard that the Nazarene had threatened to destroy the Jewish Temple, and then rebuild it again within three days.

"Some threat," Martius remarked with a smile.

"Some builder," young Venerius added.

It was also said that the prisoner claimed to be a descendant of Davidus, an ancient King of the Jews, Aristarchus went on, and that he had been sent by their God to reclaim this Davidus' crown as King of the Jews. He said that when the chief priests brought the prisoner before Prefect Pilatus all they wanted from him was a sanction of their sentence of death by stoning.

"The prefect refused the Great Sanhedrin's petition?" Varro asked.

Aristarchus nodded. The chief priests were sorely disappointed, he related. Pilatus would have none of their finding. He examined the priests' witnesses himself, and these men only contradicted each other. With the consequence that Pilatus dismissed the Sanhedrin's charges against Jesus. The priests were not at all pleased."

"Was another charge brought?" Varro asked. "That of bearing arms?"

Aristarchus said that had been the case, and two swords had been presented in evidence. He said that before that occurred, however, after the initial interview with the prisoner at the Judgment Hall, Pilatus sent Jesus to Herod Antipas, the Tetrarch of Galilee. Antipas was at Jerusalem for the Passover and staying at his own palace, a stone's throw from the Antonia Fortress. This was done partly as a matter of courtesy to Antipas, and partly because of a dream of the prefect's wife the night before.

"A dream?" Varro knew all about dreams.

Aristarchus revealed that the prefect's wife held great store in the predictive power of dreams, and the prefect always strove to respect his wife's wishes. Aristarchus then claimed that Pilatus had confided to him that, as he was leaving the Palace of Herod to attend the hearing at the Judgment Hall, his young wife had urged him not to condemn Jesus. Her dream had warned her against harming a holy man from Nazareth. Antipas had subsequently interviewed the Nazarene, then sent him back to Pilatus with a message to say that he found the man guilty of no crime. The chief priests had been incensed by this, and, soon after, the two swords had been produced by the Captain of the Temple Guard. Testimony was given that one of Jesus' accomplices had struck and wounded a member of the High

Priest's arresting party. The witness was heavily bandaged. He claimed that his ear had been sliced off by the blow. The Guard captain's testimony that the prisoner had been found in possession of the two swords had been confirmed by his officers.

"What did the Nazarene say in his defense?" Varro asked.

"Nothing. He spoke barely a word. He offered no testimony to contradict the priests, or the wounded man, or the officers of the Guard. Pilatus had no option. He had to declare the prisoner guilty of sedition. He was not altogether happy about it. I think his wife's likely reaction weighed heavily on his mind." But, said the scribe, the evidence had been clear, and as neither the prisoner nor anyone else could or would offer contradictory testimony, Pilatus had no choice but convict him. His wife was unhappy with him afterwards, so Aristarchus later heard. Yet the law had to be upheld. Pilatus sentenced the Nazarene to die that same day with the other condemned men. "I myself wrote the execution warrant, which I then took to the prefect, for him to affix his seal."

Varro, surprised, clarified the man's testimony: "You personally wrote the warrant for the execution of Jesus of Nazareth?"

"That I did, questor." The Greek didn't consider the fact of importance.

Varro called for Artimedes to produce the warrant found in the archives at Caesarea, and it was presented to Aristarchus. "Is that the warrant written by you?".

"This seal, the lion's head, this is Pilatus' seal, my lord," Aristarchus said at once, pointing to the yellow wax seal on the reverse bottom edge of the roll of parchment. "Let me consider the warrant itself." After studying the document at length, he said, "This is the warrant that I wrote. My writing has matured since then. It is however without doubt my penmanship. The certification at the bottom is by Longinus. He was the centurion in charge of the execution." He returned the warrant to Artimedes.

Instructed by Varro to continue with his testimony, the scribe said that the condemned man had then been taken into the assembly hall of the Antonia, stripped, and bound to a whipping post. The guard maniple was paraded to witness the punishment, and in front of the soldiers he was given thirty-nine powerful strokes with wooden rods, as the law prescribed. After personally witnessing this punishment being exacted, Aristarchus had returned to the Palace of Herod. He believed that the prisoner would then have been chained to a man of his escort in the usual manner, and, in the second hour, taken out of the city to be executed with the two other condemned men.

Varro frowned. "*Two* other condemned men? You testified that three other men had been sentenced to death. Explain."

All three of the other men had been prepared for execution, he said. They too had received beatings with rods. They were about to be led down the sixty steps from the Antonia to the street when a pardon was delivered for one of the men. "I know this because it was I who delivered the pardon into the hands of Centurion Longinus."

"Who was the pardoned man?"

"He was one Joshua bar Abbas, if I remember correctly, a leader of the rebel band of which the other two prisoners were members, the *Sicarii,* the Daggermen."

When asked why this Bar Abbas had been reprieved, Aristarchus answered that it was in accordance with an arrangement that Prefect Pilatus had come to with the Sanhedrin. Late during the first hour, he said, after the Nazarene had been handed over to Centurion Longinus, Pilatus had summoned him and instructed him to write a pardon in the name of Joshua bar Abbas, which he would endorse at once. The scribe had been careful to clarify that the pardon was for Joshua bar Abbas and not Joshua bar Josephus, then penned the document. Once he had added his seal, the prefect sent Aristarchus to the garrison commander with the pardon. The prisoner Bar Abbas was released into the custody of the Sanhedrin. The other three were taken out and executed.

"Did you witness the execution?"

"I did not, my lord."

Varro thought for a moment. "Are you aware that the Nazarene's followers claim he rose from the dead, following his crucifixion?"

"I have heard that said since, once or twice."

"What do you think of such a claim?"

"It is a nonsense, my lord." There was a positive ring to the Greek's voice.

"His body was delivered to the Nazarene's family for burial?"

"It was given over to the Jews, yes."

"How can you be sure that he was dead?" Marcus Martius called.

Aristarchus replied that he had absolutely no doubts in that regard. He went on to explain that he had been with the prefect that same afternoon, at the bathhouse in the Palace of Herod, in the west of the city. This palace was where the prefect and those who came up from Jerusalem with him stayed when visiting the city. After lunch, Pilatus had exercised by throwing javelins from the Palace wall, after which he had bathed. Aristarchus had been taking dictation from him while he was undergoing a massage at the bathhouse when a member of the Great Sanhedrin came to him. Pilatus was on good terms with this man, a Pharisee by the name of Josephus of Arimathea, who came from a village lying twenty miles from Emmaus. Josephus of Arimathea sought the prefect's permission to have Jesus of Nazareth's body taken down from his cross, reminding Pilatus that the Jews could not pollute their Sabbath with the dead. Josephus had assured the prefect that this particular prisoner, Jesus, was dead, and asked for permission to take the body down and inter it without delay.

"What was Pilatus' reaction to this?"

"He was surprised, my lord. Very surprised. As Your Lordship will be aware, it takes several days for a crucified man to die. That is the whole point of this form of punishment. To die within a matter of hours is unusual, and undesirable."

"Were you not suspicious that perhaps the Nazarene was not dead?"

"Like the prefect, I was surprised at Josephus' claim. Pilatus sent for Centurion Longinus, the officer in charge of the executions that day." Aristarchus said that Longinus soon arrived at the palace, which was quite close to the execution site. At that time, he remarked, it was possible to see the three men on their crosses from a palace balcony. Prefect Pilatus had asked Longinus whether the prisoner Jesus was dead. In answer, the centurion had confirmed that the man was indeed dead. "And one does not doubt the word of a Roman centurion," he added.

"Quite rightly," Martius remarked.

"Let us be clear," said Varro. "Pilatus accepted that the Nazarene was dead?"

This Aristarchus confirmed. He said that Centurion Longinus then informed the prefect that the other two condemned men were still alive. To hasten their deaths he sought permission to break their legs. This would prevent the crucified men from supporting their weight with their legs, and they would soon asphyxiate. Pilatus granted permission for the legs of these two to be broken, and for all three bodies to be brought down from their crosses.

"A physician was not present?" Varro asked. "No one with medical knowledge certified the deaths of the prisoners?"

Aristarchus replied that no physician had been present at the executions. That was not normal practice, he reminded his listeners, because the bodies of crucified men were usually left up on their crosses to rot. Had the crucifixion of Jesus of Nazareth taken place at any other time, his body would have been left on public display for at least a week. It was only because the execution was rushed through on the eve of the Passover Sabbath that his body could be taken down so soon after being put up, said the scribe.

Varro was nodding. From his readings of the Lucius Letter and the Marcus and Matthias documents it seemed likely that Jesus had come to Jerusalem in the week leading up to the Passover with the fixed intention of being crucified, and specifically on the day before the Sabbath. Jesus would have known that his body would be taken down before sunset on the Friday, to prevent the pollution of the Sabbath. When put up on his cross that morning, Jesus had known that he would only be left up there for six or seven hours. "Let us be sure about this, Aristarchus," the questor said, fixing his eyes on those of the witness, "as far as you were concerned there was absolutely no doubt in the prefect's mind that the Nazarene was dead when he was taken down from his cross?"

"None, my lord. Longinus informed the prefect that to ensure the man was truly dead he had stabbed him with a spear. This convinced Pilatus, and he gave permission for the body to be taken down, in the ninth hour, toward the tenth hour."

"So, two to three hours before sunset, the body was handed over to the Nazarene's family, allowing time enough for the body to be disposed of before day's end?"

The witness replied that the receivers of the body had not actually been the Nazarene's family. Josephus of Arimathea had told Pilatus he was providing his own tomb for the interment of the prisoner, a new tomb in the vicinity of the execution place, in a garden just to the northwest of the city.

"The Jews do not cremate their dead, like ourselves?" Varro queried.

"I understand that outside Jerusalem the Jews used to cremate their poor on a large communal pyre, my lord, a rubbish dump which burned perpetually. Those who can afford a family tomb are interred."

Varro had become suspicious. He heard King Agrippa's words in his mind. "The body was handed over to Josephus of Arimathea," he said. "What then?"

Aristarchus said that he could not testify to exactly what happened once the prefect gave Josephus permission to take charge of the body. No one seemed to know precisely what followed, and he was not an authority on Jewish burial customs.

This comment prompted Varro to instruct Callidus to fetch the expedition's expert on Jewish customs, Antiochus. As much as he disliked the man, his knowledge might be invaluable. When Antiochus arrived soon after, Varro directed him to a place on one of the couches and instructed him to listen carefully to the witness' testimony. In this interim Varro provided a stool for Aristarchus, and the Greek gratefully took a seat. The concession had the effect of putting the scribe more at his ease. Once Antiochus had sulkily taken his place, the questor resumed the questioning. "Scribe, we know that two days after the execution the Nazarene's body disappeared from its tomb. What was Prefect Pilatus' response to that?"

Aristarchus said that Pilatus was annoyed by this, particularly because the Sadducee members of the Great Sanhedrin created a great stir. They had asked Pilatus for men from the Roman garrison to guard the tomb against body snatchers, but Pilatus had told them to use their own Temple Guards, which they did. It came to light that someone bribed these sentinels to later say that they had fallen asleep, and this was when the body had been removed. The Sadducee members of the Sanhedrin then accused their fellow councilor Josephus of Arimathea of having been involved in a conspiracy to remove the body, and put Josephus in chains and lodged him in the Temple cells. He was released a day later, after the other Pharisees on the Sanhedrin had gone to Pilatus and protested.

"If I may make a comment, questor?" Antiochus spoke up.

Varro looked over at the Jewish magistrate. "If it is pertinent," he agreed.

"It occurs to me," Antiochus began, "that perhaps Pharisees on the Great Sanhedrin, led by Josephus of Arimathea, planned to wrest control of the council from the Sadducees by claiming that the Nazarene was the Messiah, proving that their philosophy was superior to that of the Sadducees. But this plan failed; the Sadducees continued to control the Great Sanhedrin right up to the time of the Revolt."

"The plan failed," said Martius, "because the Pharisees were unable to produce a walking, talking Nazarene following his execution."

"How could they?" commented young Venerius with a laugh. "If he was still alive, we would have arrested Jesus and nailed him up a second time, and we would have crucified the Pharisees into the bargain, for harboring an escaped criminal."

"Was Josephus of Arimathea acting alone," Varro pondered, "or was there a broad conspiracy?"

"If I may speak, questor?" said Pythagoras. "In relation to the documentary evidence relating to the man Josephus of Arimathea." When Varro assented, he went on: "To refresh your memory, the Marcus document identifies Josephus of Arimathea as a member of the Great Sanhedrin, and a Pharisee, one who was expectant of the appearance of the Messiah. The Lucius Letter goes a little further, stating that Josephus did not vote for the execution of the Nazarene when the Great Sanhedrin heard the accusation of blasphemy. The Matthias document describes Josephus of Arimathea as both a rich man and *one of the Nazarene's disciples*."

"He was one of the seventy?" Varro raised his eyebrows. "Then Josephus had to be a *secret* disciple. The chief priests would not knowingly have tolerated one of the Nazarene's elders on their council."

"The document indicates as much," Pythagoras remarked. "Whether Josephus of Arimathea was acting alone, or whether he represented or led a group of Pharisee conspirators, he was in a particularly influential position to orchestrate a secret plot. He had a foot in each of three camps. As a follower of the Nazarene, he was Jesus' spy in the Sanhedrin, being privy to the deliberations of the chief priests. He had the ear of the Roman prefect, and, as a rich man, Josephus of Arimathea could afford to offer substantial bribes to parties to a subterfuge."

"A number of rumors circulated to the affect that Josephus of Arimathea did bribe the centurion Longinus, my lord," Aristarchus volunteered.

Both Varro and Martius straightened.

"Bribed him to do what?" said Varro.

"Watch what you say, scribe," Martius cautioned. "You tread dangerous ground when you impugn the reputation of a Roman centurion."

"There were two principal rumors," Aristarchus cautiously advised. "One had it that Longinus had taken money from Josephus of Arimathea to hand the body over. The second rumor had Centurion Longinus accepting a bribe to make it look as though Jesus of Nazareth had died on the cross, without actually going through with the execution."

This revelation was met with a momentary stunned silence.

Martius was the first to speak. He was angry. "I will not have it! That Longinus might accept payment to hand over the body I can accept; that is not uncommon. But a criminal act on such a scale I find difficult, if not impossible, to accept."

"A man who can be bribed on one thing, tribune," Crispus chimed in, "can be bribed on all things."

Martius scowled at Crispus. "Longinus risked his own neck to fabricate the death of the Nazarene, for money?" he countered. "Could Longinus have been that foolish?"

"The centurion was arrogant," remarked young Venerius. "All centurions are arrogant. This one would deny any complicity and lay the blame at the feet of the Jews. Whose word would be taken? That of a Roman citizen and centurion, or that of a Jew?"

Martius, Crispus, and Venerius all began to talk at once.

As anarchy threatened, Varro clapped his hands to end the clamor. His colleagues fell silent. "This is not a rhetorician's classroom," Varro scolded them. "I am questioning a witness. Besides, at this point we have nothing but an unsubstantiated rumor." He returned the focus to Aristarchus. "Was any proof offered that such a plot existed?"

The scribe shook his head. "The rumor about a sham crucifixion did not circulate until later that same year, after Centurion Longinus was himself executed for desertion."

"See!" Venerius sneered in Martius' direction. "Your 'law abiding' centurion could desert, but could not be involved in a conspiratorial crime? I think not!"

"Hold your tongue, Venerius," Varro cautioned. "Go on, Aristarchus."

"The rumor had it that Josephus of Arimathea and Centurion Longinus had been complicit in a plot, and that Jesus of Nazareth was not dead when he was entombed."

"There would have been many witnesses to the crucifixion," said Varro, "none the least of whom would have been Sadducees from the Great Sanhedrin. There can be no doubt they wanted the Nazarene dead, as he was a threat to their power. Any hint of foul play would have attracted their attention, Aristarchus."

"If I might put a question to the witness, questor?" said Martius. "Aristarchus, for all we know, your colorful tales regarding this rumor and that rumor may be nothing but fictions. Is there anyone who could support your claims?"

Aristarchus thought for a time, then replied, "There was a Jewish apothecary at Jerusalem. According to one rumor, which I heard from several different sources, this apothecary was paid by Josephus of Arimathea to provide Centurion Longinus with a soporific drug which Longinus in turn administered to the Nazarene on the cross. This drug supposedly created the appearance of death. The apothecary could tell you himself."

"Why did you not tell us about this before?" Varro demanded.

"I was about to, my lord, but I was interrupted." Aristarchus cast his eyes to Martius, Crispus and Venerius, his interrupters.

Now that the subject of a drug had been raised, Varro regretted not calling Diocles the physician to be present for the questioning. He momentarily contemplated suspending the session again to summon the doctor, but decided against it rather than interrupt the flow of evidence. "Do you know what drug was supposedly employed?"

Aristarchus replied that he had only heard that the drug in question had the capacity to induce a deep sleep and slow the heartbeat, so that any person taking it had every appearance of being dead. He added that the drug had been mixed with vinegar to disguise it, and in that form it was given to Jesus to drink at the time of the execution.

"Name this apothecary," said Martius irritably.

"His name was Matthias," Aristarchus replied. "Matthias ben Naum."

Varro sat bold upright. "What name?"

"Matthias ben Naum," the Greek repeated.

Varro looked over to Artimedes. The secretary nodded. He too recognized the name of Naum as the same the questor had heard in his first dream. "Naum?"

"Yes, Matthias, the son of Naum," the witness replied, looking mystified.

Oblivious to Varro's new train of thought, and antagonistic toward the scribe for implicating a Roman centurion in a significant crime, the tribune fixed his gaze on Aristarchus. "I believe that the scribe has concocted all this nonsense, questor," he said accusingly. "If not for a reward, then to ingratiate himself. Or, is there another reason? Could it be that he is out

to slander Gaius Pontius Pilatus? Is that your game, Greek? You have held
a grudge against your former master all these years. You saw the questor's
visit as your opportunity to make Pilatus look a fool. What better way to
achieve that end than to create the impression that Pilatus was hoodwinked
by the Jews?"

Aristarchus looked appalled. "Not true, my lord," he said earnestly. "I
swear it!"

"You know the penalty for giving false evidence before a magistrate, do
you not?" said Martius in a low, threatening voice. "It is a capital offense,
scribe!"

"Every word I have uttered here today has been the truth, my lord,"
the Greek protested. "I harbor no grudge against Prefect Pilatus. Nothing
could be farther from the truth. I have every reason to be eternally grateful
to Pontius Pilatus. Before he returned to Rome, he set me free from the
bonds of slavery. I have my lord Pilatus to thank for my freedom. Surely,
there is no greater gift, no greater reason for gratitude."

His accusation demolished, Martius sat back, folding his arms.

"Tell me about the apothecary Naum," Varro resumed, now that his
deputy had flung his accusations, and missed the target. "Could he still be
alive?"

Aristarchus replied with a shrug that it might be possible; Naum may
have survived the Revolt, could be among the last prisoners being held by
General Bassus. He knew for a fact, he said, that Matthias ben Naum was
still practicing his art at Jerusalem just before the Revolt broke out. He had
seen him there, at his business premises on one of the streets of the Upper
City, advanced in years but apparently in good health.

"You could recognize him again if you saw him?"

"Oh, yes, my lord, I am certain of it."

Varro nodded slowly. "You have been most helpful. You shall have your
endorsement, and a cash reward besides. I will have one of my secretaries
pen a suitable testimonial. You can display it in your premises. Does that
meet with your approval?"

Aristarchus was beaming. "Indeed it does, my lord. Thank you, my
lord."

"There is, of course, the matter of your credentials. Before I can entertain
the matter of a reward, I will need confirmation of your identity."

"I have my manumission certificate, my lord, issued by Pontius Pilatus."

The scribe reached to the leather bag on his belt in which he normally carried a small wax tablet and stylus, like all members of his profession.

"Yes, you can show that to us," Varro responded, "but do you have any documentation to prove that you were the prefect's secretary at Jerusalem?"

"Well, no. That information would be available in the archives at Caesarea."

"Very well. One of my secretaries will return to Caesarea, to confirm that information." Varro looked over at Artimedes, who nodded to affirm that he understood.

"Very good, my lord," said Aristarchus with a continuing smile. "The secretary will have no trouble finding the necessary record."

"In the meantime, you will be placed in the custody of Centurion Gallo."

The smile dropped from the scribe's face. "I am a prisoner?"

"Not at all," Varro replied. "You shall be my guest, Aristarchus."

"I may retain my money?" Aristarchus' hand went to a bulging purse on his belt.

"Of course. Only prisoners are deprived of their possessions. I will ask you to remain with us only as long as it takes to ascertain whether Matthias ben Naum is among General Bassus' prisoners," Varro replied. "You did say you would recognize Ben Naum if you saw him again."

Aristarchus looked suddenly unwell. "Yes, my lord," he acknowledged.

"Then you will be able to pick him out from among Bassus' prisoners. We march in the footsteps of General Bassus and the 10th Legion."

"With free transport, food and lodging in the meantime," said Martius with a wink Varro's way, "courtesy of the questor."

As Callidus led the scribe from the tent, Varro and his officers came to their feet.

"Another stray dog joins our wandering band," young Venerius sneered. "All we need now is a snake charmer."

"A lying dog," said Martius, stretching. "You mark my words, questor, he may well have been Pilatus' secretary, but the scribe's slandering rumors are pure invention."

XVII

THE SCENE OF THE CRIME

Jerusalem, Roman Province of Judea. May, A.D. 71

Viewed from the Mount of Olives, the scene was one of serenity. There was little to advertise the fact that a famous city thousands of years old had once spread from the foot of the mountain. The giant Temple Mount was still to be seen, a rectangular, flat-topped man-made monolith flanked by walls of massive white Judean stone. Of the so-called Second Temple itself, a vast complex of buildings erected on the Temple Mount by Herod the Great where once an older structure built by King Solomon had stood, nothing remained. On a rise to the west stood a fortress built by the 10th Legion in the ruins of the Palace of Herod, around three ancient towers left standing by Titus. This legion fortress provided the only sign of life. Auxiliary light infantry were visible at sentry posts and moving along the walls. Their cloth standards fluttered in the breeze from the fortress' tallest tower. Between fortress and Temple Mount lay a valley of broken stone, dirt, and dust. Among the rubble, hints of once mighty buildings protruded. Titus and his legions had devastated Jerusalem during their five month siege. In their wake, Varro's cousin, Rufus, had leveled the ruins they left behind, earning himself the Turnus epithet.

"A million Jews died down there last year, questor," said Decurion Alienus, as they took in the view from the mountain slope, "and thousands of Roman soldiers."

Unlike Alienus, whose mind was filled with the faces of Roman friends and colleagues who had perished here at Jerusalem, Varro's mind was on his investigation. "So," he said, "you were quartered here on the Mount of Olives during the siege?"

"Yes, questor. The men of the 10th Legion had their camp up here, and my Libyan troopers and myself camped with them. Down in the valley, over to the northwest..." He pointed to the spot. "Titus had his main camp there, with the 5th, 12th and 15th Legions."

"And we are standing on the likely site of the olive press, the one called Gethsemane?"

Alienus cast his gaze to left and right. Clustered behind them stood Varro's officers and officials, talking among themselves. "I cannot be entirely sure, my lord. When we first arrived here last spring this mountainside was covered with olive trees. We cut down every single one. There were several olive presses on the mountain when we arrived. The one here would have looked directly down on the Temple, and was within an easy walk of the city. If I had to hazard a guess, my lord, this was Gethsemane."

Varro nodded. "Then, in all likelihood, this is where the Nazarene was arrested in the early hours of the Friday morning prior to the Passover, forty-one years ago. Lead on, Decurion. We shall trace Jesus of Nazareth's last hours from here, step by step."

Under a frying May sun, the guide led the questor and his party down from the red stone and dry earth of the denuded mountain, across the Kedron Valley, and up into the Lower City. They went first to the site of the house of the former Jewish High Priest Ananus. This location was fixed for the questor by Antiochus, who had visited Jerusalem several times in his youth as a Passover pilgrim and knew the city layout well. From one rubble-strewn site to another, Antiochus guided the party to a corner where once the house of High Priest Josephus Caiaphas had stood. From there, they walked beside the towering western wall of the Temple Mount, past its blockaded staircases, to the place, at the northeast corner of the Mount, where the Antonia Fortress had once stood. A single course of massive stones gave an impression of the layout of the rectangular fortress built by Herod the Great. According to Antiochus, the fortress had originally been called the Baris but was renamed by Herod in honor of his great Roman friend Marcus Antonius.

"The legionaries of the Roman cohort garrisoning the Antonia were massacred when the Jews launched their uprising without warning," Alienus commented with disgust. "Our men stood no chance at all. Last summer,

Titus had the fortress reduced, stone by stone, before we launched the final assault on the Temple."

Varro called for Aristarchus, the former secretary to Prefect Pilatus, brought to Jerusalem chained in a cart with Philippus the Evangelist. Now, released from his manacles, the scribe was led to the questor, who asked him: "It was to this place that the Nazarene was brought, to be questioned by Pilatus?"

Aristarchus nodded. "This is where the Antonia stood, yes, my lord. A long flight of steps, here, led up to an iron gate. I find it hard to believe that nothing remains. Quite astonishing. The city that I knew, the handsome Antonia and the Temple, all gone."

"A city of fools," commented Antiochus acidly behind him.

The scribe pointed to a mound of earth two hundred yards away; this had been the palace of Herod Antipas, he said. Each of the four legions involved in Titus' siege had built massive ramps of earth against the northern and western walls of the Temple Mount for the final Roman assault. Rufus had pulled down the ramps and distributed the earth among the rubble. This mound, where Antipas' flat-roofed pyramidal palace had once stood, was the remnant of one of those ramps. King Agrippa and his sister Berenice had later acquired the palace, and used it whenever they came to Jerusalem.

"The Nazarene was then returned here to the Antonia," said Varro, thinking aloud. "Pilatus endorsed the warrant which you wrote, Jesus was flayed, then three prisoners were brought out, down the steps to where we now stand, on their way to their execution. Take us to the place of execution, Aristarchus."

As commanded, the scribe led Varro and his companions to the execution site. Their route took them over the worn cobblestones of a narrow street which ran across the excoriated landscape to the west. As they went, Alienus indicated a spot to their left, where, he said, the men of the 10th Legion had unearthed a huge trove of buried Jewish treasure weeks after the end of the siege. Beside the white stone fortress where the Roman military banners flew, and where the expedition members had made their quarters on arrival the previous day, the stumps of gateway pillars marked the city's Water Gate.

"The prisoners and their escort would have emerged from the city at this point, questor," said Aristarchus as the party passed through the opening.

"There, where the fortress now stands, that was the Palace of Herod, where I spent the middle part of the day with Prefect Pilatus. The execution site is that rocky rise over there." He pointed away to their right. "It was called *calvaria*, or, as the Jews say, Golgotha."

"The Skull? Varro remarked. "It most certainly looks like a skull."

He led the way, following the road inclining up to a rise and which a northbound traveler would take on the first steps on a journey to Galilee or Syria. It took just a few minutes to reach the base of the rocky outcrop.

"There were dead trees up there," said Aristarchus. "Condemned men were required to carry the cross beams on which they were to be crucified. The cross beam would be nailed to the trunk, and the prisoner would be lashed to the cross so formed."

Varro clambered up onto the rocks. On the rise he found the sawn-off stumps of dead trees embedded in the dry, rocky earth. Even the dead trees had been cut down during the siege. Here, on this rock, hundreds of men had met their deaths over the years. Yet, to Varro, it did not seem a haunted place. Not like the Temple Mount and the Antonia, which had made his skin crawl. The questor looked back toward the site of the city. This would have been the Nazarene's last earthly vision: the city walls, the Temple, the Mount of Olives rising behind it, assuming he was crucified facing Jerusalem. Perhaps, Varro thought, he had been deliberately faced the other way, with his back to his holy city. On this rock, the Nazarene had died. Or had he?

The questor and his party spent an hour in the area. Within a half mile radius of the execution site there were a number of Jewish tombs cut into the terraced rock. During the Revolt most had been damaged, some destroyed. One of these tombs would have been that of Josephus of Arimathea, the sepulchre used for the interment of Jesus, but there was no way of knowing which tomb it had been.

✠

Varro had dined with his officers and the prefects of the auxiliary units based at Jerusalem. Now, in the moonlight, he and Martius climbed the succession of wooden ladders which took them to the top of the tallest tower of the fortress. Called the Hippicus by the Jews, the tower was said to be twice as old as Rome. The standards of all the units currently at Jerusalem were displayed here, among them the blood red *vexillum* of the questor's 4th Scythica Legion detachment and the white banner of his Vettonians.

"Did you know, Julius, that no Roman standards were put on display here in the years before the rebellion, to appease the Jews?" said Martius disapprovingly when they reached the stone tower's crenellated summit and looked out over the desolation below.

"I have heard," said Varro, gazing out to the Temple Mount glowing silver in the moonlight, "that when Pilatus first arrived at Jerusalem, at the beginning of his posting, he installed his standards up here. The Jews rioted, and followed him back to Caesarea in their thousands. They refused to budge until he relented, which he did in the end."

Martius shook his head. "We should not have given in to the Jews over the years the way we did. It only primed them for revolt. We gave them exemption from military service, we gave them coins without Caesar's image, we allowed them to collect their Temple tax from their people across the Empire and to remit it to the priests here. Worst of all — preventing a legion from displaying its standards — that is going too far."

"Our procurator did steal from their treasury," Varro returned. "That was what set off the Revolt, Marcus. If Cestius Gallus had punished Procurator Florus for his thievery and given the Jews back the gold he purloined, there would have been no uprising."

"If it had not been that, it would have been something else. The Jews would have found some pretext or other to rebel. It was our own fault. A handful of Caesars gave them concession after concession. We gave them a taste for freedoms, and in the end they could not be content with what they had. What a self-destructive people they are."

"They couldn't have imagined, ten years ago, that it would come to this." Varro's eyes traversed the silent valley that was now the graveyard of a city. "Who could?"

Martius was looking up at the moon. "Ten years ago, you would not have imagined yourself here today," he mused. "And in these circumstances."

"I certainly would not. Ten years ago?" Varro stopped to reflect. "I was twenty-four, and commanding the 2nd Wing of the Pannonian Horse, on the Rhine. All the talk then was of the revolt of the Britons the year before. Nero was emperor…"

"And we loved him," Martius chuckled. "No one then believed that he had murdered his own mother and was losing his mind."

"What of you, Marcus? Where were you, and your dreams, ten years ago?"

"Home, a thin-striper fresh from the 14th Gemina Martia Victrix in Britain."

"You served with General Paulinus during the revolt of Queen Boadicea? I was unaware of that." Varro was impressed. "The 14th's victory is the stuff of legend."

Martius nodded. "I never expected to survive, outnumbered twenty to one. We won that last battle more by Mars than Minerva, I can tell you."

"My manservant Hostilis was made a prisoner in Britain during that revolt."

"A Briton, is he? He looks too slight to have been a fighter. We made a great many Britons slaves after that revolt. The Britons don't believe in slavery, you know. They killed their captives. No sense of commerce, those people. The Britons will never amount to anything." He moved to the other side of the tower. Away to the south-east, the waters of the Dead Sea shimmered on the horizon. "After our victory I decided the gods must have chosen me for the soldiering life. I found my future on that battlefield."

Varro joined him. "The soldiering life is still your ambition?"

"A general's standard, famous victories, a consulship, and then a conquering expedition to some exotic land to expand the borders of the Empire — in that order. That should keep me occupied for the next ten years."

"You will make a fine general, Marcus. You command respect. The way you handled the men during the tremor, on the road from Lydda… I could never do that. I am no soldier. And I have no desire to be a soldier."

"What then does the future hold for you, Julius? Senator, pretor, and consul?"

"That is the plan," Varro said without enthusiasm. "My mother is relying on me. I am the man of the family; much is expected of me. But should the chance present itself, I would like to write. History."

"History? Any subject in particular?"

"Historical mysteries have always interested me. The mystery of the murder of Germanicus Caesar, for example. Then there is the case involving his daughter and his grandson - Nero, and the murder of his mother Agrippina. Mysteries of that nature intrigue me. The ability to ask questions is the one thing that sets us apart from the beasts, after all, Marcus. Without questions, mysteries will always remain unsolved."

"I like matters clear-cut."

Varro smiled. "The soldier's way."

"Once we expose the Jew's crucifixion plot and you deliver your damning report to Collega, the affair of the Nazarene's death will be clear-cut, the mystery resolved."

"Possibly so." Varro looked to the dark south. "The solution is perhaps down there, with Bassus. I must find the apothecary Ben Naum. His evidence will be crucial."

"We shall find him. Then you shall have the evidence you need. Mark my words, Julius, my friend — in ten years time no one will have even heard of Jesus of Nazareth."

XVIII

THE ESCAPEE

Roman Province of Judea. May, A.D. 71

The hill town was fire-blackened and deserted. Bet Lehem, the Jews called it — the House of Bread. To the Romans it was Bethlehem. Centurion Titus Gallo and his eighty soldiers of the 4th Scythica moved in and out of the ruins of Bethlehem, poking here, nosing there.

Questor Varro had decided not to wait for Artimedes to rejoin him from Caesarea with his report on Aristarchus' background. He had pushed on, following the trail of General Bassus and his Jewish prisoners. The senior cavalry prefect stationed at Jerusalem had informed the questor that Bassus intended to secure Hebron twenty miles south of Jerusalem and then move east of the Dead Sea to take the rebel-held fortress of Macherus. Once that had been achieved he would wrap up his campaign by retaking the Masada fortress to the southwest. Telling the prefect to direct Artimedes to follow once he returned from Caesarea, Varro had marched the few miles from Jerusalem to Bethlehem. While his soldiers secured the silent ruins, Varro walked the dusty, sloping streets of the village with his retinue close behind.

A hundred yards distant, a skeletal dog ran across the street and disappeared briefly into the rubble of a crumbled house, then emerged from behind it and bounded away down the rocky gradient where once the goats of the villagers had grazed. One of Gallo's soldiers threw a javelin at the canine, but the animal dodged the missile, which lanced into the hard ground and bent behind the head, as it was designed to do.

Centurion Gallo boomed a loud reprimand at the legionary for wasting a javelin.

"But, centurion, it was a rebel Jewish dog," the young soldier protested in his defense, bringing a laugh from his comrades.

According to the Matthias document, Jesus had been born here at Bethlehem. It was also the birth place of Davidus, King of the Israelites, from whom the Nazarenes claimed Josephus, the Nazarene's father, had descended. No good reason had been given for the Nazarene's birth to take place here, although it was not uncommon for a pregnant woman to be confined for a birth away from her home town. The Lucius letter also gave Bethlehem as the birthplace of Jesus. It added that Josephus had come here to his home town with his pregnant wife Miriam to pay a new poll tax levied in Judea by Caesar Augustus that year, and Jesus' mother had given birth while they were here. According to the Lucius Letter, the birth had taken place in a stable behind an inn in the town, because the inn was crowded with fellow taxpayers.

Gray-bearded Pythagoras was walking at Varro's shoulder as he roamed the village. "Questor, I cannot reconcile the Lucius Letter's claim regarding the tax of Caesar Augustus with the records," the chief secretary gravely advised. "According to the official records held at Caesarea, the year in which the new tax was introduced by Caesar Augustus was twenty-four years before the year in which the Nazarene was executed. That would make him twenty-four years of age at the time of his death. Yet, both the secret reports of the High Priests and the Lucius letter state he was in his thirties when he died."

Varro nodded. There was nothing to be found in the empty village. After a brief pause at Bethlehem, the questor ordered the column to resume its march.

✠

On the rocky Dead Sea shore, they made camp within the earthworks of a much larger marching camp built here several years before by Vespasian. The advance guard had reported no sign of General Bassus' army at Hebron, so Varro guessed that Bassus had turned east and skirted the Dead Sea to the north, planning to cross the Jordan River and join the main north-south highway in the Perea region. That highway would take him down to Macherus, a fortress held by rebels since the first month of the Revolt. Varro had decided to follow an overland course to the Jordan. From there he would take the highway south to Macherus, where he should find General Bassus. Now, a day's march east of Jerusalem, the expedition prepared to spend the night.

While their infantrymen made camp and the cavalry stood guard, Varro and his officers and freedmen walked down to the water's edge, where they were flanked by multicolored ridges of sandstone layered with chalk, clay, and gravel; yellow over white, then orange, with a top level of ochre red. Green was a color totally absent from the scene in the lifeless landscape.

"The only thing that would grow around here," said Callidus caustically as they made their way toward the lake, "is a man's beard."

They had all heard of the Dead Sea. Every educated Roman knew of this lake. Fifty miles long and eleven miles wide, it was many hundreds of feet below sea level. Its main claim to fame rested on its content. Reputedly, the Dead Sea was so salty a man could easily float in it.

"The story goes," said Martius as they stood looking at the rippling waters with a breeze blowing into their faces from the south, "that when Caesar Vespasianus was here a few years ago with his army he had some Jewish prisoners trussed up and tossed in, to see whether or not they would float. Caesar was quite tickled when they bobbed around like apples in a water pot."

"The prisoners would have not been unhappy that they floated, either," Varro suggested, generating laughter from his companions.

✠

Varro rose before dawn as usual. Seated on a stool, he was about to submit his face to Hostilis' razor in the torchlight when Centurion Gallo burst into his tent.

"The scribe Aristarchus has escaped from custody, questor!" Gallo reported.

Leaving the shaving stool, Varro hurried through the darkened camp with the centurion, following a soldier bearing a spluttering torch. The first rays of dawn were beginning to brighten the horizon above the bare hills east of the lake when they reached the baggage carts. Soldiers of the watch stood around one cart with guilty looks on their faces. Philippus the

Evangelist, still the questor's 'guest,' sat with folded arms and closed eyes in the vehicle, partly covered by a blanket. Philippus was still proving useful, with Varro occasionally asking him new questions on their travels, such as recently when the questor had asked whether Josephus of Arimathea had been one of the Nazarene's followers; Philippus had answered that he could not say, although he did state that Josephus had not participated in the disciples' public gatherings. Philippus' traveling companion since the expedition left Emmaus had been Aristarchus the scribe. The cart's rail on one side, where Aristarchus' chain had been fastened, had been broken away.

"What possessed him to escape?" Varro pondered, before giving a command. "Sound 'Assembly.' Search the camp. He must be in hiding here."

As the centurion hurried off bawling orders, Varro looked down at Philippus, whose eyes remained closed. "I know you are awake, Evangelist," he said. "No one could sleep through all this commotion."

Philippus opened one eye. "Let a man sleep," he croaked.

"How long ago did Aristarchus make his escape, Philippus?"

"I have been asleep," Philippus replied. Opening the other eye now, he changed position, jangling the chain connecting his manacled left wrist to the side of the cart.

"You must have heard the scribe break free," Varro persisted.

"I heard nothing. I saw nothing." Philippus fixed Varro with a steely gaze. "I was blessed with a deep sleep." The Evangelist, unhappy at being dragged along on the expedition, had apparently decided to be uncooperative.

"That slyboots Aristarchus!" exclaimed Marcus Martius, arriving on the scene.

"Philippus would have us believe that Aristarchus simply melted away."

"Another miracle!" Martius exclaimed with a wry smile in Philippus' direction.

Philippus rolled over, pulled the blanket up over him, and closed his eyes again.

As a trumpet sounded 'Assembly' nearby and the camp burst into life, Varro began to make his way back to his tent, and Martius fell in beside him. "Why would Artistarchus venture to escape, Marcus? Could it be that his credentials are false, that he was lying to us all along, and he bolted before Aristedes returned to denounce him?"

"Either that," the tribune replied, "or the mole-faced scribe could take no more of the Evangelist's preaching."

Back at the *pretorium,* Varro resumed his seat and motioned for Hostilis to proceed with his shave, as, outside, the camp became a hive of activity. "It is perplexing, Hostilis," the questor said, as the slave, standing behind him, dampened his skin. "Aristarchus the scribe, escaped. He must have lied about his past."

"Yes, master." As Hostilis spoke, he applied the razor to his master's throat.

"It is possible that he was not in Prefect Pilatus' service after all."

"No, master."

"Perhaps he merely repeated gossip about the Nazarene's execution."

"That is possible, master." The slave expertly slid the iron razor over his master's tanned skin.

"Do we discount his testimony altogether? The conspiracy between Josephus of Arimathea and Centurion Longinus; did Aristarchus concoct that story?"

"It is difficult to know, master."

"What of the apothecary Matthias ben Naum? We only have Aristarchus' word that Ben Naum provided Longinus with a drug to make it appear the Nazarene died on a cross. If Matthias ben Naum exists at all. This is very troubling, Hostilis."

"It is, master."

"Everything fitted together. The conspiracy between Pharisee and centurion. The apothecary. The drug. Not to mention the name of Naum, the name from my dream. If Aristarchus' story is a complete fabrication, where does that leave us?"

"Confused, master," Hostilis succinctly remarked.

By the time that Varro was coming to his feet with his tingling skin soothed by a balm of fragrant valerian lotion administered in the last stage of his shave, Centurion Gallo entered the *pretorium* once again. "It appears the scribe has escaped the camp, questor," Gallo unhappily advised.

Varro frowned. "How could he have managed that?"

"You had best come take a look for yourself, my lord."

Gallo and his commander emerged into the new day. Daylight now flooded the camp. Martius, Crispus, and Venerius fell in with Varro as the centurion led the way to the north-facing *decuman* gateway, where 4th

Scythica sentries bearing embarrassed expressions quickly stood back out of their way. A pair of spindly wooden sentry towers flanked the gateway. Gallo pushed the gates open and led the officers outside. He pointed to the ditch running around the wall. A ladder stood in the ditch, propped against its outer wall. "Aristarchus must have waited until the sentries were distracted by the discovery of his disappearance," the centurion explained, "then climbed the ladder, pulled it up after him, threw it over the wall, then followed it, and used it to negotiate the ditch."

Martius was appalled. "The sentries left their posts?"

"The men heard the alarm raised and rushed to the baggage carts, tribune," Gallo hurried to explain, "leaving the gate temporarily unattended. They are inexperienced..."

"Half the remaining rebels in Judea could have entered the camp while the sentries were away from their posts, man!" Martius snarled.

"The guilty men will be punished, tribune," Gallo quickly responded. "They'll feel my cudgel across their backs..."

"No, no, no, that will not do," Martius retorted. "Your recruits must learn that if they desert their posts, for whatever reason, they put the lives of their comrades at risk. In battle this is a capital offense. They would lose their heads, as you well know, Gallo."

"Yes, tribune," the centurion returned grimly.

"Have *every man* of the last watch, including the cavalry patrol on duty last night, report here to me," Martius ordered. "They will draw lots. One man will be stripped, and each of the others will give him ten lashes. They will not leave their posts again. Go!"

Furious, with his own men and at being countermanded by the tribune, Gallo strode away, yelling orders.

Venerius watched him go. "That was telling him," the junior tribune said with a leer, and loud enough for Gallo to hear. "He should also draw a lot. He shares their guilt."

"Mind your business, thin-stripe," Martius snapped. He looked over to Varro. "The scribe has a start, Julius, but we should be able to track him down."

Varro nodded. He turned to Crispus. "Quintus, take your troopers and scour the district for Aristarchus. Venerius, you can make yourself useful; ride to the cavalry post at Qumran. Alert the commander there to be on the lookout for the scribe. If we have not secured Aristarchus by the time you return, you will take ten men and ride to the Jericho road and patrol it to east and west in search of our fugitive. Away you go, the pair of you. Remember, I want Aristarchus brought back alive!"

XIX

THE APOTHECARY

Macherus, Territory of Perea, Roman Province of Judea.
May, A.D. 71

Black smoke billowed above the walls and four square towers on the apex of the cone-shaped hill. The fortress of Macherus had been burning all day long. Part way down the chalky northern slope, the town of Macherus was also ablaze. On the flat below, a stone wall ten feet high ran for two encircling miles. Punctuating this wall every so often on rises and ridges were busy Roman camps, and, in the depressions, guard posts. Within the ring of stone and steel, and just to the west of the hill, a huge pile of stones rose up, the beginnings of an assault ramp which was to have run all the way to the summit of the hill. The ramp had not been needed. Lying on the ground in grotesque death poses, between the encircling wall and the hill, sometimes in piles, sometimes singly, were the bodies of seventeen hundred Jewish men. The siege of Macherus was at an end.

"Ten days we were ahead of you, Varro." The speaker was General Sextius Lucilius Bassus, commander of the 10th Legion for the past two months. Bassus was thirty years of age, tall, pale, and gaunt. There was a redness about his eyes, as if he suffered from a lack of sleep. "Ten days we spent building the siege works, and then, last night, the townspeople tried to break out. But we knew to expect it from an informant, and we were ready for them."

Varro stood with the general on the tribunal in the bustling main 10th Legion camp within the siege works, looking up at the smoking hill.

"No survivors, general?" said the questor with a worried frown.

"Too many damned survivors, Varro," Bassus cursed. "We think at least nine hundred slipped past us in the dark. But even they will fall into our clutches before long."

"Nine hundred?" Varro brightened. There was still a possibility that Jews with information might be located. "Where do you think they went?"

"South. To join the rebel leader Judas ben Jairus. Without a doubt."

"At Masada?"

"No, Ben Jairus is at odds with the Daggermen at Masada. The damned fool Jews have spent more time fighting themselves than the Roman army during this damned war."

"Where is Ben Jairus? Do you know?"

"My scouts have spotted some of his people down in the Negev Valley. We will be marching for the Negev tomorrow, once we are finished here."

"General, if I cannot find what I looking for here, would you object if my party and myself were to join you for the march to the Negev?"

"If you must." Bassus looked at him from the corner of his eye. "As long as you and your people keep out of my way."

"We will do our utmost not to inconvenience you, I assure you. How many Jews does Ben Jairus have with him?"

"Hard to tell. The few who escaped with him from Jerusalem, the nine hundred from last night, and the three thousand or so I allowed to leave the fortress of Mecharus."

Varro looked at him with astonishment. "You allowed them to leave? Why?"

"I had my reasons." Bassus swung around and stepped down from the tribunal, then began to walk back toward the *pretorium* of the 10th Legion, forcing Varro to jump down and then trot to catch him up.

Varro drew level with the general. "Can you share those reasons with me?"

"I…" Bassus suddenly gasped and stopped in his tracks. Then, draping his left over Varro's shoulders, he put his weight on the questor. His right hand he put to his own belly, pressing hard.

The surprised questor looked into Bassus' face. It was contorted with pain. "What ails you, general? Is there something I can do?"

Bassus failed to reply for several long moments, and then the pain seemed to pass. His face relaxed, but the pallor of his cheeks was now gray. "Something you can do, Varro? Not unless you can prevent me from shitting fire and blood daily!"

Varro was horrified. "That sounds vile. You must see a physician."

"I have seen a physician!" the general irritably returned. "I see the fussing fool of a legion physician every morning and every night, and I am sick to death of his damned purgatives and potions. The cure is worse than the ailment, Varro." He started forward again, slowly, gingerly, and still with an arm around Varro for support. "It will pass," he said. "A change of diet, a change of air. As soon as I have rounded up the last of the rebels I plan to take myself up to the hot spring near Tiberias. I hear that it has a most rehabilitating affect on the constitution."

"I have used that hot spring myself, and I can say that it certainly is stimulating." Varro was trying to be kind. It was obvious to him that, whatever Bassus was suffering from, a bathe in a hot spring would do little if anything to help.

"Good, good. Now, what was it we were discussing?" The sentries either side of the entrance to the general's pavilion stiffened at their commander's approach. "Come inside, out of the sun, Varro," Bassus urged.

As the pair passed into the large tent, two of the general's servants anxiously rose up from the floor where they had been waiting for their master's return. Taking Bassus from Varro, they helped him to his camp bed then carefully lay him on his back.

"There is no position that I find comfortable for long," the general confessed, as Varro came to stand looking down at him and the servants began to towel the general's perspiring brow. "I am as happy on my feet as in any other position."

"How long have you been suffering like this?"

"Not long. I live with it, and plow on with the business of soldiering. Mind you, I do find that riding can be an agony at times, which is just a little inconvenient for a soldier. Still, every problem has its solution. I sent down to Caesarea and had the procurator send me up the chariot and pair he was so proud of."

"Procurator Rufus sent you his chariot?" Varro suppressed a smile. He knew how enamored his cousin had been with chariots since childhood, and guessed that Rufus had been far from happy to part with his plaything.

"I drive it myself. It allows me to stand, and makes travel almost tolerable. Now, where were we, Varro? Remind me of what we were talking about."

"You were explaining why you let the rebels at the fortress go free."

"Of course. While we were building our encirclement, the partisans would send out raiding parties to harass us. One day, a youngster by the name of Eleazar, a member of one of these raiding parties, was captured alive by one of my Egyptian auxiliaries. I tied this Eleazar up on a cross, for all his comrades up in the fortress to see. It eventuated that Eleazar was the son of a leading Jewish family, and the rebels sent envoys down, offering to evacuate the fortress if I returned this Eleazar to them alive. I agreed."

"I see."

"It meant that I could take possession of the fortress without losing a man, while the partisans were left to flee into the wilderness. You see, Varro, I knew that the rebels at Masada would rather cut these peoples' throats than take them in. In my own time, I will track them down, in the open, and I will deal with them once and for all."

"A clever strategy."

"I thought so. To complicate matters, the people in the town refused to leave, so we continued siege operations, until last night's fun and games. Of those we intercepted we killed everyone bearing arms, of course. The unarmed and the women and children were put with our existing prisoners."

"It is the prisoners that interest me, general. Do I have your permission to seek out several Jews among your prisoners?"

"Help yourself, Varro. Give my camp prefect their names; he'll rake them up for you if they are here." Bassus suddenly let out a pain-filled groan. He sat up, as if propelled by an unseen hand, and, doubled over. Clutching his midriff with one hand, he grabbed at a slave with the other. "The medication," he gasped. "The medication!" Another slave ran to him with small stone bottle. Bassus drank, then, with a twisted face, waited for the potion to go to work. As the pain drained from his face, he slowly eased back down to the supine position. "That's better," he sighed, with relief.

✠

By night, Bassus' three thousand Jerusalem prisoners, now joined by a similar number of women and children from Macherus, were housed in miserable slave camps on the Macherus perimeter. By day, they were on the road to Jericho, hauling water in clay pots strapped to their backs, like pack animals, watched over and goaded by auxiliary cavalry.

In the evening of the day on which Varro and his column had linked up with the twelve thousand troops of Bassus' army, the questor stood at the gate to the largest of the camps for male prisoners, flanked by his deputies and with men of his 4th Scythica Legion detachment drawn up in ranks behind him. Led by centurions, parties of 10th Legion soldiers were moving through the camp with torches held high. Every now and then the centurions would halt among the collection of pathetic shelters formed from clothes and blankets, and call out the names of three men: "Matthias ben Naum, an apothecary of Jerusalem. Baruch bar Laban, a native of Tiberias. Tobias, his son."

Varro stood with folded arms, watching and waiting as the centurions repeated the names time and again, hearing them add that a reward awaited these men if they came forward. Varro had promised old Laban bar Nahor that in return for information he would seek his son and grandson among the Jerusalem prisoners, and he was keeping his word, although he held little hope of finding either. But the main focus of Varro's quest was the apothecary Ben Naum. The escapee Aristarchus had not been apprehended by the search parties. It was anyone's guess where the Greek scribe was now. Varro had recalled Crispus and his men, but he had left Venerius and a small cavalry detachment out patrolling the Jericho road on the lookout for Aristarchus. In the meantime, the questor was proceeding in the hope that the scribe's evidence was reliable. Yet, severe doubts now occupied his mind about the very existence of Ben Naum.

If any of the men the questor was looking for were located, Varro expected that they would be in poor health; all the prisoners appeared to be in a state of physical exhaustion. With that in mind Varro had instructed Diocles the physician to be present. The doctor stood with his assistants in a group to Varro's right. Now, while he waited for results to be generated in the compound, the questor beckoned Diocles. "A question of a medical nature for you, physician," he said once Diocles had waddled to his side.

"If it is in my power to answer, my lord questor," fat Diocles replied.

"If a man were to regularly pass blood," said Varro, "what would be the nature of his complaint?"

Diocles rubbed his chin, looking like a philosopher contemplating a matter of significant gravity. "It would depend on which of the five orifices of the body provided the outlet for the blood, questor," he answered, with an air of importance. "In the case in question, are we talking about the mouth, the nose, the ears, the penis, or the anus?"

"The anus."

"The flow is regular, you say? In quantity?"

"Regular and in quantity, accompanied by a fiery sensation, and with a gripping pain in the abdomen."

"Oh, my goodness. We are not talking about yourself, are we, questor?"

"No, not me. This is a purely hypothetical question."

"Ah, well, I am relieved to hear that. Your hypothetical man would in all probability be suffering from a cancerous growth."

"A cancer?" Varro nodded slowly. He had feared as much.

"A cancerous growth in the bowel, I would fancy."

"I see. Can it be treated?"

"Treated, yes. Cured, no. It is a death sentence, questor. A death sentence."

✠

Varro reclined beside Bassus in the general's *pretorium*. Senior officers and leading freedmen from both camps were arrayed on couches around two dining tables in the large tent. Most were enjoying a sumptuous dinner, but, as Varro noticed, Bassus only nibbled at his food. Varro guessed that Bassus must have realized the cause of his medical condition by now. If Varro's drunkard of a physician could diagnose the general's illness from a description of the symptoms, then the physician treating the general would have known what he was dealing with. Besides, Bassus was no fool; even without a doctor's prognosis he would have known that he was a dying man.

With a sigh, Varro took up his drinking cup, and looked absently into the diluted wine. Knowledge of Bassus' awful and terminal illness was enough to depress anyone, but the questor's own life was not exactly panning out the way he would have liked either. As things stood, his investigation was in jeopardy. The exercise in the prisoners' camp had proven to be a waste of time. No one answering the name of Ben Naum had come forward. Neither had the son or grandson of old Laban been located; not that they would have been of any assistance to him. When, as a last resort, Varro had sent Gallo back through the camps calling for anyone with information about the death of Jesus of Nazareth four decades before, not a single soul had responded. Figuratively, Varro had reached a river, and, for the life of him, he could not see a way across.

"Begging the questor's pardon?"

Varro looked up from his cup, to see Centurion Gallo standing at the open end of the dining table. "Yes, centurion?"

The normally taciturn Gallo managed something approaching a smile. "The questor will never believe it," he said, "but, after we left the prisoners' camps, several men came forward and identified themselves to the guards."

Varro's spirits instantly rose. "Fortuna smiles at last."

"It was the promise of a reward that brought them out from under their rocks, questor," Gallo remarked with a cynical elevation of the eyes. "You can be sure of that."

"Who do we have?" Varro asked with anticipation.

"Interestingly, questor, we have not one, but three Matthias ben Naums."

Before long, three salivating Jewish prisoners stood in front of the dining table, taking in the sea of exotic dishes being served to the Roman officers. One prisoner was elderly, one middle-aged, the third in his twenties. All were well-built, which was why they had been allocated to General Bassus' slave labor parties. Each was chained to a soldier of the 10th Legion. The officers continued to eat while the prisoners were questioned; to them, this was entertainment.

"You are all Matthias ben Naum?" Varro asked.

All three nodded, but none spoke.

"You all practice as apothecaries, and you are from Jerusalem?"

Again the prisoners nodded in affirmation.

"Obviously, Varro," said Bassus beside him, "two of these men are liars. Or the Jews have a shortage of names and should think about inventing some new ones!"

This brought a hearty laugh from many of the diners.

"Either that, or all Jewish apothecaries are named Matthias ben Naum," said Marcus Martius, tearing at a pigs trotter, with juice running down his chin.

There was another gale of laughter around the table.

All three prisoners were looking extremely uncomfortable. Each had come forward independent of the other, in separate camps, and it had only been when they had been led into the general's tent that they had learned that were not the only claimant to the name of Matthias ben Naum.

"That man is too immature to be the one I am looking for," said Varro, indicating the youngest prisoner, who stood to the left of his two companions. "My man had to be alive and practicing in Jerusalem forty-one years ago. This man was not even born then. For that matter, the man on right would have only been a babe in arms at that time."

"How old are you, Ben Naum on the right?" Bassus demanded.

"Er, sixty years of age, I think, my lord," the man answered.

"Liar!" Bassus snarled. "You would not be a day beyond forty-five."

"I look young for my age, my lord," the man countered.

"Liar!" Bassus said again. He looked over to the camp prefect of the 10th Legion, who stood by the door. "Have these two imposters crucified at dawn."

"No!" the middle-aged man cried as the soldiers of the escort went to haul him away. "I am truly Matthias ben Naum. These other two are the imposters! I swear it!"

"Wait!" Varro called. "He may be older than he looks, as he says."

"Then take the young one away," Bassus instructed.

The youngest of the prisoners was hauled from the tent. Hanging his head in defeat, he went without a word. This left the two older men standing before the officers.

"How do you propose to test this pair, Varro?" Bassus asked.

Varro looked over to Diocles at the second dining 'U.' "Physician," he called, "how would you sort the wheat from the chaff here? What question would you ask these men to determine their qualifications as an apothecary?"

Diocles, who had Callidus beside him to ensure that nothing stronger than water passed his lips all night, thought for a moment, then fixed his eyes on the middle-aged prisoner. "Younger Jew, answer me this," he began, projecting his voice as if he were a lawyer posing a question in court. "I am conducting a surgical operation to repair an injury caused by a blow to the head. I have made an incision, to separate the flesh from the bone where it is united to the *pericranium* membrane and to the bone." The prisoner stared at him, blank faced. "I intend to fill the whole wound with what we physicians call a tent, to expand it, causing as little pain as possible." Diocles was enjoying being the focus of the attention of everyone in the pavilion. "Along with this tent I will apply a cataplasm. I come to you and ask you to prepare it. Of what would your cataplasm consist?"

The middle-aged prisoner did not reply. His eyes flashed around the faces in the tent, as if half expecting someone to offer their help, or their pity.

"Well?" General Bassus demanded. "You say you are Matthias ben Naum the apothecary. Answer the physician."

"It is difficult, my lord," the prisoner stalled. "I need to think on it."

"Liar!" Bassus scoffed. He looked at the older prisoner, who had yet to utter a word. "You, old man. How would you answer the physician's question?"

"I would make a cake of fine flour, pounded in vinegar," the older prisoner immediately replied.

One of Bassus' freedmen at the second table laughed at this.

"An alternative to pounding?" Diocles asked the prisoner.

The question wiped the smile from the face of the amused freedman.

"As an alternative preparation, I would boil the cake of flour and vinegar, to render it as glutinous as possible," came the old man's reply.

"Very good," said Diocles.

"Remind me not to suffer a head wound," Marcus Martius remarked. "I'll not have you physicians playing at bakers and cooks with my skull as the oven."

"The older man is an apothecary, in your judgment, physician?" said Bassus.

"The old man appears to have had some training, general," Diocles replied.

"Very well. Take the other one to join the first imposter on a cross."

"I would do the same!" the younger prisoner cried. "I would boil the flour and vinegar, as he said!"

"Take him away!" Bassus ordered.

Protesting loudly and struggling with his guards, the second man was dragged out.

Varro looked at the last remaining prisoner. "You are Matthias ben Naum, apothecary of Jerusalem?" he asked.

"I am," the man replied.

The questor was feeling elated. Everything was pointing toward Aristarchus having spoken the truth. For all that, he knew he had to proceed calmly and methodically with his next questions. "Were you present in Jerusalem forty-one years ago?"

"Er, yes."

"You sound unsure."

"It was many years ago, my lord. I sometimes left Jerusalem, to visit relatives."

"The time that Jesus of Nazareth was executed. Do you know of whom I speak?"

"I have heard the name."

Varro knew that if this genuinely was the apothecary that Aristarchus had referred to, and if he had participated in a conspiracy involving the death of the Nazarene, he was unlikely to implicate himself, let alone confess. If the questor was to gain the answers he needed, he had to proceed with some cunning. "How old are you?" he asked.

"This is my seventy-second year of life. But my mind is still sharp, my lord."

"I'm glad of it. Until made a prisoner, were you practicing as an apothecary still?"

"I was."

"What drug would you administer as a general painkiller?"

"Myrrh, as a rule," the old man replied.

"Myrrh is overrated," Bassus growled. "It has only minimal affect."

Varro suspected that the general was speaking from experience. "Apothecary, how would you disguise the taste of a soporific drug?" the questor asked

"Why would you do that?" the old man asked suspiciously.

"Answer the question, if you please."

"Vinegar," the old man replied with a weary sigh. "Vinegar has many medicinal uses and is regularly administered. It would disguise the taste of another preparation."

Varro looked over to Pythagoras at the second dining table.

The secretary could read his mind. "Lucius writes of vinegar, questor," he said across the tent. "Marcus writes of vinegar, and of myrrh mixed with wine. Matthias writes of vinegar, and of vinegar mixed with gall."

General Bassus looked perplexed. "This makes some sort of sense to you, Varro?"

"It does, yes," Varro replied. "Apothecary, I want a patient to be so relaxed that to an observer he is to all intents and purposes dead. What drug would you administer?"

The old Jew again looked guarded. "There are several which might be applied."

"Give me an example."

"Well, deadly nightshade for one. I cannot be certain about the result. I would caution that the dose would need to be exact, in proportion to the size and weight of the patient, and to their constitution. Too large a dose, and the recipient would die."

Varro was feeling confident that he had found his man. The trick now was to link the apothecary with the death of the Nazarene. "Let us return to the year that Jesus of Nazareth died. It was in the reign of Tiberius, the consulship of Sejanus and Longinus."

The apothecary nodded warily. "I remember the year."

"There was a legion garrison quartered in the Antonia Fortress at that time. Which legion were those soldiers from?"

"The 12th Legion, if I remember correctly."

"Correct." The next question was a key one. "Be sure how you answer this. What was the name of the senior centurion of the Jerusalem garrison at that time?"

The old man swallowed hard, conscious of the fact that all the eyes in the room were on him, conscious of the fact that Varro waited on his answer with intense interest. "I, I am not sure," he replied, with obvious unease. "I cannot remember."

"Who was the Chief Priest of the Jews at that time?"

"It would have been Joseph Caiaphas."

"Good. Before him?"

"Simon ben Camithus, I think."

"After Caiaphas?"

"Er, Jonathan ben Anunus."

"Well then, the Roman centurion in charge wielded more power in Jerusalem than the High Priest. Surely, you remember his name?"

"Antonius." The apothecary almost vomited out the name. "Centurion Antonius was in charge at that time."

Varro suppressed a wave of disappointment. "It was not Antonius. Think again."

"It was so many years ago," the old man said in his defense. "I cannot remember."

"If you can remember of the name of the High Priests, you can remember the name of the senior centurion. This particular senior centurion was stationed at Jerusalem for at least three years, and probably much longer. Think again."

"It may have been Ventidius. Was it Centurion Ventidius?"

"You are guessing," said Varro, disappointed. If this man was Ben Naum, and if he had been involved in a conspiracy with the centurion in charge of the execution of the Nazarene, he would not have forgotten his name. Yet, he may have only been foxing. Varro tried another tack. "Does the name Josephus of Arimathea mean anything to you?"

"No. Should it?" The apothecary looked genuinely at a loss.

"Think again on the name of the centurion."

"Truly, I cannot remember." Now the old man was sounding desperate.

"I will give you a choice. It was either Centurion Coponius or Centurion Longinus. Which of those two? Before you answer, think on this. If you are pretending not to know, to throw me off the track it will not work. If you tell me the wrong name I will know that you are not Matthias ben Naum. Tell me the right name, and I will know that there is a good chance you are Ben Naum. Now, was it Coponius or Longinus."

The old man hesitated, and then he said, "The name Coponius is familiar. The centurion was Coponius. I am certain now. It was Centurion Coponius."

Varro shook his head. "Coponius was the name of a procurator of Judea," he said, unable to hide his disappointment. "The name I was looking for was Longinus."

"Another damned liar!" Bassus declared. "This one we shall put to the torture, to see how much he does know. Then he will join the other two on a cross."

"No, please!" the old man dropped to his knees. "No torture, I beg of you, my lords." His manacled hands were clasped in front of him. "I confess, I am not Matthias ben Naum. I am an apothecary, but I am not Matthias. My name is Saul ben Gamaliel."

"Why would you lie," Varro demanded, "and claim to be Ben Naum?

"For the reward." Tears welled in the Jew's eyes. "To perhaps win my freedom."

"You must have realized that we would find you out," said Varro.

"I was an apothecary, and I knew the real Matthias ben Naum." Ben Gamaliel returned. " I thought I could make a success of the deception. And if I had said the centurion was Longinus, you would have believed me. If only I had chosen correctly…""

"You say you knew the real Matthias Ben Naum?" Varro's interest renewed. "How can I be sure you are not lying again?"

"I knew him, I swear. He was staying under my roof until only a few nights ago."

"How can that be?"

"Get up, get up, you sniveling apology for a man!" Bassus called. He motioned to the soldier at the end of the old man's chain, who dragged Ben Gamaliel back to his feet.

"I am a native of Macherus, not of Jerusalem," the Jew rushed to explain. "Matthias and myself were in the same guild, and when he fled Jerusalem last year he came to Macherus and I took him in. Last evening, we both tried to flee the town. He escaped with the fortunate few, I was apprehended by your soldiers."

"You've only been our prisoner for a day?" said Bassus. "This is hilarious!" he hooted with laughter. "A day! And you try to trick your way to freedom!"

"How old is Matthias ben Naum?" Varro asked.

"Close to my age. Perhaps a little older, perhaps a little younger."

"Is he in good health?"

"When I last saw him he was in good health. He has a robust constitution."

"Would you recognize Matthias ben Naum if your were to see him again?"

"Of course."

Varro nodded. That answer had just saved Saul ben Gamaliel from an appointment with General Bassus' executioners.

✠

As the sun rose behind the hill of Macherus to introduce another sweltering day, the Roman army was on the move, proceeding down the Nabatea road toward the south. An army this size took several hours to vacate its camp site. Five thousand men of the ten cohorts of 10th Legion. Five thousand auxiliary light infantry in ten cohorts. Four wings of auxiliary cavalry and the one hundred and twenty men of the 10th Legion's own cavalry unit, totaling two thousand troopers. Six thousand prisoners. And trundling along in the rear, fifteen hundred mules with their handlers, two hundred wagons and carts, a herd of cattle for fresh meat, a mob of sacrificial goats.

Varro and his party would tag onto the end of the main column. The questor had gone through his camp to check that his column was lined up and in readiness to march. Now he strode out the gate, to where his mounted colleagues waited. Once Hostilis had helped him up into his saddle, he sat watching the passing parade. Soon a chariot came surging down the road beside the marching column, drawn by two superb white horses with plaited manes and tails, and adorned with gold horse ornaments.

"A chariot, questor," Callidus called.

Varro nodded to his freedman. He knew that, rather than stating the obvious, Callidus was referring to the questor's last dream, the one involving a chariot.

Standing, uniformed and armored, with his scarlet general's cloak flowing behind him, General Bassus drove Procurator Rufus' handsome chariot, a vehicle decorated with scenes of beaten gold depicting Mars the Avenger. The general reined in opposite the questor. "Have you seen, Varro?" Grinning, Bassus pointed down the road, to a myrtle tree at the roadside. Two cross-beams had been nailed high on the trunk, and the two prisoners consigned to their deaths the night before for masquerading as the apothecary Ben Naum had been lashed up with arms outstretched. "Ben Naum trees," Bassus said, with a roar with laughter. "The Jews make Ben Naum trees!" Then, with a lash of the reins along the backs of his steeds, he sent the chariot lurching off down the road again.

Members of the questor's party were smiling at the general's pun, but Varro was not amused. He looked away from the two crucified men, but he could not escape the sight of death. Close by, on the plain spreading before Macherus, lay the corpses of the Jewish men slaughtered two nights before, naked, bloated, and reeking. There they would remain until they rotted away. Their bones would litter the plain for ever more. Varro was beginning to tire of the useless waste of life. He wished that the Jews had never revolted and cost Rome and themselves so dearly. He wished that the rebels who remained at large surrendered and spared themselves and their families. Death was no answer. Surely, he thought, while a man lived he could always hope for better times.

The line of advance stretched for two miles down the road when in the third hour the questor's column finally began to move off. Varro remained at the roadside and watched his people file past. Behind the freedmen on their mules came Miriam and Gemara astride Antiochus' horse. Miriam's eyes focused straight ahead, but young Gemara looked the questor's way. The child gave Varro a smile as she passed, a smile that warmed his heart. In the last cart of his baggage train sat Philippus and Saul ben Gamaliel. The cart had been repaired and Ben Gamaliel was chained to the side. He looked miserable as the cart bumped and jolted along. The Evangelist raised his eyes when the cart drew level with Varro.

"Do you expect your quest to end in the Negev, questor?" Philippus called.

"Possibly so," Varro replied, easing his horse in beside the moving cart and keeping pace with it. "Once I have my report, you shall have your freedom."

"My fate is in God's hands," the Evangelist replied, sounding much more congenial than in recent days. "Your investigation is progressing well?"

"With the help of Ben Gamaliel, your traveling companion there, I hope to soon locate a key witness, one who will cap my inquiries."

"May God guide you," Philippus returned serenely.

Beside him, the apothecary bore a hang-dog expression.

"Be of good cheer, apothecary," Varro called. "Soon we should overtake your friend Ben Naum, and you shall have your freedom."

"If it is so ordained," the man gloomily replied.

Varro was about to kick his horse to the trot when he heard shouting to the rear of the column. Following the pointing arms of cavalryman of his rearguard, he could see a small group of riders galloping from the direction of Jericho. At their head he recognized Venerius. Varro turned his horse toward the rear, and went to meet the horsemen.

Several hundred yards behind the column the questor and Venerius came together. The junior tribune's Vettonian troopers had a spare horse with them, and, as Varro converged on the small party he saw two bloodied bodies tied to the back of the animal. One body was clothed, the other, naked. Both hung head down.

"I found him for you, questor!" Venerius crowed. Jumping down to the ground, he strode to the horse with its double load. Around him, his Spaniards grinned down from the backs of their horses. "I found the scribe."

"You found Aristarchus?" Varro also dismounted.

Venerius slashed the ropes holding the two corpses in place. They fell onto the road, landing with a fleshy thud, like sides of beef. There they lay, arms splayed, face up. The trauma of their last living moments was reflected by their wide eyes.

Standing, looking down, Varro did not recognize the clothed cadaver, a dark-headed man. Blood soaking his white tunic and a narrow horizontal rent at breast level indicated that he had died from a thrust to the heart from a bladed weapon. On the other hand, the round face of the bald, naked corpse was unmistakable. The mole on the right cheek provided confirmation. This was Aristarchus, the scribe of Emmaus. The flesh of his throat lay open in a deep incision which ran from ear to ear.

"I said I wanted the scribe alive," said Varro with displeasure.

"He was already dead when we found him at the roadside, five miles outside Jericho," Venerius advised, "throat cut, and denuded. The other man we came across a little later, walking the road. I recognized his tunic as the one that Aristarchus had been wearing. Obviously, this rogue had been one of the robbers who killed the scribe, so I dispatched him on the spot." He said it with an air that exuded a certain pleasure.

"He may have been a Roman citizen," Varro remarked with a scowl. The execution of a citizen without the benefit of a properly constituted trial was illegal.

"He was no citizen," Venerius confidently replied. "He wears a freedman's plate."

Varro knelt beside the second body. Sure enough, there was a small, round bronze disc at the end of the leather strip, a freedman's proof that he was not an escaped slave.

Martius and Crispus now rode up. "So, the mole-faced scribe is dead?" said Martius, resting forward on a horn of his saddle to look down at the bodies.

Varro came to his feet. In his mind he pictured Aristarchus the last time he had seen him alive. "This was not the scribe's tunic, Venerius," he said. "It is similar, but not the same. This man was not Aristrachus' killer. Not on the evidence of the garment."

"No!" Venerius shook his head. "I will not have it. It is the same tunic."

"If the questor says it is not so," said curly-headed Crispus, "it is not so."

"It is not the scribe's tunic," Varro reiterated. "You killed an innocent man."

"Well, when all is said and done, does it matter?" Venerius countered with a nervous laugh. "I probably saved him a life of pain and sorrow. Who would want to live the life of a freedman, after all? He would probably thank me, if he could."

"You truly are a low, murdering piece of work, Venerius," Martius growled.

The young man's eyes flared. "I take exception to that, tribune! You, who slit the throat of the Vettonian, accuse me of murder?"

"I took no pleasure from it. Unlike you."

"You have one rule for yourself, and another for everyone else!" Venerius spat.

"Take me on at your peril, boy!" Martius snarled.

"Enough, the pair of you!" Varro intervened with a glare. "The damage is done. Dispose of the bodies, Venerius."

A faint smile came over Venerius' lips. He called to the troopers with him, ordering them to fling the pair of corpses from the road.

"No, cremate them," Varro snapped. "It is the least you can do."

As Varro went to remount, another trooper came galloping up from the direction of the column. When he drew up he reported an accident in the column, and a fatality.

"Who?" Varro demanded. His immediate concern was for Miriam.

"The prisoner," the soldier replied. "The apothecary."

Leaving Venerius to make a funeral pyre at the roadside, Varro and his companions rode back to the column. Varro's baggage train had come to a halt, and dismounted men of the rearguard stood around. Diocles the physician knelt beside the body of Saul ben Gamaliel. The apothecary hung from the chain attached to the manacle on his right wrist, partly over the right side of the cart, partly under the wheel. The chain, six feet in length. was looped around his throat.

"A broken neck," Diocles pronounced, coming to his feet with the help of an assistant as Varro slid from his mount.

"How?" Varro queried testily.

"Suicide. Or so it would appear."

Philippus sat in the cart with a disinterested look on his face.

"What took place, Evangelist?" Varro demanded.

Philippus shrugged. "I was beginning to doze off. The first I knew of it, your soldiers were shouting all around me, and my companion was dead."

"The apothecary appears to have wound the chain around his neck and then thrown himself over the side of the cart," said Diocles. "I recommend that the other prisoner's chain be shortened, to prevent a similar occurrence."

"Agreed," Varro returned absently. He looked at the dead apothecary, and wondered why the man would take his own life. With both Aristarchus and the apothecary dead, he had lost his two best informants. Even if he did locate Matthias ben Naum now, who would identify him?

XX

THE ROAD TO THE FOREST

Kingdom of Nabatea. May, A.D. 71

In the darkness, Varro stood with General Bassus and a group of their officers on the camp wall, looking west toward the Dead Sea. During the day the army had marched out of Judea and into the kingdom of Nabatea, a small state bordering the south-eastern corner of the Dead Sea, a kingdom allied to Rome and dependent on her. Behind the Roman officers, the marching camp set up beside the highway twenty miles south of Macherus was full of life. Cooking fires blazed, thousands of troops dressed casually in their tunics moving about the tented streets, conversation hummed on the night air.

"Do you see it, Varro?" Bassus pointed into the gloom.

"I see it, general," Varro confirmed. On a mountaintop on the far side of the lake, a light flickered, as faint as a distant star.

"Masada," Bassus announced. "The Daggermen, advertising their presence."

"You think they know that we are here?"

"They know we are in the vicinity. They have lit a bonfire up there on the fortress ramparts to taunt us, to rub our noses in the fact that they have held that place since they cut the throats of the 3rd Gallica garrison five years ago. I hope they enjoy their fire; they will not be up there for much longer. A month or two at most." With an arm around the shoulders of his deputy, the twenty-eight-year-old military tribune Quintus Fabius, General Bassus gingerly made his way back down to the floor of the camp.

Varro and the others followed. "I'm looking forward to that visit to the hot spring at Tiberias we spoke of, Varro, once the last rebel is dead or in chains," Bassus resumed. "As soon as we deal with Judas Ben Jairus and his band, I will address our 'friends' over there at Masada."

"We do know where Ben Jairus is?"

"My scouts are certain that he is hiding in the Forest of Jardes, in the Negev Valley, accompanied by between two and three thousand men. Tomorrow, we will march another twenty miles down this road. After that, Varro, we turn west, and it will be an overland journey into Idumea, to the Negev. Leave your heavy baggage behind at tomorrow night's camp. I plan to divest myself of my carts and wagons, and of the prisoners. Those damned people make a speedy march impossible, dragging their feet the way they do. I will leave a thousand auxiliaries to guard baggage and prisoners, and take the remainder of the army after Ben Jairus. If you still intend keeping me company all the way to the Negev, be prepared to march light."

As they were nearing the general's tent, where they were due to dine, Callidus came hurrying up to Varro. "Artimedes had returned from his mission to Caesarea, my lord," the freedman advised. "The secretary and his escort are just now dismounting at the *decuman* gate."

Excusing himself from the general's company, Varro hurried away, accompanying Callidus to the camp gate. As they approached, the double gates swung open. Artimedes walked stiffly in through the opening. Decurion Pompeius and six cavalrymen followed, leading the party's horses. On seeing the questor, Artimedes gave him a wave.

"Welcome back" called the relieved Varro. Hurrying forward, he embraced his secretary and former tutor.

"Steady on, my boy." Unaccustomed to such a display of warmth, Artimedes quickly pulled out of the embrace.

"I was beginning to think we had lost you, noble Greek," Varro said, hurt that his display of honest affection had not been reciprocated.

"You are a hard man to track down, questor. At Jerusalem they told us we might find you at Hebron. From Hebron we retraced our way back to Jerusalem, only to be redirected to Macherus and the road to Nabatea, and here we are at last, exhausted and saddle-sore."

"But safe and sound," said Varro gratefully.

Artimedes rubbed his numb backside as they walked toward their tents. "I would not lead the cavalryman's life for any amount of money."

"Was your mission a success? Was Aristarchus telling the truth?"

"You are impatient, as always." Artimedes used a scolding tutor's tone. "To begin with, you should know that Terentius Rufus is no longer Procurator of Judea."

"Rufus has left the province?"

"He set sail from Caesarea while I was there. His replacement Liberius has arrived, and has taken up the post." He sniffed. "I rather think I preferred your odious cousin. Liberius has not a lot to recommend him."

"He will not be a cause of concern to us. Come, come now, what of Aristarchus? You keep me in suspense, ancient Greek. Well, give me the answer! Or do I have to have it tortured out of you?" Varro broke into a grin.

The diminutive Greek frowned. "I do believe you would do it, too, young man, to repay me for schooldays punishments. Much deserved schooldays punishments, I might add." This was as close as the secretary would come to sharing a joke with the questor. "Yes, the mission was a success. Prefect Pilatus did have an under secretary by the name of Aristarchus, and Pilatus granted him his freedom just before his return to Rome."

"Was it the same man, the man we knew as Aristarchus?"

"It was clearly the same man. As it happened, the freedman in charge of the archives at Caesarea had been acquainted with Aristarchus; both were in the same profession, and both were servants of the province's administrator. He was able to describe Aristarchus, right down to the mole on his cheek." A frown formed on his brow. "Tell me, is there something I should know? You speak of Aristarchus in the past tense."

"Aristarchus is dead," Varro announced, with obvious frustration.

"Dead?" the shocked secretary came back. "How?"

"A long story awaits you over dinner, my dear Artimedes. Suffice it to say that we are heading for the Negev Valley in search of the man Aristarchus identified as Matthias ben Naum the apothecary. Last night we found a man, another apothecary, who could identify Ben Naum, but this morning he too died."

"Another death? You have either been very unlucky or very careless in my absence, questor. What were the circumstances?"

"He took his own life," Varro replied, sounding dispirited.

"Why would he do that?"

"That is what I have been asking myself. My fear is that there is no Matthias ben Naum, and that my witness chose to escape his punishment before he was found out as an inventive liar. He told me that he knew Ben Naum, and that Ben Naum had escaped to the south with the last of the rebels."

"Where then lies the problem?"

"He began by claiming to himself be Ben Naum, so it is difficult to know where his lies ended and the truth began, if his lies ended at all. We must face the possibility, good secretary, that this apothecary concocted everything."

"The possibility exists, clearly, but why would he have lied? What could he have hoped to achieve?"

"Only he could tell us that, and the apothecary has gone to ashes." Varro went on to confide his concerns. He still did not know why Aristarchus had run off, and had to assume that the scribe had feared being found out for some deception. Through Artimedes' efforts he now knew that the Greek was who he claimed to be, but how much of his story could be believed? Did both the scribe and the apothecary lie, and was Matthias ben Naum nothing more than a figment of their combined imaginations? That being the case, Varro feared that in traipsing all over the wilds of Judea and Nabatea in search of a non existent Matthias Ben Naum he had embarked on a fool's errand.

All the while, walking behind the pair, Callidus had been listening in to the conversation, and now he spoke up. "If I might remind the questor, there was the matter of his dream, and the name of Naum. You must agree, my lord, in the light of that it would be a considerable coincidence if there were no Ben Naum."

"Callidus has a point," Artimedes agreed. Coming to a halt at the end of the camp street containing their tents, he looked his former pupil in the eye. "Clearly, there is only one way to find out, questor. Follow it through to the end. All the way to the end. As I have always taught you."

XXI

THE WITNESS IN THE FOREST

The Forest of Jardes, Territory of Idumea, Roman Province of Judea. May, A.D. 71

The heat pressed down on him like a giant hand. Oppressive heat, thick with humidity. As Varro stood on the camp wall, wearing armor and a sword for the first time since the expedition had begun, perspiration flowed like a river from beneath his bronze helmet. It ran down the back of his neck, it trickled into his eyes, it made salty inroads into the corners of his mouth. Wiping his eyes with the back of a clammy hand, he focused on the scene in front of him.

Spread around the forest in battle order, the soldiers of General Bassus' army stood frozen in their ranks, silently anticipating the order to go in after the partisans hiding in the trees. The majority of Bassus' two thousand cavalrymen encircled the small forest. Troopers drooped in the saddle, horses shook their heads and occasionally pawed the ground in their boredom. Just behind their line, auxiliary infantrymen bearing small, light shields decorated with spiral motifs stood in eight cohorts that were distributed every few hundred yards. Their cloth standards hung damp and limp in the humid Negev air. In the forest, the partisans had the benefit of shade, but here, standing in the open for hours on end in their chain-mail jackets, the auxiliaries, some from Egypt, some from the Balkans, some from the Rhine, were baking in the heat. The Egyptians were accustomed to this climate, the Germans were as tough as oak, but several Pannonian infantrymen wilted like delicate flowers, collapsing in their ranks, to be carried away by orderlies.

East of the trees, occupying a grassy rise overlooking a stream, the heavy infantry of the 10th Legion was formed up, in three lines, each line ten men deep. The soldiers of the 10th, all Roman citizens and natives of western Spain, were olive skinned and dark-haired. The identical outfits, the shining segmented armor, the even rows of glinting helmets, the legion's charging bull emblem repeated on five thousand long, curved wooden shields, all combined to give the formation a uniformity and an anonymity which reduced lines of men into mere components of a death-dealing machine.

In front of the formation stood the eagle-bearer of the 10th Legion, proudly holding aloft the golden eagle standard of the 10th. Directly behind him stood the legion's trumpeters, all in a line, waiting for their general to give the order to go forward, an order they would relay by sounding 'Advance At The March' or 'Charge.' But General Bassus was lying in a tent in a camp hastily thrown up behind the legion. For the past hour, the general had been only semi-conscious and incapable of giving any order.

It had taken the column the best part of four days to reach the forest. Even after leaving the heavy baggage at the Nabatea road, the column had made little better than ten miles a day to begin with, over difficult desert terrain in blistering heat, until the wheat-growing district of the Negev Valley provided easier going. The cavalry had preceded the foot soldiers, and had quickly surrounded the forest while the infantry came up.

Bassus had been impatient to seal off all possibility of escape and then move in quickly before dark and kill or capture every last rebel hiding in the forest with Judas ben Jairus. Delayed on the march by severe abdominal pain, the general had himself arrived on the scene some hours after his army, coming up in his chariot and with a cavalry escort. Seeing that the forest of evergreens stood thicker than he had imagined, Bassus had second thoughts about a full-on frontal assault. Legion formations were at their best in the open or storming a rampart, but in tightly-packed trees their ranks and their discipline would suffer, and heavy casualties might result.

The general's mind was already on Masada, last Jewish bastion in Judea and a reputedly impregnable fortress. He would need every man he had to take Masada and draw the curtain on the Jewish Revolt. Once that was done he could rest, secure in the knowledge that he had fulfilled his orders and done his duty by Caesar. To achieve his goal, and rapidly so, Bassus could not afford heavy casualties here at the Forest of Jardes, and the general had decided to consult the gods before launching an attack.

In the quest for guidance a goat had been sacrificed to Mars, god of war. The entrails of the animal had been found to be deformed. Reading this ill omen as a danger signal, Bassus had held off giving the order to advance into the forest. His anxiety had brought on an excruciating attack of pain and abdominal cramps, and the general had collapsed.

Varro heard shouting in the camp behind him. He and his colleagues, who stood on the camp rampart by the *pretorian* gate, looked around. Tribune Fabius, deputy commander of the 10th, had emerged from the general's tent and was issuing orders to waiting centurions and prefects. Varro looked to Martius, who stood farther along the rampart, closer to the *pretorium*. "Did you hear what was said, Marcus?" he called.

"No, but I will find out," Martius replied, before shimmying down a ladder. He soon collared one of Fabius' centurions. The pair spoke animatedly for a few moments before Martius climbed back up to the ramparts.

"Well?" Varro queried impatiently.

"It seems the general mentally rejoined us long enough to instruct Fabius to arm the auxiliaries with axes," said Martius with an amused smile. "Bassus has decided to cut down the Forest of Jardes. Defoliating the Jews, and eliminating our firewood shortage at the same time. Very clever really."

Now Crispus called out. "Questor! Look!" He was pointing toward the forest.

Varro and Martius both followed the prefect's gaze, to see a lone rider slowly coming out of the trees. He wore a white tunic and rode with his arms horizontally outstretched, to signify that he was unarmed.

"A Jewish envoy, it seems," Martius remarked. "This should prove interesting."

They watched as Tribune Fabius was summoned to the camp wall. Once he came up onto the ramparts and sighted the rider for himself he issued an order. A troop of Roman cavalry galloped to the rider and surrounded him. The man dismounted, was searched for weapons by two troopers, and was then led through the 10th Legion's ranks toward the camp. As he was brought in the *pretorian* gate, Varro and his officers came down off the wall and joined Tribune Fabius and several of his subordinates who had also descended. The combined group stood just inside the gate, waiting for the Jew.

The envoy was an athletic figure in his twenties, with curly black hair and a perfectly sculpted face. "My name is Jacob," he said in a firm voice as he came to a halt in front of Fabius. "I claim the neutrality afforded ambassadors of peace by all nations."

Fabius, himself a handsome-faced man, although slim and slight in comparison to the young Jewish ambassador, folded his arms. "You bring a message for my general, Jew?" he tersely inquired.

"My leader, Judas ben Jairus, seeks terms for an honorable cessation of hostilities," Jacob replied. As he spoke, he ran an analytical eye over the assembled Roman officers, assessing their rank and caliber.

"General Bassus offers no terms," Fabius haughtily replied. "He will accept only total and immediate disarmament and unconditional surrender." As Fabius knew, this had been Bassus' tenet since embarking on his campaign.

Jacob's eyes returned to Fabius. "Judas will not agree to unconditional surrender," the envoy advised unemotionally. "He is prepared to disarm, if you let the people with him go free into the desert, to start a new life."

"Impossible!" Fabius snapped. "Go back and tell your leader that his options are twofold: unconditional surrender, or death."

"Sent to receive terms, I won't return without them," Jacob defiantly declared.

"Impudent Jew!" Fabius exploded. "You will not dictate to me!" He nodded to the cavalrymen of the escort. "Lash him to a cross up on the camp wall, where his friend Judas ben Jairus can see him. That will be General Bassus' answer."

"You violate the neutrality of an ambassador!" Jacob angrily retorted as troopers grabbed his arms.

"You Jews have violated your word at every opportunity during this war," Fabius bitterly replied. "More than once you have ignored the neutrality of Roman ambassadors. Like for like, Jew."

"Wait!" Varro spoke up. "The man is right, Fabius. No matter what the other side does, we are Romans and we ought to observe the neutrality of envoys."

The troopers who were in the process of hauling Jacob away looked uncertainly from questor to tribune.

Eyes blazing, Fabius swung on Varro. "These people have lost the right to civil treatment," he snarled in the questor's face. "Not that I need excuse myself to you, Varro. You have no standing here. General Bassus has only tolerated your presence out of the goodness of his heart. So, mind your business." He turned to the cavalrymen. "Take the Jew away! Give him a slow cross."

Annoyed by the tribune's attitude, Varro could have made an issue of it. Yet, he told himself, if he was to pick a fight with Bassus or his officers it would have to be a fight that he badly needed to win, because once he went down that road he might sour relations with the general and lose his valuable cooperation. So, as the hotheaded Jacob was dragged away yelling deprecations against Fabius and Romans in general, Varro kept silent. He watched from a distance as two lengths of wood were formed into a large 'X' by Fabius' men. This was propped up on the camp rampart facing the forest. Jacob was then stripped and spread-eagled on the cross with his arms and legs tied in place. Varro was familiar with 'slow' cross. It was intended to draw out the agony of execution. The victim would die from a combination of starvation and exposure, lingering for many days before expiring. Varro had never personally consigned anyone to a slow cross, although such a punishment was within his power. He thought it enough that a prisoner paid with his life, it had never been in his nature to inflict unnecessary pain.

Fabius then sent several of his centurions riding to the edge of the forest where they called into the trees that Jacob would be freed alive if and when the remaining rebels gave themselves up. All the while, Jacob yelled at the top of his voice, warning his comrades in the forest not to trust these Romans who had violated his neutrality, and urging them not to surrender. Tribune Fabius soon tired of the prisoner's voice and ordered him gagged.

Now Pedius, Varro's lictor, came to the questor. With military operations pending, Varro had put Pedius in charge of the welfare of Miriam and Gemara. "Miriam is asking to see you, my lord," Pedius advised worriedly. "A matter of urgency."

Accompanied by Pedius and Martius, Varro strode to where the expedition's baggage animals were tethered. The veiled Miriam had been sitting on the ground with Gemara. She quickly came to her feet when she saw the questor.

"Pedius said that you wished to see me," Varro began.

"I think that the man who has been put on the cross on the wall is my brother," she announced. There was a slight quaver in her voice. "Please, will you help him?"

It was the first time Varro had detected a hint of emotion from her. It was also the first time she had sought his aid. Yet, he did not entirely believe her. "How do you know he is your brother?" he asked, suspecting she was merely aiming to help a fellow Jew.

"I heard him crying out. I recognized his voice."

He looked into her beautiful dark eyes, trying to read them. "You recognized his voice? From here? I find that hard to believe."

"Would you not recognize the voice of *your* brother?" she countered.

"Both my brothers are dead." His voice was a monotone, his impassive reaction conditioned by years of grief for his two brothers, killed in Rome's recent civil war.

"Five years ago, my brother Jacob, a free man, went to Jerusalem to celebrate the Passover," Miriam went on, seemingly ignoring his comment. "He disappeared there, and I have not seen him since. I have thought him dead all this time." Now she made her salient point. "Would you not recognize the voices of your dead brothers?"

Had he given her a direct answer, it would have been in the affirmative. His brothers' voices lived eternally in his memory. Instead, he asked her a question. "How is it that your brother was free and you were not?"

"My father sold me into slavery."

Varro was shocked. "Your father did that?"

"My brother was also in Queen Berenice's service, but as a free man. The queen always permitted her free Jewish servants leave to take part in the Passover Festival. That last year, Jacob did not come back. I had always thought that he must have died in the war. Then, today, I heard his voice. To me, it was like a voice from Heaven."

Varro looked questioningly to Martius, who nodded. Martius believed her.

"Come with me," Varro instructed.

Leaving young Gemara with Pedius, Varro and Martius conducted the Jewish woman up onto the camp ramparts. Soldiers' heads turned disapprovingly as she passed along the narrow boardwalk behind them. Varro knew that it was considered unlucky by Roman soldiers for a woman to mount a camp's walls, but at this moment that was the least of his considerations. Seeing Antiochus among officials a little further along the wall Varro motioned for the Jewish magistrate to join them. When they reached the wooden cross and stood before the crucified man, Miriam suddenly burst into tears. Falling to her knees, she pulled aside her veil, and began to kiss the prisoner's feet. Tears also began to form in Jacob's eyes.

Varro did not need Miriam to tell him that this was indeed her brother. He ordered the nearest soldier to remove the gag from Jacob's mouth. Once the gag had gone, Jacob began to converse rapidly with Miriam, and she with him, in Aramaic. Varro had anticipated this. He turned to Antiochus. "What are they saying?"

For a time, Antiochus listened to the emotion-charged exchange between brother and sister, before providing Varro with a commentary in Latin. "The girl reveals that she is a Nazarene," he said, turning up his nose with distaste.

"Miriam is a Nazarene?" Varro remembered her interest in the house at Nazareth.

"Her brother is also a Nazarene," Antiochus went on. He listened a little more. "No, he *was* a Nazarene, but he turned his back on the Nazarene's doctrines, wise fellow. He tired of turning the other cheek, he says, and turned to armed rebellion against Rome instead. He was with Judas ben Jairus and his brother Simon during the fighting at Jerusalem — they were both leaders of one of the Jewish factions. He used tunnels beneath the city to escape with Judas in the last days of Titus' siege."

After a time, Miriam, on her knees still, turned and looked up at Varro with tear-stained cheeks. "Please, save him," she implored. "You have the power."

"He can save himself," Varro replied, "if he will go back to Judas ben Jairus and convince him and all those with him to surrender."

"I will not do that!" said Jacob vehemently.

"It would mean you will live, brother," said Miriam slowly coming to her feet. "Save yourself. For me, and for our mother."

Jacob shook his head back and forth "I cannot!"

"Why not?" She was angry now.

"Judas sent me to negotiate terms. He told me that if I came back without terms he would kill me. I may as well die here, now."

Martius put a hand on Varro's shoulder. "Julius, a private word." Varro and Martius moved away. Once the pair was out of earshot of the others, Martius spoke confidentially. "Your primary concern in all this is finding the apothecary Matthias ben Naum, is it not? So, the last thing we want is Bassus' troops killing all the Jews in the forest, because one of their victims could be our man Ben Naum. Agreed?"

"Agreed."

"What if we were to send jolly Jacob there back to his unpleasant friend Judas, with the proposition that I go into the forest and negotiate terms with them, if they hand Ben Naum over to you for questioning? Then, even if the negotiations come to nothing, at least you have secured Ben Naum. If they refuse to produce Ben Naum, you can be reasonably certain that the elusive apothecary is not with them."

Varro was shaking his head. "No, Marcus, I am not letting you venture in there alone. Besides, I doubt they would hand over one of their own. All the same, thank you for your original thought and your brave offer, my friend." Then an original thought of his own occurred to Varro. "However, if I were to offer to go into the forest to negotiate with them, on condition that they allowed me to question Ben Naum, in there, in the forest, that might prove to be a workable proposition."

"*I* am not letting *you* venture in there alone!" Martius countered.

Varro smiled. "Then we shall go together."

"Done!" Martius returned, clapping his friend on the back.

They returned to the cross.

"Jacob, I will have you freed if you agree to go back and tell Ben Jairus that I will personally enter the forest and negotiate terms with him, on condition that he produces a man by the name of Matthias ben Naum, an apothecary of Jerusalem, and permits me to question him in the forest, on a matter dating back forty years."

Jacob looked at the questor, uncertain about the trustworthiness of the offer.

"Agree!" Miriam urged her sibling. "Agree, brother, and live!"

Jacob looked away for a long moment, thinking hard, then turned back to Varro. "I am to tell Judas that you are prepared to come into the forest to negotiate terms?"

"On condition that I can question Matthias ben Naum," Varro reiterated.

"Question him in the forest?"

"Yes, in the forest. I will venture in there with just a handful of companions, if Judas ben Jairus is prepared to give a guarantee of safe passage both into and out of the forest. Unlike some of my colleagues, I am prepared to trust the word of Jewish people."

Jacob looked at his sister, searching her eyes for an answer.

"Agree, Jacob" she said, softly now, pleading now. "Please agree."

Jacob dropped his eyes. "Very well," he said, almost inaudibly.

✠

Tribune Quintus Fabius came clambering up onto the ramparts in a rage. "Who told you to free that man?" he yelled to the soldiers of the 4th Scythica Legion around the cross.

Jacob was standing free. His clothes had been returned, and he was flexing his arms, which had been burned and bruised by the ropes that had held him on the cross.

"*I* ordered him set free," Varro declared, pushing through the legionaries.

"I warned you, Varro!" Fabius was close to screaming. His fists were clenched. "You have no power here. You cannot countermand my direct order!"

"Shall we see General Bassus about the matter?" Varro asked.

Fabius grinned. "Yes, let us do that."

Following Fabius, Varro and Martius climbed down from the wall. As Fabius strutted toward Bassus' *pretorium,* Varro called over Callidus and whispered in his ear. Callidus nodded, then hurried off toward the questor's tent. Varro and Martius then continued on in Fabius' footsteps. Bassus was resting on one elbow on a low campaign bed in his bare pavilion. As anxious servants hovered around, the general's physician, Polycrates, a tall, elegant Greek with silver hair, stood mopping Bassus' perspiring brow.

Tribune Fabius dropped to one knee beside the bed. "General, the questor has overreached himself," he declared. "You must order him to obey me."

"How are you feeling, general?" Varro asked, as he and Martius came to stand at the end of the bed.

"The pain comes and goes, Varro," the white-faced Bassus weakly replied. "It comes and goes." His clarity of mind seemed to have returned; for the moment at least. "What have you been doing to upset my tribune?"

"Varro countermanded my orders," Fabius fumed.

"Is that true, Varro?"

"I am sending the Jewish envoy back into the forest with an offer to negotiate terms," Varro informed the general.

Bassus shook his head. "No terms. Unconditional surrender, or the Jews die."

Varro had made up his mind. "I am sorry, general, but I need all those Jews alive. One of them may be instrumental to the success of my investigation."

"I cannot help that, Varro." Bassus' tone was harsher now. "I am under orders to speedily terminate the rebellion. And I have Ben Jairus' Jews where I want them."

"I understand your situation, general." As Varro spoke, Callidus slipped into the tent. There was a small scroll in the freedman's hand. "However, you must also understand my situation. I will do my best to convince the Jews to surrender themselves to you, but above all I must do everything possible to interview the man I seek."

"I am senior here, Varro," Bassus growled. "I won't have it. The Jews surrender unconditionally, or I send my troops into the forest with orders to kill all who resist."

"Yes, you are senior to me, general," Varro acknowledged. He held out his hand to Callidus, who lay the scroll in it. "However, with respect, as Acting Governor of Syria and Judea, General Collega is senior to you. I have here an Authority from General Collega. My tribune will read it aloud." He passed the document to Martius.

Martius unraveled the scroll and recited the contents for all to hear. "'Gnaeus Cornelius Collega, Legate of Caesar Vespasianus Augustus, to all persons in the Province of Syria and the Sub Province of Judea. It is hereby certified that Julius Terentius Varro, Questor to the Propretor of Syria and Judea, has my Authority to require and command all things in my name.'" It was short, it was to the point, and it was incontrovertible. Collega was indisputably the more senior man; his appointment as a general of *legatus* rank predated that of Bassus by four years. With the departure of Titus, and in the absence of a governor of consular rank, Collega was the most senior representative of the emperor in Syria and Judea. Martius held the Authority out to the general, so that he might authenticate the seal as that of Collega.

Bassus waved the document away, a look of resignation on his face. "Very well, do as you will, Varro," he sighed. "Just bear in mind, my 'friend,' if just one Jew escapes from that damned forest as a consequence of your actions I will haul you before Caesar once we both return to Rome, and you can answer to him. That is a promise!"

It was not a promise, or a threat, that worried Varro. He did not intend to let any rebels escape.

✠

Nightfall would claim the forest in under two hours. General Bassus' army was still in place, still encircling the Forest of Jardes. The eleven thousand soldiers continued to stand in their places as they had since the middle of the day, enduring the heat.

"There he is!" someone on the wall called.

All heads turned toward the trees as a lone rider emerged from the forest. An hour after he had been given back his horse and sent on his way, Jacob was returning.

"That's a relief," commented Martius beside Varro, on the ramparts. "I was beginning to think that Judas ben Jairus had slit the young envoy's throat."

"On the other hand, Jacob could be returning to tell us that Judas will not parley."

"He would not be fool enough to come back if that were their answer."

Outside the camp gate Varro and Martius mounted up. They and ugly Decurion Pompeius and ten of his troopers filed down through the stationary ranks of the 10th Legion. They met the envoy on the gentle slope half way between trees and Roman lines.

"Well, Jacob?" Varro asked as the Roman horsemen encircled the Jew's horse. "What does Judas ben Jairus have to say?"

"Judas agrees to your offer," the young Jew replied with a stone face. "He promises safe passage in and out of the forest for you and four companions."

"What of the apothecary Matthias ben Naum?" Varro asked. "Am I to have my interview with Ben Naum?"

"You may interview Ben Naum. In the forest."

"Then, Ben Naum is in the forest with Judas and the others?"

"Yes, he is there."

Varro was elated by the news, but he tried not to show it. "Very well. Four companions and myself."

"At dawn tomorrow."

Varro did not like the sound of that. The rebels might attempt to break out in the night. "There is time enough for a meeting before sunset," he responded.

Jacob shook his head. "Tomorrow, at dawn, or not at all." He went to turn away.

"Very well," Varro called. "Tomorrow at dawn."

"I will meet you here as the sun rises," Jacob advised. With that, he pushed his way out of the circle of horsemen.

"Bassus will not be pleased with the delay," said Martius as the Romans turned back toward their camp.

"Neither am I," Varro returned. "It will be a long night."

Returning to the camp, Varro and his deputy dismounted. They went directly to General Bassus' *pretorium*. Fabius was there, looking like a child who had lost his favorite toy. Bassus was lying flat. He did not even turn his head as the two officers entered his tent. "Well, questor, to what have you committed us?" Bassus asked.

"My party will go into the forest at dawn tomorrow, General," Varro answered.

"No, no, no!" Bassus painfully rocked his head back and forth. "The Jews are up to their old tricks, Varro. They will attempt to escape once darkness arrives."

"To prevent that you will have rotate all your troops in three watches through the night, distributed evenly around the forest with burning torches."

The questor's plan for the night watches was subsequently adopted. Varro returned to his quarters, and he and his senior men dined apart from Bassus and his officers; the general no longer wished to mix with the questor or his subordinates. As Varro had anticipated, by exercising his Authority he had alienated himself from Bassus. He had done what he had to do, and could live with the consequences. Having traveled light, Varro and his colleagues dined on benches made from strips of turf laid one on another, around a table of similar construction. It was an uncomfortable experience, sitting to eat, as slaves did, rather than reclining. At least questor's silver plate had found a place on several pack mules and could be used to add a touch of civility to the meal.

As Hostilis and the other personal servants moved in and out of the questor's tent, serving the food being prepared outside by the cooks, Varro

ran his eyes around his dinner companions, who sat elbow to elbow, four
to a bench around the earthen table. Martius, in good spirits, talking
convivially with the poetic Crispus, reviewing the day's events. Venerius,
in discussion with Alienus the guide and Pompeius the cavalry decurion
about the superiority of Roman horsemanship. Gallo, a solitary figure, only
speaking when spoken to. Pedius, discussing remedies for footsoreness with
Diocles. Pythagoras, aloof, distant. Artimedes, embroiled with Callidus in
a conversation about horoscopes. Antiochus, sitting at the end of the 'U,'
shunned by all present.

"A word with you all," Varro called. "A word!"

The conversations ebbed away, and all heads turned toward the
questor.

"In the morning, at sunrise, I shall enter the forest to meet with the
rebels and to interview the apothecary Matthias ben Naum," Varro began.
There was sudden tension in the *pretorium*. All present knew that the Jews
could be laying a trap for their questor. "As you will have heard, the rebels
have agreed to provide safe passage for myself and four companions. I have
decided who those companions will be."

"As your lictor, my lord," Pedius spoke up, "I will of course accompany
you."

"Take me, my lord," said Crispus.

"No, take me, questor," the one-eyed Pompeius chimed in, his voice as
deep as a grave. "We need someone to give the Jews a fright, not a poem."
This brought a laugh from several of the diners and a characteristic cackle
from Venerius.

Varro dispensed the aggressive decurion a reproving frown, before
continuing. "I shall take two military officers," he announced. As he said it,
he noticed Venerius shrinking back, as if to exclude himself from selection.
"Tribune Martius…"

"I plan to make a study of the flora and fauna of the forest while we are
there," Martius joked, raising smiles around the table.

"The other…" Varro's eyes came to rest on Decurion Alienus, the
Egyptian provided to him by his cousin, "shall be you, Alienus. You are
familiar with this part of the world, and you understand a little Aramaic."
Varro had also chosen him because he looked as if he could take care of
himself in tight situation, and for one other reason — Alienus was not a
member of the little 'family' that Varro had brought down from Antioch.

If any of his companions on this risky venture in the forest were to meet an unpleasant end, Varro preferred it to be an outsider.

Alienus nodded. "Very good, my lord. We will be going in armed, I take it?"

"Yes, armed."

"Questor, I am prepared to go with you," said Crispus. He sounded hurt at being left out. "I will go wherever you go, face whatever dangers you face. I am unafraid."

"I need you to stay with the expedition, Quintus. If Marcus and myself were to fall, command would devolve to you. In that event, you must complete this mission."

Crispus nodded vigorously. "I would not let you down. I swear."

"I shall also have need of a secretary, to record Ben Naum's testimony."

"Naturally," said Pythagoras, "as senior secretary that task shall be mine."

"No, Pythagoras," Varro returned, causing a deep frown to appear on the secretary's brow. "Whatever transpires, you must write the report that Gnaeus Collega is expecting, using the notes taken to date."

"Ah, of course." This explanation pleased the white-bearded Greek.

"That leaves the post of secretary in this little party to you, faithful Artimedes."

Artimedes gave an accepting nod. "I understand, questor."

"Then I am the last member of the party, questor?" Pedius said expectantly.

"No, Pedius. Your task is the guardianship of the woman and the child, and of the Evangelist. Philippus is to be released once the expedition returns to Caesarea. If I do not return, the females are to be sent to the household of Paganus, a freedman of Antioch."

Pedius was gratified by his assignment. "Yes, questor."

Varro looked over to the centurion of the 4th Scythica. "Centurion Gallo…"

Gallo's eyes had dropped while the questor was speaking. Hearing his name, he looked up. "Questor? Am I to be the fourth man?"

"No. Select one of your trumpeters as my fourth companion. One who can ride."

"Er, yes, questor." Gallo's mystified expression mirrored the thoughts of everyone in the room apart from Varro. "A trumpeter? May I ask why?"

By way of replying, Varro turned to Crispus. "Command, until I make my return, is yours once I enter the forest, Quintus. If you should hear my trumpeter sound 'To Arms' from the forest, you and your men are to come to our aid, at the gallop."

Crispus smiled. "I understand, questor. At the gallop! Faster even than that."

"Then…" Varro lifted his drinking cup. "Good Fortuna be with us all tomorrow."

His companions raised their cups. "Good Fortuna be with us all!" they chorused.

✠

An eerie ring of light circled the forest. Holding burning torches, Roman soldiers stood every few yards. Now and then, fresh torches were distributed around the line. The watches of the night had been reduced from the traditional four to three. At four-hourly intervals the watch changed with a chorus of trumpets, and a fresh line of almost four thousand men moved in to relieve the weary sentinels who had marched all morning, dug a camp in the middle of the day, and stood motionless in the sun through the afternoon.

In the fourth hour of the night, after taking in the unique sight of the illuminated circle from the camp wall, Varro and Martius strolled through their camp. "Now that we know Miriam is a Nazarene," Varro remarked as they walked, "I have told Pedius to allow her to spend time with Philippus during the day. If she so desires."

"I would not want to spend my days with that old charlatan," Martius returned.

Three figures now came bustling down the camp street toward them. Tribune Fabius led the way, with a freedman and a servant bearing a lantern close behind.

"Varro! A word!" Fabius called agitatedly as he came up.

"Be careful, Julius," Martius counseled his friend in a low voice. "This turbulent fellow Fabius will not let sleeping dogs lie."

"What can I do for you, Quintus Fabius?" Varro asked.

"I want you to assemble your freedmen, for inspection," Fabius announced. "I suspect that your party harbors a criminal."

"You really do tire my patience, Fabius." It was obvious to Varro that the petty Fabius was in search of revenge for coming off second best to Varro during the day.

"You are reputed to have picked up a number of suspicious characters."

"You are misinformed, Fabius. Apart from a Nazarene informant who joined us in Caesarea, all my people came down from Antioch with me."

"You will forgive me if I satisfy myself?"

"You seek someone in particular?"

"As a matter of fact, I am — a Greek swindler by the name of Alcibiades. He tricked me out of a large sum of money at Caesarea."

"Just how did this Alcibiades manage to swindle you, Fabius?" Varro was unable to disguise his mild amusement.

"Well, if you must know, I had arrived at Caesarea at the beginning of the spring and was waiting for General Bassus to arrive in the province when this fellow came to me with the information that he had discovered the ancient book of an Egyptian priest called Bolos which revealed the secrets of turning silver into gold."

"Alchemy?" Varro stifled a laugh. "You believed this fellow?"

"Not at first, but when he provided an example of the science of Bolos…"

"What manner of example?"

"Before my very eyes," Fabius continued, "he turned a silver sesterce into gold. He placed it one end of a device, and it came out gold at the other end."

"You genuinely believed that he turned silver into gold?" Varro was incredulous.

"It was gold sure enough, Varro," Fabius fumed. "Then he asked me to give him one thousand silver sesterces, so that he could turn them into gold for me."

Varro could not believe his ears. "You gave him one thousand sesterces?"

"No, I did not give him one thousand sesterces." Fabius' eyes flashed guiltily away. "I gave him five hundred. And then he disappeared. With my money."

Martius roared with laughter. "Five hundred sesterces!" A military tribune was paid forty thousand sesterces a year. A legionary, meanwhile, earned nine hundred a year. Fabius had given the swindler the equivalent of more than half a year's pay for a soldier. "I knew you to be a simpleton, Fabius," Martius declared, "and now you have proved it!"

"I will have you know I took a precaution against thievery!" Fabius countered.

"What manner of precaution?" Varro asked.

"The fellow gave me share scrip as security; scrip in the corporation running the largest horse farms in Syria, with hippodrome and army remount contracts."

"And, of course," said Varro, "the scrip was a forgery?"

Fabius lowered his head. "Yes," he conceded.

Again Martius roared with laughter.

"An excellent forgery, but a forgery just the same," Fabius said with a sigh. "As I discovered too late. Alcibiardes, or whoever he is, must have a scribe as an accomplice."

"This all seems so blatant, Fabius," Varro remarked, shaking his head. "How could you have allowed yourself to have been taken in by so obvious a deception?"

"Damn it all, Varro, I was the most senior Roman officer at Caesarea at the time! It did not occur to me that anyone would have the gall to thieve from me, of all people."

"That was what your thief was counting on," said Varro. "The most skilled deceivers set their sights high." As a magistrate, he spoke from experience.

"I scoured Caesarea for the fellow. But what better way to escape than to fall in with a visiting official's party? I must insist that you turn out your people for inspection."

"What does your Alcibiades look like? Describe him to me."

"A Greek. A good-living Greek, with a paunch. Bald. Round-faced, and with a distinctive mole on his cheek. A man with a way with words."

Varro and Martius looked at each other.

"A mole you say? Varro touched his own cheek. "Here? The size of a sesterce?"

Fabius' eyes widened. "You do have him!"

"No. You will find your man outside Macherus, beside the Nabatea road," Varro advised. "His name was not Aclibiades, but Aristarchus, and he was a scribe by profession. He would have been the one to forge your share scrip."

Fabius beamed. "Beside the Nabatea road you say? I will send a cavalry detachment to apprehend him at once."

"There is no hurry," said Varro. "Aristarchus is going nowhere."

"Only as far as the wind will blow him," commented Martius dryly.

Fabius frowned. "I fail to understand."

"The man is dead, Fabius, and cremated," said Varro "Someone cut his throat for his money. Your money. When he thought that his crime would catch up with him he fled my expedition, and into the arms of some cutthroat on the Jericho road."

✠

Varro and Martius had gone to the camp wall, for one last look at the ring of fire before they turned in for the night. Fabius had left them in the camp street, feeling the fool he was, and feeling cheated of his revenge on the man who had swindled him.

"It all makes sense now," said Martius, inclining his head and taking in the stars. "Aristarchus was indeed a liar and a deceiver."

"Aristarchus knew it would only be a matter of days before we overtook the 10th, and its tribune, his victim Fabius. That was why he fled our camp."

"Did his escape have everything to do with Fabius and alchemy, and nothing to do with his testimony to us about Pilatus and the Nazarene? How much of what he told us about the rumored Nazarene execution conspiracy can we believe, Julius? If any of it?"

"About the Nazarene, Centurion Longinus, Matthias ben Naum, and the drug? How much indeed, my friend? Let us hope that Ben Naum can answer that tomorrow."

XXII

THE HOLE IN THE GROUND

Forest of Jardes, Territory of Idumea, Roman Province of Judea. May, A.D. 71

Morning had arrived, and clad the earth in her saffron robe. All eyes tracked to the forest. In the dawn's low light, a single rider could be seen emerging. Varro settled his helmet on his head, fixed the chinstrap in place, then eased his horse forward. He led the way at walking pace through the line of troops with their spluttering torches, down the grassy rise toward the distant rider. Artimedes came next, followed by Martius and Alienus. Publius, a pale, curly-headed legion trumpeter of sixteen years of age whose instrument curled over his left shoulder, came last of all.

The brother of Miriam sat waiting for them. As they joined him in the open, Jacob looked past the quintet. Like a flooding river, Roman troops were flowing from the camp and spreading to left and right behind the encircling line at double time. "What are they doing?" Jacob queried suspiciously.

"Reinforcing the line," Varro replied. "As a precaution. If your people play the honest game, the legion will not interfere. Is Matthias ben Naum waiting?"

Jacob returned his attention to the questor. "Yes, he awaits."

Varro nodded toward the forest. "Then lead on."

Jacob turned his horse around and headed for the trees at the trot.

"Alienus and I will go first, questor," Martius called, spurring his horse forward.

Varro let the two officers precede him. With Artimedes at his side he came along close behind. As before, the boy trumpeter brought up the rear. Holding his reins with the right hand and his trumpet at his shoulder with the left, the youngster looked anxiously all around him as the Jewish envoy led the way into the trees.

Easing back to the walk, Jacob followed a narrow track just wide enough to allow passage to a wagon or cart. The track meandered in a generally westerly direction. Two by two, the Romans followed him down the track at a short distance. The track climbed onto a rise, then fell away sharply to the left on the far side. There was no sign of life in the foliage to left or right. No animal stirred. No bird beat its wings among the branches. No partisan raised his head.

Varro's muscles were tensed. He was prepared to defend himself at the first sign of threat. Yet, despite feeling more vulnerable than at any other time in his life, he projected an aura of calm indifference. As a Roman magistrate should.

After several minutes riding, they came to a natural clearing, roughly round in shape and some two hundred and fifty feet across. The grass had been pressed down, and there were circular piles of charcoal at regular intervals. It appeared to Varro that until recently there had been tents and cooking fires in this clearing, but he detected no movement in the surrounding trees. In the middle of the open space there was an oblong hole, freshly dug, ten feet long and four feet across. The earth from the hole had been thrown onto the ground behind it, forming a low mound.

Jacob dismounted at the edge of the clearing.

"This is the meeting place?" Martius called, as the Romans reined in around him.

"This is the place," Jacob confirmed. "Here we dismount." He slipped from the saddle, and following his lead, Varro dropped to the ground. His four companions warily did the same.

"What is the purpose of the hole in the ground?" Martius asked. With his left hand he held his sword scabbard, securing it so that he only had to reach over with his right and draw his sword with one swift, smooth motion.

"You will see soon enough," Jacob answered.

"Probably intended to be our grave," said Alienus with a wry smile.

"We came in good faith, Jacob," said Varro impatiently. "Where is Ben Jairus?"

Jacob nodded toward the far side of the clearing. As he did, three darkly-bearded men stepped from the trees. "That is Judas ben Jairus."

None of the Jewish partisans wore a weapons belt. Nor were there weapons in their hands. The central figure wore armor with silver and jet inlay, the armor of a Roman centurion he had killed in the Sanctuary of the Temple during the battle for Jerusalem. This was Judas, son of Jair, leader of the second last Jewish rebel force under arms.

"Can they speak?" said Martius. "Or are they dumb?"

"You must disarm before Judas will enter into any discussion," Jacob advised.

Varro shook his head. "First, I will speak with Matthias ben Naum. Where is he?"

"Look in the pit."

All five Romans looked toward the excavation at the center of the clearing. From where they stood none could see into it. Varro tethered his horse to a bush. As the others did the same, the questor walked toward the pit. Alienus quickly joined him.

With his right hand Martius grabbed Jacob by the back of the tunic. "You come with us," he growled, hauling the Jewish envoy with him as he followed Varro.

Artimedes and the trumpeter quickly fell in behind.

When Varro and Alienus reached the edge of the pit and looked down they could see it was some seven feet deep and that a lone figure swathed in a brown cloak sat on the earth floor. The man was big-framed, gray-headed and gray-bearded, with well-tanned skin. He might have been aged in his sixties, or seventies. Looking up, and, seeing faces appear around the perimeter of his place of confinement, he smiled. "You are the Romans? Come to question me?"

"You are Matthias ben Naum?" Varro responded.

"I am he," said the man, effortlessly drawing himself to his feet.

Varro looked down at the Jew with a mixture of curiosity and suspicion. He had marched across Judea to find this man, yet, the questor was strangely unexcited by what he saw. He had not imagined Ben Naum like this; he had pictured him small and wizened. This fellow was tall and powerful. The Jew held his right arm against his chest, as if it were injured.

"What is your occupation?" Varro asked him.

"Apothecary," came the immediate rejoinder.

"From where do you hail?"

"From Jerusalem. Help me out of here, my lords. Judas put me in this hole so that I might not run away. I give my word, if you help me out, I won't run."

"Will you answer my questions, about the death of the Nazarene?"

"Of course. I will tell you all you want to know. Just help me out of here, good lords." Smiling broadly, the man stretched up his left hand to Varro. But the questor, feeling that something was not quite right — precisely what, he could not put his finger on — held back. So the smiling Jew turned to Alienus beside him. "Give me a strong right hand, friend, and pull me out of here."

Decurion Alienus dropped to one knee. While holding the long scabbard of his cavalry sword in place at his side with his left hand, the Egyptian reached down to the Jew with his right. "Here, take hold."

The Jew wrapped his large, callused hand around Alienus' right wrist, clasping it with an iron grip. "Pull away, my lord," the man urged, grinning up at Alienus.

As Alienus went to stand and haul the Jew from the pit, Varro, looking down at the man still, was overcome with a growing feeling of unease. The Jew had reached up his left arm, apparently because his right was weak or useless. He had grasped Alienus' right wrist, on the decurion's sword arm. Alienus was now prevented from drawing his sword. All Roman soldiers were trained as right-handed swordsmen, reserving the left arm for a shield. With this simple act of grasping his right wrist, the Jew had for the moment rendered Alienus defenseless.

Yet, something else bothered Varro. Something about the Jew himself did not ring true. Even if the questor accepted that an apothecary could be tall and well-built, the man's skin seemed oddly out of character. Surely, Varro now thought to himself, an apothecary worked indoors, making his potions and his preparations with his mortar and pestle and all the other equipment that an apothecary employed in his work. The skin of Saul ben Gamaliel, apothecary of Macherus, had been milk white. Yet, this man was so tanned by the sun his skin was like leather. This man had spent a lifetime out of doors. This man was no apothecary! "Wait, Alienus!" Varro yelled. "He is not Ben Naum!"

Even as the words were leaving the questor's lips, the Jew's right hand, the hand that had been seemingly useless only moments before, reached beneath his cloak. A sword slid from a concealed scabbard. The weapon shone like new; a Roman legionary *gladius*, twenty-two inches long, double-edged, with the short sword's distinctive sharp pointed end. With hate in his eyes, the grinning Jew thrust upward with the weapon.

"No!" Varro bellowed.

Alienus had no chance to escape his fate. As the point of the sword came up at him he drew back his head and tried to pull away. But the Jew's grasp was like a vice. In a desperate and instinctive act of self-defense the Egyptian went to reach for the sword's razor-sharp blade with his bare left hand. His fingers reached the blade as the blade reached his neck. With all his strength, the Jew pushed the end of the sword up into the decurion's exposed throat. At the same time, he dragged on Alienus' right arm, pulling him onto the sword. The blade penetrated beneath Alienus' jaw. The decurion's eyes bulged, his mouth gaped open. The Jew withdrew the sword. The cavalryman hung on the edge of the pit, open mouthed, wide-eyed. Blood spurted from the entry wound. The Jew tugged with the left hand, and Alienus tumbled into the pit. Alienus had been right; this was indeed his grave.

All around the clearing, a victorious roar arose from a hundred throats. Varro looked up. Across the clearing, Judas ben Jairus and his two colleagues had dropped to their knees. They were scraping away loose dirt. Then they were rising to their full height once more, bearing swords and shields unearthed from hiding places at their feet. Judas was grinning at the questor. All around the clearing, scores of partisans were crashing through the trees, yelling at the top of their voices. Most did not have the luxury of armor. Many did not carry swords but were armed with simple spears, tree saplings with fire-hardened points. One or two were equipped with bows. Once in the open, the rebels came to a halt, and fell silent. Lining the perimeter of the clearing, they surrounded the five Romans in the same way that the Roman army surrounded the forest.

"By the thundering spouse of Juno, touch us, and you are all dead men!" Martius declared, drawing his sword.

"Yes, we are dead men!" Judas ben Jairus called back across the open ground in a rasping voice. "But we shall have the corpses of Roman officers to decorate our graves!"

Members of the partisan ring yelled in concert. All expected to die; they would die happy if they could take a Roman questor, tribune, and decurion with them. Seeing a chance to escape to his comrades, Jacob now broke away from Martius, ran around the pit and toward Judas Ben Jairus. Martius bounded around the opposite side of the pit to cut him off. Jacob, focused on reaching his leader, did not see the tribune coming. Martius raised his sword on the run. He swung it in a slashing motion.. The middle of the cutting edge caught Jacob on the right side of the neck, just below the ear. Driven by the force of the tribune's blow, the steel cleaved through flesh and bone as if it were butter. Jacob threw up his hands, and fell forward. Martius came to a halt, standing over the fallen Jew. Jacob's head had all but been cleaved from his body. In his death throes, the arms and legs of the youth were quivering.

There was an uncanny silence. The stunned partisans had watched the execution without a sound. Varro was the first to react. Turning to Publius the trumpeter, who stood beside him with a look of abject horror on his face, he grasped him by the arm, yelling, "Blow, boy! Sound 'To Arms!' Lose neither your courage nor your breath! Blow, boy!"

"With all your might," Martius added, "so that even the gods might hear you!"

✠

Prefect Quintus Crispus stood beside his horse. Behind him, Decurion Pompeius and his twenty-nine Vettonians also stood by their steeds, ready to mount up on the prefect's order. In front of Crispus spread the ten cohorts of the 10th Legion in their battle lines. Away to left and right, three and a half thousand auxiliary foot soldiers, many carrying axes, stood in a line which circled the forest behind the inner line of mounted cavalry.

Immediately in front of Crispus, Centurion Gallo stood with his eighty men of the 4th Scythica Legion. In ten compact rows of eight men, they were ready to go into the forest with General Bassus' army when and if the order was given. Junior Tribune Venerius stood with the centurion. To Crispus' right, between the 10th Legion's last line and the camp entrenchments, stood General Bassus' chariot, its two horses waiting calmly in their traces with a groom holding the bridle of one. The chariot itself was empty. Soon after the questor and his companions had entered the Forest of Jardes, General Bassus had been hit by severe pain, and had been carried back into the camp.

Crispus cocked his ear. The distant sound of musical notes wafted on the still morning air. A trumpet call, faint, but unmistakable. The legion call 'To Arms,' sounded over and over again. Crispus went cold. He was suddenly afraid. Not for himself, but for his questor. He whipped around to Decurion Pompeius. "You hear it?"

"I hear it," said Pompeius gravely, nodding.

"Mount up!" Crispus ordered breathlessly.

Hostilis, Julius Varro's servant, had been standing close by, watching and waiting for the questor's return like everyone else. He came running, to help Prefect Crispus up into the saddle. Behind Crispus, the Vettonians mounted their steeds. The detachment's standard-bearer reached to the white standard of the Vettonian Horse that stood planted in the earth, lifted it up, and raised it high.

"Column of two's!" Decurion Pompeius ordered.

As the cavalrymen were forming up in pairs behind Crispus and Pompeius, several horsemen came galloping toward them from the front of the 10th Legion formation — Tribune Quintus Fabius and an escort. "Where do you men think you are going?" Fabius called as he rode up.

"The trumpet call," Crispus said urgently. "The questor's signal for help!"

"No one may enter the forest without General Bassus' express order," said Fabius.

"But the general is not here," Crispus returned, nodding to the empty chariot. "You can give permission in his stead, tribune. There is no time to waste!"

Fabius shook his head. "Roman troops will only enter the forest when General Bassus gives the order," he declared. "And General Bassus is currently indisposed." There was a supercilious smile on Fabius' lips.

Decurion Pompeius now found voice. "We have our orders, from Questor Varro."

"I am giving you a new order," Fabius retorted. "Do not enter the forest! I should not have to remind you that I am the senior officer here. And I say we shall await General Bassus' instructions, whenever he is in a position to pass them on to us." Roughly pulling the head of his horse around, Fabius galloped back the way he had come, to the head of the 10th Legion formation, with his escort flying after him.

Crispus, astounded, looked at Pompeius. "I don't believe it! That swine!"

"We can't leave the questor to his fate," Pompeius returned.

Crispus made a spur of the moment decision. "Wait here!" he commanded. Throwing his legs over the horns of his saddle, he jumped down to the ground. Holding his scabbard at his side, the prefect ran back toward the camp gate.

Standing nearby in front of the 4th Scythica men, Centurion Gallo and Tribune Venerius had been witness to these exchanges. Now, as Crispus hurried back to the camp as fast as legs would carry him, Gallo saw a figure dash toward the general's chariot. The man, wearing the red-striped tunic of a servant, leapt up into the chariot, freed the reins in an instant, then lashed them along the backs of the pair of horses. The groom holding the bridle fearfully let go and jumped out of the way as the chariot lurched forward. Now Gallo recognized the driver. It was Hostilis, the questor's handservant. As the chariot came rolling along the front of the 4th Scythica formation, Gallo stepped out in front of the horses. Showing no fear, ignoring the risk of being run down, he grasped the bridles of both horses and planted his feet. The momentum of the animals' progress dragged him a short distance until the chariot came to a halt.

"Let go, Centurion!" Hostilis called angrily. "The questor is in trouble!"

"What do you propose to do about it?"

"In my native Britain I was trained to drive the chariot," Hostilis earnestly returned. "I know what in am doing, centurion. Stand aside!"

Gallo hesitated a moment. Then he turned to Venerius, standing just twenty feet away. "Get up in the chariot with the slave!" he called.

Venerius stared back at him, aghast. "What?"

"Get up in the chariot," Gallo repeated. "The questor told me that he wanted you to lead any rescue effort if it became necessary."

"He did?" Venerius went white with fear. "You're sure? He said nothing to me."

"You are wasting time, damn you, thin-stripe!" Gallo cursed. "Or do you propose to disobey the questor?"

Venerius gulped. Many times he had wished that he had not come on this expedition, but never more than now.

"Move, boy!" Gallo bellowed.

His legs feeling like lead weights, his mind numb with fear, Venerius walked to the back of the chariot then pulled himself up behind the standing driver.

Gallo let go of the bridles and quickly stepped back. "Go like the wind, slave!" he called up to Hostilis.

With a slap of the reins and a cry of encouragement to his steeds, Hostilis set the vehicle in motion. The chariot went charging along behind the last line of the 10th Legion. When Hostilis saw an opening between cohorts which offered an avenue all the way to the front he tugged the reins to the right. The animals responded immediately. The chariot curved right, executed a bumping turn, then sped down the avenue.

As Gallo walked back to his place at the extreme left of his detachment's front row, Optio Silius called out to him from the ranks. "Did the questor really say that, centurion? Did he really tell you he wanted Soupy Venerius to lead his rescue?"

"Something to that affect," Gallo replied, unable to hold back a smile. "I can't recollect his exact words, but I'm sure that was what the questor had in mind." It had only taken Centurion Gallo a matter of weeks to have his revenge on Gaius Venerius.

In the chariot, Hostilis was learning on the run. Apart from the fact that they possessed two wheels and were drawn by two horses, the British war chariot and the Roman *biga* were quite dissimilar. The chariot that Hostilis had learned to master was open-ended. He had knelt to drive, with a warrior standing behind him, on a rectangular wooden floor suspended by pliable leather from the chariot sides. The Romans only employed chariots for racing and as the private conveyances of the rich. Open at the rear, with closed sides rising to a high, curved, closed front, Roman chariots had no suspension and were uncomfortable to ride in and difficult to manage.

Uncomfortable they might be, but Roman chariots were fast, very fast, as Hostilis soon found to his satisfaction. As he raced out through a gap in the 10th Legion line, members of Tribune Fabius' mounted escort attempted to cut him off. He charged by and left them in his wake. Rather than try to stop him, the men of the auxiliary line parted to let him pass through, some even raising their javelins in salute and cheering, thinking the uniformed officer in the chariot with the driver must be General Bassus.

Hostilis swiftly mastered the art of driving standing up. The techniques for turning horses were the same as he had learned back at home in the kingdom of the Iceni, although he realized after his first turn that in a Roman chariot the driver had also to lean well into the bend or risk taking the vehicle over on its opposite side. Balance; it was all a matter of balance.

His passenger was not helping. Hostilis looked back over his shoulder. A white-faced Venerius was clinging onto the side rail. "Stand in the middle. Plant your feet either side," Hostilis yelled to the junior tribune.

Venerius gingerly complied, securing new handholds to left and right.

"Have your sword ready!" Hostilis then called, focusing his attention on the fast approaching trees. He aimed for the same track that he had seen his master take only a short while before. He did not slacken speed, driving the chariot into the forest at full pace. The horses were fit, trained, and willing. They charged down the narrow thoroughfare between the trees, sending clods of earth flying from their pounding hooves. Hostilis glanced over his shoulder again, into the petrified eyes of the junior tribune. "Your sword! Your sword!" Both their lives might depend on Venerius' swordsmanship.

Venerius nodded numbly, and drew his sword, before clutching at the rail once more with his free left hand.

The track inclined to a rise. At full pace, the chariot came up the gradient. At the summit, just where the track dipped on the other side and jagged away to the left, the vehicle became airborne. At the same time, Hostilis spotted the turn to the left. As he leaned hard left and drew on the reins, the chariot came back down, landing with a jolt on just its left wheel. The concussion sent the chariot up on its side. In the back, with sword in his right hand and only holding on with his left, and unprepared for the crashing landing, Venerius was jolted free. As the chariot tipped over, the junior tribune was thrown out, ejected like a drunkard from a tavern. The chariot teetered on one wheel briefly, then, lightened by Venerius' departure, dropped back down onto two wheels and went careering on its way.

Venerius turned over in the air, and landed heavily on his back. The wind was knocked out of him, the sword flew from his grip. Dazed, trying to catch his breath, he lay there in the middle of the grassy track. He heard the drumming of the chariot-horses' hooves growing fainter. Rolling over, he looked down the track. There was no sign of the chariot. It occurred to him that Hostilis had been so engaged with the task of keeping the chariot upright that he had not even noticed that Venerius had been thrown out. Either that, or the slave had deliberately left him behind.

Fear gripping him, Venerius sat up. His head was spinning. He looked around. His sword lay ten feet away. Dragging himself to his feet, he stumbled the several paces to the weapon, stooped, and picked it up. He looked down the track, and then back the way he had come. He asked himself whether he should follow the chariot. It did offer a speedy means of escape. Then he told himself that the chariot had been heading into the forest, toward the enemy. Safety lay in the other direction, away from the enemy, toward the Roman lines. He took two steps back up the track, then stopped, wincing as pain shot from his right hip. He realized that he had probably dislocated or broken something in his fall. Cursing his luck, he resumed his progress, limping painfully up the track.

As he broached the rise, he stopped abruptly. Ahead, three hundred feet away, between him and safety, Jewish partisans were coming out of the trees and standing in his path. Hearing a noise in the trees beside him to his left, he spun about. Several partisans bearing spears were emerging from the foliage, leering at him. Venerius turned, and began to lope along the track, heading deeper into the forest, following the departed chariot. "Hostilis!" he bawled. "Hostilis, come back!" The trees absorbed his cries.

Then ahead, more partisans began to walk into the open. These men took up station in his path, smiling, and beckoning him to come to them. Venerius swiveled around, looking back up the track. The partisans he had first encountered were closing in on him from the east, closing the distance and picking up the pace of their steps. One Jew in the lead was energetically swinging a sword back and forth.

Eighteen-year-old Venerius dropped to his knees. Flinging away his sword, he burst into tears. His entire body shook with his sobs. "The gods help me!" he wailed. A Jew came to stand behind him. From the corner of his eye, Venerius saw the flash of a sword. He lowered his head, and closed his eyes, and tensed for the blow he expected to come at any moment. "Please, I mean you people no harm," he sniveled. "I am Gaius Licinius Venerius. I am the nephew of Licinius Mucianus, the most powerful man at Rome beside Caesar himself. I can pay you." He remembered the valuable Equestrian ring on his left hand. "Here, my gold ring…" He began tugging at the ring.

The sword, a former Roman sword, came down on the neck of Gaius Licinius Venerius, nephew of Licinius Mucianus. It cleaved the head of the boy named for Venus goddess of love from his shoulders. The decapitated body collapsed to one side. The head, still wearing a richly decorated helmet, toppled off and rolled down the track for several feet, over and over, before coming to rest. Venerius' lips continued to move.

The trumpeter had sounded 'To Arms' a dozen times. Martius had rejoined Varro and the others. Both Martius and Varro had swords in one hand, daggers in the other. Artimedes and the trumpeter stood behind them. The petrified trumpeter still had his instrument over his shoulder.

"I'll take care of the boy," Martius said to Varro, casting his eyes around the clearing as the partisans began to edge forward, slowly tightening the ring around them. "You look after your Greek."

"I would prefer it if we had shields," said Varro, carefully watching the nearest partisans, expecting them to dash forward to the attack at any moment.

"Are you ready to make a break for it?"

"Which direction?" Varro asked.

"Toward the horses," Martius replied.

"They will expect that," Varro came back.

"We ignore the horses, and in the confusion keep running, with the speed of Mercury, along the track. Agreed?"

Varro decided it was better than no plan at all, and the track would lead them out of the forest. "Agreed."

"You other two, take hold of our belts," Martius instructed, "and do not falter."

Artimedes and the trumpeter took hold of the officers' sword belts.

"On your word," said Varro.

"Mars, Minerva and Fortuna, don't desert us this day! Ready, Julius? Now!"

With Martius and Varro running side by side and dragging the two non-combatants along behind them, the quartet charged toward their horses, whose reins had been taken by rebels. Letting out a shout, the partisans of the ring ran forward, with several launching spears in the direction of the running Romans. Their hasty, poorly directed volley missed the Romans. Arrows whizzed by, too high to hit their targets.

Martius ran toward a Jew in front of the horses who jabbed a spear at him with an overhand thrust. Martius easily knocked aside the spear then brought his sword up into the man's groin. The Jew went down, clutching at his groin and screaming. Martius and the trumpeter ran right over the top of the downed man.

A short, bare-headed partisan with a round shield and short sword came at Varro, swinging his weapon wildly. The sword swished past Varro's nose; Varro felt the wind of its passing. As Varro's running momentum carried him forward he crashed his own sword down onto the man's head. It sliced into the partisan's skull, split it, and exposed the brain matter. The man dropped. He was dead before he hit the ground.. This was the first time that Julius Varro had physically killed anyone. He had sent men to be executed by others, he had led auxiliary units which had killed German raiders, but he himself had never inflicted a lethal blow. As a youth, he had wondered what it would feel like to kill a man. Now he knew. It felt like nothing. He was so focused on staying alive that the act of homicide simply did not register. At that moment it held no more significance for him than the need to draw breath.

Martius swung at a teenaged partisan in his path who raised a wicker shield. The tribune's blow shattered the wickerwork. The shield disintegrated. Martius swung again, and sliced off the man's left arm at the shoulder. The limb fell to the ground. Blood gushed from the stump just below the man's shoulder. Screaming with horror, the youth dropped his spear, grabbed at the stump of his arm with his right hand, and reeled away.

In the face of this fierce Roman onslaught, other partisans in their path fled to left and right, some throwing away their weapons to run unencumbered. Jews who had secured the five Roman horses quickly led them into the trees to prevent their riders from regaining them. This permitted a gap to suddenly open in the partisan line, as Martius had hoped. Martius and Varro dived through the opening, dragging Artimedes and the young trumpeter with them. As they ran along the track, Varro, looking over his shoulder, past the panting Artimedes, could see Judas ben Jairus himself leading a group of ten or twelve determined and well armed pursuers.

"I cannot run, questor!" Artimedes gasped, clutching at his chest with his left hand as he struggled along, slowing himself and Varro.

"You must!" Varro yelled. "Keep going!"

"I cannot…" As Artimedes spoke, a spear lanced into the middle of his back. The secretary let go of Varro's sword-belt, staggered, then came to a stop, reaching around ineffectually for the spear between his shoulders with his right hand, as if he might pluck it out like a splinter. As Martius and the trumpeter kept running, unaware of Artimedes' injury, the little bald man looked at Varro, who also came to a halt. There was an innate sadness in his eyes. "I am sorry, my boy," he gasped, before crumpling to the ground.

Dropping his dagger to free one hand, Varro grabbed the end of the spear lodged in the secretary's back and yanked hard. It had no barb and came free without difficulty. Flinging the spear away, he stooped to lift the secretary to his feet. As he bent, he felt a spear glance off his armor. "Get up, Artimedes!" he yelled, reaching under the Greek's arm. Artimedes was limp. His shiny head sagged like the head of a straw doll. He was unconscious, or dead.

"Julius!" Martius was running back to the pair, sheathing his dagger as he came.

The musician had stopped in the track, and stood watching in horror. "Hurry, my lords!" the terrified trumpeter bawled as he saw Ben Jairus and his party drawing closer.

Varro tried to lift the Greek, but with just one free hand, he could not.

Now Martius joined him. "Is he dead?"

"I hope not."

Martius switched his sword to his left hand, then each of them took one of Artimedes' arms and between them they half carried half dragged him at the run. Publius fell in with them once they reached him. But they had only gone fifty paces when a band of twenty or more partisans washed from the trees and into their path.

"We can't fight our way through them carrying the secretary," Martius declared

"I will not leave him," said Varro determinedly.

"Then we make a stand here," Martius declared.

"If that is what we must do."

They came to a halt, and lay Artimedes face down on the ground. Varro and Martius then stood back to back, the questor facing west, the tribune facing east.

"What should I do?" cried the terrified trumpeter.

"Stay with Artimedes," Varro said. There was no other course he could advise.

The two partisan bands quickly linked up and flooded around the four Romans. At a distance of twenty feet they exchanged comments in Aramaic, laughing, pointing.

"What they are saying?" Martius asked as they tensely watched and waited.

"Does it matter?" Varro came back.

"Probably not. As a matter of interest, Julius, am I to take it that there was no Matthias ben Naum?"

"Apparently not. That was definitely not Ben Naum in the pit."

"So, coming here was a waste of time?"

"So it would appear."

Martius laughed. "Well, I would not have missed it for anything."

"These have been an interesting few months," Varro remarked.

"It has been a pleasure knowing you, questor."

"It is not over yet, Marcus."

"Trust in your luck, and pray to Fortuna? Is that it?"

Now there came the sound of pounding hooves behind the partisans, to the east. Jews on that side of the track began to scatter in sudden panic.

"What is it?" Varro called, unable to see what was happening in that direction.

"Fortuna shines on you, questor," Martius returned, sounding elated. "Come!"

Varro turned, to see General Bassus' chariot surging down the track toward them. As it came up, the chariot slue to a halt three hundred feet away, with the horses lifting up on their hind legs and pawing the air. Now Varro recognized the driver. "Hostilis!"

The Briton eased his horses around, coaxing them into backing up then going forward, making the seemingly impossible task of turning the chariot on the narrow track look easy. Very soon the chariot faced back the way it had come, with the open end beckoning Varro and his companions. "Hurry, my lords!" Hostilis anxiously called.

Now, seeing that the chariot was not going to run them down and that it was not accompanied by other chariots or cavalry as they had feared, partisans rediscovered their courage. Spears were loosed at Hostilis, who ducked out of harm's way. But the rebel focus was on finishing off the Roman officers. With a yell, partisans came at Varro and Martius. Varro dodged anonymous blows and jabbed at contorted faces. He was soon separated from Martius. A spear went shooting past his ear. Something hit his breastplate. A sword glanced off his helmet as he sidestepped. There was a sudden, stinging sensation on his left upper arm. Seeing a round shield lying on the ground, he dropped onto one knee to grab it up. A bloodied hand and forearm were still attached to the shield's handles, courtesy of a slicing blow from Martius.

A gray-headed man came at Varro. Forgetting the shield, Varro thrust upward and caught the man in the stomach. The Jew dropped his long Roman shield and went reeling away. Grabbing the fallen shield with his left hand Varro came to his feet. As he did, he instinctively spun around, just in time to use the shield to parry a blow from a sword. He swung at his assailant, missing. He swung again, and again. The partisan turned and fled.

Suddenly, Varro was alone. Bodies lay everywhere around the scene of combat. Martius was to his right, fighting two men simultaneously. He too had found himself a Jewish shield - square, small, but effective. Publius the trumpeter was bleeding from a head wound and trying to fend off three attackers by frantically swinging his trumpet around and around. Sword blows glanced off the metal of the instrument with hollow clangs. Between the two struggles, the questor could see a clear path to the waiting chariot. Artimedes lay where he had fallen. The back of the Greek's skull had been battered into red, bloody mush by club or stone. If Artimedes had not been dead before, he was now. Varro sprang forward to go to aid of the trumpeter. In that instant he saw an arrow enter the boy's throat. Young Publius dropped his trumpet, and fell backward to the earth clutching at his throat. A Jew began hacking at the fallen youth with a sword.

Angry for the first time that day, Varro ran at the Jew, bellowing: "Leave him be!" The partisan, bending over the body of the trumpeter, looked around, to find Varro's sword sweeping across his face. The blow sliced through his jaw. Screaming, the man dropped to his knees with hands to his bloodied face. Varro looked toward the chariot. The path was still clear. "Now, Marcus!" he yelled on the run. "Now is our chance!"

Martius had dispatched one attacker with a thrust into the mouth. Now he knocked the other down with his shield. But instead of going in for the kill, he pulled away and ran after Varro. The questor tripped as he reached the chariot; dropping his shield he literally fell into it. Looking up, he saw Hostilis with a broken spear skewering his thigh. The slave reached down and dragged his master into the back of the chariot. Martius came running up, covered in blood, but smiling. He seemed uninjured; it had to be Jewish blood. Varro reached out to Martius.

"Fortuna be praised!" the grinning tribune exclaimed. Dropping his shield, he reached up to grab Varro's hand. In that moment, an arrow pierced him, entering just above his armor at the left armpit and penetrating his chest. Martius looked down at the arrow jutting from his body. "That was not part of the plan!" he said, almost in disbelief. Sheathing his sword, he grasped the arrow and broke it off, casting away the piece in his hand. He looked up at Varro, and smiled again. "Nothing serious," he said, "thanks to the gods." His smile disappeared. Martius collapsed into the back of the chariot.

Varro sheathed his sword and hauled his friend in beside him. Looking down the track, he saw Judas ben Jairus and others coming at the wide-eyed run, swords raised.

"Hold tight, my lords!" Hostilis called back over his shoulder, lashing the reins along the backs of his steeds. The chariot surged forward. Varro grabbed the rail with his left hand. With his right he gripped Marcus Martius' armor, to keep his friend from falling out. Martius lay face down, feet hanging out the back of the bumping chariot.

"Marcus, we will soon be out of this," Varro assured his friend.

Martius looked up at him with glazed eyes. "Soon be out of it," he slowly, mechanically repeated.

XXIII

THE MASSACRE

Forest of Jardes, Territory of Idumea, Roman Province of Judea. May, A.D. 71

Naked and bloodied, Marcus Martius lay stretched out on a table in the physician's tent. Diocles' assistants were washing down the tribune's body, while he stood looking down at his patient, with Varro at his side. Regaining consciousness, Martius opened his eyes.

"Can you hear me, Marcus?" said Varro.

"I hear you," Martius replied weakly. "What of the Jews? Are they dealt with?"

"They rushed from the forest on our heels," Varro advised, "and threw themselves onto our auxiliary line. Once they had exhausted themselves, the 10th was sent in against them. Not a rebel survives, Marcus. They were killed to the last man."

"Fools," Martius commented, his voice as soft as a breeze.

"Worry not, you will come out of this, Marcus," Varro assured him. "Your wound is not fatal." Varro had no medical training, and was not qualified to make such a statement. It was more a profound hope than a known fact.

"It's the physician who worries me," Martius responded. "Is he sober?"

Varro smiled. At least his friend had his wits about him. Not that he could necessarily say the same about Diocles. The physician was white-faced; he appeared to tremble, faintly, but perceptibly. "Listen to me, Diocles," he said, in a steady, controlled voice. "If the tribune dies, then so do you. Do you hear me?"

Diocles did not look around. "He will not die," he replied, in a quavering voice which failed to inspire confidence.

"Then do what you are trained to do. Save my friend."

Diocles now instructed his assistants to roll the patient onto his right side. Martius groaned as he was turned. Blood was seeping from the wound caused by the Jewish arrow, with the arrowhead still embedded beneath the left arm, and also from a second wound, an incision near the arrow's entry point; at some point during the fighting, Martius had been jabbed in the side with a spear. Diocles looked down at his hands. Momentarily they quivered, the combined result of weeks without a drop of wine, the status and condition of his patient, and the questor's threat. The doctor inclined his eyes to the tent ceiling, and offered up a silent prayer. 'Asclepius, son of Apollo, god of health and protector of physicians, many times I have sought your aid, but I have never needed it more than today. Steady my hand and sharpen my eye so that I might save this man.'

"Are you capable, physician?" Varro called. "Can you do this?"

Diocles returned his eyes to the patient. "There is nothing to be concerned about," he responded. He nodded to an assistant, who placed a roll of cloth between Martius' teeth. One assistant then held the patient's wrists, another, his feet. "Scalpel." Handed a scalpel, Diocles hesitated above the arrow's entry point. 'Asclepius, do not fail me,' he implored the heavens one last time, before commencing to dig into the wound. The arrowhead was in deep; he had to burrow like a termite around the jagged shaft. He felt his patient tense from head to foot with the pain, and knew that Martius was biting hard into the cloth, but the tribune did not make a sound. Beside him, Varro watched his every move.

It took time, but eventually Diocles, perspiring freely, was able to dig out shaft and arrowhead, which he cast into a bowl. He then smeared ointment from a jar into the wound. "Bandage," he gasped. There was still the risk of the patient bleeding to death. The bandaging must be proficient. In his head, Diocles could hear the voice of his first medical instructor, Philemon of Athens. 'Strength is imparted by the compression and the number of folds of the bandage. In one case the bandage effects the cure, and in another it contributes to the cure. For these purposes this is the rule — that the force of the constriction be such as to prevent the adjoining parts from separating, without compressing them much, and so that the parts may be adjusted but not forced together; and that the constriction be small at the extremities, and least of all in the middle.'

Varro watched the physician wind a lengthy bandage around Martius' torso. Martius' eyes were closed. "Marcus?" he anxiously called.

"Still here," came a wheezing reply. Martius' face was becoming flushed.

Varro nudged Diocles. "He seems to be having difficulty breathing, physician."

"He was also speared," Diocles replied as he worked. "The spear may have punctured the left lung. He will breath more easily momentarily, I assure you."

Minutes later, once the bandaging was complete, Martius was rolled onto his back once more. He began breathing with less difficulty.

"The arrowhead is removed, and the flow of blood stemmed," Diocles announced.

"What now?" Varro asked.

"We are in the hands of the gods, questor. Pray that infection does not set in."

Varro looked at his friend. "You are strong, Marcus. You can come through this."

With his eyes still closed, Martius nodded slowly. Then he stopped moving.

"Marcus?"

Diocles put an ear to the tribune's chest. "He breathes; the tribune has again lapsed into unconsciousness, questor," he pronounced, "because of the blood he has lost. The body will replace the blood naturally. All he needs now is rest."

Varro felt comforted by this. "I know that he will recover," he said positively. Now, he saw Hostilis standing to one side. The broken shaft of a spear protruded from the servant's right thigh. Varro himself had a flesh wound on the arm, which one of Diocles' assistants now tended to. "Look to my man Hostilis now, Diocles," Varro commanded.

Diocles instructed Hostilis to lie on another operating table. Once the Briton had complied, the physician prepared to withdraw the stump of the spear.

Varro looked over to Pythagoras. "Hostilis saved my life today," he told him, "and Tribune Martius' life. You will prepare manumission papers for Hostilis. He is to be granted his freedom the moment that we return to Antioch."

Hostilis had overheard. "Thank you, my lord," he called, before crying out with pain as Diocles began to pry the offending length of wood from his leg.

"I shall prepare the manumission document for your seal, questor," said Pythagoras. "May I ask, is there is no possibility that Artimedes might be found alive?"

"Artimedes is dead," Varro replied with a sad sigh. "As are Alienus and the boy trumpeter. I saw them all die." A thought hit him. "Can anyone tell me, how did Venerius come to be in the forest? As we were coming out, we passed a naked body lying beside the track. It had lost its left hand and its head. I swear, I recognized the face as belonging to Venerius. How was it he was there?"

"Tribune Venerius volunteered to come to your rescue, my lord," Hostilis called, before letting out another howl of pain. Hostilis knew perfectly well that Gallo had tricked Venerius into joining him in the chariot, but he saw no point in disparaging the dead officer cadet, or the live centurion. Hostilis was not one to do anything without carefully thinking through both the consequences and the advantages of his act.

"He volunteered?" Varro was astonished. "Who would have credited it? Venerius found his courage. Wonders will never cease!"

✠

It was the afternoon. In his *pretorium,* Varro sat at Artimedes' compact, folding writing table, penning the last of two letters. Hostilis had brought Artimedes' writing instruments to him: the table, a writing frame, a box of quills and inks, and the questor's seal, that of a bearded Neptune, god of the sea, with his trident. This was Varro's family seal, first used by his grandfather after he had served Caesar Augustus as an admiral. This seal was Varro's signature. On letters it informed the recipient of his identity. On death warrants it sealed a condemned man's fate. On manumission papers it set an enslaved man free.

The first letter that he had written was to his mother, to tell her that her favorite, Artimedes, was dead. In describing the morning's events, Varro had claimed full culpability for the secretary's death, writing that he had foolishly led Artimedes into a trap, that he should have known better than trust the rebels. The second letter was addressed to the family of Gaius

Licinius Venerius, to inform them of the junior tribune's death, stating that Venerius had died bravely while trying to save the questor's life.

Centurion Gallo entered the tent. Behind him came a centurion of the 10th Legion.

"Begging the questor's pardon," Gallo began. "We think we may have identified the body of the rebel leader. He was found wearing the armor and helmet of a Roman centurion. Is this Judas ben Jairus, my lord?"

As Varro looked around, the centurion beside Gallo lifted up a wooden spike of the kind that usually topped entrenchments. On the end of the spike sat a decapitated head, that of a darkly bearded man in his thirties. The centurion's hand was red from the blood that had dripped from the dead man's severed neck.

Varro took in the head, with its staring eyes and bloodied open mouth. He recognized the face of the man who had led the rebels in the forest that morning. "Yes, that is Judas ben Jairus," he confirmed with a sigh before returning to his writing.

"We thought as much," said the centurion of the 10th. "We have counted three thousand and ninety seven dead Jews. For ourselves, and apart from your thin-striper and the decurion, we lost just ten men of the 10th killed today. A paltry price to pay."

Varro nodded glumly. He had seen enough death this day. He continued writing.

Gallo and his companion looked at each other, shrugged, then took their leave with the gory trophy, only for another visitor to enter the tent almost immediately.

Impatient with the interruptions, Varro looked up with a scowl, to see Pedius standing before him. "Yes, what is it, lictor?"

"You asked for Miriam to be brought to you, my lord?"

Varro lay aside his pen. "Bring her in." He was not looking forward to this.

Pedius withdrew, only to return moments later with Miriam.

"You may remove your veil if you wish," said Varro, coming to his feet.

"I am perfectly comfortable as I am, thank you," she said, haughtily.

He cursed her to himself. Why did she have to be so difficult? This woman confused him. Before now no one had ever made him feel so angry and yet so completely benevolent at the same time. He had not suggested she remove her veil for any significant reason, he would simply like to look on her face. Still, it was not important. Coming out from behind the writing table he stood in front of her. "Your brother led us into the forest this morning," he said. He waited for a reaction, but when he received none he continued. "He led us into a trap." Another pause. Still no reaction. "Artimedes is dead, and so are Alienus and Venerius. Tribune Martius has been injured; severely injured."

"I am sorry to hear about Tribune Martius, and the others."

Varro thought that she did sound genuinely sorry. "You have heard, Miriam," he went on, "that every Jew in the forest has been killed? Every one?"

"Jacob may have escaped," she came back.

"He is dead." Varro had planned to be kinder, but it came out matter-of-factly.

"How can you be so sure?"

"I saw him killed."

"By whom?"

"By Martius."

She did not say anything.

"Your brother is dead, Miriam. I am sorry, but he brought it on himself."

"If Tribune Martius truly did kill my beloved brother," she now said, with a voice taut with emotion, "then I hope that he too dies."

He sighed. "I am sorry you feel that way."

"May I go now?"

"Very well. Pedius, take her back to her quarters."

Varro slouched unhappily back to the writing desk and resumed his seat. When he looked up, Miriam and the lictor had gone, and Hostilis was limping in the doorway bearing a water ewer. There was a bandage around his thigh, his face was white.

"Sit down, Hostilis," said Varro grumpily. "Rest your leg."

Hostilis put the ewer down and then settled on the tent's earthen floor.

When Varro finished the Venerius letter Hostilis quickly hopped up. He brought a lamp so that his master could drip sealing wax onto the back of the document, forming a small yellow, streaky mound which had the appearance of liquid onyx.

"How long have you been able to drive a chariot?" Varro asked as he applied Neptune to the melted wax.

"I was trained to drive in my youth, master, in Britain."

"Well trained, at that. Fortunately for me."

"In my younger days, I was able to run out onto the pole while the chariot was in motion and then run back to the driving position, without losing my balance or losing control of the chariot." This was unusual loquacity for Hostilis.

Varro smiled. "Quite a trick." He realized that in all the years that Hostilis had served him he had known very little about the man's past. Not that he had been interested enough to inquire before now. "Your name was not Hostilis when you were in Britain," he said, as he waited for the wax to harden. "That is your Roman name."

"Yes, master." Hostilis fanned the wax to make it dry more quickly.

"What were you named before?"

"My name was Mordoc."

"Mordoc? Does it have a meaning?"

"Son of the Sea, Master."

Varro looked surprised. "Why Son of the Sea?"

"My father was a fisherman. He was training me to also be a fisherman when King Prasutagus' Horse Master came to our village by the Sunrise Sea and chose me to train as a charioteer, in the king's service."

"Why were you chosen?"

"The Horse Master said that I had the look of a charioteer, whatever that meant."

"He must have seen the talent you displayed today when you saved my life, and your courage. In addition to your freedom, on our return to Antioch you shall have one hundred thousand sesterces, Hostilis, for the talent and the courage you showed today."

Hostilis looked at him in astonishment. Manumission had been at the back of his mind when he had leapt into General Bassus' chariot that morning, but he had never given a moment's thought to a financial reward should he succeed in conveying his master to safety. "That is too much, master," he protested.

Varro shook his head. "It is a pittance to a man like myself. You are of course welcome to remain in my service, my paid service. But you will be free to choose your future course. You might choose to go into business, for instance."

Hostilis looked at him with even more surprise. "Could I?"

"Buy yourself a fishing boat, Hostilis," said Varro earnestly, clapping the servant on the back. "Or a fleet of boats. Either that, or join one of the chariot racing teams." He smiled. "After the display I witnessed today, there is no reason why you could not achieve fame and fortune in the hippodrome."

Hostilis was nodding. Hopes and dreams had been ingredients missing from his life for the past eleven years. "I will think on it, master." For the first time in all the years that Varro had known him, Hostilis smiled. "Thank you, master." And for the first time in years, Hostilis dared to think about his home, and family, on the other side of the world.

✠

Hostilis was asleep under a blanket on the floor—dreaming his dreams, Varro thought to himself as he continued to write. The questor was now penning a eulogy to the men who had died in the forest, the men he would be cremating come the new day. Artimedes in particular, he felt, was deserving of his finest words, his most heartfelt sentiments. As he sat with pen in hand, his mind was drawn back to the last moments of Artimedes' life. Invariably, those thoughts strayed to his own brush with death. He saw the face of the man he had killed, and saw the horror struck realization in the man's eyes as Varro's sword came down on him, the realization that he was about to die. Varro saw his sword plunge into the stomach of the gray-headed man, saw his blade destroy the face of the trumpeter's assassin.

As the events contained in those minutes in the clearing and on the track came crowding back, it seemed to Varro that he must have killed ten men and wounded a hundred. Yet, when he analyzed it, he had killed just the one, had wounded a handful more. Now that he thought about it, it seemed a miracle that he himself had come out of that morning with nothing less than a nick on the arm. Three of the four men he had led into the forest were dead, the fourth was fighting for his life. Why he had been spared he could not say.

His thoughts returned to Artimedes. What a waste his death seemed; so pointless, so unnecessary. Everything now pointed to the fact that Ben Naum had either never been in the Forest of Jardes or had died with the three thousand and ninety-six other Jews who perished in and around the forest that morning. Either way, the questor's trail had ended at the forest. Now, he had no more witnesses to pursue, no more evidence to collect. He must turn his expedition around and return to Antioch. Somehow, he had to write his report for General Collega, a report based on gossip and hearsay, much of it from unreliable witnesses. It was not what he had hoped for. Such a report would not convince him, and he doubted it would convince any other thinking person.

✠

Smoke plumed up from the funeral pyre behind them as Varro and his retinue walked solemnly back in through the camp gate. As his colleagues dispersed, Varro, carrying the eulogy he had read beside the pyre, walked toward the baggage section of his camp, accompanied by Pedius.

Outside the tent of the Evangelist, Philippus sat on the ground. He was talking to Miriam and young Gemara, who likewise sat cross-legged in the sunshine. At the approach of the questor and his lictor, the trio respectfully came to their feet, with the females helping the elderly Evangelist up.

"I have just cremated my tutor and secretary," Varro sadly announced, "and those who died with him." He focused on Miriam. "I have also sent Prefect Crispus to the forest, to find the body of your brother among the Jewish dead, and to bury it. Crispus knows your brother's face."

Miriam did not reply. To Varro's frustration she merely looked away.

"I shall now return to Antioch," Varro continued. "You, Philippus, will be released at Caesarea along the way."

"Your investigation is at an end, questor?" the Evangelist inquired.

"It is."

"How is Tribune Martius faring?"

"He spent a comfortable night, but he is still gravely ill."

"What of General Bassus?"

"As well as can be expected."

Philippus nodded sagely. Then he said, "There is a city, not far from here. A Nabatean city. It is located on the southern edge of the Dead Sea. They have boats at this city. From there, you could gently take the general and the tribune north by water. After that, it would only require a day's cross-country journey to Jerusalem. Much more comfortable for them than the overland route."

This suggestion made sense to Varro. Perhaps, Varro thought, Philippus saw the water journey as a means of speeding his own return to Caesarea, but whatever his motive, his advice seemed sound. "And the name of this city?" Varro asked.

"Sodom," Philippus replied. "The city is called Sodom."

XXIV

THE SINS OF SODOM

Sodom, Kingdom of Nabatea. May, A.D. 71

Sunlight was slicing in through gaps in the closed shutters of the eastern windows.

"A new day, Marcus," Varro said softly, as his friend opened his eyes.

"Where is this?" Martius asked, breathing with difficulty as he lay in a comfortable bed. "Where have you brought me, Julius?"

"You are in the commandeered house of a merchant in the city of Sodom, at the southwestern end of the Dead Sea," Varro answered. Sitting on the bed beside Martius, he wiped his friend's perspiring brow with a cloth soaked in vinegar.

Martius nodded slowly. "The Dead Sea?" he said after a time. "Appropriate."

"You are not going to die."

"Am I not?" Martius smiled weakly. "We all have to die, sometime, Julius. I shall die in Sodom."

"You will not. Today we shall put you in a boat and take you across the lake to Jerusalem. You will be more comfortable there. This barren city is too hot, too humid. The air is sulphurous. It would be injurious to any man's health to spend too long here."

"A boat trip? Sounds diverting. Be sure the boat does not sink, Julius. I might drown, and then where would we be?" He tried to laugh, but that only brought on a violent coughing fit which seized his entire body and shook him from head to toe.

Diocles quickly moved in, and standing at the head of the bed, which had been moved out from the wall, he grasped Martius' shoulders and held them, as if that might ease the coughing spasm. "You must not laugh, tribune!" he warned Martius once the coughing had come to an end.

"Why?" Martius rasped. "Afraid I will laugh myself to death, physician?"

"You heard him," Varro scolded. "No laughing."

"He is right, of course," Martius responded. "Death is no laughing matter."

Diocles moved around to the far side of the bed and lay his ear on Martius' chest. He could hear fluid rattling in Martius' one remaining good lung. It was not an encouraging sign. "There is nothing more I can do for him, questor," he confessed with sad resignation, standing back. "It is out of my hands."

Varro reached over and took his friend's right hand, clasping it at the wrist. "You have been my strong right hand, Marcus," he said, determined not to sound emotional.

"You can always find another right hand," Martius replied.

"Not like the one I have."

Martius lay quietly for some minutes. Then he said, slowly, a few words at a time, "Did I ever tell you, about the beggar, in Caesarea? The one I cured, of lameness? He predicted, a cruel and painful death, for Alienus and myself. There, is a salutary lesson, for you. A fellow, should never, waste, his miraculous powers, on beggars."

"He should not talk," said Diocles. "He should preserve his strength."

"Did you hear?" Varro asked his friend. "Preserve your strength, Marcus."

"I heard. Tell the simpleton, I have no strength to preserve."

"You should rest," Varro urged. "Please rest."

"I will be at rest soon enough. You know, Julius my friend, I have one regret."

"What is that?"

"I regret, that I did not bed the slave girl, Miriam. You, were never, going to get around to it. You have made a goddess of her, in your head."

Varro smiled. "Is that so, Marcus?"

"She is only, a woman, my friend. Only a woman."

"My lord questor?" It was the voice of Pedius.

Varro looked around. His subordinates were in the room with him. They had been sharing his vigil since before dawn. "What is it, Pedius?"

"The girl, Miriam, she has asked to see Tribune Martius."

Varro raised his eyebrows. He turned back to Martius. "Did you hear that?"

Martius nodded. "Why not?" he said. "Bring the goddess to me."

Varro agreed, and Pedius hurried away. Miriam, Gemara and Philippus were all being kept at the marching camp set up outside the hot, steamy little city. It was half an hour before the lictor returned. When he did, he ushered Miriam into the room. All heads turned when she entered. Varro beckoned her to the bedside.

The young beauty voluntarily removed her veil. "I have come to help you, tribune," she said, looking down at Martius with pity in her eyes.

"How?" he responded, looking back up at her with eyes which drank in her beauty. "By dying, in my place?"

"By showing you the way to salvation. Accept Jesus Christ as your savior!"

"Is that all, you have to offer?" Martius wheezed. "I expected better."

"Please, tribune, I beg you, have them carry you to the lake; permit Philippus to baptize you. Accept the Lord Jesus as your own personal savior."

"Can he save me, now?"

She dropped to her knees beside the bed. "He can save your soul," she said, almost in a whisper.

"It is not my soul, I am interested in, my beauty."

"You must beg the Almighty's forgiveness for slaying my brother."

His smile faded. "Would he forgive, those who injured me?"

"Of course."

"Well then, your God, is more magnanimous, than I." Martius' good humor had departed him. Now, he sounded angry. He tried to lift his head from the pillow, but only fell back. "I do not forgive! They, have deprived me, of my life."

"You must beg forgiveness! You must!"

"Enough!" snapped Varro. Taking Miriam by the arm, he lifted her to her feet and steered her toward the door. "If this is your way of punishing him…"

"I wish to save him, before it is too late," she said earnestly, looking into the questor's eyes with conviction. "If he will accept Jesus…"

"No more of this," said Varro angrily. He motioned to Pedius. "Take her back," he said. "This was not a good idea."

✠

Varro sat beside Martius' bed, clasping his friend's hand. Martius' breathing now came in labored gasps. Polycrates, General Bassus' physician, had come to see Martius, and he agreed with Diocles that the tribune was now too ill to be moved. On hearing this, Bassus had canceled the plan to take to the water that day for the journey north. Only when Martius' condition had improved, the general decreed, would they set out from Sodom. It seemed a generous decision, but generosity played no part in it. Bassus was hoping that his own condition would improve sufficiently to enable him to discard the plan to return to Jerusalem, a plan pressed on him by Varro, and allow him to march on the last rebels at Masada as he had originally planned.

"I, shall have, a merry time of it," Martius suddenly said, opening his eyes. He had not spoken for an hour. Now, his voice was no more than a hoarse whisper.

"When, Marcus?" Varro asked. "Where?" He put his ear closer to Martius.

"The fields of Elysium," Martius whispered. "Or Hades."

Gritting his teeth with frustration Varro watched his friend struggle for breath.

"I think, that I, am going, to icy Hades, after all," Martius wheezed after a time.

"Why, Marcus?"

"Cold. So cold."

As Varro watched, Martius ceased to breathe. Varro waited, hoping to see the chest rise again, but after a minute or so he knew that it would not. He lay Martius' hand by his side. Then, he stood, and leaned over the tribune's still form, and kissed his deathly cheek. "Good bye, my friend," the questor whispered.

✠

Varro built a funeral pyre for Marcus Metellus Martius on the broad, flat roof of the merchant's house where he had died, overlooking the small harbor of Sodom and the waters of the Dead Sea. The questor read Martius a long funeral oration. It was the least that he could do; Martius had no family; the civil wars had robbed him of parents and siblings, had made him an orphan. Apart from the few souls who gathered on the lonely rooftop at Sodom, there was no one to hear Marcus Martius described as the most honorable Roman since Marcus Cato, the most faithful deputy since Marcus Agrippa, and the most courageous soldier since Marcus Antonius.

All the expedition's surviving luminaries were there on the rooftop to hear the questor's oration. Crispus, Gallo, Pompeius and Silius represented the military, Pythagoras, Callidus, Pedius, Antiochus, and Diocles represented the civil offices. Tribune Fabius and his officers also attended. General Bassus could not; he had taken a turn for the worse; as Varro had told Martius, Sodom seemed not to be a healthy place. Varro also invited Miriam and Gemara to be there, knowing that, despite the fact that Miriam had upset his friend on his deathbed, Martius had been fond of both. As Varro was walking away, toward the steps which descended down the side of the house, and with Hostilis and Martius' own servants setting the pyre alight behind him, Philippus, who had come as chaperone to the two females, came up and took his arm.

"Questor, Miriam has something to say to you, in private," said Philippus. "Will you hear her? I would deem it a favor."

"Very well," Varro sighed. "Bring her to my quarters shortly."

The questor was using a large ground floor room in the merchant's house as his office and bedroom. He retreated there immediately after the funeral. Removing his ceremonial white toga he passed it to Hostilis. Wearing just a belted tunic now, he was perfunctorily washing his face and hands when Philippus appeared at the open door with Miriam and Gemara.

"You have something to say to me?" said Varro brusquely to Miriam as he dried his hands on a towel provided by Hostilis.

Miriam nodded. "Yes, questor, but what I have to say is for your ears only."

Varro, in no mood to be dictated to, pursed his lips as he contemplated sending her away unheard.

"Please," she added softly. "It is important. For us both."

Varro shrugged. "If you must; but a few moments only," he conceded, before motioning to Hostilis to leave the room.

The servant quickly departed, shepherding Philippus and Gemara into the next room and pulling the door shut behind him. "My master will send for you," he informed the Evangelist, taking up sentry duty at the door and folding his arms.

Once the door closed, Varro glared at Miriam. "Well? Be quick. I have much to address before leaving Sodom."

She removed her headscarf, allowing her shining black hair to tumble down over her shoulders. "I must apologize," she began.

"Oh?" He was taken by surprise. "Apologize?"

"It was wrong of me to have wished Tribune Martius dead." She took a step toward him, to shorten the physical and emotional distance between them.

"Yes it was," he said tersely. "Very wrong."

"I was distraught, at the news of the death of my dear brother. I hope you will forgive me, and that I will be forgiven by the Almighty. It was Heaven's will that my brother should die, as Philippus has pointed out to me. In wishing for revenge I gave in to human weakness. Jesus would not…"

Impatiently he interrupted her. "The desire for revenge is natural. Was that all you had to say?"

"Revenge is for sinners. To forgive your enemies, that is the greatest blessing."

"For myself, Miriam," Varro responded with growing irritation, "I cannot forgive the Jews who lured me into the forest, then killed my four companions." His voice was becoming sharper, louder. "Among them my best friend and the man who had been my adviser since I was a boy."

"It would take great strength to be able to forgive the perpetrators of such a terrible deed. But you have the strength, questor. Believe me, you have the strength."

"A secretary who would not harm a fly. A boy, a mere musician." The questor, becoming angrier by the minute, paced back and forth in front of her, clenching and unclenching his fists. "I saw them killed, before my very eyes, unarmed, and wishing their murderers no harm! It was only through the loyalty of my courageous servant that I was saved from a similar fate."

"It was God's will. Perhaps He has plans for you."

Glowering, he swung to face her. "Is that so? A god I do not even believe exists cannot possibly have plans for me!" His anger, usually slow to rise and easy to control, fueled by grief and frustration now, was boiling to the surface. "What nonsense is this you speak?"

She looked up into his eyes. "Accept that what will be, will be. God makes it so."

"Your God willed the deaths of Marcus, and Artimedes, and the others? Of your own brother?" He grasped her by the shoulders, and began to shake her, as if to shake sense into her. "Is that what you are saying? He wanted them dead?"

She did not reply. Her serenity, her self assuredness, the very certainty of her beliefs, were enough to annoy him all the more.

"How can you believe in such a malevolent god?" he demanded, shaking her again like a man demented. "How? Tell me!" He could feel her breath on his face; soft, and warm. "Your infernal God took away those I loved!" he raged. "After your people lied to me, they broke their word, they lured my friends to their deaths! Damn your God! Damn your people! And damn you!" As far as Varro was concerned, this woe-filled quest of his had become a pointless wild goose chase. It had achieved nothing but death and misery. And he was powerless to change a thing.

A feeling came over him which he could neither fully comprehend nor control. In his anger he was suddenly filled with twin desires, to punish Miriam, and to ravish her. And in that moment he let go of all restraint. "Damn you, girl!" Hauling her close, he fastened his mouth over her soft, damp lips.

Miriam tried to resist. "No!" came her muffled cry. Her headscarf fell from her hand as she tried to push him away.

In response, his right arm slid behind her back and pressed her hard against him. His mouth slid from her lips and down to the smooth, olive skin of her elegant neck. The more she struggled, the tighter his hold became. Julius Varro was a powerful man, and she, just half his size and strength, was in his power.

"No!" she gasped. "Please! This is wrong," she said, now trying to reason her way out of her predicament. "You know it is." But, beyond reasoning, he paid her no heed. Fleetingly she thought of calling out for help. But Miriam was only a slave. At best, she would be ignored. At worst, Varro could have her punished. "You don't really want it to be this way," she cried, desperate now, and hoping that an appeal to his heart might bring him to his senses. For she knew that Varro was in love with her; she had known for months.

"Silence!" Varro growled, his voice almost unrecognizable, as he dragged her toward the bed in the corner of the room.

"Please…" she whimpered. "Please, do not do this."

With one hand he roughly reached down and grasped her light, linen robe, and tried to unceremoniously drag it up. But, pressed closely together as they were, the garment would not respond. Cursing under his breath he pushed her back, so that she fell onto the bed. For a moment, he stood looking down at her sprawled there on the coverlet, fragile, unprotected, looking back up at him with fear in her eyes. Then he unfastened his belt and let it fall. "This is nothing less than you deserve!" he snarled, bending and pulling up her gown with such violence that the linen ripped.

As he cast the robe aside, Varro paused momentarily to take in the sight that now met his eyes. Miriam was totally and spectacularly naked. Her flawless, trim, curvaceous body shone as if it had been oiled. Her breasts were round and firm, each areola and nipple was dark brown. Her pubic hair was thick and the color of jet. As for her legs, they were stubbornly clamped together, but her last defense was not going to stop him. Reaching down with both hands he wrenched her legs apart, just as he would part a stubborn young bough from an olive sapling in the pruning season.

She made no sound, but her eyes spoke volumes; of her dread of what was to come, of her disappointment in him. He drew his tunic over his head and threw it to the floor, revealing a muscle-toned body, a smooth, well-defined chest, and his physical readiness to take her. Miriam had seen naked adult males in the flesh before. What slave had not? But in the sheltered surrounds of the court of Queen Berenice she had never seen a man fully aroused. Varro's erect penis shocked and surprised her. Now he lay full length on top of her, crushing her beneath him so that she had to take short, sharp breaths. Taking her wrists, he pinned them back. Again his mouth found hers. She closed her eyes, and let his kisses smother her. But her eyes soon flashed wide, as, with a gasp, she felt him enter her, driving himself into her body. She cried out with shock and pain, as her hymen broke. Sad tears trickled down her cheeks.

He began thrusting in and out, his face contorted. She found herself gripping onto his back. Her head nestled next to his. But, silently, she prayed that it would soon be over. His thrusts became more urgent, his breathing more rapid. And then he was arching his back, and letting out ecstatic groans of pleasure. Unable to resist the urge to draw him closer, she gripped his arms. He tensed, quivered from head to foot, let out a cry of exaltation, then collapsed clumsily onto her.

Briefly he lay on top of her, breathing hard, and dripping perspiration, before rolling away and lying beside her until his breathing returned to normal. He did not look at her, nor she at him. Then he rose to his feet. Finding her gown on the floor, he snatched it up and threw it in her direction. "Get dressed," he snapped, angry, not with her now, but with himself. He turned his back on her as he himself dressed, overwhelmed by shame for forcing himself on her, and unable to look at her lest she see the guilt written on his face.

✠

A thick mist surrounded Varro and Callidus as they crunched over the gritty orange beach to the waiting boats. As they walked Varro brushed his hands together to remove the last of the gray ash that still clung to his skin. He had just spent his last minutes at Sodom distributing his friend's ashes on the Dead Sea, from a promontory little farther around the foreshore.

"According to the Sodomites, my lord," Callidus remarked as they walked, "this mist hangs over the lake for a considerable time in the warmer months, often until the middle of the day." He was pleased to be leaving this unpleasant place, pleased to be beginning the journey back to Antioch, and to his Priscilla. "They say the mist has something to do with the lake's salt water." Then, a new thought hit him. "I was thinking, my lord, after the funeral of Tribune Martius yesterday, we now know the significance of your dream. The one involving the chariot."

"We do?"

"Well, yes, my lord. Obviously, it was General Bassus' chariot. The figures in black were those who died with you in the forest. The charioteer was Tribune Martius."

"The driver looked nothing like Martius," Varro returned shortly.

"He did not? Oh."

Six boats were drawn up on the narrow, half-moon beach. A seventh had gone ahead the previous day to make arrangements for the main party to be met by litters and horses at the northern shore. Each boat was equipped with twelve oars. Allocated one of the craft by General Bassus, Varro had Centurion Gallo send him twelve of his men as rowers, and had chosen

Callidus, Pythagoras, Pedius, Miriam, Gemara, Philippus and Hostilis to squeeze into the boat with him and the oarsmen. His party was assembled and waiting when Varro came down the beach with Callidus.

Fair-headed Prefect Crispus stood with the others. It would be Crispus' task to lead the remainder of the questor's column back to Jerusalem via the overland route. As before, the expeditioners would march in company with General Bassus' army, led now by Tribune Fabius. It was likely to take the column seven days to make the journey. As for the party on the lake, if they met with calm waters all the way, they could be in Jerusalem that evening, after continuous travel all day and well into the night.

Varro reached out an ashen hand. "Take care of our people, Quintus," he said, "and we shall see you in Jerusalem in a week's time."

"You can rely on me, questor," Crispus earnestly replied, grasping his superior's hand. "A safe journey to you."

Varro ordered his party into their boat. On his order, the rowers, who had been standing in the shallows at the prow end, heaved the craft out into the water. Ten of the twelve legionaries then took their seats on board; two held the craft stationary just off the beach as Varro walked through the mist to the other boats. Four boats were laden with General Bassus and his staff, the fifth with provisions. A bed not unlike a covered litter had been prepared in one of these craft. Varro pulled back the side covering and peered into the interior. On the bed lay Bassus, pale and perspiring. His eyes were closed. Polycrates, the silver-haired physician, sat at his side.

"The general?" Varro asked.

"Weak, questor," the physician answered gravely. "Very weak."

Hearing the voices, Bassus opened his eyes, then turned his head toward Varro. He lifted his face toward the figure beside the boat, and squinted at him. "Tell Caesar that I am doing my duty," he said, before falling back and closing his eyes once more.

Varro looked at Polycrates.

The physician shrugged. "Delirious," he said. "I cannot imagine who he thinks you are. He thinks that *I* am his wife."

Varro nodded. "Your boat should lead," he said. "I shall bring up the rear."

Varro crunched his way back to his craft through the damp, clinging mist, then splashed out to his boat and hauled himself in over the prow. As he took his seat in the bow, he ordered, "Push off!" The two remaining soldiers heaved the boat out into the shallows, then clambered inboard. It was a tight fit. There were not seats for all; Miriam, Gemara and Hostilis huddled on the ribbed floor between seated passengers and rowers. Miriam sat with her back to the questor; Varro, wearing his guilt like a stinking, soiled cloak, was grateful he would not have to look her in the eye during this journey.

"Prepare to row," the questor called. As his oarsmen readied their oars he looked over to his left, to the five shadows in the mist; once those other craft were under way and disappearing into the gray void, he ordered, "Rowers on the right, pull together!" The six legionaries on the right side dragged on their oars. The nose of the boat came around. Varro's last sight of Sodom was of white rooftops protruding through the mist, lit golden by the rising sun. The vision swung to his left, and then was gone. "Now, *all* pull together!"

All twelve rowers now dipped their oars. The boat began to slide over the glassy surface, out onto the lake in the rippling tracks of the craft which had preceded it.

Standing on the shore, Crispus watched the boats melt into the mist. Even after they had been engulfed by the soft gray cloud, he could hear them, could hear the rollicking of the oars and the swish of their blades, could hear disembodied voices out on the lake, ghostly, dull and empty. Once the questor's craft had slipped from view, the prefect let out a deep sigh, then turned and walked up the beach toward the city, and the column waiting on the far side of it. Crispus envied his colleagues in the boats; he was not looking forward to his overland journey.

✠

No one spoke in the eerie stillness. Passengers sat with cloaks wrapped around them as a protection again the clawing damp air, and with heads bowed. Occasionally someone would cough, as the airborne brine tickled their throat. Perspiration rolled from the rippling arms and bare brown legs of the legionaries working with precision at the oars.

After they had been rowing through the mist for little more than an hour, keeping the shore on their left and the next boat within sight, all the time veiled in silence but for the rolling of the oars and the gentle, rhythmical splashes generated by the gouging blades, a surreal voice called out from the distance. "All stop!"

Passengers' heads came up. The dripping oarsmen ceased to row. Even though Varro's boat began to lose way, it went gliding across the water still, with oars raised, as if propelled by magic.

"What's happening?" someone in Varro's boat asked.

"Questor!" came the distant voice again. "Questor Varro, come alongside the general's boat, if you please." It was the physician's voice.

Varro ordered his men to resume rowing. Slowly he edged his craft past the four boats ahead of him, one at a time. The passengers sitting in the other craft, emerging briefly from the gloom and seeming to Varro to have the appearance of ghouls journeying across the Styx River on the journey to the underworld, watched the questor pass. As he came up to the general's vessel, lying dead in the water and with its oars levitated, its features materialized from the mist like a mirage on the desert; first the long shape of the hull, then the distinctive canopy.

"Raise oars!" Varro ordered.

When his men lifted their oars to the vertical, the lengths of timber looked like a grove of limbless trees.

"Why did you summon me?" Varro called as his craft bumped alongside the other with a hollow clunk of wood on wood. "Do you wish to link the boats with ropes, so none becomes lost in the mist?"

"No," came a reply. The face of Polycrates the physician appeared from under the canopy, just a few feet away from Varro.

"What is it then, physician?"

"General Bassus is dead."

XXV

THE TWO SWORDS

Caesarea, Capital of the Roman Province of Judea.
June, A.D. 71

The sea air! The wonderful, embracing, cleansing sea air. Away below the questor, as he stood on the citadel terrace taking in the vista, the port of Caesarea was a hive of activity. He could hear the laughter of laborers, could smell the aroma of landed fish wafting up from the quay. Out on the glittering Mediterranean he could count the billowing sails of at least ten large craft, merchantmen and warships. How different this was from the tomb-like atmosphere of Jerusalem, the bloodied grass of the Forest of Jardes, the clammy, salty air of Sodom. There was sadness too. The last time that he had stood on this terrace it had been with Marcus Martius at his side, and Artimedes had still been full of life. Yet, somehow, Varro felt that both would forgive him for enjoying the return to Caesarea. The questor took one more deep breath of sea air, then turned and walked back into his apartment in the white fortress. Pythagoras the secretary sat at a writing table, with pen poised, waiting patiently for Varro to resume his dictation. Two days earlier, the questor had commenced writing his report on the death of Jesus of Nazareth.

It was difficult working with so much hearsay and so little fact. For all that, in his methodical way Varro was attempting to put what he had into the most coherent form possible. He and Pythagoras had begun by laying out all the wax tablets containing the record of the testimonies of the numerous informants, and categorizing them by subject matter: pre-arrest,

arrest, trial, execution, and post-execution. From that foundation he had begun to dictate to Pythagoras, prowling his day apartment and speaking his thoughts while Pythagoras sat at his writing table working in fresh wax. Every now and then Varro would pause, and both he and the secretary would consult the previous shorthand notes to refresh their memories about a particular point, before the questor resumed his dictation. Varro planned to spend a few more days here, working on the report, before resuming the journey back to Antioch, polishing the report along the way.

He was considering taking the coastal route north. The new Procurator of Judea, Lucius Liberius Maximus, a small, round-faced Spaniard and a former slave freed by the emperor Otho, had reminded Varro that on the coastal route stood Mount Carmel's Sanctuary of Apollo. Liberius had recommended that the questor pay a visit to the sanctuary and seek a prediction from the priest of Apollo about his future. This priest was said to possess remarkable oracular powers; he was widely known to have accurately predicted the future of Caesar Vespasianus before he became emperor. Yet, Varro was not so sure he wanted an insight into his future. What if his life was all downhill from here? The way this mission was panning out, there would be little to look forward to either in Antioch or back at Rome.

"Begging the questor's pardon?"

Varro, deep in thought about the future, looked up absently at the sound of his chief freedman' voice. "Yes, Callidus, what it is it?"

"Forgive me for interrupting your work, my lord," said Callidus from the door, "but there is someone to see you, someone I think you should see."

"Oh? And who would that be, Callidus?" Varro replied, a little impatiently.

"He says that he is Jesus, my lord."

"What?" Varro raised his eyebrows at Pythagoras, and instructed Callidus to bring the man to him at once.

Callidus led in a tall, slim man with gray hair and beard. He was severely wrinkled, and Varro, sitting on a chair now, guessed that he might be aged in his seventies, perhaps older. "Who are you?" the mystified Varro asked. He, Pythagoras and Callidus eyed the man intently.

"My name is Jesus," the stranger replied in a deep, mellifluous voice.

Varro and his companions looked at him in astonishment.

"You truly are Jesus?" Varro said. "Jesus of Nazareth?"

A smile broke across the man's face. "I am Jesus of Cana, my lord. More precisely, Yehoshua bar Annas, or, if you prefer, Joshua. Jesus, the humble rope maker."

Varro could not help but laugh at himself for having believed, if only for a moment, that Jesus of Nazareth had indeed survived his execution and walked in the questor's door forty-one years later. "What can I do for you, Jesus the rope maker?"

"I heard some little time ago," said Bar Annas, "that the questor was offering payment for information about events surrounding the death of Jesus of Nazareth many years ago. By the time that I had learned of this and came to the citadel, I was told that Your Lordship had left Caesarea. Today, I heard that you have returned. So, here am I."

"You have information?"

"How much is Your Lordship paying?"

"I am a fair man, and will pay a fair price if the information is of value."

Bar Annas smiled mischievously. "If a man cannot trust a questor, who can he?"

"What did you wish to tell me?"

"I once knew a bandit, a Daggerman, of the band led by Joshua bar Abbas, who sold two stolen swords to a man by the name of Simon, a Galilean also called Simon Petra." The informant cocked his head to one side. "Does this interest the questor?"

"Perhaps. When was this?"

"Just prior to the Passover during which Jesus of Nazareth was executed. It was of course against the laws of Rome to carry a sword, as it is now. Even the common soldiers of the Temple Guard were only permitted to go armed with staves. Although, I am sure I do not need to point that out to Your Lordship, a Roman magistrate." He smiled again.

"Go on."

"I always remembered this story, because my friend tried to sell more swords to this Simon of Galilee, but Simon, who was a follower of the Nazarene, he said. 'Two swords will be enough to ensure two men are arrested, and that is all my master will require.' I thought it strange that a man would want to be arrested."

"Could it be that you were the bandit who sold the swords to Simon of Galilee?"

Bar Annas looked horrified. "Oh, no, my lord. Not I, my lord. I am an honest man. I love Rome. Caesar be praised!"

Varro was not impressed with the theatrics. "Is that all you have for me?"

"That is all, my lord."

"Go with my man Callidus. He is the keeper of my purse. He will pay you for your morsel of information."

"How much?" Bar Annas demanded.

"Give him a hundred sesterces, Callidus," said Varro dismissively.

"Is that all?" Bar Annas retorted. "I thought it worth five times as much."

"Have a care for your own safety, storyteller," Varro growled, "and remember who you are talking to. Your information is not new to me; I have a document which also mentions the acquisition of the swords and the fact that only two swords were considered necessary to attract the attention of the authorities. Therefore, your information it is not particularly valuable to me. One hundred sesterces or nothing."

The artificial smile reappeared on the face of Bar Annas. "Thank you, my lord. You are most generous," he said, sounding neither genuine nor happy. "Now you mention it, one hundred sesterces was just the figure I had in mind."

"Then we are of one mind. Take him out and pay him, Callidus."

Once Callidus had led the informant from the room, Varro drew himself to his feet. "A one-time bandit and malefactor, if I am not mistaken," he said, half to himself. "His confirmation of the story of the swords is useful, just the same, Pythagoras. There can be no doubt that Jesus set out to have himself arrested for bearing arms."

✠

The following day, Varro sent for Philippus the Evangelist. The Nazarene stood before him as Varro reclined on a divan eating figs for lunch during a break in report-writing.

"Your report goes well, questor?" he asked cordially. He had expected to be released by this time, but he made not mention of his continued detention.

"Well enough," Varro began. He held up a letter. "I have received a petition seeking your release, Philippus, from a Roman citizen, Quintus

Pristinus, a former legionary of the 15th Legion now resident in Caesarea who was awarded two gold crowns by Caesar during the Judean war, for his bravery. Pristinus thinks highly of you."

Philippus smiled warmly. "As I think highly of him. Pristinus is a good man; he follows the way of our Lord."

Varro nodded slowly. "I thought as much. One of your converts is he?" He shrugged. "Each to his own, Nazarene. I may not agree with your philosophy, but I cannot fault your humanity. I had intended keeping you with me until I had completed my report. However, give me your word that you will remain in Caesarea and make yourself available to me should I have any further questions, and you are free to go." In reality, Varro had decided that Philippus could add nothing more to his investigation.

Philippus nodded. "I will of course place myself at your disposal, questor."

Varro called to Callidus at the door. "This man is free to go, Callidus." He returned his attention to the Evangelist. "May good Fortuna attend you in future. You may yet make that visit to your daughter at Tralles."

Philippus shrugged. "Who can know what Heaven plans for us? With respect, may I ask, what plans do you have for Miriam, and the child?"

"They will return with me to Antioch, and possibly also to Rome."

"To Rome?" There was a note of concern in the Evangelist's voice. "Would you not consider granting Miriam her freedom?"

Varro frowned, annoyed. "At some future time, yes, I shall manumit the slave. Miriam was gifted to me by Queen Berenice, Philippus. I will not insult the queen by divesting myself of her gift. Not in the immediate future, anyway."

"The child is no slave."

"The child is an orphan. I will ensure that she is well cared for." Varro's changed tone mirrored his annoyance at Philippus' intervention. "Was there anything else?"

Philippus' eyes strayed to the wax tablets on a nearby table. "You have found what you were looking for, questor?"

Varro was unsure whether Philippus knew the exact nature of his report, although he would have been surprised had the Nazarene not guessed the reason behind the questor's visit to Judea. That being the case, he had no doubt that Philippus would not be happy with the report once it was published. "I have," he replied.

"Then it only remains for me to wish you well on your journey back to Antioch. Might I recommend that you travel by way of Capernaum?"

Varro frowned. "I have already been to Capernaum."

Philippus smiled. "You may yet find answers at Capernaum."

This brought a perplexed look to Varro's face. "Why? What do you know that I do not? Is there a particular reason that I should visit Capernaum?"

Philippus shrugged. "Miriam was born at Capernaum," he said.

Varro focused on the Evangelist's face, trying to discern any implied scorn or condemnation. The face was serene, as always. "What of it?" Varro returned.

"It would be good for her to see her home one last time, if she is to go to Rome."

Varro did not respond. He motioned to Callidus. "Escort him to the gate," Varro instructed, coming to his feet and walking to a window, turning his back on the Nazarene.

"May God go with you, Julius Varro," Philippus called as he took his leave.

✠

Varro leaned on the balustrade, looking out at the sea silvered by a rising moon. Hearing movement behind him, he looked around, to see Quintus Crispus approaching along the terrace, sallow faced and weary. As ordered, Crispus had led the expedition back to Jerusalem from Sodom. He would never forget that journey. Excruciating heat and draining humidity had dogged the column every step of the way during the first five days. Pack mules had dropped dead. Hundreds of Jewish prisoners also perished before the column reached Jericho. Sunstroke had caused fit soldiers to crumple in their tracks; an addle-brained Pannonian auxiliary had run wild, cutting down his own comrades before a centurion caught and killed him. On the last few days of the march, it had rained, non stop, saturating everything and everyone. By the time he reached Jerusalem, Crispus had looked ten years older than when Varro last saw him on the beach at Sodom, and had become more convinced than ever that soldiering was not for him.

"You wished to see me, questor?" said the prefect, who was now Varro's deputy.

"I've decided to take the inland route, Quintus," Varro advised, "via Capernaum."

"Oh?" Crispus sounded disappointed. "You will not be visiting Mount Carmel, my lord?" He had been looking forward to himself consulting the oracle of Mount Carmel.

"I would rather remain ignorant of my future. Prepare to march by week's end. We will be back in Antioch before the autumn. This mission will soon be over."

XXVI

THE GOATS OF CAPERNAUM

Capernaum, Northern Galilee, Tetrarchy of Trachonitis. June, A.D. 71

The water lapped gently at his feet, washing over his military sandals and soaking his toes. Sitting on a gray-white rock beside the lake, Questor Varro gazed contemplatively out onto the Sea of Galilee. Water seemed to have dominated his life of late, from the Jordan to the Mediterranean, from the Dead Sea to this inland sea. Here, the still waters had a restful effect on him, as he watched fishermen in their boats half a mile out, dragging in their nets. Peace was what he sought now. Increasingly he had come to feel that his mission was a waste of time, and a waste of life. Martius had died, Artimedes and others had died, and for what end? He was close to completing his report, but he considered it a feeble document which in no way justified the cost of its compilation.

"My lord?"

Varro jerked from his discontented thoughts and looked around, over his shoulder, to see Callidus, standing on the rock behind him. A little further back, in the shadow of the town wall, a veiled Miriam stood, with her hands clasped in front of her.

"Thank you, Callidus. That will be all. I shall see you back at camp."

Flashing Miriam a disapproving glance, Callidus motioned for her to join the questor, then headed off toward the town's Water Gate.

Varro smiled at Miriam. "Will you not sit beside me?" he called. "Please?" When she failed to move, he tried again. "Come and tell me what

Jesus of Nazareth did here. I have read of it. There are letters, documents, which talk of him here at Capernaum."

Slowly she approached, halting a little behind him.

"Sit," he urged, patting the rock beside him. "I will not harm you. I swear, by all I hold sacred, I will never as much as lay a finger on you again." What he had done to her at Sodom had never left his mind. It had haunted him ever since that day.

Without a word, she settled on the rock, leaving a gap of several feet between them. While he looked to the southeast, she looked to the southwest.

"Philippus told me that you had been born here at Capernaum," he said.

"As I was brought here to you, I passed by the house of my birth."

"What was your father's occupation?"

"Mostly he was a rogue."

"He must have been a rogue to sell you into slavery."

She shrugged. "He was one of those men who valued only sons. He had four daughters, and just the one son. Jacob."

He could feel sadness washing over her at the mention of her dead brother, and quickly tried to divert her thoughts. "What did Jesus of Nazareth do here? I have read and heard a great deal concerning the Nazarene, but I am still struggling to know him."

"Those who accept Him come to know Him," she returned.

"I read that Jesus taught here."

"Once, Jesus taught a multitude of people on the shores of this lake, and He took five loaves and two fishes, and fed them all. Then, He sent Simon Petra and the other apostles back across this lake, in a boat belonging to Simon Petra, toward this very shore. In the night, as they rowed, a storm blew up, and the apostles encountered great difficulty rowing. Then, they saw Jesus walking past them, on the water..."

"He walked on the water?" Varro smiled gently at her. That anyone could believe such fantastic stories he found incredible. Were it any other person telling him this he would dismiss them as either gullible or unstable, or both. Yet, Miriam believed, and coming from her it seemed different somehow. He found her passion captivating.

Turning to him she saw his smile. "You are mocking me," she said unhappily.

"I would never mock you, gentle Miriam. Tell me more. Please."

"I know why you sent for me. You want me to forgive you. For Sodom."

"I, er, no, no, I want to learn more about the Nazarene." He lied badly.

"I do forgive you," she said. "As the Lord forgives all those who seek His forgiveness. Sin comes from weakness. Repentance takes great strength. And I know that in your heart you now repent."

He was hardly able to believe what he was hearing, as much as he had wanted to hear it. "You forgive me?"

"Truly."

✠

Callidus dawdled through the town, with Miriam on his mind. This girl was undeniably fetching. He had seen Marcus Martius' eye taken by her, but, worse, he had seen the questor's head turned by her. Callidus was certain that his master had fallen for Miriam, but up till now Varro had appeared not to recognize the depth of his own feelings for her. Over the past week or so, Callidus had sensed that situation beginning to change. His alarm had been heightened when he had overhead the questor telling Philippus the Evangelist that he might take Miriam to Rome. In what capacity, Callidus had wondered, and worried. If Varro took the girl to Rome merely to be a member of his mother's staff, that was one thing, but if he had thoughts of making her his mistress, that, to Callidus was a different matter, a considerably different matter, and a threat to his own plans.

Callidus felt no loyalty to Octavia, daughter of Paganus the merchant. If, however, Callidus' master were to leave Octavia in Antioch, taking Miriam to Rome as his mistress instead, not only would Octavia not go to Rome but neither would her buxom servant Priscilla, and that did concern Callidus. A great deal. In that event he could leave Julius Varro's service to remain at Antioch and be near Priscilla, but only a fool would give up such an influential post with a man who was on his way up the ladder, a man with superb connections and who was obviously destined for great things at Rome.

There was only one answer. Rather than remove himself from the picture, Callidus felt that it was Miriam who should go. To his mind, if he could somehow disenchant the questor with the girl, so that Varro's affections were once more directed wholly and solely to Octavia, then Callidus' problem would be solved. There was already the revelation that Miriam was a follower of the Nazarene. Callidus wondered if he might not somehow exploit that to his advantage. As he ambled along, deep in scheming thought, he found himself outside the same back street tavern that he had frequented with the questor and his lictor several weeks before.

For the first time, he noticed the tavern's name, The Two Goats, painted on a board suspended outside the wine house together with a rudimentary but recognizable illustration of two horned billy-goats butting each other. Looking at the sign in mild amusement, Callidus was suddenly struck by the recollection that the questor's first dream had featured a pair of goats. Intrigued, he walked up to the counter. The same two elderly tavern keepers were there, the two white-haired veterans of the 3rd Gallica Legion.

Recognizing him, they smiled broadly. "Welcome back, my good lord," said one.

"Can we tempt you to a good wine, at an even better price?" said the other.

"Why not?" Callidus settled on a stone stool across the counter from them. "Fill me a cup. Four parts water to one part wine." He watched as one of the tavern keepers directed servants to fill the order. "Tell me, how did the tavern come by its name?"

The second tavern keeper laughed. "We are the two old goats of the establishment's title," he said.

"We thought it apt, considering the name of the town," called the other.

Callidus frowned. "How so?"

"*Caper,*" said one.

"And Naum," said the other, returning to the counter.

Now it dawned on Callidus. *Caper* was Latin for goat. "Ah, it is a title of considerable wit. Considerable wit."

"Not that we have the slightest idea who Naum was," the first veteran laughed. "Some Jew or other." His partner also laughed.

"You both seem in good humor," said Callidus. "Business is on the improve?"

"No better than the last time you were here," one old timer lamented.

"Very poor," the other added, as a servant placed a full cup in front of his customer. "We need Germans in this town, drinking their wine undiluted and by the bucketful. We make so little profit we can barely feed ourselves, let alone our servants."

"A shame," Callidus remarked, taking up the cup. "A considerable shame." There was a pause as he sipped his wine.

"My good sir," one tavern keeper began again, sounding hesitant, and glancing at his companion for reassurance, "when you and the questor were in Capernaum before, there was mention of a financial reward. For information."

"Yes, concerning the death of Jesus of Nazareth," Callidus acknowledged.

"How fares the questor's investigation in that regard?" asked the second old man.

"Well, a considerable amount of water has flowed under the bridge since the Nazarene was executed, of course," Callidus returned. "It seems that all the witnesses who might have aided the inquiry are either dead or have disappeared. Why do you ask?"

The veterans looked at each other. "The reward?" asked one. "It would be large?"

Callidus shrugged. "The better the information, the larger the reward."

The pair nodded to each other, as if in silent agreement.

"What if we were to tell you," one began, "that *we* could have information?"

Callidus raised an eyebrow. "You two? You have information?"

"We did not always serve with the 3rd Gallica Legion," said one.

"Like all centurions," the other continued, "we were transferred from legion to legion as we were promoted. We retired from the 3rd Gallica, but we were with seven legions in all over the years, following each other from posting to posting like brothers."

"In the year that Jesus of Nazareth was executed," said the other, "we were still rank and file, serving with the 2nd Cohort of the 12th Legion. At Jerusalem."

Callidus was so surprised that his mouth dropped open and he loosened his grip on the cup in his hand. Red wine spilled down the front of his tunic. "You were at Jerusalem? He set down his cup. "At the very time that Jesus of Nazareth was executed?'

"We were not only there…" said one tavern keeper, glancing at his comrade.

The other looked Callidus steadily in the eye, so there was no mistaking what he was about to say. "We were members of Jesus of Nazareth's execution squad."

✠

Callidus found the questor where he had left him, although now he was deep in conversation with the Jewish girl beside him. Their intimacy only raised the freedman's ire. Still, he consoled himself as he came up behind the pair, the news he was about to impart would swiftly take the questor's mind off Miriam. "My lord, great news!"

Varro and Miriam broke off their conversation. "What news, Callidus?" said Varro with a scowl.

"The two goats, my lord! The two goats in your dream. They are running a tavern in Capernaum."

Varro looked at him as if he were mad.

Callidus burst into a grin. "You yourself met them when last we were in this town, my lord: the proprietors of the Two Goats Tavern. Little did we know then, but during the reign of Tiberius the two old goats were with the 12th Legion at Jerusalem. They crucified Jesus of Nazareth!"

Miriam let out a gasp.

Varro instantly came to his feet. "They will willingly give testimony?"

"Willing, my lord. It was the promise of a reward that bestirred their memory."

Varro strode off toward the Water Gate. "Take Miriam back to the camp," he ordered. "She is to assist Pythagoras. Then return quickly to me."

Callidus looked down at Miriam. "Up!" he snapped, stooping and taking her arm and dragging her to her feet. Miriam shook free of his grasp and went stomping off in the questor's wake. Smiling to himself, Callidus followed. This latest turn of events, he told himself, had very nicely put the cat among the pigeons.

Varro meanwhile hurried through the town toward the Magdala Gate and the expedition's camp beyond it. For this testimony he would summon Crispus, Pythagoras, Pedius, and Antiochus to join him. This time too, he would have Diocles present. In the past he had regretted not having the benefit of the physician's expert medical knowledge when questioning informants; he would not make the same mistake twice.

The revelation that the two old tavern keepers had executed the Nazarene had come as a shock. After becoming resolved to an incomplete investigation and an insufficient report, to have two such important witnesses materialize at the last moment was, to Varro's mind, either a gift from the gods or a cause for suspicion. He was conscious of the fact that Philippus had steered him to Capernaum. He had suspected that the Evangelist had sent him here to become closer to Miriam, a Nazarene; perhaps Philippus thought she could convert Varro to their faith, as she had vainly tried to convert Martius on his deathbed. But as fond of the girl as he was, Varro had no intention of letting her steer him toward adopting the Nazarene doctrine. As far as he was concerned the wild stories surrounding Jesus of Nazareth such as the fanciful tale of a walk on water could find no place in an intelligent mind. Miriam could say what she liked, she could not change the beliefs of Julius Varro. His defenses were sound: a solid wall of rationality, a deep *fosse* of self reliance.

As he walked, the possibility also occurred to the questor that Philippus had put Miriam up to influencing the questor in another way. Perhaps he had given her the task of subverting Varro's report, or even of trying to convince Varro not to deliver his testament to protect the myth of the resurrection of Jesus of Nazareth. Varro would not put such a ploy past the wily old Nazarene, but not even the heart-stopping Miriam could make him do what he did not want to do. There was of course another possibility, that Philippus was somehow behind the sudden appearance of these two new witnesses. Could Philippus have used contacts in the town to bribe this pair to come forward, to give false witness to a story which supported the myth of the resurrection? It was with increasing doubt that Varro reached the camp and ordered Centurion Gallo to take a detachment of his men to the Two Goats Tavern in the town, there to secure the two tavern keepers and then bring the pair to the questor without delay.

✠

The white-bearded secretary methodically and deliberately set out his writing instruments on the table in front of him. On the floor beside him knelt Miriam, unwrapping wax tablets from their damp linen coverings. The questor had assigned her to the secretary's staff. She was educated, and like Antiochus was fluent in three languages. She may or may not prove useful. Not that it mattered to Pythagoras; as far as he was concerned the girl was the questor's plaything, and Varro had obviously given her this appointment to please her. What did concern Pythagoras was the appearance of these new witnesses. This was a promising turn of events.

Pythagoras wanted the questor's Nazarene report to achieve General Collega's objective, to totally and irrevocably slay the myth that Jesus of Nazareth had risen from the dead. But he had his own motive for such an outcome. Licinius Mucianus had left Pythagoras at Antioch to help Collega administer his provinces, taking Pythagoras' deputy Sophocles to Rome with him. Now, Sophocles ran the Palatium and its one hundred and thirty-two under-secretaries, and, in effect, ran the Empire. This worried Pythagoras. When he returned to Rome in the new year, would Mucianus, who admired efficiency and embraced expediency, relegate Sophocles in Pythagoras' favor? Or might Mucianus suggest to Pythagoras that he go into retirement instead? He dreaded such a premature end to his career. A report which demolished the doctrine of the Nazarenes could save that career, or even project it to new heights.

Pythagoras glanced up to see two elderly, white-haired men being escorted into the *pretorium* by Gallo. On the testimony of this pair could hang Pythagoras' future. More than once he had heard Mucianus declare of philosophers and prophets: 'These people band men together to air seditious thoughts, to insult those in power, to incite the multitudes, to overthrow the established order of things and bring about revolution. Such men are a danger to Rome and her stable government.' Yet, to the secretary's mind, the report that he and the questor had compiled to date was like a toothless lion. Despite the months devoted to this enterprise, the notes on the wax tablets piled high in an expedition cart did not contain the incontrovertible evidence that would satisfy Collega or Mucianus. The two old tavern keepers now standing before the questor could change all that.

"In consideration of your age you may both sit to give your evidence," said Varro.

The two veterans gratefully took a seat on a wooden bench facing the questor's table. Their eyes took in the gathered officials, and rested briefly on locked chests stacked at the rear of the *pretorium*, containing the annual tax collection of the province of Judea, which had been handed over to the questor at Caesarea by Procurator Liberius and was being taken up to

Antioch. The questor himself sat on the couch at the head of the 'U.' His servant Hostilis knelt on the floor behind the couch. On the couch to the left of the questor sat Prefect Crispus, Pedius the lictor, and Callidus. To the right sat the Jewish magistrate Antiochus and Diocles the physician. Pythagoras was installed at the writing table in the corner; a servant knelt beside him to provide fresh tablets of wax as required. Centurion Gallo stood at the *pretorium* door with hands clasped behind his back.

"You say that you are Sextus Atticus and Lucius Scaurus, natives of Cisalpine Gaul," the questor began, " and you are discharged veterans of the 3rd Gallica Legion."

"We are they, my lord," the two tavern keepers replied in unison.

"You have provided Centurion Gallo with your notices of military discharge," Varro nodded to two thin bronze plates lying on the table in front of them; each had been inscribed by hand with the date and place of the ex soldier's enrolment, a list of the units with which they had served, including the 12th Legion, and the date and place of their honorable discharge from the Roman army. Both notices had been authorized by the military tribune of the 3rd Gallica Legion. "None the less, I must confirm that you did serve at Jerusalem at the time you say. Firstly who commanded the Jerusalem garrison at the time of the execution of Jesus of…"

"Centurion Longinus," Scaurus enthusiastically interjected.

Varro nodded. "Where was the *pretorium* located at Jerusalem?"

"In the Antonia Fortress," Atticus advised without a moment's thought.

"There was a judgment hall in the Antonia. What name did the Jews give this?"

Atticus and Scaurus looked vaguely at each other. "We cannot recall the Hebrew word for it," Scaurus then said.

"In our language," said Atticus, "it was The Pavement."

"Very well, I accept that you served at Jerusalem. However…" He still sounded guarded. "I must ask why you have come forward with information at this time."

Atticus and Scaurus looked at each other, before Atticus spoke. "My lord, we did consider coming forward when last you were in Capernaum."

"At that time we decided against it," said Scaurus. "Our present depressed economic state convinced us that perhaps this time we should not be so reticent."

"We have been finding it difficult to deal with our mounting debts, my lord," his colleague clarified with an embarrassed smile.

"On that subject, might we raise the matter of a reward, my lord?" said Scaurus.

"The inducement shall be considerable, should the information you provide be truly valuable," Varro advised, "and truthful. Now, tell me, how old are you?"

"Begging the questor's pardon," Atticus persisted, "but might we put a number to the figure of the reward."

Varro scowled at the pair. "Very well. Between ten and twenty thousand sesterces," he impatiently advised. "Now, kindly answer my question."

"Twenty?" Atticus responded, raising his eyebrows as he looked at his elderly comrade. "A most attractive number."

"Most attractive," Scaurus agreed, having quickly calculated that this was two thousand sesterces more than the emperor's bonus that they had taken into retirement, a bonus eaten up by the acquisition of their first business.

"My question," Varro prompted. "An answer, if you please?"

"What question was that, my lord?" said Atticus. In his mind, he was busy spending his half of twenty-thousand sesterces.

"Your age?"

"I was born eighty-four years ago, my lord," Atticus proudly answered, "and so was he. I am the eldest. We did tell you this once before. We could pass for sixty-four, would you not agree?"

"We think we're still twenty-four," Scaurus chuckled.

"You have reached a fine age," said Varro. "Yet, you propose to provide me with information about an event which took place four decades ago, the execution of the man known as Jesus of Nazareth. Many people your age have great difficulty with their memory. Even people of my own generation sometimes have misty recollections. How can I be sure that you can remember with clarity an event which took place so long ago? You must have participated in a great many executions over the years."

"That we did, my lord," Scaurus agreed. "A great many."

"But none was like the execution of the Nazarene," said Atticus with a chuckle.

"We have encountered followers of this Jesus over the years who actually believe that he was a god and rose from the dead," said Scaurus. Both men began to laugh.

"May I share your joke?" Varro asked.

"It is just that we know the truth," said Scaurus.

"We were there, you see," said Atticus. "We put the Nazarene up on his cross."

Varro was beginning to think it was just possible that Atticus and Scaurus would provide the eye-witness evidence that he had been seeking all along. "Very well, you had better tell me what you did, what you saw, and what you heard."

"Can first we prevail upon the questor to provide the pair of us with a guarantee of immunity?" Atticus asked.

"Against prosecution for a criminal act, forty-one years ago," Scaurus added.

"Regrettably, my lord, we cannot say what act without incriminating ourselves," said Atticus with a pained expression.

"You will have to take us on trust, my lord," said Scaurus, shrugging helplessly.

Varro eyed the pair for a long moment. He had not embarked on this mission to secure prosecutions. It was information that he needed. "Very well, any complicity in a crime that may emerge from your testimony, involving either or both of you, will not be acted upon. You have my word on it. In return, you must be entirely truthful with me. Now, begin your testimony."

XXVII

THE EXECUTIONERS' TALE

Capernaum, Northern Galilee, Tetrarchy of Trachonitis. June A.D. 71

Now that doubts about the authenticity of the witness' testimony had been allayed, the attention of most of those present was glued to the two old men. The exception was Diocles the physician, who was nodding off to sleep.

"Three years after the 2nd Cohort of the 12th was posted to Jerusalem," Atticus began, "Centurion Longinus selected eighty men of the cohort to escort four condemned prisoners, all Galileans, to the place of execution."

"From those eighty, four men would physically carry out the executions," said Scaurus. "We were two of those four executioners."

"Longinus paid all four of us to participate in what we came to realize was the fabrication of the death of the man called Jesus of Nazareth," said Atticus.

Varro blinked. "You did say 'fabrication' of the man's death?"

"Fabrication, my lord," Atticus confirmed. "This was the crime we spoke of. We were paid a thousand sesterces between the four of us. Two hundred and fifty each."

"Close to three months pay," Scaurus underscored.

"I see. How were you to undertake this fabrication?"

"The plan, as Longinus revealed to us in stages," Atticus replied, " was to drug the prisoner, so that he would appear to die on his cross."

"A drug?" Varro queried. The feeling in the room was electric. Here was confirmation of the testimony that had been given elsewhere, testimony that had previously been thought questionable by the questor. "What drug?"

"The prisoner was to be given a soporific preparation," said Atticus.

"We were then to take him down from his cross, alive," said Scaurus, "and pass his 'body' to his friends for disposal."

"The execution place at Jerusalem," Atticus continued, "was at a site just to the northwest of the city called by the Jews the Place of the Skull, or just the Skull, as we called it. There were a number of dead trees there, just trunks in the ground, and each condemned man was required to carry a cross beam from the cells of the Antonia to the Skull, and he was then put up on the cross beam on one of these trunks."

"Is that what took place in the case of Jesus of Nazareth?" Varro asked.

"We knew him as Joshua of Nazareth," said Scaurus. "We only heard him referred to as Jesus, the Greek form, much later."

"Tell me the process that you went through on the morning of the execution," said Varro. "From the Antonia to the Place of the Skull."

"All the condemned men were beaten with rods in the Antonia, with the duty maniple drawn up to witness punishment," said Atticus. "As we took the prisoners out that morning, with each man carrying his cross-beam, we found that Joshua, or Jesus, if you prefer, was extremely weak."

"So much so," said Scaurus, "he could not carry his cross-beam like the others."

"Centurion Longinus had a Jew among the bystanders dragged into the column to carry the cross-beam of the Nazarene," said Atticus.

"At the time," said Scaurus, "I assumed that Centurion Longinus had already administered the drug, or part of it, and this was why the Nazarene was so much weaker than the other prisoners. After all, they had all received exactly the same number of strokes from the rods as prescribed by law, and Jesus was a healthy fellow aged in his thirties. I could see no other explanation."

"How did Centurion Longinus come by the drug?" Varro asked.

"Longinus told us the drug came from a Jewish apothecary," Atticus replied.

"An apothecary by what name?"

"Matthias, I think," said Atticus. He looked at his companion for confirmation.

"Yes, it was a Matthias," Scaurus agreed. "His last name escapes me."

"And me," Atticus added.

"Could the apothecary have been a Matthias ben Naum?" Varro asked.

"Ben Naum?" Atticus looked at Scaurus. "Yes, I believe so."

"Yes, that was the man," Scaurus said definitely. "Matthias ben Naum."

"Do you have any idea what became of Matthias ben Naum?"

"He died," said Scaurus.

Varro looked at the old man intently. "When did he die?"

"It was a year or so after the Nazarene's execution," Scaurus advised. He turned to his colleague. "Remember?"

"I remember," Atticus agreed. "You were promoted to centurion and transferred to the 6th Ferrata, and I followed soon after. The apothecary was killed in a fire in the city, just prior to your leaving."

"How can you be so sure it was Ben Naum?" Varro queried.

"We took note of all events relating to the Nazarene's execution," said Scaurus.

"We were nervous of apprehension, you see," said Atticus. "You sometimes take a bribe, for this or for that, but we never engaged in something quite as dangerous as that, before or since."

"It did not seem dangerous at the time," Scaurus added. "You never think of being caught. Only other people are stupid enough to be caught."

"We also had the security of knowing that our centurion was involved in the deception," said Atticus. "We thought ourselves invulnerable."

"That was until Centurion Longinus deserted," said Scaurus.

"Once he was caught," said Atticus, "we were in dread of him giving us up, but he held his tongue and went to his execution with the secret of what we had done. After that we began to worry that the story would come out, from someone else involved."

"We were quite relieved to hear of the apothecary's death," Scaurus confessed. "It was one less tongue to wag."

Varro nodded. Now he knew that Aristarchus the scribe had told the truth about Matthias ben Naum's involvement in the execution plot. At the same time, he now also knew that Saul ben Gamaliel had lied when he had said that Ben Naum had shared his house at Macherus as recently as a month ago; Ben Naum had been dead for years. As the questor's column had drawn closer to the Forest of Jardes, and closer to the probable revelation that Matthias ben Naum was not only not with the rebels there but had died long before, Ben Gamaliel, dreading the drawn out agony of a crucifixion that his fellow Ben Naum imposters had suffered, had decided to end his own life, quickly. That was why the apothecary from Macherus had wound his chain around his neck and thrown himself under the wheel of the cart on the Nabatea road. How Varro wished that Marcus Martius and Artimedes could have been here to hear all this. "Continue with your account," he said, with a wave of the hand.

"Where were we?" said Atticus.

"The Nazarene was unsteady on his feet," his colleague reminded him.

"I remember," Atticus said with a nod. "The prisoners were led from the Antonia to the execution place. A soldier of the 12th marched in front of each condemned man bearing a sign on which his name and crime were described. The Nazarene was described as 'Seditionist' and 'King of the Jews.'" He turned to Scaurus. "Whose idea was that?"

"Prefect Pilatus' idea, I supposed," said his colleague.

"As was the usual practice," Atticus resumed, "each prisoner was manacled at the wrists and attached by a chain to a soldier of the escort…"

"To whom was the Nazarene chained?" Varro asked.

"It was myself," Scaurus advised. "Jesus of Nazareth was chained to me. A mock crown made from a thorn bush arrived for him while we were still at the Antonia. We assumed that the Jewish priests wanted to humiliate him. Apparently because he had claimed to be the descendant of one of their ancient kings."

"If I might offer an observation at this point, questor," Antiochus interrupted, "in relation to this reference to the crown of thorns. I now have no doubt that the Nazarene quite deliberately strove to match the predictions of the Jewish prophets relating to their so-called Messiah. This crown of thorns relates to the Messianic writings ascribed to a Jewish prophet by the name of Zechariah. If you remember, the Lucius Letter and the Marcus and Matthias documents all mention that prior to entering Jerusalem for the last time the Nazarene had arranged with someone in the city for an ass and its foal to be awaiting him. Jesus then rode into Jerusalem on the ass. All this was done to conform with a prophesy of Zechariah. As was the crown of thorns."

Varro nodded. "We can take it, then, that whoever sent the crown of thorns to the Antonia wanted the ancient predictions to be fulfilled."

"That conclusion seems inescapable," Antiochus agreed. "Some member of the Great Sanhedrin were undoubtedly in sympathy with him and his goal to be recognized as the Messiah predicted by the ancients. More than in sympathy; in league with him!"

"So it would appear. Continue, Atticus and Scaurus."

"We had been told that four prisoners were to be executed that day," said Atticus.

"This was why there were four of us," said Scaurus. "One to each prisoner."

"At the last moment," said Atticus, "as we were leading the prisoners out of the Antonia, there was a holdup."

"A servant of Prefect Pilatus arrived with a pardon for the prisoner Bar Abbas," said Scaurus, sounding disgusted that one man had been allowed to escape justice.

"Longinus released the prisoner into the custody of the Sanhedrin," said Atticus.

"During the delay, my man, the Nazarene, delivered a speech from the Antonia steps to the Jewish women gathered behind the escort. Longinus soon put a stop to that!"

"Now," said Atticus, "we were down to three prisoners. Our fourth comrade was soon employed supervising the Jew who had been chosen from the crowd by Longinus to carry the Nazarene's cross-beam. Along the street we went, to the Water Gate, with a large crowd of wailing Jewish women following along behind us."

"The Nazarene was very weak, and staggering," said Scaurus. "I had to literally drag him to the execution place."

"It was the fourth hour, I think, when we reached the Skull," said Atticus. "The remainder of the escort surrounded the execution place and we set about our duties. We knocked off the manacles of all three prisoners and stripped each man, then put up my man and the other. These two had been members of Bar Abbas' Daggermen band. We next turned our attention to the Nazarene, under Centurion Longinus' watchful eye."

"Before we put the Nazarene up," said Scaurus, "we offered him a bowl containing wine mixed with myrrh, to help numb his pain."

"This was not uncommon," said Atticus. "Often, a condemned man's family would pay for this to be done."

"Did the Prefect of Judea know about these bribes?" Varro asked.

Atticus laughed. "The prefect received a share," he said.

Varro raised his eyebrows. "Is that so?"

"It was neither here nor there," Atticus remarked. "The prisoner still died."

"And the payment you received to fabricate the execution? Did the prefect also receive a share of that?"

Both men vehemently shook their heads.

"Longinus made it clear that this was between him and the Jews," said Atticus.

"Let us return to the bowl you offered the Nazarene," said Varro. "You say that it contained wine and myrrh. How did you know that?"

"Longinus told us so," said Scaurus.

"Longinus provided the contents of the bowl," said Atticus. "It was always wine and myrrh, or something similar, on these occasions."

"Therefore, it may have contained something more potent?" Varro suggested.

"Yes, but the Nazarene declined to drink from the bowl," said Atticus. "I assumed that the prisoner wanted to keep a clear head for what lay ahead."

"For my part," said Scaurus, "I thought that the Nazarene declined this because he was already feeling the affect of the drug that Longinus had given him at the Antonia and expected it to soon take its full effect. After all…" He began to laugh. "He would not want to kill himself with the combined effect of the two drugs."

"Then," said Atticus, "we nailed him up. We nailed up Jesus of Nazareth."

"You nailed all the prisoners to their crosses?" Varro asked.

"We tied the others up," said Scaurus. "The Nazarene, we nailed."

"Why was he alone nailed? Why was he the exception?"

"On some occasions prisoners were nailed, if the officer in charge wanted to inflict more pain than usual," Atticus answered.

"We have heard," said Scaurus, "that during the siege of Jerusalem, General Titus Vespasianus always nailed his prisoners to crosses."

"Nails being cheaper than rope," said Atticus with a grin to his colleague.

"We have also heard," Scaurus went on, "that Titus sometimes nailed his prisoners two-by-two; one on either side of the cross."

"Because he had more Jews to execute than he had crosses," Atticus explained.

"Why would Centurion Longinus have wanted to inflict more pain on Jesus, if he was involved in a plot to save his life?" Varro queried.

"The centurion did not tell us why," said Atticus.

"My theory," said Scaurus, "is that Centurion Longinus thought that the intense pain would cause the prisoner to pass into unconsciousness, making it easier for the drug that he used to take effect."

"The Nazarene seemed not to feel the pain of the nails," said Atticus.

"Which only convinced me that the man had indeed been administered a powerful drug in the cells of the Antonia," Scaurus revealed.

"The centurion had told us," said Atticus, "that the Nazarene's family were not to receive his clothes."

"This was a surprise," said Scaurus. "The families of condemned men were usually permitted to claim the clothes. If the clothes were not claimed, they were sold and the proceeds distributed among the members of the execution party."

"Centurion Longinus told us that we four could divide the Nazarene's clothing between us by drawing lots for it," said Atticus.

"So we drew lots," said Scaurus.

"Another prophesy of the ancients, questor," Antiochus spoke up. "'They parted my raiment among them, and for my vesture they did cast lots.' Someone, a Jew, must have told Longinus that this had to be done to fulfil the prophesy."

The questor nodded.

"His other clothes were worth little," said Atticus, "but the Nazarene had been wearing a rich robe of purple, and we were all vying for that."

"Herod Antipas, the Tetrarch of Galilee, he had given it to Jesus," said Scaurus. "In the early hours of the morning, the prefect had sent the Nazarene to Antipas, at his palace next to the Antonia."

"It was said that Antipas was afraid of the Nazarene," said Atticus, "that he was convinced the Nazarene was Johannes the Baptist reborn. He sent him back to the Antonia wearing this robe, as if he was hailing him as some sort of royalty."

"We took the robe from him at the Antonia," said Scaurus, "before he was led out to the execution place."

"Neither of us won it," Atticus lamented. "One of our two comrades did."

"We were never lucky like that," his colleague said, shaking his head.

"What took place once the Nazarene was up on his cross?" Varro asked.

"Once we had him up," said Atticus, "we had expected the Nazarene to soon lose consciousness. He must have been up there three or four hours, and then he called out."

"The centurion was prepared for this eventuality," said Scaurus. "He had told us to expect him to perhaps call out, if the drug did not succeed in rendering him unconscious. When we heard the signal, we were to immediately alert the centurion."

"What was the signal?" the questor asked.

"He was to call out, 'I thirst,'" said Atticus. "We were to then offer him a drink."

"I ran to the centurion," said Scaurus. "He had a bowl of liquid prepared."

"What was in this bowl?"

"It looked and smelled for all the world to be vinegar," said Scaurus, "and this is what Longinus instructed us to say it was."

"Vinegar being a familiar medicine," said Atticus, "one which would not arouse suspicions yet with its bitter taste could disguise a second ingredient."

"We understood it to conceal another dose of the centurion's soporific drug," said Scaurus. "I soaked a sponge with it, put the sponge on a reed, and held the reed up to the Nazarene. He drank his fill then called out, 'It is over,' and lapsed into unconsciousness."

"Finally," Atticus added.

"Another three hours passed," said Scaurus. "Centurion Longinus had told us that the drug could be expected to lose its potency within six or eight hours of its taking effect, after which time the prisoner would regain consciousness."

"We had to bring him down within the next few hours," Atticus added.

"Centurion Longinus instructed me," said Scaurus, "to take a javelin from a member of the escort and jab the Nazarene in the side."

"The centurion had discussed this with us previously," said Atticus. "The intent was to show onlookers — the Great Sanhedrin had people watching us all this time — to prove to them that the Nazarene was 'dead.'

If we could put a javelin in him and he did not flinch, then it would appear that he was dead."

"The trick was not to cause the Nazarene a grievous injury," said Scaurus.

"Nor to kill him," said Atticus with a smile.

"So I pushed the tip of the javelin up into his side, causing a flesh wound," said Scaurus. He illustrated how he had done this, by putting his right arm vertically above his head and pushing up with an imaginary spear.

"Thankfully, the Nazarene did not flinch," said Atticus. "He was well and truly in the grip of the drug."

"I saw blood run from the wound that I had caused," said Scaurus. "It was only a flesh wound; I had been careful to ensure that. Still, blood flowed and ran down his leg."

"The centurion was close by, on his horse," said Atticus. "He saw the result of the wound, and he turned to the crowd and called out, 'Water and blood. He is dead. Yet, truly he died with courage.'"

Varro looked perplexed. "Water and blood? Is that what he said?"

Atticus nodded. "Water and blood."

"Did you see water and blood?"

"Blood only," said Scaurus.

"Blood only," Atticus affirmed.

"How odd," Varro commented. "Continue."

"One of the priests of the Sanhedrin then hurried back toward the city," said Scaurus, "toward the Water Gate and the Palace of Herod."

"This priest," said Atticus, "as we knew from Centurion Longinus, was called Josephus of Arimathea. He was a Pharisee, and a friend of the Nazarene. He was the one who had secretly arranged everything with the centurion."

"Longinus told you this Pharisee's name?" Varro queried. "Why?"

"The centurion was no man's fool," said Atticus. "He did not entirely trust these Jews. A man could not afford to, as we Romans found during the Jewish Revolt. Centurion Longinus would have been well paid for his leading part in all this…"

"Do you know precisely how much Longinus was paid?"

Atticus shook his head. "He did not tell us. Thousands and thousands, I expect. He did tell us he wanted to be sure that nothing unexpected happened to him, either an accident or an arrest through a false accusation from the Jews. He was taking precautions against a calamitous event designed to remove the plot's chief actor from the stage."

"He wanted the Jews behind all this to know that those of us who carried out the crucifixion knew who they were," said Scaurus. "They could not conceivably do away with us all, so there would always be one of us to point the finger at them and wreak revenge if anything were to happen to any of us."

"For this reason," said Atticus, "the centurion told us the name of the leading players on the Jewish side — Josephus, Matthias the apothecary, and Nicodemus."

"Nicodemus?" Varro queried. "Who was Nicodemus?"

"Another Pharisee," Scaurus advised.

"We will come to him in the course of the story, my lord," said Atticus. "Shall I continue with the account from the point of the departure of Josephus of Arimathea?"

"Please do."

"We knew that Josephus of Arimathea had gone to see Prefect Pilatus, and before long an auxiliary of the prefect's bodyguard came to fetch Centurion Longinus."

"We had been expecting this," Scaurus chimed in.

"Centurion Longinus hurried off to the palace," said Atticus. "Before long he returned, and ordered the legs of the other two prisoners broken, to hasten their deaths."

"These two were still alive, of course," said Scaurus.

"Using a cudgel, another member of our quartet broke their leg bones," said Atticus. "Crack! Crack! It is easy done, with just a heavy blow."

"While this pair was meeting their end, the centurion ordered us to take down the Nazarene," said Scaurus, "and to hand the 'body' over to a waiting Jewish funeral party. It was obvious to us that he was still alive, of course."

"How could you be sure that Jesus was still alive when you took him down from the cross?" Varro asked. "Be precise with your answer."

"He was still warm, for one thing," said Atticus.

"The blood from the wound I had put in his side, that was another sure sign," said Scaurus. "Dead men do not bleed. I have seen enough men die over the years to know."

"Perhaps we should take expert medical advice at this point," said Varro, turning to Diocles the physician. Diocles was fast asleep, slumped against Antiochus. "Wake the physician," Varro commanded crossly.

As Antiochus shook the flabby doctor, Hostilis took him a cup of water. Diocles was awoken with difficulty, and when he did wake it was in a daze. "What is it?" he called, sitting up and looking around with a perplexed expression. "What is wrong?"

"Drink the water that Hostilis has for you," said the scowling questor.

Diocles gulped down the water then thrust the cup back at Hostilis, who returned to his post behind the questor. Wiping his mouth on the back of his arm, the physician realized that all eyes were on him. "I was drowsy," he said, with an embarrassed smile.

"Have you taken in any of the testimony of these two witnesses?" Varro asked.

"Two witnesses?" Diocles looked to the two old men on the bench. "Ah, yes, the two veterans. I perhaps missed a little of what they had to say, questor. Only a little."

Varro guessed that most of what Atticus and Scaurus had to say had eluded the doctor. "Your expert opinion, physician, if you please," he said. "Do dead men bleed?"

"Do dead men bleed?" Diocles laughed. "I think not," he said disparagingly. "A dead man's heart no longer pumps blood through the body."

"If a crucified man who has been declared dead receives a wound in the side, and someone claims that he has seen blood and water flow from the wound...?"

"Not possible, questor," said Diocles. "You can have watery blood, and you can have bloody water, but not blood and water both. If the man is dead, neither is likely."

"Why then, would the centurion claim to have seen blood and water flow?"

"It is a mystery to me, questor. Unless he were trying to give the impression that a deep wound had been inflicted, that the bladder had been pierced, perhaps. But a jab in the side will not puncture the bladder. I cannot imagine what his purpose was."

"I see."

"You say that our man was crucified, questor?" Diocles inquired. "In the normal standing position was it? And he received a flesh wound to the side, you say?"

"That is so."

"Mmmm." Diocles pensively rubbed his chin. "You see, questor, the blood of a man who dies in the standing position will ordinarily settle in his organs and his legs. As I have said, once the heart stops pumping, blood cannot continue to flow through the body, and certainly will not leak from a wound in the side. Only a living, breathing being can bleed from a wound of that nature."

"I knew it!" Antiochus exclaimed triumphantly beside him, slapping his knee. "All this nonsense about rising from the dead! The Nazarene was not dead!"

"Thank you, physician," said Varro. "The evidence points to the likelihood that whatever drug was administered, it had the effect of making the Nazarene wholly insensible, so that there was every appearance of death." He looked at the two old soldiers. "You are definitely unable to identify the soporific drug used by Longinus?"

"One of our comrades did make mention of gall," said Scaurus, "but that was mere speculation, I think; soldier's gossip. You hear of all manner of preparations and their various effects, but we have no knowledge in that field."

"The Matthias document states that gall was used," Antiochus piped up. "And at the risk of being repetitious, questor, I would note that the ancient Messianic prophesies also stated, 'A bone of him shall not be broken,' and, 'They shall look on him whom they pierced.' Longinus had obviously been told by the plotters to ensure the Nazarene's leg were not broken and that his skin must be pierced in some way."

Varro nodded. "Apparently so." He turned back to the physician. "Can you speculate on what drug was employed, Diocles? A drug capable of rendering a recipient unconscious for up to eight hours, and which equally renders him insensitive to pain?"

Diocles screwed up his face. "If you were to ask me for a sleeping draught, that is one thing, but if you were to ask me to render you unconscious for eight hours, and to render you insensitive to pain at the same time…?" He shook his head. "You see, this sounds to me as if two different preparations have been utilized. One for the deep sleep, perhaps also slowing the heart rate. Another for the desensitizing effect. There are various plants which produce one or other effect; deep sleep on the one hand, a paralysis on the other. But none that will do both at the same time that I am aware of. No, no, I would not hazard a guess. This is more in an apothecary's realm."

"Two drugs?" said Varro pensively. "Administered separately?"

"One would have thought so," Diocles agreed.

"One administered prior to leaving the Antonia," Antiochus suggested, "the other administered on the cross. It is in the realms of possibility, questor."

Varro turned back to the two witnesses. "Resume your account. You had brought the Nazarene down from the cross…"

"That we had, my lord," said Atticus. "We then handed the Nazarene over to the Jewish burial party, which wrapped him in linen and took him to his tomb."

"Who had charge of the burial party," Varro queried. " Josephus of Arimathea?"

"The burial party was led by another priest of the Great Sanhedrin," said Atticus. "Another Pharisee, Nicodemus by name. This was the same Nicodemus that we made mention of earlier, my lord."

"Centurion Longinus told us that this Nicodemus was a practiced embalmer," said Scaurus, "and that he was a secret admirer of the Nazarene who had enjoyed clandestine meetings with him, without the knowledge of the chief priests of the Sanhedrin."

"How did Longinus know this, about these clandestine meetings?"

"Nicodemus or Josephus of Arimathea must have told him so," Atticus surmised.

"Longinus also told us of the plan to secrete the Nazarene away," said Scaurus. "This was after we had expressed concern that Jesus would later be seen and recognized."

"In which case we would have been in deep trouble," said Atticus. "This is a man we had supposedly put to death. Suspicion would have immediately fallen on us."

"Our centurion told us that once we handed over the 'body,'" said Scaurus, "Jesus would be wrapped in a linen shroud and taken to a tomb in the hillside close by."

"This tomb was actually owned by Josephus of Arimathea," said Atticus.

"It was his own tomb," said Scaurus, "not previously used."

"Centurion Longinus told us that Nicodemus would prepare one hundred pound weight of myrrh and aloes, which he would take to the tomb to dress the 'body.'"

"A hundred pound weight?" said Varro. "That seems an excessive amount."

"They needed an excuse to take several pack mules to the tomb," said Atticus.

"Sturdy mules carrying deep panniers," Scaurus added, "containing the jars."

"The jars of myrrh and aloes were unloaded and taken into the tomb," said Atticus, "leaving the panniers empty."

"Once they had the 'body' of the Nazarene in the tomb," said Scaurus, "they would administer a draught if necessary to revive him and would dress and bind his wounds. Then, Nicodemus or his assistants would shave Jesus of his philosopher's beard and shorten his hair, to give him a more Roman look."

"This was to make him less easy to recognize," said Atticus.

"They would then dress him in clothes brought in the panniers," said Scaurus.

"Nicodemus would then conceal the Nazarene in an emptied pannier," said Atticus, "and secrete him away when the embalmer and his assistants departed."

"Supposedly after embalming the body," Scaurus added. "If anyone had looked in the tomb late that same afternoon, my lord, they would have found it empty."

"Where did they take the Nazarene?" Varro asked.

"To begin with, to a house on the Lydda road, two or three miles outside Jerusalem," said Atticus, "then to Emmaus."

"The house of Nicodemus," said Scaurus. "Or so we thought."

"It must have been Nicodemus' house," said Atticus. "Otherwise he would have aroused suspicion, traveling to Emmaus with his pack mules so soon after the execution."

"Nicodemus, being a Jew," said Scaurus, "had to make the journey to the house outside Jerusalem with some speed, to complete it before the sunset, when the Jewish Sabbath began. The Jews did not allow themselves to perform any labor on these days. Strange people, the Jews. I never could comprehend why they think the way they do."

"The Nazarene would have spent the first night following his crucifixion at this house," said Atticus. "On the Sunday, they would have moved him to Emmaus."

"There were guards placed outside the tomb," said Varro. "What of them?"

"Nicodemus paid these sentries to look the other way when he and his assistants departed the tomb," said Atticus, "with the Nazarene hidden in a mule pannier."

"What was the plan, once the Nazarene was spirited away from Jerusalem?"

Scaurus shrugged. "We were not told the details." He turned to his companion.

"We understood that he would leave Judea," said Atticus. "We did hear a rumor, some time later when we were stationed in Syria, that he met some of his followers near Emmaus and in Galilee in the days following his crucifixion."

"They supposedly did not recognize him at first," said Scaurus with a chuckle. "Not without his beard."

"If it was indeed him," said Atticus.

"Centurion Longinus did not give you any details about the Nazarene's escape plans once he had been spirited away from Jerusalem?" Varro persisted.

Both men shook their heads.

"If it had been me," Scaurus suggested, "I would have gone east, into Parthia, to escape Rome's jurisdiction. There are any number of Jews in Parthia. He could have lost himself among them. He could not afford to fall into Roman hands again, after all."

The two old soldiers looked at Varro expectantly.

"That is all we know, my lord," said Scaurus after a pause. "Once the bodies of all three Jews had been taken down, our century marched back to the Antonia. That was the end of our part in the day's events."

"Yes, that is the extent of our information, questor," said Atticus. "With respect, was the information not worthy of twenty thousand sesterces?"

"A pity that Longinus did not acquaint you with the complete escape plan," said Varro thoughtfully.

"If I might make another observation, questor?" said Antiochus.

"If it is relevant," Varro responded.

"The evidence points to Josephus and Nicodemus masterminding a conspiracy. They were the Nazarene's secret supporters on the Great Sanhedrin. Josephus arranged for the ass and the foal for the entry into Jerusalem. He arranged for the crown of thorns to be sent to the Antonia. He told the centurion to be sure to have the executioners draw lots for the Nazarene's clothing, to refrain from breaking his legs, and to pierce his skin, all to fulfil the ancient Jewish prophesies and so make the Nazarene appear to be the promised Messiah. Josephus provided his own tomb for the burial and subsequent subterfuge revolving around the tomb, and he arranged for Nicodemus to spirit the Nazarene away. Josephus was the key to this entire plot. The testimony of these two eye-witnesses makes only one verdict possible, questor. Jesus of Nazareth did not rise from the dead, and this is what you must write in your report!"

Varro eyed him ambivalently. He did not like the man, but he had to admit, what Antiochus said did make rational sense.

XXVIII

THE NEWS OF DEATH

Capernaum, Northern Galilee, Tetrarchy of Trachonitis. July A.D. 71

'In the time of our fathers, there arose a man of Galilee, a Jew, who won the hearts of those who came to know him, in life, and in death, as a gentle, kind and righteous man, a man said to possess miraculous powers. Not the least of those powers, it has been claimed, was the ability to rise from the dead. What follows is the report of Julius Terentius Varro, Questor to the Propretor of Syria and Judea, into the events surrounding the life and death of this man, called Jesus of Nazareth, or, the Christus. This report, undertaken after the exhaustive interview of witnesses throughout the provinces of Syria and Judea and adjoining lands, will show that the man called the Christus did not rise from the dead. Further, it will show how a small group of conspirators combined to subjugate the laws of Rome and the minds of men with a subterfuge of such audacity that even the greatest criminals in all our history would have shied away from complicity in its execution for fear of discovery, ridicule, and death.'

This was the opening paragraph of the questor's report, his second report, after the first had been discarded. Following the testimony of Atticus and Scaurus, Varro and Pythagoras had started afresh. With Pythagoras' forbearance the questor had labored long and hard over this opening stanza. Artimedes had taught Varro that the opening paragraph of a book, any book, is as a door is to a house.

With the opening made to his satisfaction, the questor had moved into the report proper. For seven hectic days now since the testimony of the two old goats, Varro and Pythagoras had been working steadily, almost frantically, in the privacy of the questor's canvas pretorium at Capernaum. Every morning, from the first hour, Varro would dictate, pacing back and forth, while Pythagoras consigned his words to wax in Roman shorthand. During the afternoon, while Varro bathed at the principal bathhouse of Capernaum, Pythagoras would write out the latest section of the report in full with ink on parchment while referring to his notes. At night, following dinner, the secretary would read the day's output aloud to the questor, who made any corrections deemed necessary. Pythagoras felt sure that General Collega would require hundreds of copies of the report to be made, for distribution throughout the Empire, with the first copy sent by fast ship to Gnaeus Licinius Mucianus at Rome.

This was the seventh night of the seventh day of report-writing. Varro was both exhausted and exhilarated by the process. The mental labor was taxing, but being able to see the story of the crucifixion plot take shape on the page was a graphic reward for effort. The story that Varro was telling his future readers began with the last two years of the Nazarene's life, when Jesus served as a deputy to his cousin Johannes the Baptist. It moved to the death of the Baptist, when Jesus took over the leadership of his sect. From here, Varro painted a picture of a well-intentioned and gifted man becoming increasingly frustrated by the loss of many of the Baptist's followers.

It was then, Varro had written, in the sixteenth year of the rule of Tiberius Caesar, that Jesus was approached by two members of the Great Sanhedrin with a desperate plan. These two men, Josephus of Arimathea and Nicodemus of Emmaus, both Pharisees and associates of the Baptist's late father Zechariah, wanted to wrest control of the Great Sanhedrin of Jerusalem from the pedantic Sadducees who had traditionally dominated the council and provided its high priest. The only way these Pharisees could achieve this was by proving the preeminence of their religious philosophy with the emergence of the predicted Messiah, a man sponsored by them, who would apparently rise from the dead to prove his God-given powers.

Varro had written that, to prove that Jesus was the Messiah, Josephus, Nicodemus and the other plotters had carefully arranged and manipulated events so that the Nazarene would be seen to have fulfilled the predictions of ancient Jewish prophets. Key to the assumption that Jesus was the Messiah was his proponents' claim that he descended from King Davidus, through his father Josephus. The prophesies clearly stated that the Messiah would be a descendant of Davidus. Conflicting genealogies had since been produced to prove that Josephus was descended from Davidus, but these had since been made irrelevant by the admissions in the Lucius Letter and the Marcus and Matthias documents that Jesus was not of Josephus' seed. Varro wrote that Jesus therefore had no blood link with the royal line of Davidus so could not have been the predicted Messiah, or Christus.

Having devoted some space to the motive for the crime, Varro's emphasis in the body of the report moved to the underlying role played by Josephus, Nicodemus and other leading Pharisees at all stages of the Nazarene's arrest, questioning, sentencing, fabricated execution, and spiriting away. Where there was no direct evidence to link them to some aspects of the crucifixion plot, so Varro had written, the certainty of their role was inescapable. He said, for example, that it was apparent Josephus, or Nicodemus, or other Pharisees on the Great Sanhedrin connected with Jesus, had been present at the initial questioning of the Nazarene at the house of former High Priest Ananus, at the later questioning before High Priest Caiaphas, and then at Jesus' several hearings before Prefect Pilatus. Only they could later have passed on what they saw and heard, information which reached the Nazarene testament writers Matthias, Marcus, and Lucius.

Unless the accounts by Matthias, Marcus and Lucius of these inquisitions and hearings had been complete inventions, said Varro's report, these leading Pharisees were the only possible sources of this information, as no other follower of the Nazarene had been shown to be present at all these sessions; not Marcus, not Matthias, nor any other apostle or disciple. In the same way, no account of the interview of Jesus by Herod Antipas had been passed down, because no Pharisee had been present at Antipas' palace.

Varro had also written that Josephus and Nicodemus would have been supported secretly by other Pharisees who contributed money to the plot. Using their combined resources they had bribed the senior Roman centurion at Jerusalem, Longinus, to stage the death of Jesus on a cross, enabling the Nazarene to apparently rise from the dead. They had also bribed guards at the tomb to look the other way and allow the Nazarene to be spirited away after the crucifixion. Although Jesus had told his apostles that he intended to be crucified to emulate the prophesies of ancient Jewish prophets, the plan of the Pharisees was not revealed to them. The exception was Judas, who, at the plotters' behest and with the Nazarene's full knowledge, had played the part of Jesus' betrayer.

Confident that he had just one more day's work ahead of him before his one-volume report was complete, Varro was thinking about turning in for the night when he heard shouting voices arise in the distance. With Hostilis shadowing him as usual, he stepped out of his tent to determine the cause. As men ran past the *pretorium* with buckets in hand, the questor spied Optio Silius. "What is happening, Silius?"

"A fire in the camp, questor," said the optio excitedly. "Among the baggage."

Varro quickly made his way to the baggage area, to find off-duty soldiers trying to battle a fire raging in one of the carts, under the direction of Centurion Gallo. The centurion had dragged the burning vehicle well away from the other vehicles, but the occasional bucket of water being thrown on the fire was having no inhibiting effect.

"We can't save the cart, questor," said Gallo when he saw his superior in the firelight. "Or the contents."

Pythagoras was among the numerous members of the expedition who began to arrive on the scene to view the conflagration. "It is one of my carts, questor," said the secretary sourly. "The cart containing the wax tablets."

Varro looked suddenly alarmed. "Not our record of interviews?"

Pythagoras nodded. "Despite the damp cloths wrapped daily around the tablets to keep them moist, the fire had much to feed on with their wooden backing."

Varro watched the flames rising ten feet into the night sky above the blazing cart. "We have lost all the records," he lamented.

"Not quite all, questor," the secretary said in his usual unemotional monotone. "I had retained the last tablets pertaining to the interview of Atticus and Scaurus, in my tent, in preparation for tomorrow's writing session."

"That is something," Varro unhappily returned. "Is the report itself safe?"

Pythagoras held up a cylindrical leather document case. "The work-in-progress is here, questor. The report never leaves my sight."

"Guard the document well, Pythagoras." As Varro and secretary took in the sight of the blaze, feeling the heat of the flames on their faces, the wheels of the cart gave way. The entire burning mass collapsed to the ground with a crash and a red-hot spray of sparks, sending soldiers jumping back. Varro scowled in Gallo's direction. "How did this occur, centurion?" he called.

Gallo again came to the questor's side. "An accident, questor," he said, pointing to the blackened remains of an oil lantern lying on the ground thirty feet from the blaze, in a gap between the row of baggage carts. The singed stump of a wooden lamp post stood nearby. "That was where I found the cart. The lantern fell, and ignited the cart."

Varro walked over to inspect what was left of the lantern, squatting beside it. Gallo and Pythagoras joined him. "Bring more light," Varro instructed.

Soldiers quickly brought lanterns, and in their light the questor surveyed the location of the lamp post. He checked the position of other nearby lantern posts. "This lamp post seems out of place," he said, half to himself. Coming to his feet, he walked along the street a little way followed by lantern bearers, as spectators quickly moved out of his way. After several paces, he stopped, and looked down.

"Have you found something, questor?" Quintus Crispus asked, joining him.

"Look at the lamp posts to the left and right of you, Quintus," said Varro. "Tell me what they tell you, in relation to the fourth."

Crispus wore an expression of total befuddlement, looking from post to post to post and then to Varro. He produced an open-handed gesture. "I am sorry, questor..."

"On your hands and knees, Quintus, and tell me what you see down there." Varro pointed to the earth at his feet.

Crispus dropped to his knees. "A hole, questor!" he exclaimed. "A post hole in the earth here, the size of the lamp posts. There was a post here, in line with the others."

Varro nodded. "Someone moved the lamp post, to put it beside the cart containing our records," he pronounced. "Perhaps with no intent of arson, but then again... Gallo, find the soldiers who installed these lamp posts. Ask them if they moved that lamp."

The centurion soon identified the men who had planted the lantern posts, and they assured him that they did not place the lamp post where it had been found. "Someone moved the lamp, questor," Gallo reported, "and placed it next to the cart which burned."

As Varro walked back to his tent, it was with the conviction that somebody had deliberately relocated the lamp post to make the fire appear an accident. Somebody in his camp, Varro was certain, had set out to destroy the records of his investigation.

✠

Varro dreamed that night. Of a blazing funeral pyre. A sword lay on the ground beside the pyre. A body writhed in the flames. When Hostilis woke him with a gentle shake of the shoulder, he found himself wet with perspiration.

"You were dreaming again, master," said Hostilis. "Shall I fetch Pythagoras?"

Varro shook his head. "No need to disturb his slumbers, Hostilis. The meaning was plain enough. I dreamed of a funeral pyre. I think it was my own."

"Perhaps the fire in the camp prompted a dream without meaning, master."

Varro looked at his servant for a long moment. "I hope you are right." He sat up, then had Hostilis bring him his writing box. When Hostilis brought the box to him, Varro opened it and took out a sealed document and a small leather cap. "Here, Hostilis, with my gratitude." Where Hostilis looked uncertain, he said, "Take them - your manumission papers, your cap of liberty. I have dated the document to take effect on the first day of August. I was planning to give these to you then, but you never know what calamity might befall me before this month ends."

"No calamity will befall you, master," said Hostilis positively.

"How do you know?" Smiling wearily, Varro held out document and cap. "Take them, before I change my mind."

The slave accepted the document which granted his freedom and the cap which he could, if he so chose, proudly wear from his day of manumission to show the world that he was a freedman. "Thank you, master. Thank you so much."

✠

Varro threw himself into an eighth day of writing. By mid morning he had come to a hurdle. Centurion Longinus' desertion bothered him. It seemed highly coincidental that Longinus had run off from the 12th Legion within months of the execution of Jesus of Nazareth, and it was surprising that an enterprising and moneyed man like Longinus was soon found and arrested. This had put the principal Roman agent in the crucifixion plot out of the way, conveniently for the Jews who had been party to the plot. Once Longinus had been removed, no one in authority remained to give credence to a claim that the crucifixion of Jesus had been fabricated. Philippus the Evangelist had claimed that Longinus had become a follower of the Nazarene, suggesting a reason for desertion, but not a particularly believable one to Varro's mind. Varro had come to the conclusion that there had to be something more to Longinus' desertion. Had word leaked out that Longinus allowed the Nazarene to escape with his life? Had such a leak come from the Jews who were party to the plot? Or had one of the four members of the execution party suffered from loose lips, over one cup too many of wine whilst on leave, perhaps?

There was another possibility. What if Prefect Pilatus had come to learn of the crucifixion plot, after the event, and eliminated Centurion Longinus on a trumped up charge? If it had become known that Jesus of Nazareth had escaped execution while under Pilatus' jurisdiction, the chief priests of the Great Sanhedrin would have demanded the prefect's head. What was more, Tiberius Caesar would have given it to them. Pilatus would have done anything to conceal Longinus' crime. Countering this possibility was the thought that if Pilatus had discovered Longinus' role in the plot, would he not have also executed the four soldiers of the execution squad, key participants in the plot, to also keep them quiet? Not necessarily, Varro told himself. To have beheaded Jesus' four executioners would have raised suspicion with the Sanhedrin. Could this have accounted for the promotion and transfer of Atticus and Scaurus, to move them out of the province? How soon after Longinus' execution had their promotions followed? Weeks? Months? Years? The pair had indicated that they had remained at Jerusalem long enough to hear of the death of Matthias Ben Naum, but no longer. It occurred to the questor that, one way or another, perhaps Atticus and Scaurus knew more than they had let on about the reasons for Longinus' desertion and execution. He sent for Centurion Gallo. "Go to the Two Goats Tavern," he instructed. "Bring me the proprietors; I have more questions for them."

Townspeople quickly moved aside as Gallo and his detachment of soldiers came marching through the narrow streets. The small column came to a halt outside the Two Goats Tavern. The shutters of the premises were drawn, which Centurion Gallo considered highly unusual for the late morning of a business day. When he rattled the shutters and called for attention, no answer came from within. Scowling, Gallo walked down the side of the tavern, to a door which led to stairs to the upper floor, where

Atticus and Scaurus had their residence. The door was closed and locked. Calling his burliest legionary, Gallo told him to shoulder down the door. After four attempts, the soldier splintered the woodwork. Leaving Rufus and eleven men outside, Gallo drew his sword then led four men in through the door. Up the narrow stairs they quickly trod, to the landing. Splitting up, Gallo and his men went from room to sparsely furnished room.

"Centurion!" came the disturbed cry of one of Gallo's men.

Gallo followed the voice to a room overlooking the street. There were two beds in the room. Sextus Atticus and Lucius Scaurus lay face up in the beds. Both were dead. Their skin had a purplish hue to it. Judged by the offensive odor they gave off, they had been dead for several days. Pulling a face at the stench, and sheathing his sword, the centurion went closer to study the bodies. There were no signs of violence, but both men were open-eyed. Gallo's hackles were up; he felt sure that foul play had been involved.

A search by the centurion and his men of residence, tavern, and staff quarters in the rear found no trace of the tavern keepers' servants. Neither did they find any valuables in the house; no gold, no silver, no cash. Gallo went back through the premises a second time, searching behind walls, in ceilings, under the floor. He was looking for something in particular. Eight days before, when Atticus and Scaurus had departed the Questor's *pretorium,* they had taken weighty leather bags away with them. The bags had contained a large sum of money — twenty thousand sesterces, the questor's reward for their testimony. Now, that money, like the servants of Atticus and Scaurus, had vanished.

Gallo reported back to the questor with the news that the two old goats of Capernaum were dead. He also told Varro it was his belief that the two former soldiers had been smothered to death in their beds by their servants, who had then rifled the premises, located the pair's newly acquired wealth, stolen everything else of value, then locked up, and fled.

Unhappy at the news of the deaths of the old veterans, Varro sent Gallo and all his men to scour Capernaum and ask questions about the tavern-keepers' servants, and about any recent visitors to the old men. Gallo's hypothesis seemed a reasonable one, yet the questor could not help feeling there was a possibility that the old men had been murdered because of the testimony they had given him. He hoped that theft had been the sole motive for the killings, but he would have preferred to have known that with certainty. He could not bring back Atticus and Scaurus, and he could no longer expect answers to his question about the desertion of Centurion Longinus, but he would like to identify their killers and establish the motive for their murders.

✠

A mounted courier of the 4th Scythica's own cavalry squadron rode up to the camp that afternoon. The dusty rider was conducted to Questor Varro at a Capernaum bathhouse.

Varro was about to enter the cold bath when the courier came to him.

"This has been following you from Antioch for weeks, questor," said the soldier, removing a letter from his dispatch case, "and half way around Judea."

Varro took the letter. Identifying the seal of his uncle with some surprise — he rarely received correspondence from the reclusive younger brother of his late father — he opened the letter and read it:

Gaius Terentius Rufus at Rome to Julius Terentius Varro, Questor to the Propretor of Syria at Antioch, Greetings.

Esteemed nephew it is with leaden heart that your humble uncle must write to you at this time with the most tragic of news. It was on the day of the Festival of the Parilia that your beloved mother was seized by a severe pain in the head and collapsed at her house on the Aventine. The physicians were summoned, but there was nothing they could do to save the noble Julia Gratiana. If it is any consolation nephew those same physicians have subsequently assured me that after the initial seizure your mother would have suffered no discomfort and that death claimed her very swiftly.

It was only very recently that I received a letter at Nola from your mother in which she had told me in glowing terms that you had been given a very responsible assignment in your province of late and that she fully expected you to make a great success of that assignment. Julia also told me of her joy at receiving a letter from you at Antioch sending her greetings on the occasion of the Matronalia.

I have now come to Rome to settle your mother's affairs as her executor. The majority of her estate she has willed to yourself, but I should make you aware that she also allowed generous annuities to

myself and to her staff and to her former under secretary and now your
secretary Artimedes. Your mother has also granted manumission to the
longest serving of her household slaves.
Nephew, this news must come as a great shock to you, as it did to me.
Your mother had by far the soundest constitution of any person of her
age I could name. Her loss I can only ascribe to divine will. Soon I am
to return to Nola. If you have any return communication for me you
might address it to me there.
Farewell.

✠

The boat rocked gently as it floated in the rippling waters off Capernaum.
It was a small craft, built in the common style of edge-to-edge carvel
planking. With just two oars, it was wide at the center, with pointed prow
and stern. Normally used for conveying paying passengers from lake town
to lake town, it contained two bench seats running transversely. On one
bench sat the rowers, Callidus and Hostilis. On the other, with their backs
to this inexpert crew, sat Questor Varro and the slave Miriam.

The news of his mother's death had devastated Varro. All thoughts of
completing his report had gone to the wind. A month before, Varro would
have shared his grief with Marcus Martius and Artimedes. Now, there was
only one person he could think of turning to. Instructing Callidus to find
him a small boat and to bring Miriam to him, he had embarked onto the
Sea of Galilee in search of tranquility and consolation. Miriam had not said
a word all the time she had been sitting by his side. She had made sure that
no part of her body touched his, although, given the limited width of the
boat, the gap between them was not large. They had not spoken since the
boat left the shore.

A small Roman warship of fifty oars had just passed by, on patrol, with
a long blue pennant trailing listlessly from its mast and with the marines
on deck looking bored. The wash from the *pentekonter* subsided, and the
Sea of Galilee returned to glass. On the questor's instructions, Callidus
and Hostilis had ceased to row. Hostilis had now closed his eyes, and sat,
half asleep, soaking in the sun. Beside him, Callidus watched the sleek,
narrow warship make its way around the lake toward Bethsaida, its oar

blades flashing as they rose and fell. Callidus was thinking about the ship that would soon be taking Julius Varro and himself back home to Rome.

"My mother has died," said Varro flatly, looking straight ahead.

"I had heard," Miriam replied. "News travels fast in camp. I am sorry for your loss, questor, truly sorry." She sounded genuine. "How did it happen?"

"She fell down dead, in our house at Rome. No warning. Just fell down dead." He was still in shock at the news. "The physicians said that she did not suffer."

"That would be a consolation for you."

"It is." He sighed. "We were close, my mother and I. She was a very wise woman. Much wiser than my father, I always thought. She would not have resigned herself to her fate the way he did. Had she been him, she would have fought to clear her name."

"Was she beautiful?"

"Beautiful?" He nodded. "I always thought so. She was admired by many men. Several of Rome's most distinguished men courted her once Nero had gone and it was no longer dangerous to associate with the widow of a Piso plotter, or an accused Piso plotter, but she vowed never to remarry."

"A Piso plotter? What does this mean?"

This question brought a wry smile to his lips. It was easy to assume that everyone in the world was familiar with the politics of Rome, but, as he was discovering, it was wrong to assume anything in life. "Six years ago, Piso, a Roman senator, formed a conspiracy to murder Nero Caesar," he explained. "The plot was discovered, and many leading men of the day were implicated. My father was one of those accused. He was innocent of the charge, but it was true that he had no love for Nero. He had held such hopes for Nero, the grandson of Germanicus Caesar, yet after a golden beginning, of early years of such promise, Nero's reign turned from a dream to a nightmare."

"Your mother did not remarry?"

"No. Her father would never have forced another marriage on her. He respected her too much for that. We all respected her. No woman of Rome was more respected than my mother. She gave me the confidence to make my own way in the world, to assume the responsibilities as head of my family, the responsibilities my father surrendered when he surrendered his life. I think, like his brother Gaius, my father was not comfortable with responsibility. Gaius escaped to the country, and his farm. My father submitted himself to the executioner's ax. He did not even have the courage to open his veins and take his own life. Nero gave him that option."

"Are you?"

For the first time, he looked at her. His eyes collided with her large, dark eyes. His heart missed a beat. "Am I what?" he responded.

"Comfortable with responsibility?"

He shrugged. "I have had no choice, Miriam." He returned his gaze to the lake. "Now, of course, with my mother's death, I have more responsibilities than ever."

"You do have a choice, you know?" she said. "In all things."

He nodded. "I am aware of that."

"You should follow your heart."

"I have a duty, to my mother's memory." His voice faltered. He cleared his throat.

"I'm sorry, that you have lost her." Reaching across, she took his hand in hers.

Biting his lip, determined not to let his grief have the better of him, he gratefully, gently squeezed her delicate little hand. They sat like that, hand in hand, for a long time, not speaking, just looking at the water. Finally, he said, "Would you come to Rome with me? When I return in the new year?"

"If you command it of me. Yet, with your mother's passing, what duties would there be for me there?"

"It is not as an ordinary slave that you would go to Rome," he said, turning to her.

She dropped her eyes. "Then, what role would I have?"

"You would only go to Rome if you chose to go to Rome." He looked at her profile, absorbed by the perfection of her features. "I shall give you a choice, Miriam. You may either go to Rome, with me, or you shall have your freedom, and a bounty, and you may go wherever your heart takes you — back to Caesarea Philippi, here to your birthplace of Capernaum — wherever you choose."

She drew her hand from his. "That is cruel," she declared.

He was hurt. "Why? Why is it cruel? I am allowing you to follow your heart."

"You say that I may have the choice of manumission, and money, against a choice of you, and Rome? That is a cruel choice to give."

"You may have your freedom, which ever choice you make. At Rome, or here."

"Freedom takes many forms," she said wistfully.

"Do you understand what I am saying? I will not force you to do anything. If you choose to go your own way, then so be it. If you choose to accompany me to Rome, of your free will, then I will know that you have done it because you want to be with me."

"As your mistress at Rome?"

"Yes."

"Questor..."

"Will you not call me Julius?"

She shook her head. "I cannot. I am a slave, you are my master."

He smiled. "That can soon change."

She shook her head. "Even as a freedwoman, I could not call you by your first name. We are from different worlds, you and I, Julius Terentius Varro."

"Do you not have feelings for me?" He was sounding exasperated. "If not, then say so, and you shall be free to go, and that will be the end of it."

"You would just let me walk away?"

"Yes."

"You would forget me?"

"No. I could never forget you, Miriam. Never."

She sighed. "This is so unfair."

"Why? Nothing can be fairer than the choice I am offering you. Do you have any feelings for me at all, Miriam? Tell me."

"I confess," she said, "that I have grown fond of you. Fonder than I dare."

"Then, could you, would you come away to Rome with me? Yes, or no?"

She turned to look at him once more. "If I were to choose to go with you...?"

"Yes...?" he responded expectantly.

""Would you accept Jesus of Nazareth into you life?"

He looked crestfallen. "You cannot ask that of me," he protested.

"Why not? Jesus was a good man. You are a good man. Do you remember the night that Queen Berenice made a gift of me to you? She called me aside, and whispered something to me. Do you know what she said? She said, 'Here is a man who will know the truth when he finds it. Help him find the truth.' Jesus is the truth."

"I do not deny that Jesus of Nazareth was a good man. A good man, a prophetic man. Perhaps, a good man manipulated by others, men with political motives."

"Why must you think in terms of politics, of worldly concerns?" Her brow furrowed as she grew suddenly annoyed. "This is about faith, about opening your heart."

"Miriam, how can you expect me to believe something that I know to be untrue?" He too was sounding annoyed now. "The religion of the Nazarene is all about ignorance, and superstition. Ignorance enslaves, superstition enslaves."

"It is the religion of the Roman gods that is based on ignorance and superstition," she countered. Then her look softened. "Please, accept Him into your heart. Choose everlasting life. Become His messenger. Destroy your evil document."

"Document? You mean my report? You want me to destroy my report?"

She nodded. "I will come with you to Rome. I will be your partner in all things. You shall be my partner in all things. There are many of the faith at Rome, some even in Caesar's own household. You will be welcomed as a brother. But you must destroy the document which slanders Him."

"You cannot ask it of me." His head and his heart were in turmoil.

"That is my price," she declared firmly. "The price of your salvation."

They sat in silence, she cloaked in self-righteousness, he in dismay.

From the south, a dark cloud came rolling toward them, blotting out the sun and sending a chill wind across the lake.

"The weather changes," said Varro numbly. "Callidus, we shall return to shore."

Callidus and Hostilis came to life and slipped their oars into the water. They were soon rowing in unison, speeding the little craft back toward Capernaum. Not a word was spoken in the boat on the return journey. The bow nosed onto the beach below the town, and Hostilis leapt over the side and dragged the craft up onto the sand. Varro jumped out. He turned to help Miriam from the boat, but she disembarked of her own accord. With a sigh, Varro turned and strode up to the Water Gate. Miriam walked in his footsteps.

Last of all, Callidus landed. He stood watching Hostilis fasten the craft's bow rope to a rusty iron ring embedded in a rock at the edge of the little beach. "Did you hear?" Callidus said with agitation. "He wants to take her to Rome, as his mistress."

Hostilis gave him a disapproving look. "I am deaf in the questor's presence," he said, "unless he speaks to me. It would pay you to have the same attitude."

"She must not be permitted to go to Rome," said Callidus, half to himself.

Hostilis glowered at the freedman. "Mind your business, Callidus," he cautioned.

"You mind your tongue, slave!" Callidus snapped back with irritation. "You are not yet a freedman, fellow. Know your place!" As the cold wind cut in off the water, Callidus shivered, then, with shoulders hunched, set off with moody strides toward the Water Gate. At his own pace, Hostilis brought up the rear.

XXIX

THE SUBJECT OF POISON

Capernaum, Northern Galilee, Tetrarchy of Trachonitis. July A.D. 71

The south wind had brought an unseasonably cold change. In the early evening, as Callidus made his way to a tent not far from his own, men swathed in cloaks huddled around cooking fires throughout the camp with hands outstretched to flames for warmth.

Columbus, the giant Numidian, stood on sentry duty outside a tent door, resting on a stave. The guardian to the chief magistrate of the Jews of Antioch eyed Callidus blankly as the freedman stooped beside him and looked in through the open tent flap. General Collega had commissioned Columbus to watch Antiochus like a hawk, to make sure that the man did not involve himself in any mischief, and that was what the former gladiator had been doing for months.

"May I enter, Antiochus?" Callidus called. He did not wait for a reply.

Antiochus looked up from a letter he was writing, the latest in a succession of secret missives complaining to General Collega about the way that Questor Varro was handling the general's commission. Not trusting anyone else with such delicate matters, Antiochus always wrote these epistles himself. As for the letters' delivery, at populated stopping places along the expedition's route Antiochus had paid suitable agents who would forward them to Antioch. Now, Antiochus hastily covered his writing frame with a cloth. "To what do I owe the pleasure, Callidus?" he said, with a frosty scowl.

"Just a cordial visit, Antiochus," said Callidus, looking around the tent.

"Is that so?" Antiochus wore a cynical smile as he came out from behind his writing table. "During the course of this expedition, Callidus, you have paid me a cordial visit how many times? Let me see. Yes, I do believe it is... never!"

"For all things, there are precedents, as they say, Antiochus."

"Is that what they say? Let us dispose of the false cordiality. What do you want?"

"Well..." Callidus lowered his voice. "This afternoon, I accompanied the questor on a diversion on the lake, in a small boat."

"How charming for you."

"We were not alone. For company, the questor took along the slave girl Miriam."

Antiochus' eyes narrowed. "Why?"

"The questor and the girl have become intimate."

"How intimate?" Antiochus demanded with concern. "Physically intimate?"

"Not to my knowledge. Although that would seem considerably imminent."

"That girl is dangerous," Antiochus growled.

"My thought exactly," Callidus responded, delighted to have seemingly found an ally. He stepped closer. "Look how she has wormed her way onto his staff. Worse than that, I overheard her ask the questor to destroy his Nazarene report."

"Destroy it!" Antiochus exploded.

Callidus put a finger to his lips. "Hush! This is between just we two."

"Did Varro agree?" Antiochus whispered anxiously. "Did he give in to her?"

"Not as yet. That is not to say the girl will cease to try, Antiochus."

Antiochus began to pace the floor. "As I have told Collega, I have feared all along that Varro would favor the Nazarenes and deliver a soft and useless report. Now you say that there is a risk there will be no report at all? Is Varro mad?"

Again Callidus put a finger to his lips.

"Is he mad?" Antiochus repeated, coming to a stop and whispering now.

"I didn't say that he had agreed to her request. None the less, the possibility remains, while she remains. If you understand my meaning?"

Suspicious, Antiochus scowled at the freedman. "What are you suggesting?"

"While Miriam remains, danger remains. It occurred to me that a man of position like yourself, a magistrate of the Jews, would have considerable contacts, and the power to remove an undesirable. You know what I mean, Antiochus?"

"You are saying that she should be removed from the scene?"

Callidus shrugged. "One way, or another."

Perspiration gleamed on Antiochus' brow. Nervously, and habitually, his hand went to the small leather pouch at his neck. Thinking hard, he did not say anything.

"It would be beneficial to the future of the questor's report if the girl were removed from the scene," Callidus reiterated. "With her out of the way, the questor can be expected to have a clear head and a more balanced view."

Antiochus was slowly nodding in agreement.

"You heard the evidence of Atticus and Scaurus," Callidus went on. "There was a Jewish conspiracy to make it appear that the Nazarene rose from the dead. You know it, I know it, the questor knows it. With the girl out of the way, Antiochus, the questor will deliver a report which confirms it, and which damns the Nazarenes." Callidus knew that Antiochus wanted the Nazarenes eliminated.

Antiochus was nodding. "We must all do everything in our power to ensure the success of the questor's mission, Callidus."

"Then, I can rely on you, Antiochus, regarding this considerably delicate matter?"

"My thanks for appraising me of the matter, Callidus. You may leave it with me."

✠

Antiochus lolled on his divan, deep in thought and absently fingering the pouch at his throat. Antiochus was an insecure man. He had seen his father and other leading Jewish citizens of Antioch burned to death in the amphitheater. The fact that it had been his information that had resulted in their cruel deaths made Antiochus no less fearful for his own life. Before the Jewish Revolt, Governor Mucianus had been tolerant of the Jews of

Syria, but Collega his replacement despised the entire race and the Revolt had given him the opportunity to kill Jews wholesale. Antiochus knew that, even though he had sworn off Judaism, Collega still considered him a Jew. It was Antiochus' dread that one mistake, and not necessarily his own, could lose him Collega's favor, and lose him his life. Antiochus had no intention of facing an agonizing death, on a cross, or a fire.. If he had to go, he would go by his own hand, rapidly, and painlessly. The hemlock seeds that he kept in the little leather pouch dangling around his neck were his guarantee of that.

Momentarily, after Callidus had left him with the problem of the troublesome Miriam, Antiochus had thought of using his hemlock to dispose of the girl, but that would only deprive him of the means of his own last resort. That was not a sacrifice he was prepared to make. Applying his mind to the problem, the resourceful Antiochus had come up with a solution. That solution now came through the door to his tent.

"You sent for me, Antiochus?" said Diocles the physician.

Antiochus smiled. "Diocles, my dear fellow. Do come in. Take a seat."

"Your man said that you were not well," said Diocles crossing the floor to stand looking down at Antiochus with a physician's eye. "What seems to be the problem?"

"A lack of sleep, Diocles. I am having great difficulty sleeping."

"Ah." Diocles seemed pleased that it was nothing more serious. "Not unexpected, living under canvas the way we have been for the past few months. I myself am not sleeping as soundly as I would prefer."

"Please, sit." Antiochus patted the divan. "Talk with me. I was most impressed with what you had to say about a bleeding corpse. Your knowledge is remarkable."

"Remarkable? Oh, I would not go that far. But, most civil of you, Antiochus. None of the other fellows on this expedition are as civil." With a grunt, Diocles settled his ample figure beside his host. "I shall prepare you a sleeping draught, shall I?"

"That would be most acceptable. Thank you, excellent physician."

"Good, good. I shall have my man Pallas bring it along to you presently."

"Is there much illness in the camp?"

"Nothing of significance. Just the usual soldiers' bumps and bruises."

"You would travel with an extensive medical chest?"

"As extensive as the expedition's limited transportation arrangements allow."

"Would you, for example, carry belladonna in your medical chest?"

"Belladonna? Yes, yes, a small quantity. I use it, sparingly, for this and that. It is quite dangerous, of course. Too large a dose and it can be fatal. Quite fatal."

"I can imagine. Diocles, I was planning to decline the questor's invitation to dine at his *pretorium* this evening and instead dine alone in my own tent."

"Oh, well, I am sure the questor would not mind. He is quite an agreeable fellow, really." He frowned, as unpleasant memories came to the forefront of his mind. "Unlike some of the people on this expedition."

"One of my reasons for dining alone, Diocles," said Antiochus, with a conspiratorial smile, "lies on the floor behind us." He turned and indicated a wine amphora lying on its side at the rear of the tent.

Following his gaze, Diocles' eyes lit up. "Well, well, well. Private stock is it?"

"Purchased from Procurator Rufus at Caesarea, at a bargain price. He was soon to return to Rome. It is a Falernian."

Diocles' eyes widened. "A Falernian? Bacchus and Jove! The best Falernian, too, I'll be bound; Rufus had expensive tastes. Oh, how I miss a good Falernian!"

"Then, join me, good physician. Dine with me tonight, here, in my tent. I have an excellent cook. It will be just you, and I, and the Falernian," he said with a wink.

"Oh!" Unable to take his eyes off the amphora, Diocles was caught between temptation and fear. "Do you think I could? The questor has forbidden me to drink, and Tribune Martius threatened me with bodily harm if I was found to have touched a drop."

Antiochus patted the doctor's knee "Martius is dead. As for the questor, what he does not know will not harm him. Or you." He clapped the doctor on the back. "You are such jolly company, Diocles, I insist that you join me. I will not take 'no' for an answer!"

XXX

THE BETRAYAL

Capernaum, Northern Galilee, Tetrarchy of Trachonitis. July A.D. 71

Varro had finished dinner and now the questor, Crispus, Pedius, and Callidus were listening as Pythagoras stood at the writing table and read aloud the closing paragraphs of the now completed report, the *Investigatio Nazarena*. As the secretary was in mid-sentence, Centurion Gallo burst into the tent.

"Questor! Diocles is rolling drunk," the centurion reported urgently.

Varro had received dinner apologies from both Diocles and Antiochus, and had thought nothing of it. Now, he was furious. "Where is the physician?" he demanded.

"In his tent, questor."

Varro came to his feet. "I warned that man…!"

"There was something else, questor," said Gallo, betraying a little nervousness.

Varro Scowled. "What now?"

"The slave Miriam, and the child," said Gallo. "They have taken ill."

Varro froze. "How ill?"

"Very ill. After eating."

"Why did you wait to tell me?" Varro raged. He strode toward the tent door. "Take Diocles to them, at once!" he ordered.

Gallo quickly stood aside to let the questor pass. Crispus and Pedius followed on Varro's heel, with Callidus bringing up the rear. Left with his report, Pythagoras returned the volume to its protective leather cylinder with deliberate care before leaving the case in Hostilis' safe keeping. Then he too departed the *pretorium* and walked in the direction of the tent shared by Miriam and Gemara, at the end of the line of tents of the freedmen.

It was all Varro could do to stop himself running to Miriam's quarters. When he arrived, a young soldier of the watch stood by the entrance with a frightened look on his face. Varro pushed back the tent's flap, bent, and entered.

In the light of a low lamp he could see two bedrolls on the floor. Miriam lay on one, with her knees drawn up into her stomach. Gemara was on the other, on her back. Both had been vomiting violently; they, their clothes, the bedding, the floor, were all splattered with foul-smelling puke. Ignoring this, Varro dropped to his knees beside Miriam. Gently, he rolled her over to face him. Her cheeks were flushed, there was a dazed, questioning look in her eyes.

"Was it the food?" he asked, his voice hushed.

She nodded slowly, and reached out and took his hand. Her grip was weak.

Pedius slid into the tent behind Varro, looking worried. Crispus stood anxiously in the entranceway.

"Pedius, you have charge of Miriam and the child. Who prepares their meals?"

"Melitus, the cook of Antiochus, my lord."

"Why him?"

"Melitus has prepared their meals ever since you put Miriam and Gemara into the care of Antiochus, questor," Pedius replied. "He does it the Jewish way."

"Do you know what they ate this evening?"

"Mushrooms, my lord. I saw Melitus bring the bowl. There it is." He indicated a bowl on the floor. It still contained several mushroom pieces. "Melitus told me that he would be serving the very same dish to Antiochus and his guest tonight."

"What guest?"

"I believe that Diocles dined in Antiochus' tent this evening, my lord."

"Oh, did he?" To Varro, this information suggested the source of Diocles' intoxication. "Are the mushrooms poisonous, perhaps?" he postulated. "Are either Diocles or Antiochus ill?"

"Not to my knowledge, my lord."

"Gallo will bring the physician. You fetch water and cloth. Quickly!"
Pedius hurried away.

Callidus came to stand in the doorway beside Crispus. "What is their condition, questor?"

"I cannot tell." Varro looked over to the child. "Gemara? Can you hear me?"

Little Gemara nodded. Like Miriam, she was flushed in the face.

"The physician is coming," Varro told her. "He will make you well." Varro looked up at Callidus. "Where is that damned physician?" he growled.

"Help... Gemara ... first." It was Miriam who spoke, one difficult word at a time.

Varro returned his attention to her. "You will both be helped," he assured her. "Can you tell me about your condition? What are the symptoms?"

"Cannot... swallow," she said.

At the door, Callidus stood aside to admit Centurion Gallo.

"My lord," Gallo began, guiltily, "the physician has collapsed."

"He has what!" Varro exploded, his voice so loud that the entire camp could hear.

"Unconscious. It is the wine."

"Where did he lay his hands on it?" Varro demanded.

"It seems that Antiochus gave him wine at dinner."

"Damn the man!"

As Varro spoke, Miriam suddenly vomited again. "I... am... sorry," she groaned when her stomach had ceased its upheavals.

"No matter," he said, gripping her hand. "If there was poison , that will eject it."

She frowned up at him. "Poison?"

"The mushrooms. They, er, may have been bad." He would not share his suspicion with her that perhaps she and Gemara had been deliberately poisoned.

"Shall I fetch the physician's assistants, questor?" Gallo asked.

"Yes, yes, do that," Varro agreed. "Bring Pallas and the others, and bring Diocles to his senses! Dowse him with water! Do whatever is necessary. But hurry!"

Gallo turned and disappeared into the night. As he departed, Pedius returned, bringing bowls of water and lengths of cloth. Using these, Varro washed Miriam's face, neck and arms, while Pedius tended to Gemara in the same fashion.

Crispus called from the door. "There may be a physician in the town. Shall I…?"

"Yes, Quintus, a good idea," Varro responded. "Search the town for a physician. Take as many men as you need. But, whatever you do, hurry!"

"I shall not fail you, questor." Crispus rushed out into the night.

Feeling helpless, Varro continued to kneel beside Miriam, looking down at her.

Miriam sensed the questor's anxiety. "Will I… die?" she asked him.

"Die?" Vigorously he shook his head. "No, no, no. Put such foolish thoughts from your head." But his fears for her made him sound unconvincing.

"There is… something… you must… know," she said weakly. "Come closer."

Frowning, he lowered his face to within a hand span of hers. "What is it?"

"I am… with child." She swallowed, with great difficulty. "Your child."

He looked at her in disbelief. "A child?"

She nodded slowly, her eyes answering his unspoken questions, confirming the truth of her statement. "It is… a gift," she added. "A Heavenly… gift."

Varro now quickly made a decision. "We will transfer them to the *pretorium*," he announced. "Pedius, you bring Gemara. I shall carry Miriam. Callidus, you bring the bowl containing the mushrooms; it warrants closer inspection." He slipped his arms around Miriam. "You will be more comfortable in my tent," he said softly, as he came to his feet with her. "Hold onto me."

Once he reached his pavilion, Varro laid Miriam on one side of his bed. Pedius placed Gemara on the other. Callidus was sent to redirect the physician's assistants, and before long the round-faced Pallas and his two colleagues arrived, only to hover uselessly around the bed. They provided the only medical expertise yet available, as Centurion Gallo had been unable to revive Diocles. Varro stood beside Miriam. Looking up at him, her large dark eyes were anchored to his.

"You will recover," he assured her. "The worst has passed." Gently he lifted her head and put a bowl of water to her lips. "Drink. It will help."

She attempted to swallow, but could not.

Varro eased her head back onto the pillow, then looked up at Pallas with a pained expression. "Is there nothing we can do?"

The physician's assistant shook his head. "Nature must take its course, my lord."

Varro lowered himself onto a bedside stool, never taking his gaze from Miriam.

Slowly, she reached up to his face, and drew it down, closer. "You know... that I have forgiven... you," she whispered, "just... as I forgive... those... who have done... this... to me. Do not... grieve... for me. For I... am saved."

He could feel tears welling. He had never cried in his life, and he was determined not to now. "I love you," he told her softly.

She nodded slowly. "I know." She stroked his face. "And I... cherish... you."

"You will not die!" he said determinedly.

"You are...a... good... man... Julius...Varro."

"Good, perhaps," he said, glumly, "but powerless. There is nothing I can do to help you, Miriam. You must help yourself. You must fight this."

"There is... something... you... can... do."

He felt sudden hope. "What is it? Tell me, and I shall do it, at once!"

"Destroy... the... false document," she returned. "I beg... of... you."

Momentarily, he closed his eyes. "Not the report; you cannot ask it of me," he responded. "It would be wrong. I have my duty to do."

She lowered her hand, but gazed up at him still. "You... were... lied to. It is... a... false...document."

"How can you be so certain of that? So much of the testimony rang true."

"It is all . . . a lie!" she gasped.

"So many have died to produce that report; I cannot disrespect their memories by destroying it."

"It is... the right thing... to do."

"How can perpetuating a lie be the good and right thing to do?" he asked her. "Surely, your Christus would not want that? I would do anything to help you. I would cut off my own right hand if it would help, if it made rational sense."

"You... do not... understand now. But... you will. When... you see... the light."

"What do you mean? Miriam?" He bent closer. "Tell me. What light?"

"You have . . . sinned. But . . . once . . . you . . . find . . . the truth . . . you . . . will . . . sin . . . no more." She had exhausted herself; her strength was fading fast.

"What light, Miriam?" he persisted.

Soundlessly she mouthed something more.

"What was that? Miriam, speak again."

She whispered several more words. With his ear close to her lips Varro could just make out what she was saying: *"Eloi, Eloi."* It was, he knew, Aramaic for, 'My God, My God.' Then she closed her eyes.

Varro gently touched her cheek. "Miriam?" When she did not respond, and her eyes remained firmly shut, Varro looked around desperately to Pallas. "What is happening to her?" he demanded. "She does still live?"

Pallas moved forward, and bent close. "She breathes, my lord. She has lapsed into unconsciousness." He stepped back. "This is not uncommon, in such cases."

"You cannot revive her?"

Pallas shrugged. "I could try." He stepped up and slapped Miriam on the face.

"No!" Varro cried, reaching up and staying the man's hand when he went to hit her again. Miriam had not flinched. "Is that all you can do?"

Pallas nodded. "Obviously, she is in a deep coma, my lord."

"What will follow?" Varro asked. "Can you tell me?"

"Recovery, after a time," the Greek gravely advised, "or death."

Varro looked at Miriam's still face. Then he frowned. Miriam's lips were turning blue. "Pallas, what is happening here? The lips, man!"

Pallas leaned in for another close inspection. "Ah," he said, straightening again.

"Well?"

"This is a telltale sign that the girl has been poisoned, my lord."

Varro's face hardened. "Are you certain? There can be no mistake?"

"No mistake, my lord."

"The mushrooms. You inspected what was left of the meal?"

"I did, my lord."

"With what result?"

"It is difficult to tell from appearance and smell alone. Mushrooms are a notoriously effective agent for masking poisons of many kind. It is said that Claudius Caesar was murdered with a dish of poisoned mushrooms."

"What would cause lips to turn blue? Is that characteristic of a particular poison?"

Pallas nodded. "In my experience it is, my lord. Belladonna, my lord."

"Belladonna? I see." Varro looked over to Gemara. Her condition appeared to be less critical; her eyes were still open, and her lips were only faintly discolored.

Pallas seemed to read his thoughts. "The child obviously did not consume as large a quantity as the slave," he surmised.

Varro looked up at the medical orderly. "Is Belladonna easy to come by?"

"Every apothecary is familiar with the plant, my lord."

"And every physician? Does Diocles carry Belladonna with him?"

"A little, my lord." Then Pallas realized the implications. "For medicinal use only. In small doses, it has sedative powers, and can be used as an antispasmodic. But Diocles watches over his medicinal supplies with great care, my lord. I can vouch for that."

"He cannot watch over anything when he is inebriated," Varro growled.

"Questor!" It was Gallo, who was just then entering the pretorium. "I am still unable to revive Diocles."

"No matter," said Varro. "Leave him. Take a party of men and arrest Melitus, cook to Antiochus. And bring me Antiochus himself."

"At once." Gallo quickly departed the way he had come.

When he emerged into the chill night, the centurion looked at the four sentries stationed outside the entrance to the *pretorium,* but thought better of using them for the task at hand. He went directly to the line of 4th Scythica Legion tents. The camp had been stirred by the shouting and frantic to-ing and fro-ing. The tents of the cavalry were now deserted; Prefect Crispus had taken the Vettonians into Capernaum on his quest for a local physician. But Gallo's off-duty legionaries sat and stood around their fires gossiping among themselves as they watched and waited for the latest developments.

"You men take up your sword-belts, and follow me," Gallo ordered as he came upon the residents of the first tent after his own.

Followed by the eight men of the randomly chosen squad, Gallo led the way along the camp street toward the quarters of the freedmen. As the centurion and his men hurried through the night, Antiochus himself burst into their path in a flowing robe. There was a look of consternation on his perspiration-soaked face.

"Antiochus! Just the man," Gallo called, reaching out to lay hold of the Jewish magistrate by the arm. "The questor will have you join him."

"Murder! Murder!" Antiochus cried, recoiling from Gallo's grasp. "Someone has killed Melitus my cook!"

Gallo's jaw dropped. "What did you say?"

"The questor must be informed!" Antiochus pushed through the group of stunned soldiers and hurried toward the *pretorium*.

"The cook's tent," Gallo ordered. "Quickly!"

As the soldiers headed down the street at the trot with the centurion leading the way, Antiochus, running in the opposite direction, reached the questor's tent. Inside, he found Varro, white-faced, at Miriam's bedside. Miriam herself lay motionless. Pallas and the other medical assistants stood around, while Pedius gave the child Gemara a drink of water from a cup with Hostilis holding her head. Pythagoras sat, bored, at the writing table. Callidus was to one side, with arms folded. When he saw Antiochus, Callidus quickly lowered his eyes and turned away.

The questor looked up and spied Antiochus in the doorway. His expression became fierce. "Antiochus! Diocles is drunk. Explain, if you will…!"

"Murder!" Antiochus exclaimed.

Varro was taken by surprise. "What?"

"My cook has been murdered!" Antiochus cried, gesticulating with his arms. "There is a murderer in your camp, Julius Varro!"

On the other side of the camp, Gallo and his men reached the tent of Melitus the cook. Gallo and two soldiers pushed in through the tent entrance. A figure lying on the floor, face down. "A glimmer here," Gallo instructed. A lantern was passed into the tent, and while one of his two companions held the light, Gallo dropped to one knee beside the prone figure, that of a short, burly, hairy man. A large pool of blood soaked the ground. When he rolled the body onto its back, Gallo recognized the dimpled features of Melitus the cook. The man's throat had been cut. Bending closer, Gallo inspected the deep wound. The centurion had no medical credentials but he had seen many a severed throat during his thirty-two years with the legions. He himself had slit a few throats during that time. In Gallo's experience, it was easier and more expedient to cut a man's throat from behind. From the wound, he now adjudged that Melitus had been attacked from behind.

Once Gallo had reported this gruesome discovery to the questor, Varro ordered that no one be permitted to leave the camp. Gallo turned out all his men, to search every tent and every cart. Every sword and dagger in the camp was also to be inspected by the centurion, for traces of blood. Varro made Antiochus remain in the *pretorium* while the search was conducted. The Jewish magistrate was sitting on a couch when Prefect Crispus returned bringing a thin old man with ruffled gray hair and rosy cheeks.

"Questor, this is Boethus, a Jewish physician of Capernaum," said Crispus.

Varro quickly rose and stepped back from the bed to allow the physician freedom of movement. "Boethus, examine the young woman and the child, if you please," he said. "I think they have been administered poison, in their food, a dish of mushrooms."

Without a word, the elderly man went to Miriam's side. He felt her pulse, put an ear to her face, listened to her chest, and put a hand on her forehead. Then he moved around to the other side of the bed to repeat the procedure with Gemara.

"We were fortunate to locate Boethus, questor," said Crispus as he watched the doctor at work. "He tells me that he has only recently returned to Capernaum, after some time away. At Caesarea, I believe."

Varro nodded absently; he was not particularly interested in the physician's travel history. When Boethus had completed his examination of Gemara the doctor stood back.

"Well?" Varro queried.

"The older one seems to be in a coma," said Boethus. "Her breathing is shallow, but she has no fever. The younger one is weak, but appears less seriously affected."

"Is there not something you can give them?" Varro asked unhappily.

"Give them water, if they will take it. That is all. In other circumstances I might prescribe a purgative for the child, but at her age it may do more harm than good."

"What of this young woman?" Varro asked, resuming his seat beside Miriam.

"As I said, a coma," the physician replied matter-of-factly. "She may come out of it, she may not. I have no way of telling."

"There is nothing you can do for her?" Varro's tone was now one of despair. "Nothing to prevent her from dying?"

"I am not a magician, my lord. You will find any number of those in this part of the world. I do not have a prescription for miracle cures. I cannot prevent her death any more than I could bring her back from the dead. Resurrection is the stuff of myth, questor. Do not let anyone tell you otherwise. Now, if that was all...?"

Varro looked at him and sighed. "Thank you, yes, that is all."

Boethus began to walk toward the door. "Keep them both comfortable, and wait," he said as he went. "That is all you can do."

✠

With Hostilis cross-legged on the floor at his feet, Varro had remained at the bedside, holding the unconscious Miriam's hand. For how long, he did not know; Varro had lost track of time. Across the bed, Pedius sat beside Gemara. Pallas and his colleagues had spread on the floor around the bed. Pythagoras was nodding off to sleep at the writing table. Crispus, Callidus and Antiochus reclined on separate dining couches, each locked in his private thoughts.

Reinvigorating the scene, Centurion Gallo came back through the tent entrance. He held a dagger aloft. "The murder weapon, questor!" he declared triumphantly.

Quickly coming to his feet, Varro hurried to inspect the dagger in the centurion's hand. "How can you be sure it is the one?" he asked.

"You can still see the fresh blood on it," Gallo said with a grin. "Mixed with the dirt. We found it half buried. I saw the hilt jutting up."

"Where?"

"Behind the tent of Callidus." Gallo cast his eyes in the direction of the freedman.

Callidus looked around, with both surprise and sudden fear written on his face. "Behind my tent? The murderer must have thrown it there."

"There had been a hurried attempt to bury it," said Gallo accusingly.

"Not by myself!" Callidus quickly protested.

"It would have been a convenient hiding place," the centurion suggested, "for someone hurrying back from the tent of the cook."

"Why would I kill the cook?" Callidus looked to Varro. "My lord...?"

"What reason indeed?" said Varro, slowly walking to Callidus' divan. "Stand up."

Callidus quickly scrambled to his feet. "My lord, I had nothing to do with this. You must believe me! I could not; I dined here, with you."

"We do not know the time of the man's death," said Varro. Miriam's condition had made Varro ready to strike out at any likely guilty party. "It may have taken place before we dined, before you joined me here."

"My lord, please, this is a nonsense. I am Callidus, *your* Callidus, your most trusted freedman. We share your secrets, we too. How could you think that I could have anything to do with the death of the Jew's cook?"

"I agree, to think that you, of all people, Callidus, could betray my trust, is unthinkable. Yet, the unthinkable has occurred in this camp."

"My lord, I know that you have been made distraught by the evening's events; considerably distraught. With respect, even a blind man could see that the murderer cast the dagger outside my tent, to cast blame my way. It is obvious!"

"Oh?" Varro folded his arms as he locked his freedman in a penetrating gaze. "Who would want to cast blame your way, Callidus? And why?"

Callidus resisted the temptation to look Antiochus' way. "I cannot say, my lord. It is a mystery to me. I only know that I did not touch a hair on Melitus' head. I ask you, what possible motive would I have for killing a cook, of all people?"

"The motive for the murder is clear," said Varro, casting his eyes around all those in the pavilion as he spoke. "The cook was killed because he had laced the bowl of mushrooms with poison. The cook was killed to prevent him naming the person who provided the poison, and who also, no doubt, provided an inducement to commit the crime. Whoever killed the cook also set out to murder Miriam with the poisoned dish." The questor returned his attention to Callidus. "Did you want Miriam dead, Callidus?"

Callidus paled, and shook his head violently. "No, my lord! Why, why would I want her dead? To think such a thing is, is, is nonsensical...."

"Is that so?" Varro turned to Hostilis, sitting on the floor. "Loyal Son of the Sea, tell Callidus what you told me this afternoon."

Hostilis came to his feet. "Master, I told you that after you had been on the lake Callidus said to me that Miriam must not be allowed to return to Rome with you."

His eyes flaring, Varro swung on Callidus, who was glowering at Hostilis. "What do you have to say to that? Why should Miriam not be permitted to return to Rome with me?" With his anger boiling over, he grasped Callidus by the shoulders and began to shake him, as if to shake the truth from him. "Well? Speak up! What is your answer?"

"Please, my lord!" Callidus cried, his face betraying his growing terror. His mind was racing. He could deny the slave's accusation, but no one was more trusted by Varro since Hostilis had risked his own life to rescue the questor in the Forest of Jardes. "My lord, it is true, I have no great liking for the slave Miriam," he admitted.

Varro released Callidus. "Why? What do you dislike about her?"

"Well, she is a Jew. A Nazarene. And she has shown no respect toward yourself."

"None of these are good reasons to want her dead!"

"I do not want her dead, my lord! I swear! I had nothing to do with her poisoning, and I had nothing to do with the death of the cook. I am no murderer! Me, Callidus?"

"I do find it difficult to picture you as a murderer, Callidus, but then again I have seen you take pleasure in the torture of prisoners at Antioch." Varro turned to Crispus. "Quintus, until this matter is clarified, Callidus is to be confined, in chains."

"My lord!" Callidus wailed.

"If it eventuates that you have had nothing to do with either crime here tonight, Callidus, then you shall have my apology."

"I have committed no crime, my lord. I swear!"

"I sincerely hope that is the case. Yet, I confess, the trust we have shared all these years has been damaged today, if not destroyed. If no guilt attaches to you in this matter I think it best just the same that we part company. You will leave my service once this mission ends."

"No, my lord!" Callidus dissented. "That will not be necessary. I am your most faithful servant, and always will be! Your interests are my interests." In that desperate moment, Callidus made a decision to play a dangerous game. Confident that he would be proven innocent of any involvement in the death of Melitus the cook, he was playing for his future more than his present. Callidus had well grounded suspicions about the identity of the poisoner of Miriam and the murderer of Melitus, but making a bare assertion would not, he knew, bring success. The questor would have to work this out for himself, with a nudge in the right direction. "Just to show how my thoughts are always inclined toward the questor's interests, my lord, I would strongly suggest that to find your murderer you should look at how and why the physician came to be drunk this evening. The key to the mystery lies in the cup."

"That remains to be seen," said Varro with irritation. He nodded to Prefect Crispus. "Take him out, Quintus."

Crispus rose up, took Callidus by the arm, and led the devastated freedman to the door and out into the night.

Varro looked thoughtfully at Centurion Gallo. "You said earlier, Gallo, that Diocles dined with Antiochus this evening." Varro turned to Antiochus, who continued to recline on a couch maintaining an air of nonchalance. "Do you deny it, Antiochus?"

"Deny it?" said Antiochus, with feigned surprise. "Why should I deny it? Yes, of course the physician dined with me." He smiled superciliously. "Is that a crime?"

Varro ignored the question. "You pressed him with wine?"

"I had wine with dinner. I imbibe sparingly myself, bearing in mind your directive in regard to excessive consumption. I did not *press* wine on the physician. I offered the Greek my hospitality, and he took advantage of it. He drank to excess, despite my cautions. He could not be persuaded to stop. In fact, the man became quite abusive. In the end, the fool could not even stand up. It was a lesson to me, not to be so hospitable."

Varro turned to Gallo. "You found the inebriated physician in his own tent?"

"I did, questor."

"I helped Diocles from my tent to his," Antiochus quickly volunteered.

"On your own?"

"Columbus assisted me." He was perspiring once more, a sign of his anxiety.

"After leaving Diocles in his tent, you then went where?"

"I returned to my own tent. And there I remained. Ask Columbus."

"Gallo, bring Columbus to me."

Columbus had his own small tent, adjacent to the much larger pavilion of Antiochus. When Centurion Gallo entered it with two men, one of them bearing a lantern, he found Columbus flat on his back, snoring.

"When we searched this tent earlier, centurion," said the legionary with the lantern, "the gladiator did not as much as twitch a muscle. Snoring his head off, he was."

"Some guardian he has turned out to be," Gallo sneered, standing looking down at the massive figure sleeping like a baby. "Who knows what Antiochus has been up to tonight while this hippopotamus slept?"

Gallo's two soldiers laughed. "Will we wake him?" asked the second legionary.

"Most assuredly," said Gallo with relish. "Is that water I see?" He nodded toward a pitcher on the ground by the door.

"If not water, then piss," the lantern-bearer guffawed.

"Either will serve the purpose," said Gallo. "Give the Numidian a soaking."

The second soldier took up the pitcher and upended it over the big man's head. Water cascaded out. The saturated Columbus opened his eyes. He tried to sit up, but only fell back again. Dazedly, he looked up at Gallo.

"More water," Gallo called. "A bucketful, this time."

The soldier ducked out of the tent. Moments later, he returned with a bronze bucket slopping with water. He poured the entire contents over black Columbus' head.

This had more of a revivifying effect. Columbus sat up, spluttering and wiping his eyes with the back of his hand. "Are you trying to drown me?" he boomed.

"On your feet, big man," said Gallo. "The questor desires your presence."

Columbus was dragged to the *pretorium*. Sitting on his couch, Varro studied the massive figure who stood, swaying in front of him. "You have been drinking?"

"One cup, my lord," the Numidian groggily replied. "The Jew gave me one cup."

Varro turned to Antiochus, who still casually reclined on one of the other couches. "You gave Columbus wine?"

Antiochus shrugged. "One cup of wine. What of it? I had an excellent

Falernian, and I was being hospitable. Apparently, the man has no head for it."

"Perhaps there was something in the wine, questor," Gallo suggested.

"I would not be surprised," Varro agreed.

"Questor, if I may speak." This time it was Pallas the medical assistant, who continued to sit on the floor at the end of the bed.

"Yes, Pallas. Speak."

"Earlier this evening, Diocles had me deliver a sleeping draught to Antiochus."

"Is that so?" Varro returned his attention to Antiochus. "Where is that sleeping draught now?"

"Somewhere in my tent," Antiochus nonchalantly replied. "Mind you, one of your thieving oafs of soldiers may have stolen it when the centurion's men searched the camp earlier. I would not put it past Gallo's pickpockets and thieves."

"My men are honest," said Gallo defensively.

Varro turned to Columbus. "You have been asleep since you drank the wine?"

"That must be the case, questor," the big man returned, putting a hand to his throbbing head. "I am sorry, questor. I do not know what came over me."

Varro eyed him with disapproval. "You were asleep whilst on duty. You are relieved of your post. You may go. Return to your quarters."

Looking desolate, the Numidian backed from the tent.

"Antiochus has been free to move about the camp all evening without his shadow," Varro said to no one in particular. Once again he fixed a steely gaze on Antiochus. "You, of all people, had the best opportunity to bribe your own cook to poison Miriam and Gemara. With your sentinel asleep, you also had ample opportunity to kill your cook, to silence him, and to then lay the murder weapon at Callidus' door."

"Nonsense!" Antiochus scoffed. "There is nothing or no one to connect me with either the illness of the slave and the girl or with the cook's death. Why would I want to kill my own cook? His cooking was not good, I will grant you…" He began to laugh; a forced, nervous laugh. But Antiochus' false bravado was unconvincing.

"You may not find this amusing before the night is out, Antiochus," the questor growled. "Suspicion hangs over you like a suspended sword."

The smile faded from Antiochus' face. His hand went to his throat. "I am tiring of all this. Accuse the Jew. Always accuse the Jew! It is the convenient course, even if it is not the just course." He pulled himself to his feet. "Do I have your leave to depart?"

Varro nodded. "Yes, return to your tent." He turned to Gallo. "Centurion, you will keep Antiochus under close scrutiny from this time forward."

"Yes, questor," said Gallo with satisfaction. "My best men will be assigned..."

"No, not your best men. You will personally take responsibility for Antiochus' security. Until further notice, you will share his tent, you will go everywhere he goes, you will observe his every move. You will even watch him defecate; I do not trust him to as much as relieve himself honestly. Am I understood?"

A scowl had darkened Gallo's face. "Yes, questor," he sourly replied.

"Search his tent before you allow him to reoccupy it. Search for weapons, and search for the sleeping draught which he says he retained."

"I told you, Varro, one of your men probably purloined it," Antiochus countered.

"Pray that Miriam recovers, Antiochus. Your two lives are inextricably linked."

✠

In the middle of the night, Varro awoke. He had fallen asleep at Miriam's bedside. Raising his head, he yawned, and stretched. Taking Miriam's wrist, he felt for a pulse. It was there, faint but regular. Her skin felt cold; not surprisingly, considering the chill of the night. He came to his feet, and pulled a blanket up under Miriam's chin. At her side, Gemara rolled over in her sleep; the little one seemed to be doing much better. A snore arose from one of the dining couches. Varro's companions were asleep. Crispus, Pedius, and the snoring Pallas had volunteered to join Hostilis and himself in keeping a vigil.

Slowly, quietly, the questor went to his portable shrine. Kneeling in front of the open shrine, he lit a taper from the flame of a lamp, then ignited the shrine's incense burner. Varro did not consider himself religious. Faithful in his obligations and his observances, yes, but not religious. Every morning he touched the statues of his Lares in remembrance of his ancestors, but that was more through habit than any sense of deep devotion. He had offered up a prayer at the news of his mother's death. Before that, his last prayer, his last real prayer, had been at the time of Martius' funeral.

Now, watching the incense smoke wind a wispy course toward the ceiling, he whispered. "All-powerful Jove, best and greatest, protect her, I beseech you." He knelt there for a time, drawing in the fragrant perfume, then came back to his feet. The prayer had seemed empty, fraudulent. It was almost as if he did not have the right. Two prayers in a year, and even then he had not been convinced that anyone had been listening. Now he was asking the gods for their help, to save Miriam? He turned for the door. Walking out into the night, he startled the four young legionaries assigned to guard the *pretorium* during this watch. They had a fire in a brazier a little way in front of the entrance, and, swathed in their red woolen cloaks, they stood around it, warming their hands and talking in low voices. On seeing the questor, the quartet quickly broke up; the soldiers scuttled back to their posts, two either side of the *pretorium* entrance.

It was eerily silent. A lamp fluttered at the water clock by the entrance, another pair of lamps glowed at the nearby 4th Scythica altar. Striding to the brazier, Varro warmed his hands. His eyes followed smoke from the fire as it trailed up into the night sky. No carpet of stars tonight. Thick gray cloud blanketed the sky. Could Miriam's God be up there, looking down on him now? What a turmoil of emotions this Jewish girl had created within him. He knew now beyond doubt that he loved her, profoundly, absolutely, unquestionably. Just as he knew that she loved her God, profoundly, absolutely, unquestionably. How, he asked himself, could her belief in a single heavenly power be so profound, so strong? His own belief in the Roman gods was . . . flimsy. How had she been able to so easily forgive him for his monstrous act against her, when he could not forgive himself? How could she believe so completely that his report was built on a foundation of lies, when the evidence seemed to him so convincing? And now, she carried a child in her womb, his child, their child, the fruit of his selfish, loveless act. And she considered it a Heavenly gift. Now, at death's door, despite having been defiled, despite being the victim of a murderous plot, this highly intelligent, well educated young woman not only still believed in her God as deeply as ever, she forgave those who had deliberately set out to end her life. What manner of faith was this, which, in the face of evidence that damned the very basis of its adherents' beliefs, in the face of foul mistreatment and painful death, held firm to the last? He envied Miriam her certainty, her calm acceptance.

With his eyes to the heavens, the questor spoke to the God of the Nazarenes. "She is one of yours. If you exist, help her. She believes. She has no doubts. I cannot do what she asks, but you could not want that. If you are what she believes you to be, you do not want lies perpetuated in your name. If you are as powerful as she believes, you will save her."

XXXI

THE STORM

Capernaum, Northern Galilee, Tetrarchy of Trachonitis. July, A.D. 71

A trumpet was sounding 'End of Watch.' Varro opened his eyes. Outside, the men of the first watch of the new day would be moving into their places as the sun began to rise over the Sea of Galilee. In the gloom inside the *pretorium,* Pedius and Pallas were still asleep on couches. Crispus was sitting up; also roused by the trumpet call.

Varro lifted his head from the bedside, where he had slept. Miriam lay, just as he had last seen her. Gemara was not in the bed; she was nowhere to be seen. Varro guessed that, feeling better, the child had risen up in the night and gone outside. Shortly, he would look for her. For the moment, he focused on Miriam. The redness had departed her cheeks. Now, her face was the color of chalk. Yet, it was a serene face. Miriam looked like the statue of a goddess. He reached for her hand. Then he frowned. He felt her wrist.

Crispus pulled himself to his feet and came to stand at the end of the bed. "How has Miriam fared in the night, questor?" he asked.

Varro slowly looked up at him. "She has gone." Varro's voice was flat. The questor was numb. "My Miriam has gone."

Crispus stared at the still form in the bed. "No!" He felt Miriam's arm; it was as cold as stone. He lay a hand on her forehead; as cold as stone. "It may not be too late! I shall fetch the physician Boethus from the town!" He turned and ran from the tent.

Pallas and Pedius now stirred. Varro was mechanically rising to his feet as the pair moved to the bedside. Pallas came and took Miriam's hand, feeling for a pulse. He looked at Varro, and shook his head. "I am sorry, questor." Beside the Greek, tears were trickling down the face of Pedius the lictor.

As if mesmerized, Varro walked to his writing table. He took up the cylindrical leather case which contained his report. It had lain there where Hostilis had left it when he retired for the night. Varro slipped the thick roll of parchment free, letting the case fall. The leather cylinder hit the ground with a hollow tone. Report in hand, the questor walked slowly out the door. Hostilis, on the floor where had slept, sat up. Seeing his master disappearing out the tent doorway, he quickly came to his feet. Yawning, stretching, and scratching his head, the servant followed after the questor.

Pale and drawn, Varro paused a little way outside the *pretorium* door. In full armor, helmets, and equipment, the sentries of the new watch stood in their pairs either side of the tent's entranceway. One member of the quartet was Rufus the orderly sergeant. Around about, the camp was slowly coming to life. If the expedition were on the move, tents would be down and the baggage train packed by this time, with the column ready to march. In the time since the questor had been encamped here outside Capernaum and engaged in his report writing only the men of the new watch were active at dawn. In dribs and drabs their off-duty comrades would come crawling from their tents, like boars from their caves, as the sun rose higher in the sky.

Lamps still shone at the water clock and at the legion altar. In front of the *pretorium,* the coals of the sentries' overnight fire glowed orange in the brazier. Varro raised his eyes to the sky. The grayness of earlier in the night had given way to a threatening congregation of clouds of inky black. In the distance, thunder boomed. A cold breeze suddenly swirled, fanning the embers in the sentries' fire from orange to red. Had Marcus Martius been here, the questor reflected as he looked at the fire, the tribune would have made the observation that the gods were not happy.

Hostilis appeared beside him. In his master's hand the servant saw the roll of parchment, the end result of the labors and losses of the past four months. He did not know what was in the questor's mind, but he did know that grief can sometimes make people do strange things. "Should I not take the report to Pythagoras, master?" he asked softly in the questor's ear, "for safe keeping?"

Varro looked at Hostilis, then looked at the fire.

"Master?" Hostilis persisted.

At that moment, Pedius emerged from the tent behind the questor and his servant. The lictor heard thunder boom, rolling closer. In the grimy light of the new day he also saw Antiochus, walking determinedly down the camp street toward the *pretorium* with the fully equipped Centurion Gallo on his heel.

"Questor!" Antiochus called as he approached "I demand that you remove this oaf from my tent! I did not sleep a wink all night. Nothing I have done warrants close custody." Now Antiochus realized that Varro had a volume in his hand, and recognized it as the *Investigatio Nazarena*. He came to an abrupt halt on the far side of the sentries' fire. "Questor?" He saw Varro's odd expression, and thought that he could read his mind. "Would you not like me to take your report from you, my lord?" His tone was appeasing now. "I will ensure that it is kept safe. I will personally place it in General Collega's hands. Let me have the report, questor." As he spoke, thunder clapped close by.

The gathering was complete when Pythagoras appeared from the direction of his tent, alerted by the voices. "Questor? What is happening?" he queried as he hurried up.

"He has the report," Antiochus said anxiously.

"Miriam has died in the night," said Pedius, his voice betraying his emotion.

"I see. That explains much." With his hand outstretched, Pythagoras walked up to Varro. "Give me the report, questor."

Varro looked at him blankly. "Miriam has gone," he said.

"You cannot bring her back," said Pythagoras in a low, soothing voice. "Nor can you cremate the guilt you feel. Here, let me have the report." Carefully, he eased the thick scroll from the questor's grasp.

Varro did not resist. He allowed the secretary to take charge of the document. For, now the questor's gaze was fixed on Antiochus, standing across the fire from him. "You killed her, Antiochus!" Varro denounced. "You poisoned her!" He began to walk around the fire toward the Jewish magistrate. "You took belladonna from the physician's tent, and had your cook lace the dish of mushrooms with it."

"Keep your distance, Varro!" Antiochus cried. He began to back away, forcing Centurion Gallo to step to one side.

"Murderer!" Varro exclaimed, still advancing, eyes blazing.

Without warning, Antiochus swung on Gallo beside him. Catching the centurion unawares, he whipped the dagger from the scabbard on the centurion's right hip then shoved Gallo away with all his might. The centurion went sprawling to the ground. Antiochus then turned on Varro, with the dagger raised.

"Watch out, master, Antiochus has a weapon!" Hostilis called.

"Take care, Varro," Antiochus cautioned, backing away, waving the dagger to and fro as the questor continued to advance on him. "Keep your distance!"

Meanwhile, Gallo pulled himself up onto one knee, and unsheathed his sword. "Soldiers!" he bellowed, "Protect the questor's report!" He came to his feet with his eyes fixed on Antiochus.

In response to their centurion's order, all four legionary sentries at the *pretorium* entrance drew their swords, and the two who were closest to Pythagoras stepped forward. As one, they grasped the shoulders of the secretary, in whose hands lay the *Investigatio Nazarena*. They anchored him to the spot.

There now came a deafening crack of thunder, so loud that it shook the ground and all that stood upon it. In that same instant, there was an explosive flash of silver-white light. It was as if a meteor had come crashing to earth. And then, there was silence.

Pedius the lictor slowly sat up. Like everyone else, he had been thrown to the ground by the lightning strike. With a spinning head he looked around about him, taking in an unbelievable scene of devastation.

Hostilis lay with his hands to his face. "My eyes! My eyes!" he was crying.

Centurion Gallo was sprawled on his back, with one bloodied forearm raised and with smoke rising from the body that was now naked beneath his armor. He was dead. The two metal-clad sentinels who'd had their hands on Pythagoras also appeared to be dead. The two other soldiers were horribly burned; one lay groaning, the other thrashed in agony. Pythagoras was also obviously dead. His body was blackened from head to toe.

Varro was just beginning to sit up. "I cannot see," said the questor dazedly.

Pedius realized that he was the only one to have escaped without even the slightest injury. He saw the questor's report lying on the ground by

Pythagoras' body. Like Pedius, it had not even been singed. Scrambling to the roll of parchment, the lictor grabbed it up. He tore a strip from the scroll, and threw it into the sentries' fire. The parchment quickly burst into flame. "It burns, it burns!" he proclaimed to the heavens.

Varro heard the sound of ripping parchment, heard the lictor's cries. "Pedius?" he called, as he dragged himself blindly to his feet. "Pedius, what are you doing?"

"I am consigning your report to the fire, questor," Pedius gleefully replied. "It is burning well, Julius Varro," he taunted the sightless questor. "This is Heaven's fire. Heaven's fire!"

"What are you saying?"

"I promised my new wife and the brethren at Antioch that I would do all in my power to frustrate your fool's errand, questor, and I have not failed them, or my Father in Heaven! This will win God's forgiveness for my sins."

"You are a Nazarene? You, Pedius?"

"I had feared that the blaze I lit under the secretary's cart would be the limit of my powers of intercession, but I need not have worried. My Lord God has shown me the way!" Slowly, deliberately, he tore another strip from the beginning of the report, and cast it into the brazier. As he looked down at the burning sheave of papyrus, the words on the page miraculously faded away, even before the flames reached them. "Burn, foul document! Burn!"

"No! It cannot be!" It was the voice of Antiochus. He was crawling across the ground toward the fire with one hand outstretched. Like Varro and Hostilis, he had been blinded by the lightning. Now, he used the heat from the fire to guide him.

"The *Investigatio* cannot be destroyed, must not be destroyed!" Antiochus cried. Coming to the brazier, he reached up into the fire in an attempt to retrieve what he thought was the entire report, only for the flames to lick his flesh. Crying with pain, he withdrew his burnt hand.

Pedius put a foot in the Jewish magistrate's chest, and pushed him away. "Too late! Too late!" he triumphantly declared. "The report shall be destroyed this day, just as Pythagoras, one of its authors, has perished! It is God's will!"

Sobbing with pain and despair, Antiochus crawled away. He bumped into the baked body of Gallo, and let out a wail. "I too am a dead man!

Collega will have my head for this. The report is destroyed. The Nazarenes prevail!"

Antiochus dragged himself into a sitting position, then reached to his throat. With a jerk, he separated his precious pouch from its leather necklace. Fumbling with the neck of the small leather bag, terrified that Pedius would see what he was doing and relieve him of his last resort, Antiochus forced an opening. Then, holding the bag with his throbbing, red-raw right hand, he emptied the contents into his left. With relief, he felt the hemlock seeds drop into his palm. In one quick movement he brought the hand to his mouth. Greedily he crunched the seeds between his teeth. Letting go of the pouch which had been his constant companion for half a decade, he swallowed, then lay back his head. "Jehovah, I am yours!" he called.

With a sudden dread that the apothecary who had sold him the hemlock seeds in Antioch had deceived him, Antiochus waited. Then, gratefully, he began to feel a numbness creep over his body, from his toes, to his legs, up his torso, and down his arms, which now sagged to his side. Antiochus smiled. His eyes closed. His breathing stopped. He sagged onto the corpse of the centurion, dead.

Report in hand, the demented Pedius had been watching the Jew take his own life. "Now Antiochus is no more!" he rejoiced. "It is all God's will, questor. The report destroyed. Antiochus dead. Pythagoras dead. Gallo dead. All God's will!"

All this time, one of the two badly injured legionaries, Rufus, had been groping around the ground. Now, he located his sword. With an effort he struggled onto his knees behind Pedius. "Protect the questor's report," he cried through his agony, repeating Centurion Gallo's last order, as, summoning all his strength, he plunged the sword two-handed into the middle of Pedius' back, falling forward to add impetus to the strike. The regularly-sharpened blade slid through Lictor Pedius' body as if it were a sack of grain.

Pedius gasped with surprise, then, with a mystified expression, looked down, to see the bloodied, pointed tip of the sword emerge through the front of his tunic in the middle of his chest. Pedius opened his mouth, and let out a wild, animal-like cry as he realized what fate had befallen him. His eyes rolled up into his head, and Pedius sank to his knees, then toppled forward, brushing the brazier as he collapsed, to lay full length with the sword hilt jutting from his back. The report slipped from his dead grasp, and lay on the ground beside his body.

"What is it?" Varro called with frustration. "What's happening now?"

"The traitor is dead, questor," Legionary Rufus informed him from where he lay. "Your report is saved."

"Dead? Pedius too? Can such carnage truly be God's will?" Varro asked in confusion, trying to keep his balance. And then he felt a hand take his. A small hand.

"Come, master," said a young voice.

"Gemara?" Varro responded. "Is that you?"

"I will show you the way," the child replied.

She led him, stumbling, from the camp, to the lake. He was unaware of anyone else but her. "Where are we going?" he asked, as he heard waves breaking on the shore of the Sea of Galilee.

The child did not answer. Gemara led him along beside the water, toward the rising sun.

It was now that Quintus Crispus came running into the camp from the direction of the town, where he had been searching unsuccessfully for the local Jewish physician. Crispus had heard the explosion of the lightning strike, and, open mouthed, he stood beside the brazier and surveyed the scene of devastation, as stunned soldiers began to join him from their tents. And then he saw the questor's report lying on the ground at his feet. Quickly he stooped and picked it up. A quick inspection told him that the opening lines had been torn away, but essentially the *Investigatio Nazarena* and its conclusions remained intact. And then Crispus saw Julius Varro being led away by the child Gemara, following the lake. The cavalry prefect went to call out to Varro, but something stopped him. Somehow, he knew that the questor would not be returning. Again Crispus glanced at the report in his hand. Then he looked at the low fire in the brazier beside him. As Varro's deputy, he should deliver the questor's report to General Collega. Or did the report have another destiny? The young man who had several months before bathed in the Jordan River to wash away his sins, gazed into the fire.

As he was led by Gemara, Varro found his vision slowly returning. Indistinct, bleached images of the ground before him began to appear, and of the smiling child at his side. Then, more of a larger picture; hazy, washed out, but growing clearer with each passing minute in the bright light of the new day directly ahead, a light which was soon so bright it almost dazzled him anew. Putting a hand to his brow to shade his eyes, he stopped. His mind was filling with thoughts of where he had come from, and all that he had left behind. He went to turn around, to look back.

"Don't look back," said the child, tugging him forward.

He smiled, and nodded slowly, feeling himself surrounded by an all embracing faith in what lay ahead. He resumed his journey, feeling strangely, unusually, calm and at peace. Julius Varro never looked back.

2-05

F
DAN   Dando-Collins, Ste-
            phen

         The inquest

DUE DATE   0305   22.95
